****

Pursuit by Fire:
1981
Soviet Endgame—Book Three

****

By Alex Aaronson and James Rosone

****

Published in conjunction with Front Line Publishing, Inc.

Copyright Notice

ISBN: 978-1-957634-71-5
Sun City Center, Florida, United States of America
Library of Congress Control Number: 2023901397

Table of Contents

Chapter 1

1 July 1981
5000 Meters over Cologne
Soviet-Occupied Germany

Lt. Colonel Dmitriy "Germes" Bogdanov felt alive as he looked at the clear blue skies over Germany. It had been six months since his MiG-25R was brought down over Giebelstadt, West Germany. *No,* he thought, *I suppose it's just "Germany" now.* It had taken two months for him to get back to the theater headquarters of the Voyenno-Vozdushnye Sily, or VVS. He had been sent to the rear for refresher training on the MiG-21R before he was able to return to service. His previous mount, the MiG-25R, was in precious short supply and the Soviets were relying more and more on the older model. While the aircraft might not be as impressive, his promotion was something he could take pride in. He was now the executive officer of the 100th Independent Reconnaissance Aviation Squadron.

Today's mission was to fly into Luxembourg and see what NATO was up to. Soviet leadership believed that NATO was taking the time to rally forces in the low countries for a counterattack, but as of yet, they had not been able to find the major concentrations. The Americans found success in using their space shuttle to intercept photo-recon satellites, so it was up to units like the 100th Recon to pick up the slack.

Germes wasn't going to be taking pictures of anything, however. Instead, his job was to lead a flight of four MiG-21s into hostile territory and dare the enemy to engage their ground radars. If Germes didn't detect any ground radars, he was sure that they would feel the touch of the American E-3 Sentry airborne warning and control system, or AWACS, aircraft. That airborne radar would vector fighters to intercept the MiGs.

Typically, he would fly a pass like this on his own. But the NATO forces had started to more or less ignore single MiG-21s coming over the border. If Germes wanted to poke NATO into action, he was going to need a bigger stick. The other three MiGs were that stick. They were MiG-21PFM strike fighters of the 88th Fighter-Bomber Aviation Regiment. They were mostly there for decoration, to give the mission the

5

appearance of an attack. But if they found any targets of opportunity, they would strike.

"Flight, come to course two-one-five," he said over the radio. He heard the acknowledgment from his comrades and double-checked his fuel state. These missions were always tricky because you never knew how long you would need to light your afterburners. The MiG-21 was plenty fast, capable of more than twice the speed of sound, but the faster she went, the shorter her legs. Of course, there was also the issue of running your afterburner for too long and damaging your engines. The latter was what had brought him down six months ago, when running from a pair of American Sparrow missiles had caused him to push his plane too far. He winced at the memory.

The four MiGs streaked through an empty sky. On the first night of the war, the idea that he would have the sky to himself seemed ridiculous. Rationally, he knew that the tempo of operations couldn't be sustained. In the moment, though, he wasn't thinking rationally. He thought he'd constantly be dodging enemy sweeps into Soviet-controlled territory. Instead, his flight was alone in the sky on a beautiful summer day over Germany. Germes consulted his watch and his map. Far below, he estimated that he was flying over the German city of Bitburg. This was the edge of the Soviet Line. He was crossing into enemy territory.

"Adjust altitude to one thousand, five hundred meters," said Germes. If they wanted the Western forces to believe that there was an incoming air strike, they needed to act like it. *If you live with wolves, you need to howl like one*, he thought, recalling the old proverb. As he dove, Germes looked at the land below. He couldn't exactly make out the lines. At eight hundred kilometers per hour, he didn't have long to pinpoint it. On his first mission over NATO lines, he expected to be engaged right away, and he was.

By this stage in the war, however, the chaos of battle and the necessity of having units stay on the move meant that you could never be quite sure when you would be engaged. They overflew the lines without incident. Almost. One of the rear fighter-bombers reported a man-portable air defense, or MANPAD, launch, but they were out of harm's way before the missile could engage.

Germes considered his mission. From the start of the war, the Soviet High Command, the famous Stavka, had understood that NATO would divide the battlefield into zones where surface-to-air missiles or

SAMs would be the primary air defense, and other zones where NATO interceptors would be the primary focus. Germes was here to test a hypothesis. Stavka believed that NATO would use their SAMs to protect strategic targets, such as air bases and supply depots, while the interceptors would guard troop concentrations. The calculus was basically this: NATO lacked highly mobile SAM systems to keep up with the main armored thrusts.

To see if this was, in fact, true, Germes and his three comrades would fly over a suspected troop concentration. If they found any targets, they would drop their FAB-500 bombs, then make a run back east. If Stavka was correct, two things would happen. First, Germes wouldn't pick up any fire control radars locking onto him and his companions. That was the good news. Second, NATO fighters would pursue them. If they were lucky, they'd get a pair of West German F-104s. They couldn't quite outrun the Starfighter, but they could easily outfight them. If fate wasn't on their side, the hated American F-15 Eagle would hunt them. They could neither run from nor fight against the American air superiority fighter.

The NATO position was a mere twenty-five kilometers across the front, and Germes and his flight were rapidly approaching.

"I have no emissions," reported Germes. "Keep your eyes out for targets on the ground, and hunters in the air." He knew that the men of the 88th didn't carry the respect for him that they would for a lieutenant colonel from their own ranks, so Germes wanted to remind them that he was in charge.

"I've got something," said the captain in charge of the fighter-bomber detachment. "Small cluster of vehicles in the tree line. Three hundred ten degrees. Looks like a scout element."

"*Sbrosit*"" came the call from all three MiGs as they dropped their bombs on the small NATO outpost. The four-ship formation raced over Bettendorf. The vehicles below them exploded and caught fire. The four MiGs performed a wingover before diving to the deck and engaging their afterburners. They ran. They weren't fast enough.

"I'm engaged," said one of the 88th pilots. "Enemy radar lock. Looks like a Phantom." The Soviet pilots had a penchant for using the NATO nicknames of enemy aircraft. Since they were public record, it was just simpler. *If those are Phantoms, they're engaging with Sparrows*, thought Germes. He'd already faced off against Phantoms firing Sparrow missiles, and it hadn't ended well. Technically, his orders at this point were to run for home. He wasn't carrying any missiles and he didn't have any advanced training in dogfighting. But he'd never been in a formation like this. Running was fine when you were on your own. In the heat of battle, he couldn't leave his comrades behind.

"Kop'ye One, take the lead," said Germes. "I'll fly your wing."

"Don't be an idiot, Colonel, you don't have any weapons," said the captain.

"Be that as it may," replied Germes, "I know that and you know that, but the Yankees have no idea."

"Understood," replied Kop'ye One. "Stay on my wing and try to keep up." Germes eased off the throttle and let Kop'ye One take the lead.

"Evading," said one of the rear MiGs. Germes followed Kop'ye One as he started a gentle climb. *Don't want to pull too many g's*, thought Germes, understanding what Kop'ye One was doing. They needed to gain altitude, but if they simply jerked back on the stick, the g-forces would bleed their energy and leave them at the mercy of their adversaries. On the other hand, with the NATO fighters having the altitude advantage, it was highly unlikely that they would be able to equalize the energy states.

Germes waited for his radar warning receiver or RWR to start screeching at him, but it never did. Kop'ye One started a climbing turn to the right. Germes followed when it occurred to him, *There must only be two interceptors coming after us. They have to guide their missiles all the way to target.* He saw the two other MiGs low on the deck with bursts of radar-spoofing chaff exploding behind them. Kop'ye One was entering a shallow dive and ignited his afterburner. Germes followed suit.

"We're getting as low as possible," said Kop'ye One, "to use the ground clutter to get in range of these fascists."

Germes pushed through the sound barrier and kept accelerating. This low to the ground, he wouldn't be able to sustain this speed. He just needed it long enough to close with the enemy. At a combined five thousand kilometers per hour, it wouldn't take long.

"I have a visual on the targets," said Kop'ye One. "Ten degrees and diving." Germes looked up and to the right. Sure enough, there were two dots coming down towards the two engaged MiGs. He watched as a missile streaked away and towards his comrades. He didn't have time to watch the missile—he needed to keep his focus on staying with his wingman. He knew that Kop'ye One would pitch up at some point to try and get within the eight-kilometer range of his R-60 missiles.

It happened suddenly. Kop'ye One pulled up. Germes followed, noticing that he was in a constant one-point-five-g climb, until they were flying towards a point some ways behind the Phantoms. *We're trying to establish a rear hemisphere shot*, thought Germes, remembering that the R-60 missiles could only effectively track enemy targets from behind. As the MiGs screamed up into the sky, one of the Phantoms broke off his attack and reclaimed as much altitude as he could. The second Phantom continued after the original MiGs.

"He's target-fixated," said Kop'ye One as the Phantom shot from left to right, still diving towards the Soviet planes. Germes followed as Kop'ye One banked right and made a gentle turn, lining up the enemy fighter and firing his missile. From this view, Germes watched another missile leave the Phantom. As soon as the missile left, the Phantom pitched hard to the left and up, spitting flares. It was too little, too late. Kop'ye One's missile exploded behind the huge American fighter, tearing out both engine nozzles and the entire tail section. Within seconds, Germes watched the same result as the American's missile exploded, destroying the MiG it was racing towards.

"Looks like the other one is running," came a voice over the radio, no doubt the remaining Kop'ye pilot.

"He's just putting distance between us to make another run with those Sparrows," said Kop'ye One. "But let's get back over the line before he can. He won't follow too far into our SAM coverage."

The remaining three MiGs fled east, to the safety of what used to be NATO's Spangdahlem Air Base.
****

1 July 1981
345th Independent Guards Airborne Regiment
Spangdahlem Air Base, Germany

Sergeant Mikhail "Misha" Kozyrev sat down at the long table in the mess tent with his tray with a chunk of bread and a portion of fish soup. The Menu-board said it was *ukha*, but the thin soup tasted nothing like what his *babushka* used to make. He must have made a face because Junior Sergeant Taras Knyazev snorted.

"It's not exactly fit for the Tsar, but it's much better than field rations."

Misha frowned at the thought.

"That's not setting a high bar," he replied.

"In this life," said Taras with a chuckle, "if you don't look on the bright side now and again, you'll go mad."

"I suppose that's so. Doubly so when you're fighting a war."

"At the start of this thing," said Taras, "could you have possibly imagined that we would still be fighting a year later?"

"I'd pretty much resolved that we were going to die on the first day," said Misha. "Once we survived that, I was sure we would die on the second. So on and so forth until today. So, no, I can't say that I could have imagined us here and now."

"And the captain," continued Taras, "he would go on and on. 'We'll be home by May Day!' Then it was 'We'll be home by Constitution Day.'"

"Yes," agreed Misha, "I don't think those proclamations did much to improve morale. I've noticed that we don't hear anything like that anymore."

"True," said Taras. "On the other hand, I think I liked his optimistic take on the war more than his current tactic of reminding us of our duty to the Rodina as motivation."

"Quiet, comrade," laughed Misha, "I would hate for someone to overhear your lack of patriotism." He changed the subject. "How is the squad holding up since we've taken up residence in this Yankee air base?"

"They are restless," replied Taras. "You know how it is. They are either steeped in the battle or nervously waiting for it to resume."

"It's true. After the first thirty-six to forty-eight hours, they wonder when their good fortune will run out."

"And their fortune at this stop has been greater than usual."

"Oh?" said Misha.

"Yes," chuckled Taras, "this base has been an absolute diamond mine of pornography. Andrusha found a giant stack of American magazines while rifling through one of the burnt-out barracks buildings.

I tell you, it's like nothing I've ever seen before, and I've seen a few things."

"Oh, of that, I have no doubt," said Misha. "Just make sure they keep that under wraps and that the lieutenant doesn't catch them. In fact, you should suggest they try to trade them for something that won't get confiscated. Surely one of those magazines is worth some of that American coffee or German chocolate that's been floating around the black market?"

"*Da*," replied Taras, "that's an excellent idea. But there will be resistance."

"I imagine so. Tell them to pick their favorite model and keep her in their helmet. That should be worth something."

"I'm sure I can convince them." Taras grinned.

The two parted ways, with Misha leaving to check in with the lieutenant. Placing his food tray in the wash pile, he left the mess tent and crossed the paved ground to the company's HQ tent. Many of the buildings on the base had been deemed uninhabitable. Either the Soviets had destroyed them in the fight, or the fascist pigs had destroyed them in the retreat. Either way, the 345th was making do with canvas field tents.

Misha pulled the tent flap and entered. The lieutenant was sitting at the desk, flipping through a magazine. To Misha's surprise, it was definitely pornographic.

"Have you seen this?" asked Lieutenant Krylov sternly as he slid the opened magazine towards Misha.

"No, sir," said Misha, looking down at it. *She's beautiful*, he thought before looking back to the lieutenant. This wasn't going to be good.

"One of your men, a Private Dezhnyov, turned this in to me. He said he found it while exploring one of the empty barracks buildings."

"I see," said Misha, waiting for Krylov to continue.

"Pornography is contraband. It weakens the mind and creates contempt and jealousy among the men. Next to prostitution, nothing will erode morale quicker than this."

"Yes, sir. It is good that Private Dezhnyov brought that to you instead of keeping it for himself."

"I'm not stupid, Sergeant Kozyrev. There is no way that Dezhnyov would have given me this magazine if it was the only one he had. No, this was given to me so that when rumors of pornography come up, he can deflect by saying that he's already turned it in."

"I can see how that is possible," replied Misha, wondering when the lieutenant would come down on him.

"I don't want to deal with this. Right now, this is contained. I don't want your squad to reflect poorly on my platoon. You have six hours to ensure that every scrap of this filth is gone. We will have an inspection at eighteen hundred hours."

"Yes, sir," said Misha. "I will verify that there is no pornography in our squad." He wondered if the lieutenant would notice that he wasn't admitting to the crime.

"Very well. Next issue. I know that we have standing orders to be ready to move out on a moment's notice. And I know that everyone is getting worn down by that. However, I have reason to believe that we will have orders in the next few days. So you need to get your men as much rest as they can. I need them fresh for the coming fight."

"Understood, sir, you can count on First Squad."

"Let's hope so," said Krylov. "Let's hope so."

Misha jogged back to First Squad's camp. He gathered up the squad and laid it out for the men.

"Look," said Misha, "I understand that you don't want to. But we need to get rid of *every* last page of this contraband. Giving one magazine to the lieutenant was stupid." Andrusha stared at his feet as his sergeant admonished him. "You're smarter than that. But that's in the past. We need to look at the very near future. The lieutenant is on the warpath. He's coming through here in three hours for an inspection. You can bet that he's going to go to the motor pool as well, so don't even think about trying to stash anything there."

"What you need to do," interjected Taras, "is to trade this shit away. This stuff currently has zero value to you, but the other squads don't know that. Even better, the other platoons don't know that. See what you can get. Food, ammo, spare parts for the tank... anything." The three younger men in the squad started to nod their heads, finally accepting that they weren't going to get to keep their favorite girls.

"Okay," said Misha, "get the hell out of here, and be back in two hours with whatever you can get, and *without* the pornography. The men scattered, each heading in a different direction, no doubt with a trading partner in mind."

"What are the odds they listen?" asked Taras.

"Zero percent," replied Misha. "They'll come back with all of the material 'gone,' but I promise there will be the image of a lovely naked woman in between their socks and their boots."

"Or between their underwear and their pants," chuckled Taras.

"Please don't make me think about that," said Misha.

"And don't forget," continued Taras, "when there's shit falling from the sky, the toilet usually comes with it."

The two went about tidying up the squad's living area. If the lieutenant was going to inspect the squad, they wanted to make sure that he wouldn't find anything to complain about beyond the pornography.

Chapter 2

1 July 1981
82nd Airborne Division
Florennes Air Base, Belgium

It was almost a waking nightmare. Specialist Marlon Reeves was reliving the scariest moment of his life. He could hear the explosion. Then the plane rolled. They lost all their altitude, struck the earth, then rolled upside down. He'd spent the entire time sure he was going to die. And now, once again, he was riding in the back of a C-130 Hercules on his way to seize an airfield. On his first combat jump, he'd had to face the fear of the unknown. Tonight he was facing a very well-known fear. He wasn't sure which was worse.

Not that it mattered. He was going to do what he was trained to do. He told himself the same thing he had on that first attack. *Just get on the ground and start killing communists.* He knew that his unit was jumping onto Bitburg Air Base. It was a smaller airfield to the west of Spangdahlem. Recon overflights showed that the Soviets weren't currently using the fields at Bitburg, concentrating their forces at Spangdahlem instead. The plan was to occupy the base quickly, then fly in the M551 Sheridan tanks of the 3rd Battalion, 73rd Armored Regiment. While Reeves hadn't been read in on the Air Force aspects of the mission, he had to assume that there would be massive fighter cover for the duration of the assault. *Otherwise, this thing will be over before it begins.*

As often happened, his thoughts drifted back to Des Moines. He wondered if he'd ever settle back down there. At this point, he knew he was a lifer, but he had yet to find a place he preferred. *Or am I just being nostalgic?* he wondered. He knew that going back wouldn't be the same as growing up there. He smiled at the memory of Christmas 1970. He'd snuck downstairs at three o'clock in the morning to see if Santa had come. He'd asked for a Lite-Brite and just *had* to know if he'd gotten it.

Unfortunately, the family cat, Bandit, was sleeping in front of the tree and young Marlon stepped right on Bandit's tail, causing the cat to screech and claw the hell out of his leg. In a panic, Marlon lost his balance and fell *into* the tree, knocking it over against the corner. The ensuing commotion roused not only Marlon's two younger sisters but his parents as well. Looking back, he imagined his parents found the whole situation funny, but as a kid, he was terrified about how much trouble he was in. In the end, his parents took away his brand-new Lite-Brite, but they gave it back to him on New Year's Day. In exchange he had to promise never to try for a "sneak peek" of Christmas.

"All right, you apes," said the jumpmaster on Reeves's side of the Herc.

Reeves stepped out of the hatch and into the night. He was jerked back as his chute deployed. He looked out over the battle space. There wasn't much enemy activity on the ground. He supposed that they'd managed to achieve surprise. If the enemy was expecting an airborne assault, they must have thought it would be at Spangdahlem. Reeves wondered if NATO signals intel had led the Soviets to believe that Spangdahlem was the target, like the Allies had done in that World War II movie *The Man Who Never Was.*

"Reeves!" shouted Staff Sergeant Felix Watkins. "Get over here." Reeves looked over and saw Watkins motioning him to fall in. The troop leader had already gathered Specialist Durant and PFC Davis. Once the rest of the team assembled, they started out for their objective at a run.

Watkins led Alpha Fire Team. They needed to reach the northeast edge of the airfield. From there, they would direct mortar fire at any counterstrike that the Soviets tried to send their way. From the briefings, Reeves knew that just to the east of the air base was the Kyll River Valley. The valley was dramatically steep and would present a significant obstacle for the enemy to cross if they wanted to take back Bitburg. This feature was the key to choosing Bitburg as the objective.

Watkins slowed the team as they neared a tree-covered hill. This was their area of responsability. As they wove through the forest, Reeves heard incoming artillery. He knew that any concentrated fire would be aimed at the airfield itself and that there was nothing he could do about an errant round, so he just focused on moving through the trees.

"Try not to fall off the cliff at the end," said Watkins. The steep valley didn't just protect them from counterattack—it also put them in danger of plunging into the river one hundred and twenty meters below them. "Okay, this is the spot. Spread out left and right." Reeves moved off to Watkins's right and pulled out his entrenching tool. While he, Sergeant Luca Kidd, and PFC Davis were digging in, Watkins and the rest of the team would be on watch. Kidd's men were dug in. They'd swap duties and get comfortable.

He heard the thumping rotors of helicopters over his left shoulder and looked up from his digging in time to see a four-ship formation overfly the river. *Hopefully they're going to give us some relief from this arty*, thought Reeves, getting back to the digging.
****

345th Independent Guards Airborne Regiment
Spangdahlem Air Base, Germany

"What the hell is that?" groaned Taras in the darkness of the tent.

"*Blyat'*," Misha cursed, more annoyed than afraid. "Everyone up, get your gear and rally at the tank." The men of First Squad scrambled out of their racks and grabbed their weapons and packs. Misha counted all five and took a breath. It had been months since they had been harassed, but he was still worried that one of his men would sleep through the artillery bombardment, or air raid, or whatever the hell was going on out there.

Outside of the squad's tent, there were men running to and fro. Every man had a place to be during an attack, and none of them had much time to get there if they wanted to mount an effective defense. The 9th Company was the one exception to this rule. As the defensive reserve force, they wouldn't have orders until the scope and breadth of the attack were known. Once the enemy showed their intentions, the 9th Company would be deployed.

"Taras, get the tank started and wait for me to return with orders."

"Understood, comrade Sergeant." There was a pause, then Taras shouted, "I serve the Soviet Union!"

Trotting towards the company HQ, Misha smiled, knowing that the only thing that could get a line like that out of Taras was the presence of a Party loyalist or the company's *polytruk*. He could see light inside the tent that 9th Company was using for a headquarters; clearly, he wasn't the first to make it here. *The captain sleeps there*, he reminded himself. He pulled the flap back and slipped in. To his relief, he was the first squad leader there.

"Ah, Sergeant Kozyrev," said Lieutenant Krylov from a rear corner of the tent, "is your squad combat ready?"

Shit, thought Misha before saying, "Sir, they are in the process of starting the BMD as we speak."

"Very well—" Before the lieutenant said anything else, the rest of the platoon and squad leaders for the 9th Company came through the tent flap. As they assembled, the company *starshina* called everyone to attention. Captain Sedelnikov stood in front of the group.

"Men, as the defensive reserve force—" An explosion cut off the rest of his sentence. As the sound dissipated, he continued, "All we know is that we have been hit by multiple flights of enemy attack aircraft. This is not a feint; this is not harassment. Something is going on. The enemy is on the move. We must be ready. You are to report to your tanks, and deploy to position Zhenya Fourteen, then shut down and wait for orders."

Misha raised his eyebrow at the order. In the first six months of the war, the focus had been on pushing and pushing more. If you weren't attacking, you were losing. To that end, they wouldn't be shutting down their tanks. Maybe there was another reason for the order, but Misha wasn't sure what it might be.

"Dismissed," said the captain, and the lieutenants filed out of the tent. As soon as they were in the open, Lieutenant Krylov pulled up to Misha.

"You had better be sure that your vehicle has been well maintained. If you have another breakdown that costs us the battle, I promise I will make your life miserable."

"Yes, sir," replied Misha. It was the only response he could make. He ran back to the BMD, scrambled up the side and slid into the open commander's hatch.

"What's the good news?" asked Taras.

"We are withdrawing to the north to prepare for a possible counterattack should enemy forces strike," replied Misha. "Taras, take us to position Zhenya Fourteen."

"Understood," said Taras, engaging the engine and beginning the lumbering journey to their rally point.

"Enemy forces?" asked Tisha, the BMD's gunner. "We're kilometers from the front line."

"Yes," said Taras with a chuckle, "and those poor bastards at Giebelstadt were over two hundred kilometers from the Czechoslovakian border when we showed up on their doorstep."

Misha smiled as the realization that airborne troops worked both ways suddenly dawned on the young gunner. He thought about the tactical situation. If the Americans were making a landing here, it was a much more conservative gambit than what his own force had launched on the opening day of the war. Spangdahlem was only thirty-five kilometers from the front lines.

"Enemy helicopters approaching from the west," said the voice in Misha's radio. There wasn't much that he could do about that, but he still wanted as much detail as he could get.

"Tisha, keep an eye out for enemy helicopters to the west."

"Understood," replied his gunner. Through his own view port, he kept watch, scanning the dark sky for any indication of the enemy attack. The BMD turned sharply to the right as Taras settled the infantry fighting vehicle into his position.

"I've got something," said Tisha, "zero-three-zero degrees." Misha looked to his right and could see the streaking missiles illuminating the helicopters as they made a pass at the defenders. His eyes followed the missiles to the ground, where they exploded. He could see the silhouettes of vehicles in the fireballs that marked their graves. To his relief, he was also able to see additional streaks, rising from the ground and reaching out for the attackers. They flew out of his sight, but Tisha rotated the turret.

"Son of a bitch!" shouted Tisha. "We got three of the bastards." Over the course of the war, every grunt in the Red Army had come to love the 9K31 Strela-1 mobile SAM launcher. Unlike the larger long-range SAM systems, the Strela didn't rely on radar to track enemy aircraft. Instead, the infrared seekers looked for the heat signatures of incoming aircraft. This was especially effective against the American attack helicopters. Even if the Americans had plastered the defenders with antiradar missiles, the Strela would still be waiting for the enemy to get in close.

"Oh, *blyat'*!" said Tisha. "They must be coordinating between the helicopters and other aircraft. A string of bombs just took out at least one of the Strelas."

18

"This is a very organized attack," said Misha. "I suspect the Captain is right: this isn't a feint."

"Isn't that," replied Taras, "exactly what the enemy would want us to think if it *was* a feint?" Misha didn't ignore the point—it was well made—but he didn't react to it. No sense in giving Taras the satisfaction. Misha looked across the battlefield and could see missiles streaking into the sky to the west. He hadn't seen streaking fire crisscrossing so fiercely since the first night of the war as he'd gently floated in his parachute.

"There's something brewing in the air," said Misha.

"Not a lot we can do about it," said Taras, stating the obvious. "Whatever our brothers in the VVS are up to, I doubt it will be enough."

"Taras," replied Misha, "that sounds like defeatism."

"It's just sound tactical thinking. Just like on the ground—when we choose the time and place of the assault, we get to pour as much into it as we can. The defender has to keep forces along the entire front. If a lowly sergeant sitting in a BMD can see that something is coming… it's going to be something big." The crew settled into silence as the battle raged around them.

"*Yob' tvoyu mat'!*" said Tisha, breaking the silent vigil. "Aircraft Inbound bearing zero-one-fife." Misha looked into his view port. Sure enough, there were incoming aircraft. He had no reason to believe that they were friendly units returning from a mission. The trail of missiles rising to meet them was enough to convince him of that.

"Everyone brace for impact," said Misha, "this could be rough." *It's in the hands of fate now*, he thought. In the pregnant pause that followed, Misha found himself wondering what type of aircraft was about to destroy his BMD. *It could be anything… they have the Jaguar, the American F-111, the Tom—*

These thoughts were cut short when the aircraft overflew the squad's position, dropping bombs as they did. The roar of the aircraft was deafening as they flew over the BMD, but the explosions that followed made everyone forget about the jets that had just passed.

The earth shook with the force of the warheads, rattling the BMD. Misha heard something pinging off the armored skin of the vehicle. It could have been rocks and debris. It could have been bomb fragments. Either way, it was a sign of life—his life. Before the echoes of the last bomb faded, the radio came to life.

"This is Saber One to all Saber units," said Captain Sedelnikov. "Form up on me, heading two-nine-zero." There was a pause as the order was acknowledged. "We are covering the deployment of the regiment's self-propelled mortars to the valley east of Dudeldorf. We must protect their northern flank." *That's one thing I like about Sedelnikov*, thought Misha, he *trusts us with more than the bare minimum of information.*
****

3rd Battalion, 69th Armor Regiment
Diekirch, Luxembourg

Sergeant First Class Don Mackintosh was ready for Operation Fullback to get started. This opinion was shared by most of the 3rd Battalion, 69th Armor Regiment. They'd been sitting in Luxembourg for months, training and preparing. Crossing back into Germany a year after the Soviets had launched their invasion seemed fitting. When the war had originally broken out, the conventional wisdom was that it would be over in a matter of weeks. Months at worst. Yet as the war entered year two, there was no end in sight. Mackintosh remembered admonishing one of the privates. "The experts and the generals always think the war will be over soon and we'll have the boys home by Christmas. Then the fighting starts and everyone is too desperate to care that they were wrong."

Mackintosh peered through his view port on the M1 Abrams tank. This would be the unit's combat baptism for the new tank. The M1 was superior to the M60 in every aspect. Even with the crash course in operation, Mackintosh felt that the company as a whole was considerably more deadly than they had been in October. Now it was time to prove it. Their column was moving out to the northeast. They would cross the shallow Our River at the village of Bettel.

While the NATO forces resupplied and prepared for Operation Fullback, the Soviets had been consolidating their positions in western Germany. While NATO was preparing their hammer, the Warsaw Pact was preparing an anvil. Mackintosh felt bad for the civilians that were about to get caught between the two.

"Come to course zero-four-zero," ordered Captain Henderson, the company commander. "Keep an eye out for the bridging units."

That'd ruin the day pretty quickly, thought Mackintosh.

"I've got 'em, straight ahead," said the driver, Cam Fletcher. Just before the unit made it to the river, the M60 Armored Vehicle Launched Bridges, or AVLBs, deployed their sixty-foot bridges across the forty-five-foot-wide river.

"Welcome to Germany," said the captain when the tank hit the bridge and pitched up. "Keep your eyes sharp, everyone, we're in Indian country." Mackintosh expected immediate action upon crossing the border, but instead they plowed forward into Germany without any fanfare. It wasn't until they neared the village of Mettendorf, five miles from the crossing, that Mackintosh saw a streak of fire rush to his left. He traced the missile to its source.

"BTR, zero-one-two degrees," he called out.

"Engage," ordered the captain. Mackintosh had already depressed the firing buttons on his gunner's yoke. The roar of the 105-millimeter main gun signaled the end of the Soviet infantry fighting vehicle.

"It's been a while since we've seen a Bastion," said Mackintosh over the intercom. During their final combat in Germany before withdrawing to Luxembourg, the Soviets had significantly reduced their use of the antitank guided missiles. Many on the NATO side had speculated that they were running short of supplies. The lull that had led up to Operation Fullback must have given them time to resupply.

The regiment continued towards Mettendorf. Their orders were to skirt the town of the north and press past it. Any pockets of resistance would be picked up by infantry units of the 3rd Infantry Division following behind them. Leadership wanted the 3/69th AR to push past them and get into the enemy's rear. As Fletcher maneuvered the tank to the north, Mackintosh trained the gun on the town, looking for more Soviet targets.

"BTR, zero-six-zero degrees, firing," said Mackintosh. Again the gun roared. "BMP, zero-six—" Mackintosh didn't get to finish his report before the entire tank clanged with the impact of an enemy round. He was rattled but was immediately back at it. "Firing!" The gun barked again. He continued looking for enemy targets.

"Fletch, whaddya got? Any damaged systems?"

"Negative, sir, she's driving like she's supposed to."

"I think that BMP got a shot off on us," said the captain. "It's a good thing he didn't take out our tread." Mackintosh grunted at the obvious statement. The regiment continued to push east, towards their objective: Oberweis. They would occupy the town and set up a defensive line to prevent the enemy counterattack from points east. Once the infantry brigades had cleared out Mettendorf, they would regroup for another push to take Bitburg.

"Intel spotted tanks in Oberweis," said the captain. "Best guess is that it's the 11th East German Armored Regiment. Keep an eye out for T-55s, but don't be surprised by anything."

T-55s, thought Mackintosh, *those tanks are no match for what we're bringing to the fight.* Within a minute of thinking the thought, he was living the reality of it. The regiment encountered a company of T-55s heading right at them.

"Holy shit," said Captain Henderson, "I expected they'd be dug in." There was a relatively flat plain to the west of Oberweis, and the East Germans were using the terrain to set up a classic battle of maneuver. They were outnumbered and outgunned by the Americans, but they relentlessly pushed on towards their foe.

"T-55, bearing zero degrees, firing," said Mackintosh. PFC Wright slammed another round into the M68A1 main gun. The T-55s were returning fire, with both sides taking hits. At this range, the 100-millimeter shells of the East German tanks didn't have much chance to crack the frontal armor of the M1s, but the closer the two forces closed, the better the odds. Every man in the M1 was focused on their job and too busy to be afraid.

After several rounds were sent downrange, the captain spoke up. "They're breaking! Fletch, give me everything you have—we need to destroy as many of them as we can before they get away." Mackintosh had a bad feeling about that. The enemy tanks were retreating in two columns, one to the north of Oberweis, the other to the south. "Stick with the northbound group, Fletch," said Captain Henderson. Mackintosh destroyed another T-55, putting a sabot right through the engine compartment.

In the heat of the battle, he almost missed it. Almost. "Fletch, come to zero-nine-zero now!" ordered Mackintosh. To his credit, Fletch didn't flinch. To the captain's credit, he didn't countermand the order. The sound of the Bastion missile hitting the frontal armor was deafening inside the tank.

"Reverse!" ordered Captain Henderson. The tank came to a stop, then lurched backward. It was clear to Mackintosh that Henderson was trying to assess the situation.

"Sir, I'd bet my farm," said Mackintosh, "that they've got a company hull down on the riverbed. They got us to show our flanks and unloaded with a salvo of missiles." Without pause, Henderson was on the radio to regimental command, explaining the situation and requesting air support from the division's attack helos. His request was denied. The unit's air assets were already assigned. He'd have to make do.

"We've got to get in there," said Captain Henderson. "Whether we get air support or not, we need to smash that line." Henderson got on the radio and gave the order. The company would form a wedge on his tank, and they would punch through the center of the enemy line. The formation crashed towards the enemy. The hull-down position of the T-55s left very little exposed. Mackintosh had to put every bit of his skill to the test. The company of Abrams main battle tanks thundered in the direction of the Enz River.

Mackintosh could make out the winking of a 100mm cannon. Several American shells, including one of his own, obscured the view of the enemy tank for a few seconds before Mackintosh could see the tank breaking from its cover and making a run for the river. Unlike the Our, the Americans wouldn't need bridging units to get across. The tanks could ford the narrow, shallow river with ease. Mackintosh focused ahead of the tank, finding another small bubble that represented the turret of a T-55.

"T-55, engaging," said Mackintosh as he sent another round east. In the chaos of the battle, Mackintosh lost track of how many rounds he'd fired at how many tanks. He just kept focusing on finding new targets. He heard what might have been heavy machine-gun fire pinging off the armor of the tank. Between the sheer number of tanks and the speed with which the Americans were attacking, the battle closed to point-blank range.

The Americans didn't slow their advance as they approached the river. Henderson's company crashed against the East German line like a wave slamming into the breakwaters. Mackintosh watched through the gunsight as Fletch guided the Abrams through the enemy line and into their rear. The line of T-55s behind them was now some other company's problem.

The tank pitched down as it headed down towards the valley below. "Keep an eye out for high-priority targets," said Captain Henderson.

"Do fleeing tanks count?" asked Mackintosh, knowing full well that they did. He fired off a round at a T-55 that was splashing into the river to the east. The Abrams was rapidly approaching the river, and the village of Mettendorf. Mackintosh heard Captain Henderson taking a report of his company disposition. They'd lost seven of their fourteen tanks. Mackintosh had no way of knowing how many men they'd lost, or how many tanks could be repaired and put back on the line. He'd save that cruel math until after the shooting stopped.

The captain barked out orders to the company. Once the other units were moving, he told Fletch, "Once we're across the river, come to zero-zero-five and get us north of the town. There's a valley about five klicks up that we're going to close off. Mack, once we get up there, focus on the village and keep an eye out for retreating enemy tanks."

"Roger that, sir," replied Mackintosh. "Good thing these new tanks don't look anything like those T-55s. I'd hate to get blasted by one of our own guys coming through town."

Chapter 3

2 July 1981
White House
Oval Office
Washington, D.C.

Secretary of Defense Harold Brown sat across from President Carter. It had been a long wait, but Carter was finally getting updated on the first day of Operation Fullback.

"Sir, by all indications, this has been a remarkable success. Even with the delay in getting the M1s in place, we've managed to catch the Soviets by surprise. The British Army of the Rhine is applying pressure near Münster. The 82nd Airborne has taken Bitburg Air Base and are waiting for the 3rd ID to relieve them."

"So, to this point, everything is going as planned?" asked the President.

"That's right, sir. There is still plenty of time for things to go wrong, but for now we seem to have Ivan on the ropes."

"What are we looking at here, Harold?" asked the President. "Is this a turning point in the war?"

"It's far too soon to make such a grand pronouncement. But if we can maximize our advantage here, it just might be the turning point."

"What does that look like?" asked the President.

"If Northern Army Group can take Kassel"—Brown pointed on the map—"and the Central Army Group can close the passes west of Frankfurt, we'll be able to smash the Soviet forces we've trapped in North Rhine-Westphalia and Rhineland-Palatinate. That would take a considerable Soviet force off the table."

"And if we fail to close the door?" asked the President.

"Then the Soviets will be able to withdraw some of their forces to the east, but they'll still be on the defensive, and we'll have taken the initiative. With more modern systems like the M1 and the new AH-64 Apache, the longer we can keep the Soviets pushed back, the more we can close the technology gap that has hindered us so far."

"I see," said the President. "I don't want you to take this the wrong way, but I'm going to be very cautious with my optimism on this."

"I totally agree, sir. But this is what passes for good news these days."

"What about Korea?"

"The Korean offensive is a bit behind the European offensive. The 1st Marine Division was sent directly into the fight in South Korea. The 2nd Marine Division is en route to land somewhere in central North Korea. By placing this force with a clear path to the capital of Pyongyang, we believe we will force the North to dedicate a massive troop investment to protecting the homeland. This will allow our beleaguered troops in the South to turn the tide."

"How confident are we," asked the President, "that Kim Il Sung will break off significant forces to defend against an approaching division?"

"We can't be completely sure until the Marines are on the beach. But Kim is a paranoid narcissist. The CIA strongly believes that he will see 2nd Marines as an assassination force."

"That's absurd," replied Carter.

"It's only absurd if you're not paranoid... sir."

"Good point. What is our chief obstacle in the landing?"

"The Soviet Pacific Fleet is a wild card. So far, they've stayed bottled up in Vladivostok. They don't want to antagonize the Japanese, so they can't attack our forces in Japan. So they haven't had much in the way of target opportunities until now. The Marine expeditionary force will present them with a very tempting target."

"What are we doing to counter the threat?" asked Carter.

"We've got *Kitty Hawk* and *Midway* with the force. We have some additional air cover from the air bases at Misawa and Chitose, Japan. With our standoff abilities, our analysts believe that any attack from the Pacific Fleet will end in a bigger disaster for them than the Battle of the Eastern Mediterranean back in February."

"Please keep me updated," said the President. "I want to know the minute there's movement on this."

"Of course, sir." With his briefing complete, Dr. Brown excused himself. As he left, Hamilton Jordan, the President's Chief of Staff, took his place on the opposite side of the Resolute Desk.

"What's on the agenda, Ham?"

"More tweaking on the draft, sir," replied Jordan. "Before I get into the nuts and bolts, please understand that I've been over all of this with Attorney General Civiletti, and this is all aboveboard and constitutional." Carter was taken aback.

"When you have to start with a warning like that," said the President, "I'm very concerned with what I'm about to hear."

"I think we're onto something. To get this straightened out. We're settling in on a force structure of about thirty percent women—"

"That doesn't sound like the fifty percent the ERA has mandated," interrupted the President.

"Okay, we're playing a little fast and loose here, but the boys at DOJ have told us that the ERA only mandates that women be drafted on an equal basis. We can issue waivers that disproportionately affect women."

The President frowned.

"That hardly seems to match the spirit of the law, Ham."

"Yes, sir. I agree. But we're trying to keep our military functioning at a wartime pace while not violating the Constitution. There are some legal remedies, basically repealing the ERA and replacing it with a new version that excludes the draft, but there's no way we can get Congress to agree on the wording, even with the war on."

"That's fair."

Jordan continued, "The best part of the plan is that if we waive twenty percent of the applicants, we can start looking for specialists. When it comes to drafting men, we can take pretty much any healthy eighteen-year-old and turn him into a rifleman. Basically, regardless of the eighteen-year-old, we can find a place for them. When it comes to the women, however…" Jordan faltered, looking for the right words.

"Just spit it out, Ham," said the President, "I won't hold any rudeness against you."

"Since we have the chance to be selective, we can afford to look for more skilled women. We can pull from the retail sector to help staff up supply, as an example. Nurses are an obvious fit as well. Anyone with banking experience, things of that nature."

"I'm not really following—what is the downside to all of this?"

"The draft is going to lean older on the female side, and it's going to hit more mothers."

"That's not going to play well. I think that the nation as a whole would rather repeal the ERA than move forward with something like this."

"I think you're right," agreed Jordan, "but we can't repeal the ERA with a stroke of a pen. We can do this." The President didn't look quite satisfied. "Sir, I know you don't like to operate like this, but we can get this moving very quietly. We can classify most of the changes under the guise of national security. And to be honest, that's exactly what it is."

"I don't like it, Ham," replied the President. "At the same time, we need to field the best army we can. We owe that to the world... Bring me the specifics when you have them, but get this going."

"Yes, sir," said Jordan on his way out.

What are we becoming? wondered the President as he turned his chair one hundred and eighty degrees and stared out over the South Lawn before another knock at the door pulled him back into his busy day.

****

2 July 1981
82nd Airborne Division
Bitburg Air Base, Germany

Specialist Marlon Reeves starred across the river valley. They'd been on the ground for twelve hours and had not been removed from their perch. By now they were well dug in and keeping out of sight. The Soviet artillery barrage was intense, but it remained behind them. Only the occasional short round would get the hairs up on the back of his neck. Otherwise, he'd really pulled great duty on this mission. He kept his eyes on his sector, and when the occasional Soviet vehicle came into view, he relayed the details to PFC Davis, who would get the word to the mortarmen.

"Hey, Sarge," said Davis, looking up from his radio. "Command is sending a runner out. I think we're going to be redeploying." Reeves looked over to Staff Sergeant Felix Watkins, the squad's leader. Watkins, in turn, looked back towards the airfield. Reeves went back to covering his assigned zone, looking for communists. Whatever the runner was telling Watkins, he'd find out when Watkins was ready to relay it. Then again, it could have nothing to do with Reeves at all.

After a few minutes, Watkins raised his voice. Reeves couldn't make out what the staff sergeant was saying, but he was clearly upset. If

Watkins was upset, Reeves was certain that he wasn't going to be happy either.

"All right, men, close it up," said the sergeant after the runner left. Reeves climbed out of his fighting position and closed with the rest of the team on the staff sergeant. "Look, Command has lost their damned minds." With an opening like that, nothing good could follow. "We're repositioning." He took a knee and unfolded his map on the ground. The rest of the squad dropped down to take a look. "They want to get eyes on Spangdahlem, so we're moving to... here."

"That's across the valley," said Sergeant Kidd.

"No shit," said Watkins. "So we're going to be doing a lot of climbing."

Reeves looked closer at the map.

"Wait, that's the highest elevation point on the battlefield."

"Good eye, Reeves. That's why they want us there," replied Watkins.

"But Ivan's been here for at least a week. Surely they've got something on that hill."

"Yes, but any spotters Ivan has are going to be west-facing. We're going to sneak around to the east face and hide out there."

"This is some real Delta Force shit," said Kidd.

"Look," said Watkins, "we've had it soft over here. The Reds are coming up from the south, but the Kyll River Valley is protecting this eastern flank. DIVARTY needs targets, and the farther behind the lines we can get those targets, the better it's going to go. They've been plastering that hill off and on since they got set up. These are not my favorite orders, but we're going to follow them, because that's what we do, got it?"

"Got it," replied the squad, as one.

"How are we getting across the river?" asked Kidd.

Watkins pointed to a spot on the map. "Command says the narrowest part of the river is here. You're the best swimmer that I've got, so I need you to swim the river with a line. Once you secure it, the rest of the squad will cross on the line."

"When are we pulling stakes?" asked Kidd.

"As soon as our relief is here," said Watkins. Before that could happen, though, the sirens sounded, alerting the base to an incoming threat. "You see anyone, Kidd?"

"Negative, Sarge," replied Kidd. "It's a ghost town over there." Watkins lifted his binoculars and looked north. His view was obscured by a ridge north of the air base, but he could see a dust cloud rising into the air. "Looks like they're coming at us from the north. But don't get distracted. Keep an eye on the east—that's our area of responsibility."

"Staff Sergeant Watkins," said a sergeant nearing their position. "Change of plans, you need to report back to the captain. Whatever this is"—he gestured to the north—"it supersedes your previous orders."

"Understood, much obliged," Watkins replied, then turned to his men. "All right, ladies, let's go see the old man. Kidd, take them in. I'll give Nichols the pass-down and meet you down there."

"Roger that, Sarge." Kidd took the rest of the squad down the hill while Watkins filled in Sergeant Nichols on the events of the past six hours.

By the time Watkins caught up with the squad, they were just about to enter the headquarters tent. There was motion and commotion everywhere as men rushed to defensive positions to repel the coming attack. Dodging another squad that was leaving the tent, they slipped in to find Captain Foster.

"I need you guys on the line," said the captain. "Take the roof of the auxiliary admin building. That should give you a good vantage point."

"Roger, sir, we've got it," replied Watkins, who then turned to leave.

"Wait," said the captain, "you're going to want to take some of these." He motioned to a crate of LAW rockets.

"Sir," said Watkins as Reeves and PFC Sebastian "Seabass" Davis grabbed two each, and they hustled out of the tent and ran for the aux admin building. They ran up the side stairwell to get roof access. The roof had a nice two-and-a-half-foot elevated ledge that would give them some cover in the upcoming fight.

"Listen," said Watkins as Reeves and the squad were taking up their positions. "Don't waste those rockets on a tank unless we don't have a choice. Save them for one of those BMPs, or a troop concentration. We've only got four of them—we need to make them count."

"Got it, boss," said Sergeant Kidd. The division artillery opened up as the enemy approached. The thunder of the guns was a stark reminder of the chaos to come.

"Here they come!" said Reeves. "Tanks, cresting the ridge."

"Division has plans for those tanks—we're here to keep the infantry out." Reeves shifted his rifle in his hands and waited for the shooters to arrive.

****

345th Independent Guards Airborne Regiment
Spangdahlem Air Base, Germany

"I think this second day of fighting is going to be significantly more dangerous than the first," said Taras, as though reading Misha's mind.

"I wouldn't have thought that possible after those strike planes nearly bombed us into oblivion," said Misha, "but I agree." On the night of the attack, his platoon had been sent out to protect the west flank of the base, only there were no enemy targets there. Instead, the attack turned out to be focused on the smaller air base to the west of Spangdahlem. That left Misha and his BMD out of the action.

"I imagine the lieutenant is going to figure out a way to blame you for our lack of combat," laughed Taras.

"Of that, I have no doubt," replied Misha. He didn't know what it was, but he must have done something to offend Lieutenant Krylov. Ever since Krylov had taken over the platoon, he'd been riding Misha hard. It seemed to Misha that nothing he could do was good enough for Krylov. At this point he just tried to keep his head down and do his job.

Tonight, they were heading northwest. There was a river crossing some twelve kilometers from the base. The 345th was coming in behind an armored thrust in an attempt to dislodge the American Airborne troops. The Soviets would make a helicopter assault south of Bitburg as a feint, but that would only buy them so much time. There was also an East German motor rifle division to the west of Bitburg. They had been slow in their response last night, and Misha didn't have much faith in their ability to get it right today.

The 7th Guards Tank Division, on the other hand—Misha had full faith that they would be up to the task today. The 7th was rolling out the latest Soviet tank innovation, the T-80. She would be making her combat debut in the effort to break into Bitburg. The division had proven itself from the start of the war, having fought in some of the fiercest fights in the North German Plain.

Misha looked through his view port and was surprised to see a flight of ungainly *Grachi* fly over the formation on their way southbound. He'd never actually seen one of the new Su-25 ground attack planes before. With their long wings, laden with bombs, and a 30mm cannon that could tear through all but the sturdiest armor, their presence on the battlefield was a welcome one. He'd been fortunate that he hadn't seen the American A-10 Thunderbolt either. The Soviet troops had taken to calling it the "Molotok," the Russian word for "hammer." *And we're all just nails*, thought Misha.

The key to this crossing was that it was the only place within fifty kilometers where the slopes on both sides of the river valley were gentle enough to allow them to cross without a span from one cliff side to the one on the opposite shore. Engineer units had demined the west bank of the river. That was necessary, but it had also given the NATO bandits notice of what was coming. Now it was up to the 7th and the 345th to make sure that it didn't matter. They would wipe out the Americans before they could establish their bridgehead.

The BMD pitched up as they climbed out of the Kyll Valley and climbed up to the relatively flat ground north of Bitburg. As the tank settled back level, Misha ordered, "Driver, come to course one-nine-five."

"One-nine-five, understood," replied Taras. The Soviet force bore down on the hapless American defenders. There would be blood spilled on both sides, but Misha was confident that Bitburg would be in Soviet hands within days. The Soviets raced south, skirting the town of Bitburg to the east. The primary objective was the airfield southeast of the town, so they chose to bypass the town.

As Misha watched through his view port, streaks of flame shot out of the easternmost buildings of the town. Antitank guided missiles. The Americans must have put some forward antitank teams in the town. That was bold, as they would be operating without the direct support of the rest of the division. But that was their problem. Misha's problem was getting to Bitburg and fighting the Yankees.

The artillery fell as the vehicles closed with the airfield. Misha's BMD was near the head of the battle line, but he could still feel the impacts of the rounds as the Americans tried to slow their advance.

"I don't think they want to give up the airfield today," said Tisha, the BMD's gunner. There wasn't much to say about that. Just the idle chatter of men facing death with nothing they could do about it.

Misha wasn't a fan of the battle plan. The closest defensive ridge the terrain offered was still two kilometers from the main airfield facilities. Command didn't want them to dismount under that cover, then try to cross in the open. It would be a mass suicide unseen since the Great World War. Instead, they were driving those final two kilometers and dismounting at the objective.

Ahead, Misha could see the tanks of the 7th Guards engaging US forces. The muzzle blasts were clear, even if the targets they were aiming at weren't. With any luck, they'd clear out enough of the enemy to give Misha and his men a fighting chance to get out of the BMD. More missile fire poured out of the air base, and many of the T-80s were taking hits. In fact, Taras was now driving past the first dead tanks as they crossed over the final ridge to make the suicide sprint for the airfield.

"Fuck," said Tisha. "Enemy aircraft inbound."

"How can you tell they are enemy planes?" asked Taras.

"Those fucking Molotki really stand out."

Misha watched in horror as a pair of the American antitank aircraft descended on the tank column with missiles pouring out of them. The effect was devastating, but not nearly as worrisome as what came next. The two aircraft wheeled over and made another pass. This time, there were no missiles. In fact, from Misha's point of view, he couldn't see what was happening, except that Soviet tanks were exploding on the ground.

"Must be a hell of a gun on those things," said Tisha.

"And you can be sure that once they've eaten all the tanks, we'll be next," said Taras.

"Where are our brothers in the VVS?" asked Misha.

"There must have been something more important to protect, further away from the fighting," Taras snorted derisively.

The airfield was taking shape as they closed. Misha was looking for a building to aim for, so that once they left the protective armor of the BMD, they wouldn't be standing out there naked with their balls in their hands.

"Taras, there's a hangar, eleven o'clock. Make for that." He then looked over to his gunner. "Tisha, put a few rounds of high-explosive in there to clear it out."

"Firing," said the gunner as the report of the 73mm cannon rang through the BMD. The smoke and debris of battle had settled into a haze that settled over the battlefield, giving the entire scene a surreal look.

"You've got about fifteen seconds," said Taras as he raced for the hangar. The BMD tore through the perimeter fence. A BMD to his left took a missile to its front armor but kept moving. Misha prepared to pop his hatch. He knew that in the meatbox behind him, Andrusha Koshelev would be getting ready to pop their hatch as well. There was a sudden shift as Taras whipped the BMD around, with the right track going in reverse while the left went forward.

"Go! Go! Go!" ordered Misha as he popped his hatch and climbed up, out, and down the BMD. He sprinted for the hangar. He was surprised to see several men still inside. He went to a knee and fired several rounds towards them. The men in the hangar seemed shocked by the presence of Soviet infantry. All but one scattered as the rounds hit, odd man out falling to the ground with a hole in his head. More Desantniks joined Misha, and they advanced on the enemy.

He watched the enemy break and run from the hangar. At first he was confused. In his six months of war, he'd never seen the enemy break so quickly. As he cleared out the hangar, he understood. These men weren't infantry. They were mechanics, or supply. As he shot one in the back, he noticed that none of them held weapons. The fact that they were unarmed didn't bother him in the slightest. They were enemy combatants, and even if they didn't have a gun right now, that didn't mean they wouldn't get one, then come back and kill his men later.

Taras had pulled the BMD out to regroup so that they could use the BMDs in a separate attack thrust. They were no match for the T-80s, or even the T-72s, but they could make an accounting of themselves, especially against a light infantry unit such as they were facing today. Misha couldn't worry about that right now, though. He'd secured this tiny piece of the battlefield, but now he had to push out. He'd wait here to link up with additional forces, but he needed to be ready to move when they did. So he needed his next objective.

The hangar was a great place for unloading the squad. It was big enough to obscure the BMD, and the men climbing out of it, but it wasn't the best for observing the battlefield. There was no way to get any elevation. He was stuck on the ground. He cautiously moved to the south end of the hangar and peered around the open door.

To the south, he could see aircraft revetments with hardened hangars to protect aircraft. From what he could tell, there weren't any aircraft there. That made sense. The Soviets hadn't been using the base, and the battlefield was way too hot for the Yankees to bring in any aircraft of their own. He estimated that it was about thirty meters to the first of the revetments, and he decided then and there that this would be his next objective. He turned to explain the plan to his squad and noticed that they had acquired several more men.

"All right, men, listen up," said Misha, taking charge of his makeshift light platoon. "There are some more hangars thirty meters that way." He pointed in the direction of the revetments. "We're going to take those. They'll provide much better protection than this tin shack." Misha was worried that someone might object to his taking over, but he could tell that most of the newcomers were just happy to have someone else in charge. "You"—he pointed at a junior sergeant—"your squad will go second. My squad will go first, and you'll give us covering fire. The rest of you follow behind. We'll regroup at the next hangar."

With that, Misha gave a quick check to make sure that his men were ready and in position. "Go!" The Desantniks broke out of the hangar and ran for their next objective. Rifle fire erupted on either side of them as the remaining paratroopers fired at unseen enemies. Enemy fire erupted from the revetment, and Misha and his squad went prone, looking for targets. A muzzle flash attracted Misha's attention, and he sent five rounds in its direction. He heard one of his men cursing loudly. It was Andrusha.

There was nothing Misha could do for him at the moment. If he couldn't neutralize the threat, Andrusha wouldn't be his only casualty. The worst part was that Andrusha had his only light machine gun. He didn't have a lot of firepower outside of that. He took a few more shots where he could see Yankees in firing positions. There was a scream followed by an explosion. One of the follow-on squads had fired a rocket-propelled grenade or RPG at the hangar.

That was the break that Misha needed. "Let's go, move it!" he yelled as he leapt to his feet and closed the distance to the hangar. He was ten yards out when he saw an American firing to his left. He cut the soldier down. Another RPG flew past him and exploded in the revetment. Misha looked over his shoulder, back to the original hangar they had taken. He could see the next squad advancing while the third squad continued pouring fire into the objective.

Misha continued his push, willing his muscles to give him as much speed as they could. He made it into the hangar and looked for targets. He found none. Inside the building, he took a knee and caught his breath before looking around for his squad. He saw no one. Some of the troops came running in behind him while others were carrying the wounded. Misha took a roll call of the wounded. Andrusha wasn't among them.

Misha turned to the junior sergeant he'd called earlier and said, "Secure this hangar—I'm going to get my friend." He and Andrusha had been in combat together since Afghanistan. They'd jumped together on the first day of the war. They'd hidden in the cold German forest during the battle of Wurzburg. There was no way in hell he was going to leave him now. He ran back into the open, to the spot where he remembered Andrusha falling.

It didn't take him long to find the young man. He ran to his friend and took a knee. Andrusha's dead eyes stared at the sky. Misha's shoulders sagged.

"I'm sorry, my friend. I was starting to think that we would survive this war. That was my mistake. But I will kill a dozen of them to avenge you. And I need to borrow this." He pulled the nylon strap of the RPKS-74 light machine gun out from around Andrusha's shoulder, freeing the weapon from his dead friend. He quickly relieved Andrusha of all of his ammunition and then placed his hand on Andrusha's cheek for a moment before sprinting back to the hangar.
****

82nd Airborne Division
Bitburg Air Base, Germany

Reeves felt small in the presence of the armor. His meatbag of a body wasn't much protection when compared to the armored behemoths that were bearing down on him. As he watched an element of A-10s tear into the tank column with AGM-65 Maverick missiles, he reflected that maybe being a meatbag on a rooftop wasn't too bad after all. The A-10s had cut the column about in half, from what Reeves could see. That left the forward section intact to make a run on the base.

"Here comes the infantry," said Staff Sergeant Watkins. Reeves looked over and saw Watkins peering through his binoculars to the north. "Seabass, Kidd, get the LAWs ready." The two soldiers dutifully grabbed two of the tubes and extended them until they clicked into place. "Enemy's about a mile out, so it's going to be a while, but don't get complacent." As if to emphasize the point, a Soviet tank round smashed into the building they were on top of. "Reeves, go check the west side, and see what's going on with those tanks."

"Roger that, Sarge," said Reeves as he walked across the roof at a low crouch. He looked over the ledge and was in awe as he watched the 3rd Battalion, 73rd Armor, engaged in a running tank battle with the Soviets. The squat M551 Sheridan tanks were supported by ATGM teams and were holding their own against the heavier Soviet tanks. Nonetheless, losses were mounting.

"Sarge, they've sent the Sheridans to stop the tank assault. It looks like it's working."

"All right, Reeves, get your rifle pointed downrange and get ready to receive our guests."

The Soviet mechanized infantry had closed quite a bit since Reeves had reconnoitered the tank battle. He raised his rifle and tried to pick a spot he thought the Russkies would use for cover. There were some buildings about three hundred yards away that would be perfect cover for an approach.

"Sarge," said Reeves, "I don't think any of those APCs are going to close to within LAW range."

"You never know," said Watkins, "we might find a hero who barges right in on us. Either way, they'll kill a troop concentration just as well as they'll disable a vehicle." As expected, the enemy vehicles began unloading their troops at extreme range. Seabass fired off a few rounds.

"Cease fire, dammit," said Watkins. "All you're doing is letting them know we're here. Hold your fire until they close within two hundred yards. This fight is a marathon, not a sprint. And nobody go full auto unless the enemy gets within fifty yards of this position. Even then, only use short, controlled bursts. Three to five rounds only. We don't have the ammo to waste."

Soviet troops advanced to the first line of buildings. It was clear to Reeves that they were clearing out the buildings, but he wasn't able to tell who was holding them. Was it German locals? Was it airborne troopers? He saw one of the Soviet APCs aim in his direction and realized that they were exposed.

"Shit, get down!" shouted Reeves as a section of the building to his left exploded with the impact of the Russian shell. Everyone went prone, as there were several more explosions impacting the building. Reeves couldn't track time. From the moment he'd seen the cannon pointed at him to this point could have been a few seconds... or it could have been a few minutes.

"Get back on the line," ordered Watkins, and Reeves sat up and looked over the ledge.

"Contact, one o'clock," said Kidd, firing. Reeves looked to his right and could see several Soviet soldiers moving towards their position. He took aim and squeezed the trigger, watching a Russian soldier fall before lining up his next target and firing. Incoming rounds struck the roofline, but it was clear that it wasn't focused fire, just the enemy shooting in their general direction. The squad was constantly ducking and moving to avoid popping up in the same position twice and giving the enemy an easy shot.

The building shook again, as it had when the enemy BMD had first fired at it.

"We've gotta get out of here," said Watkins. "There are at least four of those APCs concentrating fire on us." The squad collected up their gear, including collapsing the LAW rockets, and made for the roof access door. As they hit the ground floor, they could feel a section of the building collapse, throwing a thick cloud of dust in the air. They staggered out of the building.

"Get over to the main admin building," said Watkins. "We're going to set up outside, on the corners. Kidd, take Reeves to the northeast corner. I'll keep Seabass and Durant to cover the northwest."

"Roger," said Kidd, making eye contact with Reeves to ensure he heard the order before he took off to the east with Reeves on his heels. When they made it to the far side of the building, Kidd took a knee and scanned the battlefield. "Reeves, take the wall of the building next door, and cover from two-nine-zero to three-six-zero."

Reeves understood that Kidd was setting up interlocking fields of fire to give them the best chance of covering their entire area of responsibility.

"Two o'clock," said Kidd. "I've got movement in the hangars over there." He fired a quick three rounds before taking aim again and firing. There was nothing for Reeves to do at this point, as the enemy was beyond his own field of fire. "We better have someone holding that side of the line, or we're going to be in trouble." The thought of the enemy breaking through just to their right was sobering.

"We've got more company," said Reeves. "Twelve o'clock." There were five men sprinting towards them, coming in head-on. Reeves fired a single round. Then another, and another. Kidd was also countering the threat. Within seconds, all five were down. "Oh shit! RPG," yelled Reeves, diving away from the building he was using for cover. The wall exploded behind him, throwing cement debris everywhere.

"You hit?" asked Kidd without looking at Reeves. He was peering around the corner, trying to get a shot off at whoever had fired the RPG.

"I don't think so," said Reeves. "But I might have sprained my ankle on the landing."

"Ready those LAW rockets," said Kidd. "We should have done that when we got here."

He's right, and that's the type of detail that could cost us the battle, thought Reeves as he pulled the tubes apart. The smoke covering the battlefield reduced visibility to between fifty and seventy-five yards, depending on the wind. The orderly beginning of the battle, where Reeves and Kidd had been able to call out and engage targets, shifted into a new chaos where targets would dance in and out of the wisps of smoke. They fired at what felt like an endless number of Russians. Yet they kept coming.

Reeves began to wonder if he was actually shooting at ghosts. More often than not, he couldn't see the bodies fall in the shifting smoke. One thing that he was sure of, though, was that the enemy was getting closer.

Chapter 4

345th Independent Guards Airborne Regiment

Misha took stock of his forces. He had three remaining from his squad. In addition, he'd added seven other Desantniks.

"What unit are you with?" he asked the junior sergeant he'd put in charge of his second squad.

"Third Platoon, 7th Company," said the man. "I'm Junior Sergeant Igor Arefyev, and this"—he gestured to another junior sergeant—"is Slava Tipolov."

"Okay, we can't stay here long. We need to push forward. But tend to your wounded while I figure out our next move."

"Understood, comrade Sergeant," said Arefyev. "And I see you found your friend." He pointed at the machine gun.

"That's right," said Misha, rolling with it. "This is the type of friend you can always count on." He then turned from Arefyev and headed to the far side of the revetment. *If they want to think the machine gun is my best friend, why not let them believe it?* thought Misha. There was a copse of trees next to the revetment on the south side and what looked like a maintenance building to his right and another revetment farther south and to the left. He'd need to clear the building first before taking the next revetment.

"Arefyev," said Misha, "come here, we need to talk." When Arefyev reached him, he continued. "I'm going to slip out into these trees with my squad and set up some firing positions. Once we're in place, I need you to take that building there." He gestured towards the objective. "Once you're in, have Tipolov bring his squad in to support you. After you clear the building, you can give us covering fire to take the next revetment."

"Understood," replied Arefyev, who trotted over to the rest of the unit and passed on the plan. Misha's squad regrouped and low-crawled into the woods. With the noise and the smoke and the general chaos, they were able to set up positions about fifteen meters apart with a good view of both the building and the revetment. He signaled to Arefyev and opened up with the RPKS on the maintenance building.

Arefyev and his team bolted out of the revetment and made for the building. One of the men fell and didn't get up. Fire was coming in from the revetment to the left. Misha shifted fire and unloaded two more bursts before his machine gun ran dry. He swapped mags and went back to work. Glancing over to check on Arefyev's progress, Misha watched as the junior sergeant breached the door and one of his troopers tossed in a grenade. The explosion caused the door to pop open again, but Arefyev pushed against it to keep it shut.

Misha heard one of his men take a hit, but there was nothing he could do. For the second time in the battle, he felt helpless. But the only way he could ever render aid was to take the objectives. So he kept firing. He checked in on Arefyev. He couldn't tell much from the outside of the building. Tipolov's squad crossed to the building and entered through the same door that Arefyev had. There was nothing for Misha to do but keep pushing the Americans back. But he couldn't do that forever. He'd need more ammo soon at this rate.

He caught movement from the building and looked to see Arefyev motioning to him from a broken window on the second story.

"First Squad, follow me," shouted Misha as he rose from his position and ran for the building. The dash to the building was intense. Bullets whipped all around him while the sounds of bigger guns thundered in the background. He reached the door and saw a dead Soviet private in the hallway. He waited for the rest of his squad to catch up. Privates Kulakov and Silivanov arrived, but there was no sign of Junior Sergeant Zlobin.

"Follow me," said Misha as he cautiously entered the stairwell and climbed to the second floor. There was another dead Desantnik on the stairs. He could hear sporadic firing above him and peered around the corner at the top of the stairs. It was difficult to make out the situation. From what he could tell, Arefyev's men occupied a room across from the stairwell, while an enemy force occupied rooms on the opposite side of the building. Neither side could effectively move without exposing themselves to enemy fire.

Misha's tactical problem was that he couldn't see the enemy position. He could only hear the rifle fire and see the bullet impacts. There just wasn't much that he could do from here. He pulled a grenade from his pack, removed the pin, and chucked it down the hall. Immediately after the explosion, he ran across the hall into the first room on the opposite side. He found more bodies. This time there were both American and Soviet soldiers. Misha mentally tallied the losses and realized that nearly the entire force that had come into this building was dead.

Misha took a knee and peeked around the corner of the doorway. There was a muzzle flash and a burst of fire. He pulled back as bullets tore at the door frame above his head. *At least I know where they are*, he thought.

"Glory and honor!" shouted Misha.

"None but us," came Arefyev's reply from further down the hall. From what Misha could tell, the Russians were both on the same side of the building and the Americans were on the opposite side. Privates Kulakov and Silivanov made the dash across the hall to join Misha. Fire erupted from the far side, and Silivanov cried out.

"Dammit! I'm shot," said the private.

"Kulakov, check him out," said Misha. He then called out to Arefyev, "How many do you have with you?"

"Two—it's just Ryabov and myself."

"How many Americans are there?"

"I can't tell, but I think they are all concentrated in a single room, on the opposite side, all the way at the end of the building."

Misha turned to the privates, "How is he?" He watched as Kulakov cut a hole in Silivanov's pant leg and exposed a gruesome wound in his thigh.

"It's bad, comrade Sergeant," said Kulakov, stating the obvious.

"Get a tourniquet on that. He's going to lose the leg, but he might survive the battle." Misha dropped the magazine from his machine gun and pulled a fresh one out. He slammed it home and charged the weapon before calling out to Arefyev, "If you have a grenade left, toss it."

"If I had any more grenades," replied Arefyev, "I would have used one by now."

"Kulakov, give me one of Silivanov's grenades." If there was one thing Misha had learned in his extensive combat experience, it was that he'd much rather use someone else's grenade if he had a choice. Kulakov tossed the grenade to Misha, who pulled the pin and yelled, "*Lozhis'!*" as he tossed it to the end of the hallway. As soon as the explosive detonated, Misha fired a sustained ten-round burst into the far corner and advanced into the hallway.

If Arefyev was wrong and there were more enemy soldiers in the building, Misha wouldn't make it far. He was betting his life on his fellow Desantnik's analysis. He advanced past the room that held Arefyev and Ryabov. He could make out the doorway of the office at this point. He fired another sustained burst. He was praying to a God he wasn't allowed to believe in that the sound of the machine gun would frighten the Americans. Thirty rounds go fast, though, and as the gun went silent, he pulled his last grenade, tossed it into the room, and dove for the floor. The grenade detonated and there were shouts and cries coming from the office.

"Arefyev, take them out!" shouted Misha as he reloaded with his last partial magazine. Then, before he could get his weapon racked, the two paratroopers advanced into the hallway and towards the Americans with their AK-74s barking single rounds. Misha followed behind them. By the time Misha entered the room, the carnage was over. The Americans were all dead.

"Looks like we won't be advancing," said Arefyev.

"We'll be lucky if we can even hold this place. We need more troops, but until they get here, we need to set up defensive positions. You take the southwest corner and get eyes on that revetment that we were trying to take. If the enemy counterattacks, it'll come from there. I'll see what I can do about getting some more men to our position. Get comfortable. This is the closest thing to rest that we're going to get anytime soon."

****

82nd Airborne Division

Specialist Marlon Reeves and Sergeant Luca Kidd had been holding their position for what felt like an eternity. But something had to change, and soon. They were both running low on ammunition. The plan had called for runners to bring supplies, but up to this point, none had appeared.

"Look," said Sergeant Kidd, "we can't hold out without ammo. We need to figure out a solution."

Reeves had an epiphany.

"Cover me, Sarge," he said as he dropped his rifle and raced towards the enemy. It took him mere seconds to get to his first dead

Soviet. He relieved the man of his rifle and searched him for spare magazines. After finding three additional mags, Kidd fired a burst over his head.

"Get back here, dammit!" yelled the sergeant. Reeves obediently returned.

"Here," he said, handing over the AK-74 and magazines. "It ain't a solid M16, but it'll kill a commie just as well."

"You're crazy, Reeves, but you ain't wrong," said Kidd. "But don't do that shit again. You're lucky you didn't get your ass shot off."

"You're the one who said we needed a solution," replied Reeves.

"Okay." Before he could finish his reply, Kidd fired several rounds downrange. "But next time, we work together, not this 'cover me' bullshit."

"Roger that, Sarge," said Reeves, verifying his own ammo situation. He was down to one thirty-round mag, with a partial in the rifle. He'd lost track of how many rounds he had but couldn't take the time to drop it and take a look. Before he could worry about it any more, there was an explosion just to the north of their position. The blast was enough to knock them back but didn't cause any immediate damage.

Reeves was trying to get his bearings. The explosion had left him deaf and disoriented. He looked to where he thought the enemy would be and saw a solid wall. The blast had spun him around, and it took him a minute to put everything together. He turned to his right and saw the oncoming enemy. They were charging in force. He fired his M16, and after seven or eight rounds, it ran dry. He dropped the mag and reached for his last one, but it was too late. A Soviet soldier was running up on him.

He pulled his combat knife and jammed it in the Russian's gut as he ran past. The Russian fell, and Reeves rolled with him, twisting and ripping the knife, trying to find some vital piece of the man that would kill him. Bullets ripped into the back of the Russian, and Reeves momentarily marveled that the dying Russian had accidentally saved his life. He rolled over, putting the dead Russian under him, withdrew his knife, and relieved the corpse of its rifle.

He pulled back on the charging handle of the AK-74, found a target and pulled the trigger. Nothing happened. Another Russian came at him, and Reeves swung the AK by the barrel, striking the enemy soldier in the face with the thick wooden stock. He then went back to his knife, stabbing the man repeatedly in the heart. He was engrossed in the savagery of his own attack when he was struck from behind, and the world went black.

****

3rd Battalion, 69th Armor Regiment
Olsdorf, Germany

West of Bitburg, the fighting had been brutal for the 3/69th AR. They punched through Mettendorf, and the East German defenders there. They pushed on to Olsdorf, where they finally had to pause to allow the lines to catch up with them. The tanks were dug in, waiting for resupply during the night. In a surprise to everyone in the regiment, the 3rd Aviation Regiment was able to bring ammunition and fuel up to Olsdorf in their new UH-60 Black Hawks. This allowed them to rearm and refuel without waiting for some of the slower units to catch up. Speed was key to relieving Bitburg.

Don Mackintosh considered what Captain Henderson had told him: they were going to expect even greater resistance today. They were linking up with elements of the West German Bundeswehr's 5th Panzer Division. Intelligence reported a large infantry holding force in Oberweis with armored support. The two armored units would pass north and south of the city in an effort to locate and neutralize the enemy's armor, while the 2nd Brigade of the 3rd Infantry Division was sent into Oberweis to eject the enemy.

As the Abrams raced along with the rest of the regiment, battle was imminent. From his gunner's position, Mackintosh would see the now-familiar pattern of battle. Antitank missiles slammed into tanks ahead of him. The renewed supplies of missiles were an unwelcome event for tankers on both sides of the war. 3/69 was taking losses, but they were still pushing forward. Mackintosh had no doubt that to their north, the 5th Panzers were encountering similar resistance.

AH-1 Cobras swooped over the forested hills, letting loose salvos of unguided rockets. The rockets could cover a rather large area and destroy any antitank teams within the kill zone. *Let 'em fry*, thought Mackintosh absently. The Americans were advancing with the flow of the terrain. They slipped along valleys that gave them a degree of cover from the hills closer to the objective.

Without warning, several of the M1s in the lead of the column exploded. Tanks were swerving left and right and desperately trying to stop.

"Minefield," said the captain, mostly for PFC Wright's benefit. The loader was the only one who hadn't seen the tip of the spear get blunted. "Fletch, come to zero-nine-zero and bring us to a stop." The entire company would be executing a classic "herringbone" maneuver, where the tanks would take alternating left and right turns, allowing their guns to cover a vast area while minimizing their exposure while the engineers came forward to demine the area.

The key to the operation was speed. They wouldn't have long before the enemy started lobbing artillery at them. The new OBATs or obstacle breaching assault tanks were deployed near the lead element and were no doubt racing into the minefield. The OBATs were older M60A3 tanks that were fitted with a mine plow on the front of the tank. This plow would dig up enemy mines and either cast them aside, clearing a safe lane, or flip them over, pointing their destructive charge at the earth. Either way, it would be a lot safer once they pushed through.

Shells began exploding all around the tanks as the order was given to move forward again. There were four clearly marked paths through the minefield. The regiment was pushing hard to get out of the artillery shelling, and Mackintosh found himself hoping that the radar boys were getting a fix on the enemy guns so that some air strikes could be brought in. Close-air support was hit or miss lately. NATO could grab the sky and hold it, but the SAM coverage of the Soviet forces meant that even if they held the air superiority, the Soviet forces were not defenseless.

"Contact Armor, zero-four-five degrees," the captain called out.

"I've got it. T-55. Firing, load sabot," said Mackintosh. The enemy tanks were descending on the Americans from the hills south of Oberweis. Mackintosh could see the strategy. They wanted to slow the American attack long enough to get more elements of their infantry dug in to defend the town.

"Looks like they're trying to flank us south," said the captain. "Fletch, come to zero-nine-zero." The tank turned to the right and Mackintosh rotated the gun to the left to keep his sights on the advancing

T-55s. The battle evolved, with PFC Wright loading and Mackintosh firing. The rhythm of the battle was suddenly interrupted by a loud clanging.

"Sir, she's acting kinda funny," said Fletch. "She's pulling hard to the right." Suddenly, the tank whipped hard right. "We've thrown a track!"

"Bring her to a stop, Fletch," said the captain. "We're a mobility kill, but we're still in the fight, dammit." Now that the tank had lost the ability to move, they were sitting ducks for any East German tanks. They might survive a hit to the frontal armor from those 100mm cannons, but it wouldn't take long for them to get blown to hell.

"Firing," said Mackintosh, engaging another T-55 on the hills above them. He started scanning for another target. It took a few seconds to find one. That was when Mackintosh realized that the battle was moving away from them. The East Germans were withdrawing back to the north. Either they were breaking, or they planned to regroup for another thrust. It didn't matter which—either way, it seemed that Mackintosh and his crew would live to fight another day.

"All right," said Captain Henderson, "I've reported our situation up the chain. We'll have a support vehicle out soon. In the meantime, let's get the process started. Mack, you stay on the gun and keep an eye out for bad guys. Fletch, Wright, you're with me. Wright, grab the replacement track, Fletch, once he's got it out of the storage compartment, give it a once-over. We can't screw this one up or we'll be really done." The tank commander popped his hatch and slid out of the vehicle.

From inside the tank, Mackintosh couldn't see the men working on the track. Nevertheless, he was familiar with the process. Right now, while Fletch was inspecting the new track, Wright and Henderson would be preparing the damaged tread for replacement. They'd be pulling bolts, disconnecting track pins in preparation for the M88 Recovery Vehicle, which would lift the tank so they could get the bad track completely off, and the new track back on.

During the whole process, they were terribly exposed. If there was a bright spot, it was that the enemy would be unlikely to come rushing back this way. With the flow of the battle pushing north, there was little chance of them running into anything dangerous. *Maybe an attack helicopter*, thought Mackintosh Grimly. He popped his own hatch and looked at the sky, as though his thoughts were going to summon one of those terrible Mi-24s. He prayed that they could get the tank back online soon, because he wanted to be with the unit when they relieved the 82nd Airborne at Bitburg.

Chapter 5

19 July 1981
Jacksonville, North Carolina

Nancy Rodriguez nervously turned her coffee cup, her fingers tapping on the porcelain, while she listened to Becca dish the latest gossip. As the war dragged on and Jacksonville shifted to the war economy, both young ladies found themselves with very little free time. Between jobs—Becca had taken a shift at the Montgomery Ward at the mall—family, and all of the tiny things that you never noticed until you ran out of time, these Sunday morning coffees on Nancy's porch were the one time they took to connect. The sound of children playing in the distance contrasted with the faint hum of military aircraft overhead.

"Margaret Lee got her notice," said Becca, her eyes wide with disbelief. "Can you believe it?"

A shiver ran down Nancy's spine. "It gets more real every time I hear another story," she replied, swallowing hard. "There are younger women out there, but every once in a while they call up someone our age. I really wish I could figure out what the system is. It just seems so random."

"I suppose," said Becca, her voice lowering conspiratorially, "that if you could figure out the system, you might figure out a way around it."

"Yes," said Nancy, laughing, "you have discovered my secret plot, Rebecca Elizabeth Henderson. I will not only avoid the draft myself, but I will sell this secret for three simple payments of $19.99." That got a big laugh from Becca, and the tension in the air momentarily lifted.

"I really don't like living with the threat of the draft hanging over me, even if it isn't something that's likely to happen."

Nancy nodded, her eyes filled with understanding. "Oh, I understand. I'm right there with you. But there's nothing we can do about it."

"We could move to Canada."

"Too cold," said Nancy, "and besides, they have blue money. I don't think I could work with blue money. I'll stick with the natural greenbacks we have down here. We should have a party."

"What on earth are you going on about?" asked Becca, her eyebrows raised in confusion.

"Oh," said Nancy, realizing her non sequitur, "we should have a party for Margaret. Do you know when she ships out?"

"Fran didn't say anything about the timing, just that Margaret was drafted."

"I think we should throw her a shower," said Nancy, her eyes lighting up with determination.

"I don't know, Nancy. I think the Army gives you everything you need once you get there. I mean, what are you thinking? You'll get her a monogrammed knife or something?"

"I don't know," replied Nancy, "it just seems like we should be doing something to mark the occasion. Maybe give our friends something to look forward to, rather than the bleak prospect of getting shot by the Russians in a few months."

"Oh, Nancy, it's not that bad. They aren't sending women to the front lines, at least not yet." The Department of Defense had issued a statement prohibiting the placement of female service members in combat roles. While this had the support of the majority of the population, there were still lawsuits filed, citing the unconstitutional nature of a policy that was in clear violation of the Twenty-Seventh Amendment.

"You know what I mean," replied Nancy. She changed the subject. "Did you hear they're remaking *Pork Chop Hill*?"

"No, what's that all about?" asked Becca.

"Apparently, Sylvester Stallone approached a studio with the idea that Hollywood needs to contribute to the war effort."

"The guy from Rocky?"

"Yeah, that guy," replied Nancy.

"Yeah, that guy," replied Nancy. "From what I read in *People*, he wanted to remake *The Longest Day*, but the government pressured the studios to avoid making the Germans the bad guys."

"Yeah, I can see how that would be a mess," said Becca, shaking her head.

"And the Japanese are our allies too," continued Nancy. "So that really just left the Korean War as the only historic war we could draw from."

"Well, I don't doubt that some of those Hollywood screenwriters can just rewrite some of these World War II stories but with the Russians as the bad guys instead of the Germans."

"That's a great idea," said Nancy, her eyes twinkling. "You should look into that." Both women laughed at the notion of becoming the new queens of propaganda. "But seriously, I think our movie options are about to get pretty grim."

"I don't know," said Becca, "*Kramer vs. Kramer* was pretty grim—"

"Don't remind me," said Nancy, grimacing.

"Speaking of grim divorces," said Becca, a mischievous smile playing on her lips, "have you heard from Carlos lately?"

"You are just the worst," laughed Nancy, playfully swatting Becca's arm. "But yeah, I got a letter from him on Wednesday. He's still in Latin America somewhere."

"With the war over, is he coming home soon?"

"It doesn't sound like it. At least, he hasn't mentioned it, and I think he would. I even asked him about it, so maybe I'll hear something soon."

"Are you excited that he might come back?"

Nancy sighed, looking at the leaves rustling in the breeze. "I don't know how to feel," she admitted. "There will always be a part of me that loves the man. And we have Jennifer, so he's going to be a part of my life no matter what. Worst of all, I really miss the guy... why does life have to be so complicated?"

"Maybe it's not that complicated," replied Becca, her voice softening. "He might really be the one for you. Maybe you gave up on him too quickly?"

"Oh, now you're sounding like my parents. I'll never admit to it, but sometimes I think y'all are right." Nancy thought about it for a few seconds before adding, "I'm not sure how much it matters when compared to the fact that we could all be killed in a nuclear fireball tomorrow."

"Nope. You don't get to do that," said Becca. "You don't get to pretend that you don't have any problems just because the world has bigger ones. That's not how life works."

"I suppose you're right," agreed Nancy. "I just don't know what to do."

"Tell him," said Becca.

"What if he's seeing somebody else?"

"In a war zone?" asked Becca. "My uncle told me all about that in Vietnam. There's a word for that and it ain't *girlfriend.*"

"Oh, Becca, I didn't need to think about that," said Nancy, her face falling.

"No, probably not. For the record, while Carlos has his failings, he doesn't seem like the kind of guy to resort to prostitutes."

"I hope you're right. I don't think I want to know."

"But seriously, Nancy, you need to tell him that you might have made a mistake. Give him something to look forward to. Something more to fight for."

"But what if he's just too angry to come back? What if I screwed everything up?"

"That's a risk you need to take, honey. You made this mess; if you want to clean it up, that's up to you."

Nancy looked into her now-empty coffee cup, hoping to find an answer and failing. She took a deep breath and said, "You're right, Becca. I need to face this and take responsibility for my actions."

Becca smiled and placed a comforting hand on Nancy's arm. "That's the spirit. Life may be uncertain right now, but it's up to us to make the best of it, no matter what."

Nancy nodded, a small smile forming on her lips. "I'll write him a letter, tell him how I feel. Maybe that'll give him something to look forward to, and we can try to work things out when he comes back."

"See? That's a great first step," Becca encouraged. "And in the meantime, let's focus on the things we can control, like throwing that party for Margaret."

Nancy's smile grew. "Yeah, let's do it. We can invite all our friends, make it a real celebration of her bravery and dedication."

The two women began to plan the party, finding solace in their friendship and the knowledge that they were doing something to help one another and their community during such difficult times. As the sun continued to rise and the sounds of children playing mixed with the distant hum of military planes, Nancy and Becca held on to the hope that their love, friendship, and resilience would guide them through the uncertain days ahead.

****

25 July 1981
VA-27 "Royal Maces"
USS *Coral Sea*
Sea of Japan

Lieutenant Junior Grade Sam "Pharoah" Bell sat in the wardroom sipping a cup of coffee. He watched as his friend and squadmate, Lieutenant John "Rhodie" Charters, brought a cup of his own over to the table.

"What's the word, Rhodie?" asked Pharoah.

Rhodie shook his head. "When I know, you'll know, pal."

"You've got to at least have an idea, right?" asked the younger pilot.

"Well, sure. Nothing official, but if you think about it, the North Koreans don't have much in the way of a navy. So when the Marines get close to making landfall, we'll be running nonstop close-air support, just like when we took it to the Sandis in Nicaragua." *Coral Sea* was part of the largest amphibious task force assembled by the United States since the Second World War. They were tasked with putting the 2nd Marine Division on the North Korean shore and breaking the stalemate that was developing on the peninsula.

"Hey, 'air-to-mud' has become our specialty," said Pharoah with a chuckle.

"Hey, it's honest work," replied Rhodie. "You hear anything from your folks back home?" Pharoah was used to this. It was as though Rhodie felt it was his duty to make sure of his mental well-being. Maybe it was.

"Yeah," replied Pharoah. "I got a letter a few days back. Dad says they're doing fine, all things considered. The blackouts have eliminated the night courses he used to have to cover, so he's pretty happy about that." Pharoah's father taught political science at Los Angeles City College, a two-year school in the East Hollywood neighborhood of Los Angeles.

"More nights at home with the missus can't be all that bad," replied Rhodie. "Did he mention anything about shortages?"

"Nothing new as of late. The rationing seems to be working to keep them from going without, even if they don't have as much as they used to."

"Yeah, my old man—" Rhodie was cut off by the klaxon sounding.

"General quarters. General quarters. All hands man your battle stations. Set material condition Zebra throughout the ship."

"The hell?" said Pharoah as the room cleared out. He fell in behind Rhodie as the aviators joined the troves of sailors moving to their battle stations. Within a minute, they were at VA-27's ready room. Commander Gerard "Chops" Armstrong stood at the front of the room, waiting for everyone to take their seats.

"Gentleman," said Chops, "since we left Sasebo, we've known that Ivan might decide to make a run at us. It looks like that's exactly what's happening. Intel reports that P-3s out of Misawa have picked up the Soviet Pacific Fleet south of Vladivostok. Our best evidence indicates that the fleet is heading to intercept us before we can land in Korea." He looked across the room and made eye contact with Lieutenant Hayes. "Scooter, what can you tell us about the Soviet Pacific Fleet?" Every aviator in the room had a keen understanding of what the Soviets had, but Pharoah knew Scooter was obsessed with the order of battle.

"Yes, sir," said Scooter. "The Pacific Fleet is the second-largest in the Soviet Navy, second only to the Northern Fleet."

"Especially after that ass-whipping we handed to the Black Sea Fleet," said Heaver, getting a good laugh from the squad.

"Well, yes… sort of," continued Scooter. "The Pacific Fleet is not only larger but more capable. For starters, they have a significant standoff attack capability. We will not be able to get close without putting ourselves in range of their surface-to-surface missiles. Worse news for us is that they have a significant surface-to-air missile capability." The room got quiet. "If we're tasked with making an air strike against the fleet, we're most certainly going in harm's way."

"All right," said Chops, "on that pleasant note, the boss is sitting in with command staff and finding out what our assignment will be. Smoke 'em if ya got 'em, boys. That's all we have for now." The men knew that they wouldn't have to wait long, but with so much at stake, the waiting was torture.

"So much for that 'air-to-mud' specialization," said Rhodie.

"I'm not going to lie," replied Pharoah, "I was a lot happier with the close-air support mission. Stick to the devil you know, right?"

"Don't let Scooter freak you out. This'll be a lot like close-air support, except the targets are a *lot* bigger."

"That's certainly one way to look at it."

"Attention on deck!" The squad rose from their seats as Commander Clint "Rerun" Jones entered the room.

"At ease," said the commanding officer of VA-27 as he took Chops' place at the front of the room. "Gentlemen, we have our mission. We're trying something new today." That got everyone's attention. "We're going to lay a serious chaff barrier on the edge of their SAM range. Behind the chaff, we'll have some Prowlers out there throwing out as much interference as they can."

Pharaoh leaned over to Rhodie and said, "Doesn't sound like anything new."

"Once the EW elements are in place, the main battery is going to lob some Samsons at the enemy fleet."

"Wait, the what?" asked Chops.

"I'm glad you asked, because until five minutes ago, I had no idea either. These are Israeli air-launched drones. They have radar reflectors and transmitters that *should* fool the Russkies into thinking they're attacking aircraft. This will convince the enemy to light up their radars, allowing additional Tadpoles to launch AGM-78s to take out the radars. The Intruder squadron from Midway will be adding a layer of Harpoons to the attack, and we'll be coming in with a combination of Shrikes for any leftover radars, and MK-83s to sweep up anything the Harpoons didn't send to the bottom of the ocean.

"Our egress will be on a course of two-zero-zero," continued Rerun. "No matter what happens on our attack run, you need to return on a course of two-zero-zero from the target. The Prowlers will be jamming along that course, so if you want their help, you'd better remember that heading. Pharaoh, what was that heading?"

"Two-zero-zero, sir," replied Pharaoh.

"That's right. We'll be escorted by VF-21. The Freelancers will walk us right up to the SAM umbrella, then hang back while we do our thing. Once we drop and clear the target, we'll continue on two-zero-

zero for fifteen nautical miles before turning to a course of six-zero to return to the ship. Any questions?"

"Sir," said Scooter.

"Go ahead."

"Why Phantoms? I mean, doesn't *Kitty Hawk* have two squadrons of Tomcats?"

"I asked the same question," said Rerun. "Turns out, the flags want to keep the Tomcats on combat air patrol and ready to pounce if Soviet Naval Aviation decides to join the fight, which I promise they will." Pharaoh thought about that. It was a sure bet that in the wide-open Pacific, Ivan would throw some Tu-22M Backfires their way. The Soviets had designed the Backfire with the exclusive purpose of countering the US Navy's aircraft carriers. The Navy, in turn, had specifically designed the Tomcat to confront the threat posed by the Backfire. It was tit-for-tat, right up to today, when the effectiveness of both systems seemed likely to be tested to the breaking point.

The briefing wound down, with assignments being made and specifics drilled into. Within minutes, the aviators were checking in with maintenance control and then heading for the locker room to get suited up.

"Wouldn't you know it," asked Lieutenant "Heaver" McGuire as he pulled the top of his flight suit over his shoulders, "we get our first crack at the Russian bear and they have us going in on mop-up duty."

"You'll be lucky to drop on a sinking cruiser before it slips beneath the waves," said Lieutenant "Buzz" Barber. Pharoah wasn't sure if they were being serious or if this was just bravado before the mission.

Actually, in Heaver's case, he's being serious, thought Pharoah. Rhodie came over as Pharaoh finished strapping on his harness.

"Okay, so I was wrong about the mission," said Rhodie, "but the basics are still the same. We fly in, we put ordnance on target, and we fly out. Don't let Scooter get in your head. His opinion changes nothing. We still have orders, and that's what we're going to do!" Rhodie grabbed Pharaoh's shoulder and brought him in for a bear hug.

"Let's go! Let's go! Let's go!" came the call from the corridor.

"Just stick with me, and you'll be fine," said Rhodie.

Half an hour later the Maces were off the deck and formed up. Pharaoh brought his Corsair up to cruising altitude, along with the rest of his squadron. It was a bit of a surreal feeling as he looked out the window of Corsair at the armada of aircraft preparing to hurl themselves against the Soviet Pacific Fleet. He'd been nervous during previous operations and aerial engagements, but he'd never felt quite like this. As he thought about it, he realized something... *I'm flying with an armada into an air defense unlike anything we've fought before*...For now, the only thing he had to worry about was staying on station with his wingman and waiting to see if he'd still be alive in a few hours.

The battle may have just gotten started, but it was still miles away from VA-27. Looking at his watch and the time hack for the Intruders about to launch their Israeli-made decoys, he knew it wouldn't be too much longer before the main body of the strike force would eventually begin firing their AGM-78 antiradiation missile, which would home in on the enemy fleet's air-defense radars, hopefully giving his squadron a clean shot at the enemy fleet, or at least a seriously degraded air-defense system to have to deal with. Thinking about the chance to engage the enemy fleet reminded him of the *Kitty Hawk*'s A-6s firing off a wave of Harpoons as they closed the gap on the Soviet fleet. Shaking his head dismissively, he knew Rhodie's comments in the wardroom were likely right. They were the mop-up crew. The guys being sent in to finish off what the Harpoons failed to sink. Rhodie was right about something else—there wouldn't be many Soviet threats left if the Harpoons did their job, and that was a good thing.

It all came down to timing...everything would depend on the timing of each station getting it right.

If this operation was going to work, then each plane needed to be at the right place at the right time. If the timing was off, then the missiles and decoys could end up coming in delayed waves, allowing the enemy time to deal with them piecemeal. If that happened, then this gamble, this giant air armada he was a part of, could turn into a giant turkey shoot with them being the turkeys. For now, they'd do their best to remain in the protective cloud of electromagnetic interference courtesy of the Prowlers and hope to remain out of sight of the SAMs and MiGs that would likely be hunting them should they catch a whiff of them prior to their attack. A misstep now, like falling outside the protective shield, could cost lives.

****

VAQ-136 "Gauntlets"
USS *Midway*
Sea of Japan

While Pharaoh was getting ready to put iron on target, Lieutenant Junior Grade Jeff "Potsie" Weber was preparing to protect him. While the attack squadrons constituted the fleet's "sword," the electronic warfare squadrons were the "shield." The EA-6B Prowlers of VAQ-136 could jam enemy radar, preventing the Soviets from being able to detect the incoming attackers. The electronic warfare, or EW, suite on the Prowler was state-of-the-art. The Prowler was the best EW plane in the air. Well, to hear it from the pilots and electronic countermeasures officers (ECMOs), it was.

Potsie stood atop his bird's ladder as he surveyed the scene around him before stepping into his seat behind the pilot. His crew, the closest thing to a family he had out here in the Pacific, was with him. There was the pilot, Bill "Trashman" Palmer, and ECMOs "Loner" Dawson and "Fritz" Schneider, the rest of his flight crew.

The flight deck aboard the carrier was abuzz with activity. Aircrews wearing their different-color vests ran about in orchestrated chaos as they feverously worked to get the air wing into the sky. Unlike in the training operations he'd participated in prior to the war, the aircraft covering the deck were armed to the teeth. Missiles hung beneath wings, waiting to be locked on to some commie bastards. Settling into his seat, Potsie watched the ground crew guiding the next pair of aircraft into the catapult of the forward deck. As the cats hurled the fighters down the deck, throwing into the wind, afterburners ablaze as they clawed for altitude, the next pair was being made ready to rinse and repeat until the entire wing was airborne.

Fastening the straps to his ejection seat, Potsie readied his mind for what would likely be the largest naval aerial combat action since World War II or the First Korean War. Unlike the Phantoms and Corsairs taking off ahead of him. His Prowler, the EA-6B electronic warfare variant would wage a different kind of fight than the naval aviators of generations before him. Instead of slicing through waves of Japanese Zeros or North Korean MiG-17s, his Prowler would unleash its electronic wizardry to blind the enemy and act as a protective shield for the attackers as they closed with the enemy to deliver the knockout blow that could decide the fate of this battle.

He liked that part of his job. Something about having the ability to jam enemy radars, preventing the Soviets from detecting the incoming threats until it was too late, made him feel like a demigod unleashing his fury on an unsuspecting foe. All the training he'd gone through, and the lessons learned from the veterans of Vietnam, had assured him of the superiority of the EW suite of tricks aboard his Prowler. Even the ECMOs who worked to defeat the Soviet systems were glad they didn't have to counter the suite of tools aboard the Prowlers.

Potsie adjusted his straps, making sure they were snug should the unthinkable happen and he have to eject. He shivered involuntarily at the thought of it. The sea in this area of the world was extremely cold. *I'm still probably in the safest seat in the fleet right now*, he thought, pushing aside the thoughts of ice-cold water. They were immune to the antiship missiles that could ruin the day of the sailors aboard the ships of the fleet. Unless something went terribly wrong, his Prowler wouldn't be within SAM range of the enemy fleet.

Placing his helmet on, Potsie looked to his right. Loner fiddled with his helmet before giving him a nod and a thumbs-up. While he couldn't see his pilot, Trashman, in front of him, he knew was running through his final checklist before turning the engines on. As the two ECMOs sitting in the back, He and Loner probably had one of the most important jobs in the coming battle. It was their equipment that would blind and mute the Soviets for the fleet's air wings to land punch after punch until they knocked the enemy out. Their "Double Ugly" Prowler was about as ready for battle as they were going to get.

Double Ugly... he smiled at that. Sailors had nicknamed the bird on account of her odd-looking extended cockpit and the fact that the EW versions of the A-6Es flew with a double the crew to man their electronic warfare gear. Just then he heard a knock against the window as the plane captain gave them a thumbs-up before hopping to the deck, letting them know from outside that the bird was ready.

Watching the cats launch another pair of Phantoms down the deck and into the sky, he felt confident in their abilities to be more than a match for anything the Soviets could bring. Especially when paired with their box of tricks to blind and mute the likely MiG-23s flying out of Chuguyevka or Uglovoye air bases near Vladivostok, or the even more pathetic Yak-38s flying from the *Kiev*-class VTOL carrier *Minsk*. Finishing his equipment checks, he felt they were in good hands with the Phantoms against the likely aircraft they'd encounter. As Trashman sent the message to the air boss that they were ready to roll, Potsie sat back in the chair and played the time-honored military tradition of hurry up and wait for their slot in the launch sequence.

Chapter 6

25 July 1981
22nd Fighter Aviation Regiment
Chuguyevka, Primorsky Krai

Colonel Mikhailov walked into the hangar and paused for a moment as he surveyed the scene before him. The ground crews were conducting their final checks of the aircraft before handing it over to the pilots. He could see the crews had affixed three drop tanks to give the aircraft the additional range it would need to reach the fleet and take up an overwatch position. That left room for just one of the R-60 Aphid missiles and two of the R-23 Apexes—not much in terms of air-to-air weaponry, but it would have to do.

Then Mikhailov spotted the man he'd come to see standing off to the side. He appeared to be deep in thought as he studied a map.

Colonel Mikhailov approached his top fighter ace. "Major Sokolov," he called out.

"Ah, comrade Colonel. Have you come to wish me luck before I achieve my next aerial kill of the war?" replied Major Sokolov jovially.

Colonel Mikhailov laughed. "I think those Korean kills are only worth half credit." He then turned serious. "I have no doubt in your abilities to achieve your next aerial kill, comrade Major. This mission is important, Sokolov. The Americans have assembled a large fleet in the Sea of Japan, as you know. Our navy is going to be facing an overwhelming naval force of fighters being arrayed against it. It is our squadron's duty to prevent these Yankee aircraft from savaging our brothers-in-arms."

"*Da*, comrade Colonel. My pilots and I know what's at stake," Sokolov replied solemnly. "We will bring the fight to the Americans and do our best to overwatch the fleet while they move to attack. Just ensure our relief arrives on time. We will not have much time to loiter over the battlefield if they are late."

"Good luck, Major. I shall see you when you return."
****

Zashchitnik Flight—Soviet MiG-23s

The predawn air felt heavy and warm around Major Alexei Sokolov as he settled into the cockpit of his MiG-23. The relentless Siberian winter was a distant memory now, replaced by a July heatwave that had turned the tarmac to a shimmering mirage as he looked outside the hangar. His gloved hands tightened around the stick of his swing-wing beast, its engines rumbling with a barely contained predatory growl as he eased off the brakes and moved forward onto the tarmac. He guided his aircraft along the taxiway towards the end of the runway to line up for takeoff.

Once Sokolov had turned off the taxiway, he gave his instruments a final once-over before accelerating down the runway. His attention, keen as a hawk's gaze, checked the glowing constellation of dials and gauges that held his life in their hands, each indicator a piece of the intricate puzzle that allowed this machine to fly like a bird of prey. The fuel gauges, their needles standing proudly at maximum, were a stark reminder of the daunting task that lay ahead of him. He only wished he could carry another three air-to-air missiles instead of the external fuel tanks he'd need to reach the fleet and provide cover over them.

"Control, Zashchitnik One. Ready for takeoff," Sokolov transmitted, his voice as cool as the chilled vodka he'd downed at the officers' mess the previous night.

The reply crackled through his earpiece. "Permission granted. Good luck, comrade."

With the final words from Control received, Sokolov's heart pounded in his chest like a drum, the rhythm of warfare quickening his senses. With a deep breath, he eased the throttle forward. The roar of the engine felt like a symphony of power and precision that tore through the quiet morning.

The jump in acceleration gripped his body, pressing him back into his seat as his MiG-23 hurtled down the runway. The ground blurred and fell away, and for a moment, it was just him and the open sky. Beneath him, the vast expanse of the Sea of Japan shimmered in the morning light, a beautiful yet foreboding sight. Sokolov knew that hundreds if not thousands of airmen and sailors would likely die before the end of this day.

He leveled his aircraft out and waited a moment for his wingman, Captain Ivan Kuznetsov, who mirrored his ascent, to close the distance between their aircraft. Their silhouettes cut through the warming air in perfect harmony.

As they turned to head in the direction of the Pacific Fleet, they maintained a tight formation; the six aircraft appeared as three at these distances until they separated to engage. Twenty minutes into their flight, they received word from the fleet—they were under attack. The fleet commander revised their orders, directing them to intercept and eliminate the American EA-6 Prowlers they had detected moments before the electronic warfare aircraft had blinded their radars and reduced the detection ranges of the fleet's surface-to-air missile systems.

Activating the radio for probably the last time until they engaged the Americans, Sokolov gave his final instructions for how he wanted their flight of six to attack these aircraft. He knew the value of such planes in a battle like this, and that meant they'd be protected—likely by naval versions of the American F-4 Phantoms. He assigned two of his three pairs to go after the Phantoms, to keep them occupied while the other pair focused on the Prowlers.

As they climbed higher, opting for a top-down attack on the Americans, the gravity of their mission weighed heavily upon Sokolov. Today, they were not just pilots; they were the first line of defense—the fleet's shield against the relentless onslaught of the US task force sent to destroy their naval comrades. His pilots were not just men; they were the embodiment of the Soviet resolve, the hard edge of their nation's determination to defeat capitalism and usher in a new world order.
****

VAQ-136 "Gauntlets"

Potsie sat behind Trashman, waiting for the mission to unfold as the plane buffeted from time to time from the turbulence outside. Shortly after getting airborne, they'd topped their tanks off, ensuring they'd have plenty of fuel to stay on station for the duration of the mission. Once they had a full tank of gas, the mission seemed to get underway pretty soon afterwards. From that moment on, they were filling the sky with as much chaff as they could to deploy as they began the process of prepping the electronic battlefield for the blitz they were about to unleash.

When the radio call came for them to move back, Fritz acknowledged, then Trashman pulled back from their previous heading to start flying long, lazy ovals in the sky behind that chaff cloud they'd helped create. If Potsie had to guess, he'd say the Intruders must have fired their decoys. His digital display indicator or DDI came to life with a sudden spike in Soviet search radars lighting up, appearing on his screen as colored shapes. With the radars active, he was now generating targeting data he'd be able to use to jam them before the main event started.

This was the most dangerous part of the mission. The enemy radars were in active search mode, looking for where to send their missiles, and it was now on the shoulders of Potsie and Loner to shut them down. During the mission briefing, they'd been assigned specific radars to target based on the composition of the fleet. Potsie was responsible for jamming Peel Group radars. Whenever one popped up on the DDI, Potsie would assign a jammer to it. He had just finished the preliminary assignments when the call came in.

"This is Ironclaw Actual to all Ironclaw units: Buzzer." That was the code word for the Prowlers to begin jamming. Loner reached over and flipped the Master Rad Switch. Potsie could imagine what the Soviet radar operators were going through as their previously clear readouts were reduced to nothing but electromagnetic snow.

Within a minute of the "Buzzer" order, several of the Soviet radars went off-line.

"Looks like Ivan is trying to save a few of his radars for later in the game," said Loner.

"Not like it's going to do him any good. I mean, as soon as they start emitting, we'll shut 'em right back down." At this point, Loner and Potsie were playing the world's most expensive game of Whack-A-Mole.

With the battle to suppress and destroy the Soviet SAMs well underway, Potsie felt like time was moving both at warp speed and at a snail's pace. He'd see a pair of AGM-78s close in on a radar until the images merged. Then, sure enough, like clockwork, another would pop on to take its place and he'd have to scramble to move the jammer from the radar they'd just taken out to the new one that had turned on. In that brief moment between the time the radar went active and when he could get it jammed, the operators had enough time to catch a glimpse of what was going on.

It was during those seconds before reacquiring that he'd find himself holding his breath as he raced to be faster than the operator he was trying to jam. The first couple of times he had won out, jamming the radar before it could get a lock and fire a missile. Then he heard Loner curse as he alerted Trashman to a missile launch.

"Oh crap, Loner. Tell me that missile isn't aimed at us?" Fritz blurted before anyone could say anything.

"Come on, Loner, do I need to start taking evasive maneuvers yet or what?" demanded Trashman. His radar homing and warning system or RHAW was almost constantly blaring one warning or another as the strike aircraft were now engaging the Soviets below, making it hard to distinguish between a missile targeting their bird versus the dozens much closer to the enemy.

Finally, when it felt like time had stopped, Loner looked over Potsie as he declared for them all, "It's not headed for us. It's locked on one of the strike planes."

Potsie should have felt bad for them, having failed to get that radar jammed before its operator could snap off a shot, but right now he felt like he'd just won the lottery. They hadn't been targeted—at least not yet.

"Well, put that one out of your mind, Loner. He drew quicker than us, that's all. Focus on the next one and don't let it get inside your head. You got this, Loner," Trashman announced.

Potsie liked that about him. He was a good leader and knew now wasn't the time to beat Loner up over it. It wouldn't help the situation, and he was right. Loner needed to stay focused—they both did.

Then Potsie saw something on his radar he'd thought he wouldn't see. A contact approaching from the direction of Vladivostok. He was about to say something when the single contact multiplied into three contacts. His eyes went wide. *Oh wow, they're coming for us.* Then he found his voice, alerting, "Heads up, Trashman! I'm tracking three—shit, I'm tracking six bogeys inbound from the direction of Vladivostok."
****

Zashchitnik Flight—Soviet MiG-23s

The journey across the expansive Sea of Japan was made in tense anticipation of the impending clash. Major Alexei Sokolov wished his aircraft felt nimbler, like the predator of the sky he felt he was. He knew the sluggish, cumbersome sensation would change as he jettisoned the external fuel tanks when they ran dry—or the moment he had to react to the enemy in aerial combat. Until then, every maneuver, every change in course was a calculation, a careful balance between conserving fuel and maintaining an advantageous position until they were in range to strike at the Americans.

As Sokolov led his flight of six Floggers—that was what he'd heard NATO called their MiG-23s—he found his gaze being drawn to the radar screen nestled in his cockpit. A blip indicated that the US naval task force was on a heading towards the Pacific Fleet below. The distance was still too far for him to make out the individual carriers and escort vessels, but he knew this was a formidable fleet. What troubled him right now was the lack of aerial targets. While the naval ships had just recently come into detection range, the squadrons of fighters he knew the carriers had launched were being shielded by an unknown number of EA-6 Prowlers—the aircraft his flight had been directed to locate and destroy. Somewhere behind the Prowlers were the Phantoms, the aerial escorts protecting the strike aircraft and these electronic warfare planes blinding the fleet.

A crackle in his earpiece snapped Sokolov from his thoughts. "Red One, Red Two. I have visual on the *Minsk*," Ivan's voice echoed, a calm and steady presence beside him.

Sokolov peered through his canopy, the distant specks of Yak-38s dotting the sky as they lifted off the *Minsk*. "Acknowledged, Red Two. It's time for us to go active with our radars and find these Prowlers. Let's remind these Yanks they aren't welcome here," he responded, pushing his throttle forward as he activated the RP-23 Sapfir look-down/shoot-down radar. Their MiG-23s were the first Soviet fighters to field the advanced radar systems in conjunction with the beyond-visual-range missiles—the Vympel R-23.

Accelerating to near Mach speeds, Sokolov and the five other MiGs had closed the gap on the cloud of electromagnetic clutter when his radar was finally able to burn through the jamming, revealing the aerial armada he knew had been hidden behind it. As new contacts populated his radar faster than he could count, he felt his heart quickening with each pass of his radar. There were scores of A-6 Intruders, F-4 Phantoms, and EA-6 Prowlers. It was time to put his plan into action—to create some more aces for the Soviet Air Force.

"Zashchitnik Three, Zashchitnik Five. You are free to engage. See you back at the barn, and good luck," ordered Sokolov as he split his force to better their odds of success.

With the distances between them closing rapidly, he headed toward the first Prowler he'd detected. While he was still too far out to get a solid lock with his missiles, he knew a Phantom would likely try to intercept before he could get in range. If they were going to have any luck taking some of these Prowlers down, they'd need to take out a few of the Phantoms running interference between them.

Come on, you bastards. Try and intercept us...give me a target to shoot at.

Now that stealth was no longer a priority, Sokolov could depress the talk button. "Red Two, maintain formation," he ordered. "We're going to engage those Phantoms before we make a play for that Prowler they are guarding. Stay ready to engage on my mark."

Sokolov felt the adrenaline pumping through his veins, his focus increasing, his situational awareness heightened, the fear dulled. Following his instruments he spotted his prey, a Phantom racing towards him, closing the distance between them. They were two against many, a daunting task at hand—but nothing they couldn't handle. They were pilots of the Soviet Union, and he was an ace with eight confirmed kills; today he'd score his ninth and tenth.

His Sirena RWR squawked a warning, telling him multiple search radars were attempting to lock onto him. He needed to act, to engage before the Phantoms could. He glanced down to his hands, his eyes focusing on his weapons control panel, the ominous red glow of the armed lights confirming his missile was ready. Sokolov moved his finger to hover over the firing stub, the R-23R missile beneath his wing ready to draw first blood in this aerial ballet.

"Zashchitnik Two, I'm engaging the Phantom at your eight o'clock. Go forward on my wing trailing behind him and let's do this!" Sokolov commanded, his voice cutting through the tense silence. He pulled his fighter into a swift, shallow dive toward the Phantom. His missile achieved lock almost immediately. The American fighter broke to one side as he attempted to evade. Staying glued to his prey, Sokolov never lost lock. He squeezed the trigger, the R-23R missile releasing from beneath his wing before its engine ignited, and the missile streaked toward its prey.

The dance of aerial combat had begun in earnest as the R-23R missile tore through the sky. Sokolov stayed with the Phantom as he watched the missile chase it down. The pilot flying the Phantom kept ejecting flares and chaff, desperately attempting any countermeasure that might work. Sokolov smiled; the missile struck its mark. The proximity fuze detected the Phantom before exploding, throwing shrapnel into the rear engines and across the left wing of the aircraft. The rear of the Phantom caught fire moments before an explosion enveloped it in a giant cloud of flame. As the aircraft blew apart, the debris began its earthward fall toward the waters below.

Stupid Yankee…you should have ejected the moment you knew my missile was going to impact. Still, Sokolov harbored no ill will towards his American counterparts. They were aviators like him, defending their nation and taking orders just like he was.

Sokolov pressed the talk button, declaring with grim satisfaction, "First blood, Zashchitnik Two. What is your situation?"

No sooner had he finished the question than his RWR blared another warning. Someone was actively targeting him, and unless he reacted swiftly, he'd have a missile of his own to deal with. Breaking hard to the right as he dove toward the ground, Sokolov craned his neck around, searching the sky behind him to see if he could catch a glimpse of who was locking him up. That was when he spotted another Phantom. They'd apparently snuck up on him while he had pursued the other fighter. Knowing the enemy was about to fire, Sokolov turned hard to the left this time. He pulled out of his dive and aimed the aircraft skyward, hitting his afterburners.

The radio crackled. "Copy, Zashchitnik One," his wingman reported. "They're coming at us hard." The tightness in Ivan's voice echoed the tension that gripped them both.

Sokolov's attention snapped back to his radar; the blips of the approaching fighters were a stark reminder of the deadly dance they were partaking in.

Why am I so damn sluggish?!

He cursed to himself as the Phantom continued to trail him. Suddenly, he realized he hadn't jettisoned his fuel tanks at the start of the battle. Shaking his head at the rookie mistake, Sokolov reached for the release switch, jettisoning the spent drop tanks. He noted that his fuel gauge was as close to full as possible. Moments after he released the extra weight and drag against the aircraft, his aircraft's agility and nimbleness had returned, and just in time.

Missile warning...missile warning!

He hit the flare button. The aircraft spat out a batch of brilliantly hot magnesium flares before Sokolov broke hard to one side and dove for the ground once more. He'd barely gotten out of the area when he heard an explosion; the flares had saved his life.

Looking around for his wingman, Sokolov spotted Ivan in the distance—he was in trouble. Sokolov immediately headed toward him.

"Zashchitnik Two, break right!" Sokolov commanded, pulling his MiG's stick back hard, sending the aircraft into a vertical climb. He could see the horizon tilting wildly, the blue sky and the vast sea merging into a disorienting swirl. His stomach churned with the g-forces, the world outside his cockpit nothing but a indiscernable blur.

He felt sweat trickling down his face, stinging his eyes, but he blinked it away, his hands firmly on the controls. He could see the Phantoms, their sleek forms cutting through the clouds like hungry sharks. Then he heard the tonal sound of his missile attempting to lock onto the Phantom still chasing his wingman. *Come on, come on, lock up already*, he thought as the American pilot continued to dance outside of his radar lock.

"Zashchitnik One, Phantom on your six! Take the shot or you'll have to break off and evade!" warned Ivan, alerting him to a danger he hadn't known until his RWR suddenly came to life, alerting him to the presence of a missile attempting to lock, just as he was trying to establish a lock on the Phantom that continued to elude him.

"I'm almost there, Ivan. A few more seconds," he called out in frustration. Time was not on his side as he looked at his rear-view mirror. And there it was, the menacing silhouette of an American F-4 against the bright morning sun.

"Zashchitnik Two, break right and pop flares, then hit the afterburner," he ordered calmly as a plan came to mind.

He watched as Ivan banked his aircraft to the right in a controlled roll, flares ejecting in all directions as he rolled before his afterburner came to life. A missile leapt from the Phantom, streaking towards Ivan when it veered off to slam into another batch of flares Ivan dispensed before his aircraft began pulling away from his American pursuer.

Then Sokolov heard the RWR announce, "Missile launch...missile launch..." He'd expected the Yankee to fire and yanked his stick hard to the left, the MiG-23 responding with a swift roll, his flare and chaff dispensers ejecting decoys for the missile now chasing him. He wasn't sure given the range of his pursuit if the Phantom had fired an IR or semiactive radar-homing missile, so he'd used the two decoys in hopes one would work.

Boom!

The sound of an explosion somewhere behind confirmed the missile was no longer chasing him. It had gone for the decoy, just as he had reacquired the aircraft stick, chasing Ivan like a dog that won't let go of its bone. He wasn't sure if his own pursuer was still hot on his heels, but he didn't have time or the luxury to look. Sliding in behind the Phantom pursuing Ivan, he reactivated his final R-23R missile. He had hoped to save one of his longer-range missiles for the EA-6 Prowlers they'd been directed to shoot down, but that hadn't happened yet, and right now he had a chance to down another Phantom, one that was going to kill his wingman if he didn't act.

Take the shot before you lose your wingman, a voice his head scolded. He squeezed the trigger, watching the missile streak toward the Phantom that was closing on Ivan.

Seconds went by, though they felt like minutes, until his missile found its target. The Phantom exploded immediately upon impact. He'd scored his fifth aerial kill of the war, but his RWR was still blaring—a radar was still trying to acquire him. That earlier F-4 was back on his tail.

"Good shot, Zashchitnik One. I'm circling around to go after the bandit behind you. Can you break to your right and climb?" Ivan asked, his voice laced with tension.

"Copy that. Hold on, Zashchitnik Two," Sokolov responded, banking his MiG sharply, creating some distance and buying himself time for Ivan to maneuver.

Sokolov felt his heart pounding, feeling with each beat like it was going to explode out of his chest. He was scared; he didn't want to have to bail out over water instead of land. The likelihood of being recovered from the waves was close to zero.

Then he heard an explosion somewhere behind him.

"Zashchitnik One, got him! You're in the clear," Ivan's voice echoed in his helmet.

"Thanks, Zashchitnik Two," Sokolov said before glancing at the fuel gauge. The chaos of the aerial melee had burned through his fuel. He felt angry at himself for failing to engage the Prowlers, the primary target he'd been tasked with destroying.

"Zashchitnik Three, Zashchitnik One, what is your situation?" Sokolov called. He hoped that they might have gotten lucky against the Prowlers.

"Zashchitnik One, this is Zashchitnik Four. Red Three went down a few minutes ago. He managed to shoot down a Prowler moments before his own aircraft was destroyed. He died a valiant hero," came the somber voice of Lieutenant Romanoff.

Hot damn...maybe our mission wasn't a total bust, Sokolov thought.

"That's a good copy, Red Four. Any additional kills?"

"Affirmative. I dove on a pack of A-6s. I scored two kills with my R-23s and damaged a third with my guns before a Phantom chased me off them," Romanoff recounted. Sokolov felt his spirits soar at the news.

"Outstanding, Zashchitnik Four. We're bingo fuel. I want you to return home and forward your situation to Control once you are in range. Out."

"Wow, Zashchitnik One. That's three kills on their end and four on ours," Ivan said excitedly. His aircraft moved into position near Sokolov as they turned toward land.

"Zashchitnik Five, Zashchitnik One. Report, over," Sokolov called to his final flight of MiGs.

A few moments passed, then a shaking voice responded with more of a grunt of pain. "Um, Zashchitnik One. Five and Six didn't make it. He took a Prowler down and then blew apart moments later when a Phantom got him. I failed to score any kills. Bastards evaded my missiles...I'm hurt, though...got shot up by some guns," he coughed into the mic, clearly having a hard time trying to breathe and speak at the same time.

"I'm not going to make it, Alexei. Not this time, comrade—"

"Zashchitnik Five, cut that defeatist talk out!" Sokolov commanded, cutting in. "You'll be just fine. You'll see. Tell me where you're hit." He tried to remain calm for his friend and encourage him to keep fighting to live.

"No, not this time, Alexei. Your pep talks aren't going to fix the problem this time around. I'm losing hydraulic pressure, I'm down to a quarter tank and I'm losing too much blood…tell Nastya I'll miss her…I loved—" The message ended abruptly.

Sokolov scanned the skies around them, searching to see if he could spot his friend's plane. Then he saw a lone aircraft beginning to nose-dive towards the water below, its engine trailing smoke the entire way.

Breaking the silence, Sokolov called out, "Zashchitnik Two, form up on me if you can. We're headed home. Nothing more we can do here."

As they flew on in silence, skirting the edge of the Soviet fleet below, Sokolov took a final look at his radar screen. The blips of enemy aircraft were still thick in the vicinity of the fleet below. He gave his engine a little more power; he wanted to get past any possible Phantoms still in the area. They didn't have enough fuel to evade if they got jumped, and they were out of R-23s, meaning they'd have to get in knife range if they were going to engage their attackers.

With the world outside his cockpit becoming a blur, Sokolov pushed his MiG to the limits his fuel would allow. He felt a sense of relief. They had made it; they had even destroyed two of those dastardly Prowlers that caused so much chaos for the fleet below. They had survived another mission against overwhelming odds. He and Ivan would live to fight another day. Together, they were going home.
****

VA-27 "Royal Maces"

Pharaoh jumped as his RWR let him know that he was being painted from behind. In every other instance when the warning had gone off, he'd been preparing for evasive maneuvers and popping chaff. But today it was just another step on his way to the battle. The jammers from the Prowlers above and behind him were telling his plane that he might be under attack.

From his perch, Pharaoh had no idea how the real battle was playing out. His radar was just as blind as the enemy's right now. He imagined the decoys and missiles streaking towards the fleet. He also imagined Soviet SAMs leaving their rails as fast as they could to meet them. What seemed like hours of waiting was, in fact, just minutes when his radio came to life.

"Listen up, Maces," said Rerun. "The missile swarms were not as effective as we had hoped. So it doesn't look like we'll be mopping up the scraps. It's going to be on us to finish what they couldn't, and that means we're going to be flying towards some pretty intense SAM coverage and probably some AA guns to spice things up." There was a pause as everyone digested the news before Rerun continued. "Stick with your station and keep your course and speed steady. We need to maintain a tight formation if we're going to get through this. You don't want to wander outside of the ECM coverage and find yourself the objective of attention for those ships down there.

"You all wanted a fight. You wanted a chance to send some ships to the bottom. Well, here's our chance. So let's do it."

Once Rerun had finished pumping his guys up, the flight of Corsairs began shedding altitude to give them a better chance of scoring a hit with their dumb bombs. Not that you needed to score a direct hit with a one-thousand-pound bomb, but this tactic wasn't much different than when the Navy was dropping bombs on the Japs during World War II.

As their fighters angled in for the attack against the remaining Soviet vessels, Pharoah started to see little flashes occurring aboard the ships. It took him a moment to realize those were AA guns shooting at them. Then he saw the smoke contrails leaving some of the ships, surface-to-air missiles likely being aimed at them.

Boom, boom, boom.

Puffs of black smoke began erupting around the aircraft closing in on the ships. Then he saw what looked like basketball-sized flashes of light aimed right at him. He felt himself flinch more than once when some of the giant flashes of light zipped around his Corsair. His heart raced with each passing second, the size of the ships growing by the moment.

In this moment of battle, explosions happening around his plane as AA fire zipped around him, Pharaoh had a brief moment of calm as he considered how his current position wasn't unlike that of an infantryman in the American Revolution. Like his ancestors before him, he was facing withering fire from the enemy, with the ultimate key to success being able to stand firm throughout, not breaking ranks to run when the fear of death felt as if it was going to overwhelm him. If he could maintain his discipline, he could survive the attack.

"Almost there, won't be much longer before weapons release," Scooter announced to the group.

"Keep it down and just focus on the mission," Rerun scolded. Then, without warning, Pharoah watched as a missile streaked past him. *Where the hell did that come from...?* he lamented, unsure where it had gone other than it hadn't hit him.

"Damn, did you see that?! I think the jamming's working 'cause those missiles flew right past us," said Heaver in disbelief.

"Yeah, you're telling me. That was close. Wait until we start to get in range of their AA guns. That's when the real fun is going to start."

Pharaoh tried his best not to think about the missiles still being fired at them. He was more concerned with the Prowlers' jammers losing their effectiveness as they got closer to the enemy. The signal strength of the numerous ships' radars, particularly those aboard the *Kiev*-class aircraft carrier *Minsk* and the *Vladivostok*, a Kara-class cruiser, were particularly strong.

He remembered watching videos as a teenager of the Japanese attacks against the American fleet off the shores of Okinawa and being fascinated by the tenacity of the Japanese pilots flying dive bombers, torpedo planes, and kamikazes through hailstorms of anti-aircraft fire. Never in a million years had he imagined he'd one day share in that same experience, his own squadron of Corsairs braving the guns of the Soviet Navy. He knew the warships they were about to attack were equipped with multiple radar-guided AK-100s, which were 100mm naval cannons. These were usually supported by AK-726s, another dual-barreled cannon firing 76.2mm airburst fragmentation rounds. Should they survive the gauntlet of exploding shells and shrapnel-filled clouds, they'd have to survive the fleet's final line of defense—the AK-630s.

Each vessel in the fleet was equipped with from four to as many as eight fully automated radar-controlled, six-barreled 30mm rotary cannons. With a cyclic firing rate of four to five thousand rounds a minute, they were a pilot's worst nightmare. The automated point-defense guns were highly effective at intercepting missiles and high-speed aircraft that dared to enter their zone of control. This was the gun system that scared him the most. Flying into a wall of steel with no ability to evade or eject before turning into fish food was a terrifying reality he was about to experience.

Boom, boom, boom.

Bang, bang, bang.

All of a sudden, explosions erupted around the Corsairs as Pharaoh caught sight of the enemy ships. Gripping the controls tightly, he could feel the aircraft buffet from nearby explosions, hoping beyond hope he'd evade the burst of shrapnel filling the sky around him.

Then he heard the crackle of the radio, the voice of Heaver breaking into his thoughts as he shouted, "Maces, Magnum!"

A chorus of voices shouted the same call as each of them fired a pair of AGM-45 Shrikes at the rapidly approaching fleet.

If the strategy they'd devised days earlier worked, then the Shrikes would attract the enemy's guns, and maybe take a few of their radars out before they began their bomb runs.

With their missiles away, Pharaoh watched the scene unfolding before him like one of those films about the war in the Pacific during World War II. He saw inky black columns of smoke rising into the sky from fires raging aboard some of the ships that had taken hits from the earlier strikes by the Intruders. Knowing the fleet had already sustained damage somehow made him feel better about his odds of survival. If the pilots flying the A-6s had survived the gauntlet—so could he.

Glancing down to his instrument panel, he saw the distance to the fleet was decreasing rapidly. They'd be in range to begin their attacks soon, and that meant the sooner they got this show on the road, the sooner they could get out of Dodge, the sooner they'd be out of harm's way.

Then, as they reached twenty or so kilometers from the fleet, the entire sky around the Soviet fleet came alive with anti-aircraft fire like it was the Fourth of July. He saw flashes of light by the dozens transform themselves into clouds of black smoke. Then rapidly moving lines of red tracers arced in various directions from the different warships, the vaunted AK-630s spewing hundreds of 30mm exploding munitions into the paths of incoming threats.

He looked on his horror, shock, and amazement as the point-defense weapons swatted Shrike after Shrike from the sky before they could impact against their targets. Periodically he'd see a lone flash against a warship, a Shrike or two scoring a hit, but nowhere near enough to put a dent in the volume of anti-aircraft firing being hurled into the sky, into the direction they were approaching from.

My God...we have to fly through that..., he thought, suddenly unsure if he was going to live beyond the next handful of minutes and desperately wanting to cling to this one life he had.

"Holy crap, Pharaoh. This is insane," his wingman, Scooter, said, the fear evident in his voice.

"Yeah, you ain't joking. Let's just find our target and see what kind of damage we can do and then bug out of here," he responded, hoping if they stayed focused on the mission, it might improve their odds of survival.

The radio crackled, Rhodie declaring, "I found it. I've got a visual on the target. Bearing two-nine-two. It's the *Minsk*, the one spewing AA fire like it's going out of style!"

Pharaoh looked in the direction his wing leader called out and sure enough, there it was, the pride of the Pacific Fleet—*Minsk*. It was one of those *Kiev*-class giant heavy aircraft cruisers that made use of their VTOL naval aircraft. The ship looked like it was flanked on either side by what he thought was either a Kashin-class anti-aircraft guided-missile destroyer or possibly one of those *Kara*-class guided-missile cruisers. In either case, what he saw as they got closer was the AA guns aboard the three vessels were actively firing in various directions, blotting a Shrike or two from the sky every few minutes or so.

Then a thought came to mind, a chill running down his back. *Where are those Forgers...that carrier's got twelve VTOLs...where'd they go...?* His eyes darted briefly into the sky, scanning it quickly in search of the Yak-38s he knew had to be around somewhere. Then he saw what he thought was one of the Yaks flying some sort of evasive maneuvering before it blew apart, likely hit by a missile from one of their escort Phantoms.

The radio crackled to life as the voice of their squadron commander announced, "OK, Maces, this is it. Time to earn our pay and sink us some Russkies. Everyone has a target to hit. Go forth and rain hell on these commie bastards!"

76

Pharaoh smiled as he heard the final attack order. It was now their turn to inflict some damage on the Soviet fleet, and who knew? Maybe they'd even send it to the bottom. When the call ended, his heart raced as his mind started running through how best to approach the target he'd been assigned. This was the part of being a naval aviator he lived for, the sudden rush of adrenaline coursing through his vanes, the thrill of life and death and how aerial combat forced his brain and senses focus to focus exclusively on the task at hand.

Looking out his canopy, he saw Rhodie right where he was supposed to be. As if instinctively, Rhodie's voice came over the radio.

"This is it, Pharaoh. This is our chance to become the first aviators to sink a carrier since the Second World War. I don't know about you, but I'm ready to make some history. So here's what we're going to do. I want us to line up for an attack run that'll have us coming at the *Minsk* head-on, where she's got the fewest AA guns and gives us the entire length or nearly nine hundred meters for us to pummel with our bombs."

The pair began their descent, aligning themselves in the direction of the *Minsk*. For the attack run they were about to conduct, they'd been outfitted with a pair of Shrikes they'd used earlier, leaving them with seven one-thousand-pound Mark 83 bombs. The fortunate thing about bombs was you didn't have to score a direct hit to cause damage or knock a vessel out of service. If it exploded close enough, the shrapnel and shockwave could cause enough damage to render a vessel inoperable. Lastly, when it came down to it, they could always use their guns. The Vulcan 20mm cannon packed a punch and could shoot holes through the superstructure of a vessel if it wasn't armored.

Checking the altimeter, he saw they had descended to just under five thousand feet as they finished their final alignment towards the carrier cruiser. As the Corsairs began the second wave of the aerial attack against the Soviet fleet, the increased volume of the anti-aircraft fire mixed with last-ditch attempts by the shorter-range surface-to-air missiles was so intense he wasn't sure how any of them were going to survive.

BOOM.

An explosion erupted to his right, causing him to turn and see what had happened. What he saw was a black cloud of smoke and burning debris falling to the ocean below. He wasn't sure whose Corsair it was, but whoever it was, they had been blown from the sky before they'd had a chance to attack the fleet. Then he watched for just a moment as he saw the pair of Corsairs diving down on what he thought was a *Kara* cruiser.

The pair of strike planes dove on the cruiser, having approached from a much higher attack angle than he was going to use against *Minsk*. Watching them for a moment, he saw them unleash their collective salvo of fourteen Mark 83s. Several of the bombs scored hits across the cruiser, flashes of flame and smoke briefly erupting across the vessel. While some of the bombs had missed the ship, at least three scored direct hits against the Soviet warship.

BOOM.

When the ship blew apart in a brilliant flash of flame and fiery debris hurling into the sky, Pharaoh smiled in satisfaction at the results of their run. *Now let's hope ours is just as successful…*

"Whoa, Pharaoh! Hot damn, their gunners must have come alive all of a sudden. They're really laying it on thick now," commented Rhodie. They were now less than three kilometers from *Minsk*. "Just stick to the plan, Pharaoh, and we'll get through it."

They made final adjustments as the target grew in size the closer they got. They were also forced to weave and dodge the increasing volume of AA fire now being directed specifically at them by more than just *Minsk*. At least one or two of the nearby escorts were now focusing their guns on them. Seeing the giant vessel now less than a thousand meters and closing fast, Pharaoh squeezed the trigger and fired the cannon, sending three-second bursts of 20mm cannon fire into the AA guns and the missile launchers forward of the flight deck. It seemed like the right thing to do given that the enemy was shooting at him.

As he was about to overfly the giant Soviet ship, he released his bombs from under the Corsair, his aircraft momentarily lifting after being freed of their weight. Then he pulled up hard on the flight stick as he opened the throttle up before engaging the afterburners. Banking the aircraft into a hard turn to the right, he caught sight of the multiple strings of red tracer fire zipping through the sky where he'd just been. Something inside him had screamed at him to bank right—now he knew why. He just wasn't sure how that still voice inside him had known to do that.

The turn also allowed him to look back and check how many hits he and Scooter had scored on the *Minsk*. But as he looked at the giant Soviet ship, he was awed to see smoke and fire pouring out of her. If he had to guess, he and Rhodie must have landed three to five of the huge one-thousand-pound bombs. He couldn't be sure, but he was confident that the two of them had just sunk the pride of the Soviet Pacific Fleet.

Pharaoh heard a strange ripping sound and was horrified to see a line of tracers spitting just outside his left wing. He rolled away from the fire and did everything he could to keep himself out of the Sea of Japan as he dashed away, pulling his stick back until his Corsair was on a course of two-zero-zero. He pushed his throttle past the military power barrier and engaged his afterburner, running as fast as he could.

****

VAQ-136 "Gauntlets"

Potsie was exhausted. He also felt a little green under the gills. When the MiGs had tried to jump them, Trashman had reminded them why he was considered one of the best Prowler pilots in the fleet. One of the two MiGs had gotten a lock on them, sending a missile to chase them down, forcing Trashman into a series of aerial maneuvers Potsie might have seen at a flying circus rather than over the Sea of Japan in the backseat of a Prowler. When the missile exploded against one of their flares, he breathed a sigh of relief, catching his breath and struggling to hold what remained of his food down.

After what felt like a week of fighting, the battle looked to be over—at least for now. Potsie had heard their escorts had managed to shoot one of the MiGs down and damage another. Then a call had come out. Another pair of MiGs had slipped into the henhouse, nailing a Prowler and two Intruders before they were interdicted. By the time the MiG scare had finished and they'd been either shot down or chased off, Potsie had tallied the losses. As best he could come up with, one Prowlers, two Intruders, and four Phantoms to the Soviets' three MiGs, which caused him to wonder what the hell had happened. *Someone's going to have to figure that one out. Maybe the Soviets introduced some new missile or maybe a plane...or maybe they just got lucky, and we didn't...*

Feeling the Prowler bank out of the circular pattern they'd been flying, Potsie figured it must be time to link up with the attack squadrons and head home. As they did so, he surveyed the formations of the attack force with a sobering look of concern. While he was sure he couldn't see all the squadrons and aircraft flying around them, it was painfully obvious they were coming home with far fewer aircraft than they had started with.

"Dear Lord, we lost a lot of aircraft," said Loner, surmising what they all were thinking. "Let's hope they gave as good as they got, or this is going to be a long war."

"Amen," replied Potsie, hoping the last part of his statement was wrong, that this war wouldn't last much longer and they'd find a way to stop the Soviets so that peace could return.

With the battle behind them, the fatigue of long hours of sitting cooped up in a plane you couldn't walk around in had stiffened their muscles and worn them out. With the horizon filled with the burning smoke of Soviet fleet, the aviators of Carrier Air Wing Five limped home to Midway victorious, removing the Soviet naval threat to the Pacific for many months and possibly the remainder of the war.

Chapter 7

26 July 1981
3/6 Marines
USS *Austin* LPD-4
Sea of Japan

Corporal Philip Oliver stepped out of the shower and wrapped his towel around his waist. He was shaving when he realized that one of his team members, a new kid, was standing next to him, but he wasn't saying anything. *Jeff Jennings*, Oliver thought, remembering the name of his newest Marine.

"Something on your mind, Jennings?" asked Oliver. "Or are you just here for the show?"

"Sorry, Corporal," replied Jennings, "I'm just—I was—well, so, your tattoo... who's Samuel. Was that like your brother or something?" On the inside, Oliver was laughing at the situation, but he played it straight. The tattoo in question read: "1 Samuel 17:46."

"Which one of those idiots convinced you to come and ask me about the tattoo?"

"Nobody, Corporal, I was just curious."

"Samuel was a prophet of God, and his life was chronicled in the Bible. That tattoo is a Bible verse. It symbolizes my relationship with the Lord our God. I'm deeply religious in case you hadn't noticed it and nobody has bothered to tell you."

"I'm sorry, Corporal—"

"Just stop, Jennings. Don't dig the hole any deeper." Oliver knew that this made no sense, but a fresh private didn't need a corporal to make sense. He just needed his team leader not to be angry with him.

"But," continued Jennings, "what does it mean?"

"If you care enough to find out," said Oliver, "why don't you go find a Bible?" Jennings hesitated. "Beat it, Jennings." Jennings left, and Oliver finished shaving before heading back to his rack to get dressed.

"Jefferson was looking for you," said Lance Corporal Palmer, who had the top rack above Oliver's.

"So, you're the one," said Oliver.

"Hey, it's boring as shit on this boat," said Palmer. "Have to do something to pass the time."

"I wonder where he's going to find a Bible," said Oliver.

"I suppose he could go to the ship's library," replied Palmer.

"I doubt he knows where the library is. He's kind of a 'pull the grenade, throw the pin' type of guy," said Oliver. "Anyhow, it ain't going to be boring for long. We can't float around here forever." The excitement of the previous day's attacks had left everyone with frayed nerves and emotional exhaustion. "Pretty soon we're going to be feet wet and inbound for hostiles."

"I'll take the assault over sitting out here waiting to die," said Palmer. "I couldn't shake that helpless feeling yesterday. I kept replaying the day we almost bought it on *Guam*."

"I get that," said Oliver, "but look at it this way: on *Guam*, you had never survived a sinking ship. Today you have. You know what it feels like and that experience will help you. Sure, it's fucking terror in the heat of the battle, but you know that if we get hit again, you'll perform, just like you did last time. Of course, there's now friendly territory to divert to, so we'll have to fight the Ricos with what we're carrying. That's not going to go well."

"You're such a ray of sunshine," replied Palmer.

"You know it, Mouthwash," laughed Oliver, reminding the Marine of a nickname that was nearly dead, given all the rotation the company had had over the past year.

"Piss off, Oliver."

"Today," said Jennings, reading from a book in his hands, "Yah... Yahw..."

"Yahweh," said Oliver, throwing Jennings a bone.

"Yahweh," continued Jennings, "will deliver you into my hand. I will strike you and take your head from off you. I will give the dead bodies of the army of the Philistines today to the birds of the sky and to the wild animals of the earth, that all the earth may know that there is a God in Israel." Jennings looked up from the book. "Holy shit, that's some heavy metal right there."

"Yeah, when I was a kid at church," said Oliver, "I'd get bored out of my mind, so I decided to read the only thing available. The Bible. I started in the back with Revelation. That shit's bananas. You know the story of David and Goliath, right?"

"Sure, everyone does," said Jennings.

"That verse you just read is what David told Goliath just before he zonked his ass."

"That's some ice-cold shit," said Jennings. "But there's no way no skinny kid is going to off a giant with a slingshot. That's just silly."

"Are you retarded?" asked Oliver. "It wasn't a slingshot. Do you know what a sling is?"

"Yeah, it's that wooden handle with this rubber strap—"

"Stop. Just stop," said Oliver. He sighed and started again. "A sling is an important weapon in history. As a Marine, you should know a little history. It'll be good for you. A sling is essentially a strap and pouch. The slinger loads a rock in the pouch." Oliver cupped his left hand and placed his right fist into it. "Then he takes the strap and begins swirling it." He made a swirling motion with his right hand. "Once you've built up enough speed, you release the strap and the rock flies out at high speed. Yes, it will kill a person, even a giant, if you clock him right in the face, which is what David did."

"I see," said Jennings, taking in this new information.

"Why on earth did you get that tattooed on your shoulder?" asked Palmer, who'd never had the courage to ask until this point.

"It was after we graduated from boot camp. My boys and I all decided to get tattoos. We all wanted to have the most badass tattoo, so while the other boys were getting EGAs, flaming 'Semper Fi' tattoos and the like, I got this little representation of the most badass thing I've seen written. And everyone laughed at me, until I told them what it meant, and how much of a badass David was in the Bible." Palmer nodded in understanding.

"So you really believe all this Bible stuff?" asked Jennings.

"I don't know what to believe exactly. But I do believe in God. I don't think there's any way I could have made it this far without him. But the rest of this?" He gestured towards the Bible, still in Jennings's hand. "I have no idea."

"How different are the Norks going to be than the Sandis?" asked Palmer.

"Knock it off with that 'Nork' nonsense," Palmer. "We agreed that they were Ricos. We're going to stick with that."

"But Norks is what the locals were calling them," replied Palmer defensively.

"Oh, so now you're going to let the Army set the standards? No, thank you. They are Ricos. Red Koreans."

"That doesn't even make sense," said Palmer. "Wouldn't it be Rehcos?"

"We settled this last week. It's Ricos because it's easier to say. My God, why are you being such a pain in my ass about this?" asked Oliver, who suddenly smiled, thinking about how much of a pain in Rodriguez and Evans's asses he had been. "Anyhow, you got the same briefings that I did, but I talked to Gunny Page, and he said that the Ricos are true fanatics. Most of the Sandis weren't hard-core communists. They just hated their old corrupt government. These guys, though... they've been taught that their dear leader is a God on earth, and that we're subhuman monsters—"

"That's fair," said Palmer interrupting. "I guess they've met Marines before."

"They won't surrender at the first sign of danger. You know about the Kamikaze in World War II, right?"

"Those were the Japanese," said Palmer.

"Right," said Oliver, "Japanese who served a God-Emperor and believed that they were fighting for the very existence of their people. Gunny thinks that's the same kind of fanaticism we're going to find in North Korea."

"A ray of sunshine, I tell you," said Palmer as a quiet fell over the berthing compartment and the Marines digested what was ahead of them.

****

USS *Austin*, LPD-4
Kilo Company Leadership Briefing

First Lieutenant Marvin Bush sat in the briefing room with the other platoon leaders and Captain Omar Beck, Kilo Company's commanding officer. These meetings had become routine, where the activities of the Marines would be planned out and assignments given. Today was different.

"Gentlemen," said Captain Beck, "Major North." Beck stepped back and Major Oliver North took the center spot in front of the map of central North Korea.

"Thank you, Captain Beck," said North. "Marines, I'm bringing the orders to each company. The battalion will be facing its greatest challenge since World War II, maybe its greatest challenge ever. As soon as conditions are favorable, we will be landing north of Wonsan. I know that a lot of you have suspected as much, but now it's official."

Bush was one of many in the room who exhaled hard at that. There was no "good" place for an opposed landing. But Wonsan was a particularly tough nut to crack.

"I want Kilo Company to hear it from me. I want to give you the chance to look me in the eyes and know that I have every confidence in you to complete this mission." He paused and looked at the officers before him. "There are no easy missions, men. You mission isn't an exception to that rule. You will be landing here." He pointed to a spot of beach six miles north of Wonsan. "Once ashore, your objective will be Hill 183, here." The objective was just to the south of their landing zone. "This peak offers the enemy a clear view of our amphibious assault force. The Navy is going to plaster it, but I've yet to hear about an artillery barrage that killed everything. Kilo Company will kill whatever is left up there."

When he was finished, there was silence in the room. He turned to Beck and said, "Captain," as he held out his hand.

Beck shook it and replied, "Thank you, Major." The major and his staff left, presumably to go brief the next company. Beck got everyone's attention. "All right, now that you know the 'what,' Gunny Price and I are going to explain the 'how.'" Bush listened as Price explained to Lieutenant Leroy White that his First Platoon would be responsible for moving along the north face of Hill 183 before assaulting north. Beck then addressed all five lieutenants. "If we encounter significant resistance while we're still outside of seven hundred meters from the summit, we're going to call in naval gunfire support and, if available, air support. HQ knows how important it is for us to clear that hill, and they're giving us the tools we need to do it."

"Bush," said Beck, "you're going to take the west side of the hill. Get your men in position. When you get the order, have your squads advance by team up the hill to contact. We will clear every inch of this hill and deny it to the enemy. You've had the training for this mission, and I have every confidence that you can accomplish it."

"Understood, Captain, thank you," replied Bush. The pass-down continued as Third Platoon and the Weapons Platoon were given their orders. From there, the leaders were released to take the orders to their platoons. Bush knew that he had good NCOs that he could count on. He just had to keep up his end of the bargain and listen to them, and let them do what they did best. If he could encourage them, and stay out of their way, he knew they could take that hill. He'd have some decisions to make, and he'd be fighting alongside them, but in this arena, on this day, his men had the experience that he lacked. He wanted to live through getting that experience.

****

USS *Hawkbill*
Sea of Japan

The nuclear attack submarine USS *Hawkbill* was nowhere near the newest submarine in the fleet, yet she was sailing point for the task force. They were gliding under the surface, searching for the enemy. As Commander Robert Tyler liked to say, "The best antisubmarine weapon is another submarine." *Hawkbill* was Tyler's first command, but he'd spent the past two years preparing for this very mission.

Hawkbill had had a quiet war to this point. The North Koreans didn't have a fleet to speak of, and the Soviets weren't leaving the protective shelters of Vladivostok and Petropavlovsk. They heard the activity on the surface but didn't have a full picture of what had happened. Hopefully that was about to change.

"Dive Officer, bring us to five hundred feet depth," said Tyler.

"Five hundred feet depth, aye," replied Lieutenant Clayton Mullins, the boat's current dive officer. The floor seemed to shift under their feet as the sail planes were adjusted to decrease *Hawkbill*'s depth. There was a slight pause as the boat rose to the proper station.

"Release the buoy," ordered Tyler, who then checked his watch.

"Releasing the buoy," said the communications officer, Lieutenant Sean Burton. As he executed the order, the AN/BSQ-5 towed communications buoy was released. There was another pause as the buoy rose to the surface. Tyler checked his watch again.

"Anything, Sean?" he asked.

"Negative, sir, trying the secondary channel... bingo, we're receiving."

"All right, once it's decrypted, we might know a thing or two about what the hell happened up there," said Tyler. Fifteen minutes after the transmission started, a telex next to Burton came to life, spitting out several pages. Burton tore the pages off and handed them to the skipper.

Tyler slid on his reading glasses and gave the paper a once-over. He smiled and reached for the 1MC transmitter.

"Attention on the boat, this is Captain Tyler. In case you were wondering what the hullabaloo was yesterday, it looks like our friends on and above the surface just handed the Russkies their asses." He paused as a murmur of approval ran through the ship. Noise discipline didn't allow for anything more vigorous. "The Soviet Pacific Fleet came out to play, and we sent them home with their tails between their legs," continued Tyler. "But our job is just beginning. So as much as I want you to revel in the fleet's successes, we need to stay sharp. The Pacific Fleet has a lot of submarines, and we have yet to encounter them. I promise you all that we will, and soon. But we've trained for this, and we're ready for this. I have every confidence in every one of you. If I didn't, I would have left you in Japan. So, keep your spirits up, and be ready to perform when the moment calls. That is all." He placed the mic back on its hook and turned his attention to the immediate crew in the Control Room.

"That's not just me talking up the bad guys. If Ivan was willing to risk his entire surface force to make a run at our task force, you can bet he's committed submarines. And if I were Ivan, I'd be putting those submarines in between where we are and where they think we're going." He looked out and there were nods coming from the crew.

"We have to be getting close," continued Tyler. "If the enemy assumes, or has intelligence to indicate, that our target is central North Korea, they will have had time to deploy out there." He reached over and pointed to a spot on the main plot just east of the objective of Wonsan. "We're going to have to hunt our way in, and we cannot fail. If a submarine gets loose inside the task force, it will be a nightmare for those jarheads. So stay focused.

"Commander Silva, a word?" Tyler summoned his executive officer, Lieutenant Commander Brian Silva, who nodded and approached the captain.

"Sir?" Silva leaned in to give them what passed for privacy in the cramped quarters.

"What are you thinking?" asked Tyler. "What's Ivan thinking?"

"Sir, the closer we get to the coast, the more convinced I am that we're going to see a multiaxis simultaneous attack."

"I don't know if the Reds have the ability to coordinate something like that," said Tyler, "but that would definitely be a worst-case scenario. In that case, we just need to pray that we find at least one of those axes. We can't help what happens in spots where we aren't, so we need them to be where we are."

"If they can coordinate the submarine aspects," said Silva, "I believe they'll add in some air assets as well. Their entire naval aviation force is more or less dedicated to sinking our task force."

"Well, those that aren't dedicated to sinking our pesky submarines," corrected Tyler.

"Yes, there is that," chuckled Silva.

"This is going to be the last chance we get for any rest, and I can't even promise the next fifteen minutes. Quietly pass the word to the section heads that if they have anyone they're worried about with fatigue, to get them some rest. I don't care how they have to manage their rosters, I need the Battle Stations watch team ready to go at a moment's notice."

"Understood, Skipper," said Silva, who gave his boss a nod, then turned and left the Control Room.
****

26 July 1981
3/6 Marines
USS *Austin* LPD-4
Sea of Japan

Major Oliver North stood watch on the CIC of the USS *Austin*. His battalion was preparing to land on North Korea, but before they could, the Navy had to get them there. So far, the dreams of an uncontested landing were dashed as the Soviets threw their Pacific Fleet at them. With that threat neutralized, there were still dozens of things that could go wrong.

"Hey, we've got some interference to the northwest," said a sailor at one of the radar displays.

"What do you have?" asked the ship's commanding officer, Captain Percy Woods.

"Hard to say at this point, but it's definitely something," replied the sailor.

"Either Ivan is about to launch a major air strike, or he wants us to *think* he's about to," said Woods. North looked at the screen. Sure enough, the interference lay between the fleet's current position and the Soviet bases outside Vladivostok. North wondered how the admirals would react. Would they throw everything into the air in anticipation of a massive attack? And what if it was just a couple of jammers flying south in a bluff?

Not my job, thought North. Just like he wouldn't ask the admirals about how to deploy his battalion, he didn't waste time second-guessing them. Besides, from here, he would be able to see the battle unfold. He leaned over towards Lieutenant Commander Sims, the ship's intel officer. "Any idea what to expect?" he asked.

"It all depends on how the Russkies want to play it," replied Sims. "If they're determined that this is their best chance to take us off the board, they might throw everything they have in one big haymaker. On the other hand, if they don't really care much about their Korean fellow travelers, they might just be harassing us with some hit-and-run attacks, hoping to keep us stretched thin without exposing their own forces."

"What does the haymaker look like?" asked North.

"Well, depending on maintenance and weather, Ivan has up to four dozen Tu-22 Mikes, and maybe twice as many of the older Tu-16s."

"That's a lot of bad guys," said North.

"Damn right it is. We've got two squadrons of Tomcats and four squadrons of Phantoms, plus whatever the Air Force can get us out of Misawa and Chitose," said Sims, referring to two Japanese air bases.

"We're flying out of Chitose?" asked North.

"I don't think that's official, but I don't see how we can't be. The Japanese want us to win this war as much as we do. They don't want a belligerent DPRK right across the Sea of Japan from them." The use of Japanese bases against the Soviets had been prohibited up to this point. But North could see the logic in allowing them now.

"Yeah, in for a penny, in for a pound," said North. "The beating you guys handed to the Pacific Fleet has probably softened their tone quite a bit."

"That's right," agreed Sims. "If we can wipe out a good chunk of their naval aviation, that will give the Japanese much more flexibility."

"Captain, we're being painted by a Big Bulge radar," said a sailor at the electronic warfare station.

"Source?" asked Captain Woods.

"Definitely coming out of Vladivostok."

Sims leaned towards Major North. "If they wanted to sell the haymaker, that's how you do it."

"How's that?" asked North.

"They've put a big-ass radar bird into the air over their home base and are right now tracking this fleet—and they could be transmitting that location data to over a hundred incoming bombers."

"We're getting intermittent contact through the jamming," said the radarman. "It looks like two separate groups, one group of at least twenty-four Tu-16 Badgers and one group of at least a dozen Tu-22 Backfires."

"Looks like the CAGs had the right idea," said Sims, pointing to the NTDS screen, which indicated several groups of fighters rising from the fleet and dashing towards the enemy.

"That doesn't sound like the worst-case scenario," said North.

"Don't hold your breath, Major," replied Sims. "Those are just the ones we can detect. There could be a whole lot more in that jamming and chaff."

North looked at the NTDS and watched as the Phantoms and Tomcats that were on combat air patrol engaged the enemy. North knew that the Tomcats were specifically designed to counter this exact threat. Their long-range "fire and forget" Phoenix missiles were the most advanced air-to-air missiles in the world. They had to be in order to engage the enemy bombers before they could get within missile range.

"We don't have enough fighters airborne to stop them," said North. It was a simple matter of looking at the incoming threat and the outgoing defenders.

"We've got layers of defense, Major," replied Sims. "We have the CAP, then we have our SAM belt, then close-in systems. That's to say nothing of our defensive electronic warfare systems."

"Be that as it may," said North, "I'd much rather have more fighters in the air."

"Amen, Major. Amen."

They watched as the Tomcats started reporting missile hits. There was a slight lessening of the tension for the slightest few seconds before the call came in.

"Vampire, vampire. Missiles inbound, bearing zero-zero-seven, range one-six-zero."

"It's pucker time," said Sims. With missiles inbound, the danger had just ticked up a few notches. "Here," he said, holding out a big pair of headphones with the speaker flipped out. This allowed North to put one ear on the left speaker while Sims listened in on the right speaker.

"Captain, I have new vampire contacts, bearing zero-four-four, range one-zero-six."

"Any air contacts on that bearing?" asked Captain Woods.

"Negative, sir."

"Any idea what we're looking at?"

"Sir, the flight profile matches an SS-N-9 Siren," replied the sailor. "If I had to guess—"

"You do," replied Woods.

"They've got a sub or two over there. Maybe a Charlie or one of those up-jumped Echoes."

"I think you're probably right," agreed Woods. "Not that there's anything we can do about it." North had to agree with that assessment. The ship's three-inch anti-aircraft guns were next to useless against supersonic missiles. The tension in the room was building as the missiles bore down on their targets.

"There go the Backfires," said Sims. They'd made their launch, and now they were making their escape at twice the speed of sound. "The Badgers have to get a bit closer in to fire their AS-6 Kingfishers. Hopefully the Tomcats can take out a bunch before they're in firing range." The two men waited in silence as the missiles continued their relentless approach.

"Looks like the Badgers are turning," said North.

"At least there are fewer than there were a few minutes ago."

"Missiles inbound, starboard side." The voice from the 1MC alerted the rest of the crew to what everyone in the CIC already knew. "Prepare for Impact." Surface-to-air missiles poured out of the ships, heading towards the inbound Soviet missiles. As the groups of missiles intersected, there were fewer attacking missiles. Fewer. Not zero. No matter how many SAMs flew into the air, there were always more Soviet missiles.

"They're crossing the picket now," said Sims. A force of six frigates and destroyers led the task force. They were primarily ASW platforms, but they weren't defenseless against an air attack. Except for the *Knox*-class *Barney*, who lacked any SAMs. "The only thing that's going to save those ships is that they aren't the intended target... we are."

It was a ghastly thought that entered Major North's mind. He would gladly sacrifice those ships to save his Marine force. It wasn't that he was unfeeling or uncaring. It was just the cold calculation of war. The mission was to get the Marines on the beach. The role of the Navy was to facilitate that. He would be lucky to survive the day of the landing, but he would gladly trade the lives of a few thousand sailors to get to it.

"It's the damn trolley problem," said North, more to himself than anyone else.

"Come again?" asked Sims.

"Never mind, it's just getting hot in here," said North. He looked at the NTDS.

"Hey, Sims... look at those Badgers. They didn't turn with the rest of them."

"What the hell?" said Sims. "It looks like they bet that we'd be preoccupied with the missile threat and they could close a few more miles on us before launching."

"It looks like that bet is paying off," said North, frowning. A second wave of missiles followed the first. It was clear from the display screen that some of the picket ships had been taken out with the first wave since there weren't nearly as many SAMs meeting this wave.

"This ain't good," said Sims.

"You didn't need to tell me that," replied North. The fact that they had survived the first wave without too much of a direct threat didn't make him feel better about the second wave. He just had to stand tall in the face of danger.

The collision alarm rang throughout the ship as the missiles entered their terminal phase, reaching out for the ships. There was nothing that North could do but wait for all hell to break loose. He knew his tasking. He took comfort in the knowledge that he would know what to do to protect as many of his Marines as he could, should it come to that.

Suddenly, it was quiet. There was a heartbeat where everyone in the CIC realized that they were still alive. Then the calls started coming in from the ships that hadn't been as fortunate.

"It looks like they got three of the Gators," said Sims. That was a major blow to the task force. Yet even with the three they'd lost, there were still eight ships brimming with angry Marines to unleash on the enemy.

The CIC was abuzz with activity as the ships of the fleet began rescue operations to save as many of the men on the stricken ships and in the icy waters as they could. *Austin* would take on wounded that were flown in from helicopters. It would be a long night. Major Oliver North summoned his operations officer to relieve him in the CIC. He had to talk to his Marines.
****

USS *Hawkbill*
Sea of Japan

"Contact, torpedo!" Sonarman First Class Kent Stokes broke the silence that had fallen over the Control Room of *Hawkbill*. Once the sounds of the air battle had receded into the background, there was a pause in the tension. Stokes's announcement filled the room once again. "Bearing two-three-zero, range one-seven point four nautical miles."

"What are they shooting at?" asked Lyle Lucas, the senior enlisted sailor on *Hawkbill* and therefore the chief of the boat, or COB.

"Second contact," said Stokes, almost in response. "Submarine, sir, *Los Angeles* class." After a pause, he continued, "Sir, it's *New York City*. She's making a flank dash to the southeast." The crew held their breath. Their brothers in arms were in a race for their lives and there was nothing that they could do but watch and pray. And the prayers weren't only for the lives of the crew of *New York City*. Commander Tyler was sure that many in the Control Room were praying that they wouldn't find themselves in the same position.

"She's deployed a Nixie," said Stokes, referring to the noisemaker that mimicked the sounds of a submarine in an effort to fool the incoming torpedo. "The torpedo is homing." Now the torpedo was pinging with its active sonar. The Nixie couldn't fool the torpedo once it went active. The seconds passed. With the torpedo moving at forty-five knots while *New York City* was fleeing at thirty-four knots, the closure rate of the torpedo was agonizingly slow. Yet the seconds pounded away, and one way or another, the crew of *Hawkbill* would soon know the fate of their fellow sailors.

"Detonation," said Stokes, trying to keep the emotion out of his voice. The submarine was silent. Everyone knew that the explosion itself didn't guarantee the loss of the boat. The sonarmen would be listening to the ocean to get as much information as they could. "She's decompressing—I think she's blown her tanks." In the event of an emergency, a submarine would sometimes empty her ballast tanks to create as much buoyancy as possible. There was more silence as everyone waited for Stokes to give them the final verdict.

"She's still diving. I don't think she's coming back up," said the sonarman.

"I need everybody to keep their shit together," said Woods evenly. "We're in the middle of a naval battle, and if we make any mistakes down here, we'll be joining *New York City* at the bottom of the Pacific." There were nods among the crew. "I know what you're feeling right now. I understand that you're angry. I'm angry. I want to kill the Red bastards that did this. And I intend to do just that. But I won't do that if I act on that anger. So take that fire and swallow it. Put it down deep inside and let it fuel you. Don't let it out where it might burn all of us. Is that understood?" A quiet chorus of "Yes, sirs" wafted through the Control Room.

"Any idea what got them?" asked Woods.

"We have an unknown submerged contact in the vicinity. That's gotta be our shooter," said Stokes.

"Helm, come to five knots," ordered the captain.

"Five knots, aye," replied the helmsman.

"WEPs, confirm that tubes all tubes are loaded and flooded." *Hawkbill* had set "Battle Stations Torpedo" hours ago and was now ready to fire at a moment's notice.

"Confirmed, all tubes are loaded and flooded, aye."

"We're going to make a cautious approach. We know that he's out there, but he's probably oblivious to our position."

"I'm not a big fan of 'probably,'" remarked Master Chief Lucas.

"I agree," said the captain. "I'd much rather be certain, but those aren't the facts that I have." *Hawkbill* creeped along, stalking her prey. It took another ten minutes before Stokes spoke up again.

"Sir, we've got an ID on Contact Goblin One. She's a Victor III." That wasn't shocking news, but it wasn't good news either. The Victor III was the pinnacle of Soviet attack submarine technology. It wasn't the equal of the *Los Angeles* class that the US was putting to sea, but it was a near match for an older *Sturgeon* class like *Hawkbill*.

And this Victor just managed to send a 688 to the bottom, thought Woods. A reminder that a technological advantage was just that: an *advantage*. It didn't guarantee an outcome. It would be the crews on board the submarines that would determine who came out of this battle triumphant.

"Contact Goblin One is heading zero-five-zero, making fifteen knots." Woods looked at the map.

"She's trying to get in front of the battle group. She's just a little out of position."

"I imagine they have boats all along the approaches," said Tyler.

"Yeah, it was this guy's dumb luck that he's got to push to get ahead," replied Woods. "So much the better for us. Tell me, COB, if it were your approach, how would you make it?"

"Sir, I'd keep present speed and come to two-seven-zero. If she stays on this heading, we'll cross her bow with plenty of room to come about to port and head straight for her. If there's a change in aspect, we should have plenty of time to counter it."

"Very well," replied Woods. "Helm, come to two-seven-zero."

"Two-seven-zero, aye." At five knots, the turn was nearly imperceptible.

"Stokes, let me know the second you have a firm enough fix to fire."

"Aye, sir." With each passing minute, *Hawkbill* closed on her prey.

"Contact," said Stokes. "Unknown submerged contact, bearing three-zero-five, range fifteen nautical miles."

"That makes things interesting," said Tyler.

"Indeed it does," agreed Woods. They now had two submerged contacts in range. If they had managed to get a shot off on the first one, this second submarine, if hostile, would have had an easy shot on *Hawkbill*. "I don't mean to put undue pressure on your team, Petty Officer Stokes, but I'm going to need a fix on both of those submarines."

"Understood, sir. We're on it," replied Stokes. Woods no longer felt any confidence that his presence was unknown. But his job was to engage these submarines, and he intended to do exactly that.

"Sir, we have a firing solution on Goblin One."

"Understood, good work Stokes."

"Weapons, ready tubes one and three to fire on Goblin One."

"Aye, tubes one and three targeting Goblin One."

"Sir, we have an ID on Contact two," said Stokes. "It's another Victor III, Designating Contact Two as Goblin Two."

"Looks like Ivan is rolling out the red carpet for us today," said Tyler.

"It wouldn't surprise me if every seaworthy frontline submarine is playing a role out here today," said Woods.

"Sir, we have a fix on Goblin Two."

"That was quick," said Tyler.

"Ready tubes two and four, target Goblin Two."

"Tubes two and four targeting Goblin Two."

"Helm, prepare to come to course zero-three-zero flank speed as soon as the fish are clear."

"Zero-three-zero, aye."

"Fire," ordered the captain. The four Mark 48 torpedoes were ejected from their tubes in quick succession, each on a collision course with their respective targets. As soon as the torpedoes were clear, the helmsman executed the ordered maneuver, bringing *Hawkbill* around to zero-three-zero and increasing speed to flank.

"Torpedoes running normally," announced the weapons officer.

In the tense moments that followed, the crew listened as the torpedoes closed the distance towards their intended targets. The Soviet submarines had now detected the incoming torpedoes and began taking evasive actions, launching noisemakers and changing course to avoid the lethal weapons.

"Goblin One has launched countermeasures," reported Stokes.

"So has Goblin Two," added another sonar operator.

The torpedoes, guided by their onboard computers, ignored the decoys and continued to track their true targets. As the distance closed, the crew of *Hawkbill* held their breath, waiting for the moment of impact.

"Impact on Goblin One!" exclaimed Stokes as the sound of the explosion reached *Hawkbill*'s sensitive sonar. "She's breaking up!"

The crew couldn't help but cheer at the successful hit, but their celebration was short-lived as they awaited the fate of the second Soviet submarine.

"Torpedoes failed to get a lock on Goblin Two," reported the sonar operator, disappointment evident in his voice. "She's continuing evasive maneuvers."

"Reload tubes one and three," ordered Commander Woods, his voice steely with determination. "We're not letting that second one get away."

As *Hawkbill* pursued Goblin Two, the tension in the Control Room remained high. The submarine's survival depended on their ability to sink the remaining Soviet sub before it had the chance to retaliate. Despite the setback, the crew's resolve was stronger than ever, fueled by the memory of their fallen comrades on *New York City*.

****

White House
Situation Room
Washington, D.C.

President Carter studied the map intently. He'd served in the Navy during the First Korean War, but he'd spent all of his time on the East Coast as part of Admiral Rickover's fledgling "Nuclear Navy." Now he was the commander in chief during the Second Korean War. He preferred being a young officer in New London, Connecticut, to sitting at this desk and hearing news like this.

"We knew there would be resistance," said Secretary of Defense Harold Brown. "And we knew that the Soviets might seek to intervene. That's why we had three aircraft carriers escorting the amphibious force."

"And even so," asked Carter, "the Soviets managed to sink three of our amphibious transport ships?"

"That's correct, sir," replied Brown.

"Where does this leave us?" asked the President.

"General Barrow assures me that the force in place is more than enough to complete the objective," said Brown, referring to General Robert H. Barrow, the Commandant of the Marine Corps.

"What effect will these casualties have on the overall operation?" asked the President.

"It's impossible to say for sure," replied Brown, "but the lack of follow-on forces during the battle could lead to additional casualties taking Wonsan. The Marines that start the fight will need to be kept in the fight longer than they otherwise would have, before being pulled off the line for rest and recovery."

The answer didn't make Carter happy, but then what choice did he have?

"Are there other options? Can we get more forces there before the invasion?"

"No, sir, we're out of options. We can either hit the beach with what we have or turn the fleet around and get replacements to try this, or another plan, in a month."

"By which time the DPRK might break the stalemate in the south and push our forces into the sea."

"That's the long and short of it, sir," said Brown. "It's not the force we want for the invasion, but it's the force we have. And for the record, I'll put my money on General Barrow."

"Noted," said Carter. "What about Europe? How is this Operation Fullback playing out?"

"Both NORTHAG and CENTAG are pushing to meet their objectives. The Soviets are being steadily pushed back."

"I'm glad to hear it," said Carter. "Our boys were taking a beating at the start of this thing, and I'm glad to see us holding up our end."

"The key to this, sir, was surprise. We managed to get Ivan believing that the main counteroffensive was going to be through the south, where Italy and Greece were having success against weaker Warsaw Pact units out of Yugoslavia, Hungary and Czechoslovakia."

"How'd we sell that?" asked Carter.

"There was some of the classic 'wooden army' ruse, but it was mostly the NSA running fake signals. We even helped the Soviets 'break' one of our codes so that we could feed them bad information."

"Whatever it takes to win, Harry. Has there been any evidence of a Soviet counteroffensive?"

"The Soviets are disorganized at this point," said Brown. "Their plans for the initial offensive didn't account for being pushed back before they could finish off Germany."

"You don't have to remind me of exactly how close they came to doing just that," said Carter.

"Now that we have them on the defensive, they're having a hard time adapting to the ever-changing battlefield. Our battle plan is based largely on keeping them off-balance. We don't give the time to understand our tactics before we shift them up and try something slightly different."

"What a difference three weeks can make," said the President.

"That's true," agreed Brown before backtracking a little. "But we haven't won this thing. There are a million things that can go wrong."

"I take nothing for granted at this point, Harry."

"No, sir, I don't imagine you do."

****

USS *Hawkbill*
Sea of Japan

As the vanguard of the fleet, USS *Hawkbill* was on the prowl, looking for enemy submarines who would do her friends harm. Commander Robert Tyler checked his readings. Five knots. They'd sprinted ahead during the combat topside, trying to get some distance while the enemy's ears would be filled with the sounds of fighting. They could map where the Soviet Pacific Fleet had made their stand. But as the Soviet ships came to rest on the bottom of the Pacific Ocean, a calm returned to the depths. That calm meant every submarine, Soviet or American, was now desperately listening for one another.

"Sir," said Sonarman First Class Buddy Gallagher, "we've got several surface contacts on those fleeing Soviet warships."

"I know that, Gallagher," said Tyler, "I can read the display as well as you can."

"Well, yes, sir," stammered Gallagher, "It's just that there's something else there. Something that was blending with the noise, but now that the surface units are clearing out... there's something out there."

"Okay, I'm listening," said the commander.

"I've been trying to figure this out, sir," said Gallagher. "The last time the Soviets came after a carrier with a surface action group, it was the Eastern Med, and they got their asses handed to them."

"I appreciate the history lesson, Gallagher," said Tyler with a smile, "but where are you going with this?"

"Why would they do it again? And against three carriers?"

"I'll point out that they did manage to sink a few of our amphibs," said Tyler. "If the surface fleet hadn't been such a focus of the fleet, we would have done better against their Backfire strike."

"Yes, sir," agreed Gallagher, "but I think there's something there. I swear there are submerged contacts that were cruising beneath the surface fleet."

"XO, you hearing this?" asked Tyler.

"Yes, sir," said Lieutenant Commander Biran Silva, "I don't think anyone has a better idea. From the sounds of the battle, we can infer that the enemy knows where the fleet is. So if we can plot an intercept course from the position of the surface fleet at the time of the attack to the location of our forces during the Soviet air strike..."

"Petty Officer Gallagher," said Commander Tyler, "thank you for your crack analysis. This might not come to anything, but you've given the best lead that I've heard yet. Navigation, plot a course to intercept based on the location of the surface contacts at the time of the attack and our fleet during the Soviet air strike."

Within five minutes, *Hawkbill* was on a course of zero-three-zero, backtracking from her westerly course. What frustrated Commander Tyler was that he had full faith in Petty Officer Gallagher. He really thought that this was the most likely line of attack that the Soviets would take. But he couldn't tell anyone. Any attempt to contact the surface and warn them would ruin everything. Better to silently stalk the enemy.

"Skipper," said Gallagher, "I've got a faint contact, bearing zero-two-five. Machine noises. No ID."

"Bull's-eye," said Tyler. "Great work, Gallagher." *Hawkbill* slowly stalked her prey.

"Second contact," said Gallagher. Then, after a brief pause, "First contact is a Victor, sir. Designating Goblin One." Things were playing out exactly like Gallagher had predicted.

"Goblin One, aye," said Tyler. *Hawkbill* continued to hunt.

"Second contact is another Victor, sir," said Gallagher. "Designate contact two as Goblin Two. I'll get you more specifics as they come in, sir."

"Understood. You're doing an outstanding job," said Tyler.

As the tension rose aboard *Hawkbill*, Commander Tyler stood firmly at his station in the Control Room of his attack submarine. Sweat dripped down his forehead as he stared at the NTDS, his eyes fixated on the blips representing the two menacing Soviet Victor-class submarines. The low hum of the engines reverberated through the hull, a constant reminder of the imminent danger lurking in the depths.

Beside Commander Tyler, Petty Officer Gallagher meticulously tracked the movements of the enemy submarines. His fingers danced across the control panel, his trained ears attuned to every acoustic nuance. With a focused intensity, he relayed vital information to the captain, his voice calm and steady despite the adrenaline coursing through his veins.

As the battle unfolded, *Hawkbill*'s crew operated like a well-oiled machine. Lieutenant Commander Silva stood by Commander Tyler's side, providing real-time updates and insights into the unfolding situation. His voice carried a mix of urgency and determination, amplifying the gravity of the moment.

"Sir, we have a firm contact and a firing solution on Goblin One. We haven't firmed up Goblin Two."

"What do you think, Brian?" asked Tyler.

"If Goblin Two has no idea we're here, I take the shot. If Goblin Two thinks we *might* be here, I don't. If we surprise Goblin Two, she'll go fast and deep. That'll give us a chance at a second shot on her because it won't take long to get a solution. But if she thinks we're here, she'll stay calm and then fire at our torpedo launch points."

"I hate to reduce it to this," said Tyler, "but we have a duty to sink the sub we have in our sights. If there's another sub we have to deal with, then so be it."

"You're right, sir," said Lieutenant Sliva. "We don't really have a choice."

"Weapons, flood tubes one through four. Prepare to fire at Contact Goblin One."

"Aye, Skipper."

"Gallagher," said Tyler, "you've been johnny-on-the-spot today. I need you for one more miracle."

"Sir?" asked Gallagher.

"In the chaos of our attack on Goblin One, I need you to get a fix on Goblin Two so that we can engage." Tyler knew that he was asking for the impossible. Once the torpedoes were in the water and the enemy cranked to flank speed and popped noisemakers, the acoustic canvas would become an absolute blur.

"Sir, I'll do my best," said Gallagher.

"That's all I can ask," replied Commander Tyler. "Weps, fire tubes one and three, target contact Goblin One."

"Firing," said the weapons officer.

"Goblin Two is running!" said Gallagher.

"I need a firing solution," said Tyler.

"Loading now," said Gallagher. "Ready!"

"Fire tubes two and four on contact Goblin Two." There was a beat before Tyler said, "Helm, come to course three-zero-zero, flank speed. Dive, get us under the layer." *Hawkbill* delivered her payload and ran. She knew that even if she didn't get kills on the two Victors, she'd alerted the surface fleet that they were there—unless those topsiders were as incompetent as the submariners thought they were.

"Sir, torpedo in the water," said Gallagher. "I think Goblin Two had an idea we were there. She was ready for our attack."

There was nothing for Tyler to do. He had to fight his submarine and try his best to get out of harm's way. He'd done all the attacking he could—now it was time for some defense.

"Torpedoes are pinging," said Gallagher as he pulled one of his headphones off his ear so he could hear the crew while the enemy sonar screamed in his ear. "Explosions, sir. Goblin One is in trouble… can't tell if she's sinking. Wait. No, yeah. I have implosion." The words were barely out of Gallagher's mouth before the entire boat was rocked. Anyone not strapped in was chucked into the air.

In what seemed like an instant, the hull began to lose integrity. Bolts were popping off, water spraying inside.

"Emergency blow," ordered Commander Tyler.

"Emergency blow, aye," confirmed the dive officer. It was a desperate move. The only way it would work was if the breach in *Hawkbill*'s hull was bringing on less water than the boat could shed. Tyler looked at the boat's depth. It was going up. She was rising. Tyler breathed a sigh of relief right before reality hit him. The incoming water of *Hawkbill*'s wounds was greater than her capacity to increase ballast. *Hawkbill* continued to rise until one hundred twenty feet before she began to sink again. Those who weren't killed in the flooding were given a mild and terrifying reprise to make peace with their end.

Chapter 8

27 July 1981
3/6 Marines
USS *Austin*, LPD-4
Sea of Japan

This would be a first for Corporal Oliver. Instead of flying into battle, he'd be swimming. Second Squad was crammed into an amphibious assault vehicle, or AAV. The AAV was an amphibious armored personnel carrier, similar to the M113 on land, but a bit bigger. The Marines loaded up, and now they were doing one thing Marines just don't do well. They waited. Every warrior in the vehicle was amped up with the prospect of combat. Those who had seen the elephant knew that they had a grim job to do. The virgins were a nervous mess but didn't want to look weak in front of the veterans.

"If you're going to puke, don't," said Oliver in his most commanding corporal voice. "It's going to be bad enough fighting the Ricos. It'll be even worse if I have to do it while wearing your lunch on my uniform." Oliver was aware that the odds of them getting all the way to shore without someone losing their lunch were pretty slim. Between the nerves and the motion of the small craft in the choppy sea, it was a lot to ask.

The mission was as straightforward as it was ambitious. There was a two-hundred-meter hill just south of the landing zone. The Navy had shelled the hell out of it, and Kilo Company was going to clear it out of the Ricos if there were any survivors. *And there will always be survivors*, thought Oliver. He knew that it was going to be a battle, but he also knew that Kilo Company hadn't grabbed the toughest nut to crack. There was a three-hundred-meter hill to the west of the LZ, and that was going to be a bloodbath.

"Remember," said Sergeant Evans, Second Squad's platoon sergeant, "when we hit the sand, we need to fight our way off that beach. I don't want to see any of you assholes taking a knee, or going prone unless you're under direct fire.

"And don't bunch up out there. You know a Rico would love nothing more than to pop three of you with a grenade. Fan out when you leave the vehicle." Everyone in the vehicle knew these pearls of wisdom.

On the other hand, in the heat of battle, even good Marines could forget something obvious. Not to mention the fact that getting yelled at by leadership helped keep everyone from focusing on the insanity that was just moments away.

Ping! Something ricocheted off the AAV.

"What the hell was that?" asked a voice Oliver didn't recognize.

"Don't fucking worry about it," said Evans. "There ain't shit you can do about it no matter what it was. Just focus on the ramp and get ready to explode out of here." The AAV continued to plunge through the water towards destiny.

At least with the helos you were in and out in a flash. This waiting sucks, thought Oliver. He longed for any contact with the outside world. Any way to see what the hell was going on, to get out of his own head. *You're an NCO now, meathead*, he reminded himself. *You're an example to these grunts.* Then he felt the vehicle's tracks grab the ground, and they tipped back as the AAV made it to the beach. Before he could worry any more about that, there was daylight. The ramp dropped, and as one, the Marines pushed out of the AAV and onto the beach.

Machine-gun and rifle fire cracked all around them. In the chaos, it was impossible to tell incoming and outgoing fire apart. Oliver knew only that there was a lot of it. None of his combat experience had quite prepared him for the battle he found himself in the middle of. Shells started dropping on and around the beach. AV-8A Harriers were directed into the forested hills in search of the enemy guns.

"Second Squad, move it! Move it! Move it!" screamed Evans, trying to get his unit organized. They'd made it to the beach. That was step one. Now they just needed to secure the objective and, with some luck, survive the day. Second Squad ran to the base of the objective to get organized. Oliver's finger slid down the barrel of his M16 and passed over where his M203 grenade launcher used to be mounted. As the team leader, he was no longer the grenadier. That honor fell to PFC Randy Harrington.

Damn, I miss that little bastard, thought Oliver. *It's nice having a little extra firepower.* A shell exploding behind the squad threw bodies in the air while Oliver scanned his line to make sure his team was in order. They had to get moving. Right now they didn't have anything to shoot at, and there was nothing worse than getting shot at and not being able to shoot back.

Second Squad reached the tree line and Oliver threw himself on the ground while trying to scan the hill for any threats. Evans was doing the same thing.

"Fire Team One, let's go!" shouted Evans over the sounds of the battle. Oliver was on a knee, looking for any targets. Once Fire Team One had advanced seventy-five yards, Oliver watched them take a knee. That was his signal.

"Fire Team Two, on me!" He sprinted past Evans's team and kept going. He had eyed a spot where he was going to halt his team, but before they made it there, gunfire rang out from the forest, causing his team to go prone while Team One returned fire. Oliver had his rifle out and was scanning for targets. All he could see was the occasional muzzle flash. *Nobody can see anybody*, he thought. *They're just shooting at movement, and we're just shooting at their flashes.*

"We've got to close the distance if we want to shoot any of these Ricos," said Oliver to his Marines. "We're going to low-crawl up this hill and see if we can make contact—pass the word." He gave it a minute to make sure everyone had the order, then began using his elbows and knees to push himself up the hill. All the while, he was keeping his head down but still scanning for targets.

"Contact, left," shouted Jennings before letting off a few rounds. The flash of his rifle caught the attention of the enemy, who returned fire on the team's general location. Oliver estimated five rifles over there and wished dearly that he had his M203.

"Harrington!" shouted Oliver.

"On it, boss!" came the reply before Oliver could get the order out. Oliver heard the *foomp* of the grenade leaving the launcher and steadied his rifle on the target area. The grenade exploded, and there was a scurrying of enemy soldiers, trying to reestablish cover and concealment. That was what the Marines needed. With the enemy panicking, they were easy targets. All five Marine rifles came alive, and the enemy was cut down. There was a brief calm as no more enemy fire came their way.

He turned his head to address the team. "Don't get cozy," said Oliver, "that's just the first one. This is going to be a long day." Before he turned back towards the object, movement caught his eye. As it closed

106

the distance, he could tell it was Corporal Murphy from Headquarters Platoon. He dove next to Oliver.

"Word from Lieutenant. Bush is to hold here. Captain Beck is calling for naval gunfire support. It looks like the Ricos are using this hill as their main overlook for artillery spotting on the fleet. They're going to smoke the top of the mountain and see if they can't shake something loose."

"As long as those squids don't drop on us, that's great news," replied Oliver with a grin. They held their position and scanned for targets as the rest of the platoon closed to form a wall along the left and right of Oliver's team. From there, it was a strange stalemate, both sides on the defensive, neither advancing.

"Corporal Oliver?" The question surprised him.

"Yeah, what the hell do you—" He stopped short, realizing he was addressing his platoon leader. "Oh, shit. Sorry, sir," he said sheepishly.

"Don't sweat it," said Bush, "you're having a hell of a day. They say you made first contact with the enemy. I just wanted to say great work, Marine. Zero casualties and, what, ten dead Ricos?"

"More like five. And they could just be wounded and bleeding out, I suppose."

"Don't be too modest, but either way, great work. Keep it up." With that said, the LT shuffled off down the line, presumably to encourage the next squad. Oliver was surprised by the whole scene. But then again, there was a lull, and Bush had found a way to turn it into an opportunity. Oliver had to respect that.

They were too far away to hear the sound of the fleet's five-inch guns popping off. But they were plenty close to hear the rounds landing. The hilltop was a mere eight hundred meters from their current position. It wasn't quite "danger-close," but Oliver liked to refer to it as "danger-close-enough." The five-inch rounds arrived en masse and the ground trembled as they tore up the earth and knocked over trees. In spite of Oliver's ten months of combat, he'd never been so near an artillery bombardment this heavy.

Intermixed with the high-explosive rounds, smoke shells started dropping. Oliver didn't know if the Navy had smoke on their ships or if Marine mortars had joined the fight. It didn't matter—the smoke was a welcome addition either way. After what felt like an eternity, the explosions just stopped. And then the orders came down the line to advance. The Marines advanced in a line through the haze of smoke.

Oliver could hear gunfire off to his left but didn't take his eyes off his area of responsibility. One foot followed the other as he slowly advanced. They made it another twenty meters before encountering anything. Something moved through the trees in front of him. Oliver took a knee, relieved that his contact was movement and not enemy fire. The Rico was running towards them at full speed.

"Contact front!" he said before firing at the incoming soldier and dropping him. His team held as they looked for additional targets. *What the hell was he charging us for?* he wondered before realizing that the bombardment had likely broken the man, and he was just trying to get as far away from the hilltop as possible. He signaled for his men to resume the advance. As soon as they did, they were met with sustained machine-gun fire.

"Oh, shit, I'm hit," cried Lance Corporal Saunders.

Shit, my first casualty, thought Oliver reflexively. "How bad is it, Saunders?"

"It's bad, man, I'm gut-shot."

"Corpsman! Jennings, send word for Doc—" There was an awkward pause. Machine-gun fire rang out over their heads as Oliver called out again, "Jennings, sound off." Nothing. *Shit.* Oliver low-crawled to Saunders. The lance corporal was on his back, his rifle still in his hands. Oliver pulled Saunders's blouse apart to investigate the wound. It was bad. He'd taken two rounds to the gut. *This ain't good.* "Harrington, go get Doc Watts."

"I'm on it," replied PFC Harrington.

Oliver reached down to Saunders's left leg and pulled out his first aid kit. Opening it, he pulled out a pouch of first aid powder and sprinkled it over the wounds before adding a bandage over them.

"Hold this, man. Keep pressure on it, Harrington's getting Doc," said Oliver before turning back towards the objective to figure out what they were up against. The machine gun spat out rounds to Oliver's right. He could make out a rectangular irregularity in the terrain. *Shit, they've got a bunker set up.* It was his worst fear. The enemy had prepared this position well. A bunker this low on the hill was bad news and a sign of things to come.

Oliver thought he saw motion in the bunker and fired directly at the rectangular opening. He couldn't tell if he'd hit anything, but that would definitely keep their heads down. He didn't think he could make the throw with a grenade, so he just kept his eyes on the target as he waited for support. A second after his last shot, the machine gunner returned fire. Rounds whipped around Oliver, snapping branches from the trees and whizzing over his head. He shrunk down as small as he could, using the trunk of a fallen tree as cover. It wasn't much, but maybe it would be enough.

He didn't regret taking his shot. While the machine gun was trying to take him out, it would give other Marines the chance to close on it. As if on cue, he heard a loud bang, quickly followed by an explosion. The machine gun went silent, and Oliver risked a look over the fallen tree. He could tell exactly what had happened: someone had blown the bunker with a well-placed light antitank weapon, or LAW.

Harrington and Doc Watts came over, along with Lance Corporal Stevenson from First Squad. As Watts rendered aid, Harrington said, "Jennings is dead. He's about five yards over there." He motioned to the south of their position. Stevenson crawled next to Oliver.

"Hey, Oliver, Sergeant Evans says hi," said Stevenson. "He's sending me to beef up your team."

"Thanks, man. It's about time to get back on the clock." He turned to Doc and said, "You good, Doc?"

"Get the hell out of here, Oliver, I've got this."

"Advancing," shouted Evans from off to the right.

"Covering," replied Oliver. Oliver, Harrington and Stevenson fired low and level to the ground. This grazing fire would travel up the hill until it struck something. Most likely a tree, but you could always hope for something fleshier. The firing was really just about ensuring the enemy was more interested in not getting shot than engaging First Team as they made their dash up the hill.

After a minute, they stopped firing, and Oliver shouted, "Advancing."

"Covering," replied Sergeant Burton from Third Squad. Oliver and his men scrambled over the tree in front of them and ran up the hill while Third Squad fired uphill to his left and First Squad fired to his right. They continued up the hill Past First Squad before taking cover and searching out targets. From their briefings, Oliver knew that there were about one thousand yards between the tree line at the base of the hill and the summit. As best he could figure, they'd crossed a tenth of the distance.

Second Squad continued their advance up the hill in this leapfrog fashion. After two more rounds, Oliver was covering Evans's squad when there was an explosion ahead of him. Rifle fire erupted in the wake of the explosion. Oliver had no way of knowing what was happening, but whatever the problem was, the solution was obvious: more Marines.

"Let's go, Evans needs help," ordered Oliver as he rose and sprinted towards the sound of the violence. He dove for the deck when he could see the muzzle flashes of enemy fire. He was to the left of Evans's team, and he raised his M16 and began firing semiautomatic shots. Every time he saw a rifle flash, he gave his 5.56-millimeter reply. He had no idea how many men he might be killing, if any. It didn't matter. While killing the enemy was his official mission, right here and right now, his goal was to protect his brothers who were under fire.

"Harrington," shouted Oliver, "make contact with Team One and find out what we're up against."

"Yut!" responded Harrington, acknowledging the order.

"Stevenson," said Oliver, "make sure you're on semiauto. We need to conserve ammo, and you don't want to give these Rico bastards enough time to home in on your muzzle flash."

"Roger that, Corporal," replied Stevenson. The two continued to take shots at every muzzle flash they saw. Occasionally a round would whisk past them, snapping a tree limb or ricocheting off a rock. It might have been ten minutes, it might have been an hour—Oliver was beyond time at this point—before there was a massive barrage of rifle and machine-gun fire. Right after the barrage, Harrington returned, low-crawling back to his team leader.

"Evans's team hit an ambush. An antipersonnel mine fucked them up, and then the Ricos opened up with rifle fire. They've got casualties, but maybe the worst casualty was the squad radio. When Evans hit the deck, the Ricos put a few rounds in it."

"Better the radio than the retard carrying it," said Oliver. "Does Evans have a plan?"

"Right now, they're pinned down. It's a miracle I made it out, but I knew you needed to know what was going on."

"You're a damned hero, Harrington. If I survive today, I'll make sure the world knows." He winked as he said it. "Listen, you need to head back down the hill a few meters. Once you're past the fighting, you need to make contact with another squad. We need Lieutenant Bush over here now."

"Understood, man," replied Harrington, who scampered down the hill.

"Did he just call you 'man?'" asked Stevenson.

"After what he just went through, he could call me 'asshole' and I'd be okay with it." Something of a stalemate fell over the battle. The Marines weren't in a position to advance without additional forces, and the North Koreans weren't about to abandon their defenses. The seconds of terror were replaced by the minutes of boredom while both sides tried to figure out the next steps. The defenders had the advantage in cover and preparation, but the attackers had the advantage in force concentration and initiative.

It was another ten minutes before Oliver heard someone call out, "What do we have here, Corporal?" He turned to see Harrington returning with the LT.

"We got a problem, sir," said Oliver, "Evans and his team are cut off over there." He gestured forward and to the right. "They've got casualties, but so far the enemy hasn't been able to dig them out."

"Okay, have some water," said Lieutenant Bush, handing Oliver his canteen. "If Evans can't get to us, we're going to have to get to him. But that's not even the worst of it." There was a pause as Oliver handed back the canteen.

"What's the worst part?" asked Oliver.

"It's not just Evans's team that's cut off. It's the whole squad. I don't know what happened to Third Platoon, but we've got enemy to the rear and we're about to get rolled up if something doesn't change."

"This sucks, sir," said Oliver.

"Yes, Corporal, it does," replied Bush. "I've got Corporal Joseph's team off to the right. We're going to pop smoke, then lay down cover fire from here, so they can advance. Once they're in place, we'll join them."

"Got it," said Oliver. "Harrington, Stevenson, you apes get that?" Both Marines acknowledged the orders. Bush signaled to Joseph, then he and Oliver chucked smoke grenades up the hill. With the smoke billowing, Bush laid down a six-round burst up the hill. Rifle fire erupted all along the line as the Marines made their presence known. Harrington lobbed a few 40mm grenades to mix things up. The enemy returned fire. The rounds cracked all around Oliver's team, and Oliver thought that it was only slightly comforting to know that every bullet sent his way was a bullet that wasn't cutting down Joseph's squad.

"Cease fire!" shouted Bush after he'd calculated that Joseph's team had to have made it to the objective. They hesitated for a few seconds before more rifle fire broke out, this time from the combined forces of Fire Teams One and Three.

"Let's go, Marines," ordered Bush, and he rose and sprinted up the hill and to his right. Again, both sides exchanged fire. Oliver followed Bush. The LT was fast, and Oliver pushed himself to keep up. The violence surrounding him was disorienting, but his focus on his goal kept him upright. He had to get to the safety of whatever position First Squad had established. Through the trees, he could see the muzzle flashes ahead. This gave him a sense, an outline, of where his friends were.

He dodged between two tightly spaced trees and dove headfirst into a low clearing behind a wall of sandbags. There was something strange about the defensive position and it took Oliver a few seconds to realize that it was backwards. This was clearly a bunker built to protect units defending the hill. The Marines had cleared out the defenders and were not using it as cover against Ricos further up the hill.

Oliver looked around and noticed that Stevenson hadn't made it. Harrington and Bush were there, but no Stevenson.

"Oh shit, I'm hit," cried out Stevenson from the jungle.

"I'm on it," said Harrington, darting back the way the team had dashed. More gunfire erupted, and Oliver returned fire. Within a minute, Harrington was pulling the Marine back to their tiny sanctuary. Stevenson joined the wounded crew that was Second Squad, Second Platoon, Kilo Company, 3/6 Marines.

"Evans, what've we got? What's your status?" asked Lieutenant Bush.

"Horten and Hart are dead. Boone's got some bad shrapnel in his chest, but he's still with us and on a gun. Not sure how bad Stevenson is."

"My leg's bleeding pretty bad, Sergeant," groaned Stevenson.

"Oliver?" asked Bush.

"Saunders is down the hill with Doc last we saw him, and Jennings is dead, so it's just me and Harrington."

"Joseph?"

"Benton bought it in that last push, but me, May and Montgomery are fine."

"All right, Marines, we've got eight of us. We may be cut off, and it's going to be a long fight. Police up any ammo from the dead. Oliver, you and Harrington keep watch on our rear. If the enemy starts rolling us up, you're our first line of defense."

"Roger that, LT," said Oliver as he and Harrington moved to the downslope corners of their patch of dirt and waited for the situation to evolve.

****

Gangneung Air Base
South Korea

Captain Sun Yung-Ho was relieved at the sudden shift in mission priority. With the arrival of the F-5Gs, the Tigers were now the premier air-to-air combatant. They could outmaneuver the bigger Phantoms, but more importantly, the Phantoms could carry a much heavier air-to-ground payload. Captain Sun hurtled down the runway, gaining enough speed to leave the earth. He retracted his landing gear and headed for his squadron's rally point.

The Americans had an audacious plan to land Marines in North Korea. Sun was no land strategist, but it didn't take a lot of strategic genius to see that these Marines would be a dagger aimed right at the heart of the DPRK's leadership. With the majority of the DPRK's military fighting in the South, they would need to pull back some of those troops to stop the Americans. Once they did that, the ROK and US forces would break the stalemate in the South and start rolling the North Koreans back.

Today was the day the Americans would introduce the 2nd Marine Division to the North Koreans. Sun and the rest of the 102nd Fighter Squadron would be providing fighter cover for the Americans. Their job would be to block off any North Korean combat air support

113

aircraft from bases west of Wonsan. The American Navy would cover the beachheads, but the ROK would extend the coverage inland.

The real wild card will be China, thought Captain Sun. The last time Americans had crossed into North Korean territory, the Chinese had countered by sending over two hundred thousand troops to aid the Kim Il Sung regime. If the Chinese had been willing to face down a nuclear power in 1950, who was to say they wouldn't do it again in 1981? His flight had hardly formed up when he heard the following conversation through his headphones.

"Magpie One, this is K-9 Control."

"I am receiving, K-9 Control."

"Magpie One, we have multiple contacts inbound for the protected area. Come to course three-zero-zero to intercept."

"Three-zero-zero, understood. Estimated composition of the contact flight?"

"Unknown at this time. Assume an air threat for now until we have more information."

That made sense to Captain Sun. The enemy had to know what was going on down there, and they had to know that the enemy would have combat air patrols and fighter sweeps to ensure that no North Korean strike planes could get after the Marines. The North Koreans would want to send in fighters to tangle with the enemy and keep them off any follow-on strike planes. The commander ordered the turn and the Tigers headed for combat. Today would be the baptism by fire for the F-5G, and it would be a nasty surprise for the enemy.

After Sun had flown this course for one hundred kilometers, K-9 Control came back over the radio. "Magpie One, illuminate your radars and engage the enemy."

"Understood," replied the major leading the flight. Then to his men, he transmitted, "Switch to internal fuel, and drop your tanks." They hadn't had enough time to burn through the fuel in the single drop tank that was located on the center pylon under their plane, but it had to go. When they closed with the enemy, keeping the bulky tank would be like fighting with only one hand.

I'd much rather waste some JP-5 than get killed up here, thought Sun as he pickled the tank and switched on his AN/APG-67 radar. *The intelligence collectors from the DPRK and their allies must be going crazy right now.* This was the first time the new radar had been used in combat. It was the major upgrade that allowed the Tiger II to fire the Sparrow, and the Tiger was the only aircraft that used it. *They have no idea what they are up against.*

The radar display showed the ten contacts in front of them in what looked like five two-plane elements. Within a minute, the eight Magpies were locking and launching on the enemy. The Sparrows leapt from their rails and thundered towards the panicking enemy fighters. As the Sparrows closed, the Tigers were right behind them. When they were out of Sparrows, they would get in close with their Sidewinders.

When the first wave of Sparrows reached the enemy, Sun waited a moment to see if he could tell which enemy fighters had been hit and which had escaped. A few of the contacts disappeared, the result of a catastrophic explosion. Some of the contacts appeared to slow, either falling to the earth out of control or maneuvering in the vertical to escape the missile. He couldn't wait any longer to tell, and so he targeted one of the aircraft that were still advancing on his formation and loosed another Sparrow.

By the time the second set of Sparrows reached the enemy, they were just at the edge of visual range. A bright flash of orange at the low eleven o'clock position was his first glimpse of the enemy.

"This is Magpie One to all Magpie units, break off by team and engage the enemy."

"Understood," said Sun, and he heard his squadmates say the same. What had started as a ten-versus-eight fight was now six versus eight, and Sun liked that ratio a lot better. He spotted a MiG in the distance. "Target three hundred degrees, low. Engaging." He knew that his wingman, Yop Sung-ki, was behind him as he raced towards the enemy. The enemy was much lower than he was used to encountering them.

"Magpie Eleven, this is Magpie Eight," said Sun. "I think they're lower than usual because of those Sparrow missiles."

"Magpie Eight, can you elaborate?" asked Lieutenant Yop.

"They had to perform some high-g maneuvers to keep from getting destroyed. That depleted their energy state, so now we have the high ground, and we can control the fight." Usually the MiG-21s would have an advantage in the vertical. With a greater thrust-to-weight ratio, the MiG was able to outclimb the underpowered Tiger. *Those new engines will erase the one advantage the enemy has over us*, thought Sun.

"I'm heading down for a pass. Stay high and keep me covered," he said. It was a classic "loose deuce" two-versus-one tactic where one pilot would close in to dogfight the enemy while his wingman maintained altitude to protect his wing leader and to keep an eye out for any other enemy aircraft looking to join the fight.

Sun rolled the Tiger on its back and pulled back on the stick, making a diving pass at the MiG. He saddled up on the MiG's six, but he misjudged his pass, and before he could get a lock, the MiG started a slow left barrel roll. This took the enemy out of his sights before he could get a missile off. Even worse, it was clear to Sun that he was going to overshoot the enemy. He slammed the throttle to the wall and pulled up gently.

Just as he feared, as he flew past the MiG, a missile came off the rail. Sun didn't panic—he didn't want to pull a high-g maneuver and wind up bleeding his energy. He dropped a string of flares and watched as a line of tracers fly over his left wing. He didn't panic. He knew he'd be out of range in another second. He dipped his left wing without pulling on the stick, just trying to make himself as small a target as he could.

"Magpie Eleven, engaging," said Lieutenant Yop. Sun craned his neck and tried to catch sight of his wingman, but it was no use. He was likely behind and below him already. "Firing," said Yop. Sun rolled his plane over and looked below, watching as a Sidewinder exploded behind the MiG, tearing out most of the vertical stabilizer. The MiG pitched over and headed to the deck. Sun didn't have time to look for a chute.

"Excellent," said Sun over the radio. He flipped his plane right-side up and began searching for his next target. To his horror, what he found was another MiG, coming down fast behind Lieutenant Yop. "Eleven, check six!" shouted Sun, letting his wingman know that there was an enemy behind him. It was too little, too late. A string of 23-millimeter shells tore into Yop's Tiger. The right elevator was torn away, and the engine exploded. "Sung-ki, punch out!" said Sun, praying that his wingman would be able to get back to earth safely.

The MiG that took out his wingman had speed, but so did Sun. The MiG could outrun him and outclimb him, so Sun needed to take him out soon. The MiG came at him from the right, and Sun pulled up and to the left. The MiG crossed, climbing up and to the right. Thus committed, the combatants entered a rolling scissor fight, where the planes would cross paths as they rolled in opposite directions, each pilot trying to get their sights on the enemy. On the third turn, Sun saw a steam of rounds shoot past him, nearly striking his plane, but he knew exactly where the enemy was and, more importantly, exactly where he was about to be.

The MiG couldn't keep turning with the more nimble Tiger. The shot was a desperate one, and Sun knew it. With the MiG crossing right in front of him, Sun squeezed the trigger of his 20-millimeter cannon and was rewarded with several strikes across the enemy, including one in the cockpit.

"Magpie Four, this is Magpie One. That was the last of them. Form up and let's see what else we can find for you to kill, ace."

Ace, thought Captain Sun. *There was the probable on the opening night of the war, and the second probable and confirmed kill near Daejeon, then the Il-28 attacking the base, and these two MiGs today...* Sun had no idea how many aces there were in this war and how many of his brothers-in-arms had fallen to Soviet pilots on their way to reaching ace status.

****

3/6 Marines
Hill 183

Oliver trained his eyes down the slopes of Hill 183. The sounds of the battle surrounded him. He sincerely hoped that his brothers in Kilo Company were having better luck than Second Squad. They were still in the deadlock, with no way forward and no intention of going back. They couldn't call in fire, since they were practically on top of the enemy. Calls from Lieutenant Bush for reinforcements were met with the same reply each time: "We're working on it, and we'll send help when we can." The sun had dropped below the hills to the west. Oliver didn't want to think about what new terrors the night would bring.

"I've got movement to the left," said Evans, hesitating to fire at what might be Marines. By the time he was able to identify them as Ricos, they were just fifty yards from the bunker. Once Evans opened up on them, three other rifles came to life. Even with the four M16s concentrating fire, the enemy ran towards them.

"Movement front!" shouted Joseph as more rifles cracked the air.

"I've got movement to the rear," said Oliver, desperately willing his eyes to make out friend or foe. He felt helpless with the battle surrounding him. He could hear Marines dropping mags and reloading, knowing that every mag change represented the Marines getting closer and closer to running out of ammo.

"Oh shit, they're about ten yards away to the front," said Joseph.

"Harrington, if you can ID those as hostiles, drop a 40mm on them and I'll pivot back," said Oliver as he turned uphill and selected a target. Joseph was right—the enemy was damn near in the box with them.

"They're falling back left," said Evans. Oliver watched Evans turn and add his rifle to the forward fight. "This is my last mag," he said, dropping the mag and slapping a fresh one. Oliver kept firing at the nearest Rico he could find. They just kept coming. To his horror, he heard the *fwump* of Harrington's grenade launcher. He turned back and joined his last remaining team member in the defense of the rear of their position. He fired round after round. The enemy kept coming. He could hear the sounds of the enemy behind him, but he couldn't take his attention off his sector.

If I get shot in the back of the head, I'll know that they didn't hold, he thought. The enemy was sprinting up the hill. He couldn't stop them all, and he switched his fire selector to full auto and began unloading. Harrington added another 40mm grenade, which exploded so close that Oliver was pelted with earth and debris from the blast. He heard artillery shells coming in and wondered which side didn't care about their men. When the shells popped, though, it all made more sense. The darkness was washed away with the light of a dozen flares. Without the cover of night, the enemy were easy to target, and Oliver went back to killing them one by one. The enemy knew that they were in trouble and quickly broke off the attack.

"Harrington, keep an eye on them," said Oliver as he turned to renew the efforts to the front. As he turned, he realized that it was calm. The sounds of the battle had ceased, and the eerie quiet settled in. He saw the bodies of North Korean soldiers piled up in front of the bunker. To the left, they hadn't made it as near, but it was still too close for comfort. In the moment, Oliver realized how close they had come to getting overrun.

"I've got more movement behind us," said Harrington. The illumination flares were still slowly dropping, so visibility was a lot better than it had been during the first push. Oliver reloaded a fresh magazine and steadied his rifle at the approaching threat. They were inside a hundred yards, and his finger was inside the trigger guard, ready to squeeze.

"Hold your fire," ordered Lieutenant Bush. Oliver removed his finger and breathed a sigh of relief as he started to make out the shape of the new Personnel Armor System for Ground Troops, or PASGT, helmets that the Marines were now using. The last time he'd felt the weight lift from his body and spirit like this was when First Squad had saved his ass in Iran.

Chapter 9

14 August 1981
Ometepe Island
Nicaragua

In the nearly eight months since the Marines had liberated Daniel Ortega's compound, the war in Nicaragua had changed. The running gun battles in the streets were over. But just as the major combat operations of the US military wound down, a new and more gruesome conflict was emerging. To fight this new conflict, the CIA had appropriated Ortega's fortress. It kept them away from the locals, and it was built to a very secure standard. The Soviets had been very thorough when they'd built it.

"How are they getting all of this propaganda into the country?" asked Carlos Rodriguez, one of the CIA's shooters in Nicaragua.

"You really don't know?" asked his handler, CIA officer Fred Poole.

"I don't ask questions if I know the answer, Fred, that's more your style. I'm more of a brute force kind of guy."

"Okay, Mr. Grunt," replied Fred as he held up a pamphlet. "When was this written?" Carlos looked over the document, even taking it from Poole's hand to get a closer look. Nothing stood out about it. It was just some communist screed about the American imperialists raping the land and enslaving the people of Nicaragua.

Finally, he said, "I have no idea. It could have been printed at any time."

"That's right. Do you remember the first time you ever saw a Russian in Nicaragua?"

Carlos had to think back.

"It was just before the war with Nicaragua kicked off. We had eyes on Ayapal when the helos came in."

"And what were the choppers doing?" asked Fred.

"Unloading weapons and storing them in the town schoolhouse," replied Carlos.

"What if they weren't weapons?" asked Poole.

"I know what weapon crates look like, even Soviet ones," said Carlos.

A disappointed look crossed Poole's face.

"What was in the crates, Carlos?"

"Weap... oh." Carlos had a talent for putting things together like this, and now he was disappointed with himself.

"Don't be too hard on yourself," said Poole. "I didn't even put it together until my buddy Rick sent me an intercept from the Kremlin. You were meant to think that there were weapons being cached in local schoolhouses. It was all part of the plan to get us embroiled in a war that the Soviets knew we couldn't lose."

"How does that even make any sense?" asked Carlos.

"The rumor around the office is that this whole Nicaraguan adventure was set up by the Soviets to keep US rapid reinforcement divisions tied up at the exact moment they invaded Europe."

"Really? That doesn't sound right. Three divisions? That's what was going to give them the edge?"

"Four divisions," said Poole. "They got the 82nd Airborne tied up in Iran as well. But it's not just the size of the forces in play. It's exactly who was tied up. 1st and 2nd Marines, the 101st and 82nd Airborne? All rapid deployment units. All could have been in Europe within a month if they weren't down here dealing with the local communist infestations, or Saddam's idiots in Iran."

"Just to make sure I'm following you... the Soviets instigated a war between the United States and Nicaragua, and when they did that, they dropped off some propaganda, just in case it was useful later in the conflict?"

"Close," said Poole, "but not quite. They dropped off the propaganda because they knew they would be able to use it once the United States deposed the Sandinista regime. In 1979, Nicaragua was a Soviet satellite, second only to Cuba. In 1981, Nicaragua is a total wild card. We're trying to get a democratically elected government in place, but the Soviets are trying just as hard to get a communist regime reestablished. By deposing the Sandinistas, they can sell this fairy tale." He gestured towards the pile of pamphlets on the table.

"Why?" asked Carlos. "What's the point of all of this?"

"Best guess, hombre, is that the Soviets are gearing up for the next war. They want client states here in Latin America like they had in Europe."

"And our job is to keep that from happening?" asked Carlos.

121

"That's exactly right," said Poole with an enthusiasm that helped Carlos recover from the earlier disappointment. "There are communist movements in damn near every country between Colombia and here. Hondo is about the only ally we can count on right now. Every other nation is watching what happens in Europe. The farther west the Soviets push, the more likely that these communist movements will succeed in taking power."

"How are you and I supposed to change any of this?" asked Carlos.

"That, my friend, is exactly what we need to figure out. If there's one thing we learned in Vietnam, it's that 'winning the hearts and minds' of a foreign population is easier said than done."

"At least the war here is more or less over. That should help us win over some of the population," said Carlos.

"Not as much as you would hope. The propaganda war"—he gestured to the box of pamphlets—"is still well underway. Remember, the Soviets have been telling everyone in-country that this war was initiated by the United States. The locals have never heard of the Battle of the Caribbean."

"Maybe that's a good place to start," said Carlos. "We get some transmitters set up all over and start telling everyone about what happened. It'd be like that... you know the radio thing."

"Radio Free Europe?" asked Fred.

"Yes, exactly!"

"That's definitely something that we're going to have to work on. But that'll only go so far. Remember, the communists are spreading their message by word of mouth. That doesn't reach as many people as fast as a broadcast, but it carries a lot more weight. When you can look the teller in the eyes, the story is always more believable."

"Okay," said Carlos, "we need to infiltrate some of these communist networks. Get the details of their operations so that we know how best to counter them."

"Yes, I think that's a given. How well do you know your communist propaganda?"

Carlos laughed at that. "Not well. I learned as much as I needed to at the SOA so that I could understand the general situation down here," said Carlos, referring to the School of the Americas, where the US trained friendly militaries in an attempt to increase their professionalism.

"I think we have a starting point," said Fred. "You're about to become an expert in communism, with an emphasis on the Cuban Revolution."

"You have no idea how boring that sounds," said Carlos.

"Are you kidding? I'd kill for this assignment. If I weren't old. And white. And my Spanish didn't suck."

"Do you think any of Pedro's Rémoras would be interested?" asked Carlos.

"By Pedro's Rémoras, you mean that niece of his," said Fred, laughing. The joke around the gang was that Carlos was love-struck by the Nicaraguan freedom fighter.

"Don't be ridiculous," said Carlos. "On the other hand, she was a Sandinista, and she knows the material."

"And she is a teacher, so maybe she can cram some of this nonsense into that thick skull of yours?"

"Exactly," said Carlos with a wide grin.

****

1 September 1981
Jacksonville, North Carolina

"What the fuck?!" blurted Nancy Rodriguez.

"Nancy, language!" replied her mother, Janice.

Nancy's hands were shaking as she read the notice again.

Greetings:
You are hereby directed to present yourself for Armed Forces Physical Examination by reporting at: 1330 St. Mary's Street, Raleigh, North Carolina 27604, On Sep 12 1981...

Her eyes lost focus and she felt numb.

"Nancy, what's wrong?" asked her mother, alarmed. Nancy tried to form the words and failed. She looked again at the addressee. It was her name. She handed her mother the letter.

After reading it, Janice said, "Oh my Lord. There has to be some kind of mistake." Nancy sat down at the breakfast table and stared into space, a million things running through her mind and none of them able to break through. Her brain had overloaded and there was nothing for her to do, so she started crying. It was all she could do. Her mother rushed to her and cradled her head in her arms, pulling her daughter into a tight embrace as though to shield her from the awful reality that was assaulting her.

"Mama," was all she managed after a minute. Eleven days… that was all the time she had to fix this. That was her deadline for figuring out how the system had failed and had processed a single mother whose ex-husband was fighting for his country. Her thoughts started to line up. Her mother was right. This was a mistake. It had to be. And if she wanted to correct it, she couldn't sit here like a helpless child. She had to start getting answers. She wiped her eyes with her hand, and her mother handed her a tissue.

"Thank you, Mother," she said as she dabbed away the wetness from her eyes and cheeks. She sniffled a few times, trying to collect herself. "I think you're right. There has to be a mistake. It's been all over the news that when one parent is in the service, they won't draft the remaining parent. I just need to make some calls and get this whole thing cleared up."

"I'm going to write a letter to Congressman Rose," said Janice, referring to Charlie Rose, their congressional representative since 1973.

"I don't know that we have time," said Nancy. "I'm going to start with the local draft board. In fact, I'm going there right now. Can you watch Jennifer?"

"Of course. Go, now." Nancy grabbed her purse and practically flew out the door. She jumped into her Fairmount station wagon and tried to concentrate on the road. Each block she crossed helped her calm down. She knew that she couldn't just blow up at the people there. She'd need to be able to calmly and rationally get her point across. By the time she was turning into the post office, she had a game plan. She climbed out of the car, brushed the wrinkles out of her dress, and took a deep breath.

She walked in and turned to the left, where the arrow indicated "Selective Service System." There was a man wearing a Vietnam Veteran pin sitting behind the desk.

"Sir?" she asked.

"What can I do for you young lady?"

"I received this in the mail today." She handed him her draft notice. "But there must be some mistake. I'm exempt from the draft." The man didn't look at the notice.

"Ma'am, I'm sure you understand that I hear this a lot. And the person on your side of the counter is never right about it. They're never exempt, they just thought they were too old, or that the draft really didn't apply to women."

"No, sir," said Nancy, "I understand that the draft applies to women. But I'm a single mother, and my ex-husband is serving in Nicaragua."

"That's not very likely, ma'am," replied the man.

"It might not be likely, but it is true," she insisted.

"Okay, I'll bite. What branch is he in?"

"He's a Marine," said Nancy.

"No. That doesn't make any sense. The occupational forces are all Army. There are no Marines in Nicaragua since the end of hostilities." Nancy suddenly remembered. Carlos wasn't a Marine anymore.

"Well, you see…," she stammered, trying to remember the name of the outfit he worked for. "He's with Southern Air Services."

"So he's not a Marine?"

"No, he was in the Corps. But he took an assignment with the Southern Air Services in Nicaragua."

"Ma'am, there is no part of the military called 'Southern Air Services.' If your husband—"

"Ex-husband," corrected Nancy out of habit, horrified that she'd cut him off and most likely cost her any sympathy that he might have for her plight.

"Ex-husband," continued the man, "left military service, then you are no longer exempt from the draft."

"But he's been fighting the Sandinistas during the entire war!" She was getting a little desperate and had to tell herself to calm down. It was clear that she was losing her battle, and the only way she could hope to turn the situation around was to calm the hell down.

"Look," said the man, "there's nothing I can do to help you, but let me make a call to check out your story." Nancy was relieved to be making some progress. The man tapped in a ten-digit phone number. Long distance. That was a good sign.

"Hey, Margie, it's Vernon in Jacksonville.... No, North Carolina.... Yeah, I've got a young lady in my office saying that her husband is in the military, but he's serving in the—" He looked at Nancy. "What was it called?"

"Southern Air Service," said Nancy.

"Southern Air Service," repeated Vernon. "Yeah, that's right..." Again he turned to Nancy,

"What is your husband's name?"

"Sergeant Carlos Rodriguez," said Nancy.

"Carlos Rodriguez," repeated Vernon. There was a long pause. "She's looking it up on the computer." After a five-minute pause, Vernon picked it up again, "Yeah, that's right. Okay. And that's from the IRS?... Okay, I think that's everything we need. Thanks, Margie." He hung up the phone. "Okay, so here's where we stand. And, lady, believe me, I don't want to be the one to tell you this, but your husband isn't who you think he is." Nancy's heart fell.

"Southern Air Service is a private freight carrier who does some business in South and Central America. Again, a private freight carrier. They aren't a part of the military, or any part of the US government. Margie looked into it a bit deeper, and she found your husband's tax records. He works as a security guard for Southern Air Services." Vernon reached out and took Nancy's hand. "Your husband guards the cargo that this carrier brings into dangerous locations. I'm afraid you've been lied to for a while. He's not a Marine, and he's not in the military. You aren't exempt from the draft."

This can't be happening, thought Nancy.

"I'm so sorry, darlin'," said Vernon. "But this isn't the end of the line for you. I was drafted back in '67"—he pointed to his Vietnam Veteran pen—"and it was rough. It wasn't what I wanted to do, and it wasn't what I planned to do. But I don't regret my experience, and if you approach this with a positive attitude, you can make the most of it. You're not being punished. You're being called to serve." The almost spiritual phrasing of the statement put Nancy a little more at ease.

"Thank you, sir—Vernon," she said in a low voice. "I've got a lot to figure out and not a lot of time to do it."

"Here," said Vernon, jotting his number on a page of his notebook, then tearing it off and handing it to Nancy. "Call me if you have any questions, or just want someone who's been there to talk to."

"Thank you," said Nancy, "I will."

Chapter 10

3 September 1981
USS *Arkansas*
Mid-Atlantic

Commander Earl Brown looked out over the vastness of the ocean. He'd been in the Navy for fifteen years. He'd spent over a thousand days at sea. Yet the ocean always made him feel small. You couldn't see the end of it. It just stretched on forever. And that wasn't even the craziest part. The thought of how deep it was always caused Brown to flinch. The idea of how small his convoy was compared to the ocean. The idea of how small *Arkansas* was when compared to the ocean. All the way down to how insignificant Commander Earl Brown was.

There was no such thing as a "routine" crossing. Every trip would be contested. This transit, though, had been fairly calm. When compared to the first crossing at the start of the war, this was a milk run. *There's plenty of time for the shit to hit the fan*, Brown thought cheerlessly.

"Hey, Commander," said Lieutenant Tom Grant, the officer of the deck or OOD, "how are those Eagles going to fare this season?"

"I have no idea, Lieutenant," replied Brown.

"Sure, but you have an opinion, don't you?" He knew that Grant was trying to be annoying, but the conversation bothered Brown, who believed that the NFL season should have been canceled, what with the world spinning out of control. But, as President Carter told the nation, our cherished sporting leagues gave the nation something to look forward to. A distraction from the grim business of war.

"With the new rosters, I don't think anyone has a valid opinion on how any team will perform."

"That's true enough," said Grant, "but my 'Skins are going to crush yer Green Birds, of that I have no doubt."

"Your blind allegiance to and true faith in that ridiculous franchise will never cease to amaze me. But since you seem to need a distraction, consider that John Riggins is approximately one hundred and thirty-five years old."

"You mean to tell me that he's a wily veteran with extensive experience at the position?" said Grant. "Say it ain't so."

128

"I mean, he's one of the only ones I give credit to for taking the draft exemption. I'm pretty sure he fought in the Battle of New Orleans in the War of 1812."

"You're just being mean because you know he's going to put up huge numbers on the diluted talent." Brown wouldn't admit it, but Grant was probably right. The players who came in to replace the men who'd volunteered for military service were not of the same caliber as the men they were replacing.

"Sir," said the seaman at the ASW station, "our helo has picked up a possible contact, bearing zero-nine-five. It's faint—they're still working on a range."

Brown was relieved to be out of the conversation with Grant. He looked at the glass board where another seaman was marking the line of bearing with a grease pen. He wondered where along the line that sub, if that was what it was, would be.

"Should we wake the captain?" In the early days of the war, a faint contact like this would have merited getting Captain Stewart to the CIC. Now, though…

"Negative, let the man rest. If anything comes of this, we'll get him up then. Grant, why don't you get yourself some coffee?" asked Brown. This was code for "You may get yourself some coffee while you're refilling my cup."

"Aye, sir," replied Grant. Crossing the space and taking Brown's cup in addition to his own. In the blessed silence that was Grant's absence, Brown wondered what Yolonda was up to at this very moment. He checked his watch. It was noon back in Norfolk. She was probably having lunch, or working in the garden. He thought she spent too much time on that garden, but he had to admit to taking a certain unearned pride in it. The more he thought about it, the more he thought he was just being selfish, because time she spent in the garden was time she wasn't spending with him.

As though I have nothing to complain about. I left her by herself for weeks and months on end, he thought. It would have been better if they'd had kids. That was the plan, after all. For some families, that was just not to be, and the Browns fell into that category.

"Here you are, Mr. Brown," said Grant, breaking Brown away from his thoughts of home, and a future unrealized.

"Sir," said the seaman at the ASW station, "there are definite mechanical sounds. We've got a submarine on our hands."

"Grant, get the old man. Roberson, do we have a position?"

"Negative," replied the seaman, "still just a LOB."

"Any clue as to identification?"

"Negative, sir, there's just not enough data at this point."

"Understood. Thanks, Roberson."

Brown looked at the NTDS and the icons that represented each ship in the convoy, both cargo ships and escorts. Unless this sub was right under them, they had a pretty good chance of either killing it or chasing it off. The Soviet skippers that were still alive were the ones that understood the concept of living to fight another day. Gone were the days of the underwater "bonsai charges" of old and obsolete boats.

"What've we got?" asked Stewart as he entered the CIC.

"Unknown mechanical contact bearing zero-nine-five, range unknown," said Brown. The captain put his hand to his chin in consideration.

"Not much to do about it yet," said Stewart, "but thanks for waking me. This could go south quickly."

"Aye-aye, sir," said Brown. "I thought you'd want to know."

"What's your worst-case scenario, Earl?"

"That there's a Victor III inside our ASW screen," said Brown, referring to the latest Soviet nuclear attack submarine.

"Yeah, I tend to agree… best-case scenario?"

"An Italian patrol boat that got lost," said Brown with a laugh.

"Yeah… fair enough. I guess the days of blasting 1950s-era boats are behind us."

The crew in the CIC of *Arkansas* didn't quite relax, but they came down from their high alert and settled in to see where this went.
****

Minskiy Komsomolets
East Atlantic Ocean

"Sir," said Maks Yermolovo, the *politruk* or political officer on board *Minskiy Komsomolets*, "don't you think that this course of action is a bit, well… timid?"

"Cautious," said Captain Dmitriy Usatov, "is the word I would use."

"Well, yes, sir," replied Yermolovo, "but if we close range, the enemy will have less time to react to our missile attack."

"I'm well aware of how time and distance work, Yermolovo. But I ask that you consider the submarine that you are standing in."

"He is the greatest submarine the Soviet people have ever put to sea," said Yermolovo without hesitating.

"He is more than that," said Usatov. "He is the greatest anticonvoy weapon on the planet Earth. With *Kirov* on the ocean floor, there is no ship like him. And there are none that will be fielded soon. His brothers are still under construction and no matter how much we wish to put them to sea, we cannot ignore the laws of physics. The same with *Kirov*'s brothers. What you see as timid is simply me ensuring that the greatest ship in our fleet can continue to harass and sink convoys."

"I see, sir," said Yermolovo, rebuffed.

"If you're done second-guessing my orders, may I go back to commanding my submarine?" asked Usatov.

"Of course, sir. My apologies." Exchanges like that made Usatov's head hurt. He knew Yermolovo personally, and he even liked the man. But as often happens with political officers, he sometimes forgot that he was not the actual embodiment of the Soviet state and was, in fact, just a man.

I'm sure there are a fair few submarine captains that fall into that trap as well, he thought. He looked at the plot again. He knew the approximate location of the approaching convoy, but he didn't have an exact fix on it. He was going to need targeting information if his plan was going to work. The first attack that had sunk the USS *Eisenhower* had required an older Project 675 submarine to sacrifice his life and the lives of all on board in order to get him that information. Today, he had no such coconspirator.

Instead, he was relying on satellites, timing, and frankly, luck. As he approached the convoy, he would have intervals when he could send up the mast and receive a signal from an overflying satellite. Each pass of the satellite brought *Minskiy Komsomolets* closer to the convoy. Usatov's decision to fire at extreme range was prudent, though more aggressive commanders would have closed the gap.

He checked his watch. He still had five minutes. He thought back on the transit back to the North Atlantic. It wasn't as harrowing as the trip north, where the Soviet Air Force, the VVS, had sunk HMS *Invincible*. Every time they crossed the Greenland-Iceland-UK Gap, they were taking a significant risk. The choke points were just too narrow. There was only so much water to hide in.

That was one reason he had been pleased to receive orders to resupply in Africa once he'd expended his missiles. Apparently, *Kirov* was using Luanda, Angola, as a supply base, and he was kind enough to leave behind some P-900 missiles. There would only be enough missiles for one resupply, but that would cut out two trips through the gap, and for that he was thankful.

"Sir, we are receiving the data," said one of his crewmen. "I am loading it into the computer."

"If we have a solid fix," said Usatov, "I will immediately assign targets. We must be as accurate as we can, as we will only have one shot—and as Mr. Yermolovo so rightly pointed out, the enemy will have plenty of time to detect and defend against our attack."

"Understood," said everyone in the Control Room. The enemy shipping showed up on the threat board. A big, beautiful convoy. At first glance, Usatov estimated fifteen cargo vessels and five escorts. Not quite the spectacle from the first weeks of the war, but a worthwhile target nonetheless.

"Target one missile apiece at each of the large contacts. Select an additional nine missiles at large contacts, dealer's choice," he said, indicating that the weapons officers who were programming the missiles could select their own targets. There was a hush over the room as the weapons were readied.

"Sir, missiles are ready and programmed."

"Excellent. Fire," ordered Usatov. The submarine again rattled with the firing of a full salvo of missiles. With a feeling of satisfaction, Usatov ordered, "Come around to a course of one-three-zero, speed ten knots." And with that order, *Minskiy Komsomolets* snuck off like a thief in the night.

****

USS *Arkansas*

"Vampire!" shouted Seaman Roberson. "Missile contact inbound, bearing zero-nine-five, range two hundred thirty miles." All eyes turned to the NTDS screen, where the readout reflected a single incoming missile.

"Sound general quarters," said Stewart, then, turning to Brown, he asked, "What do you make of that?"

"I'm not sure, sir," replied Brown. "It's too far out to be a Starbright or a Siren." He was referring to the SS-N-7 and SS-N-9 carried by the most common Soviet cruise missile submarines, the Charlie I and II classes.

"And just one missile," pondered Stewart. "That doesn't make a lot of sense."

"Hang on," said Brown. "Yeoman, get me the logs for our first crossing."

A seaman in the rear of the CIC said,

"Aye XO," and began flipping through the logbooks to find the right entry.

"What's on your mind?" asked Stewart.

"There's something I remember about the attack on *Ike*. Something familiar, but I can't put my finger on it."

"Here you are, sir," said the Yeoman, extending a logbook to Brown, who took it and ran his finger along the lines as he sped through the text.

"Aha! Here," said Brown. "When the Hawkeye was tracking the incoming missiles on her look-down radar, they detected a single missile at high altitude while the rest were on the deck. Sir! That's not a single missile, that's a major salvo heading for the fleet!"

"Comms," said Captain Stewart, "get on the horn and let the fleet know that we believe the incoming vampire represents a multiple-missile threat. Explain that we believe this is a pathfinder."

"Understood," replied a Radioman.

"Now it's just a waiting game," said Stewart. The minutes crawled by, counting down to the frantic battle to come. With the threat established and no new contacts being reported, the CIC fell into a quiet lull. According to the radar, the missile was traveling at one and a half times the speed of sound. But the vastness of the ocean made it feel as though the missiles were moving in slow motion. Of course, the closer they came, the faster they seemed. By the time they were in visual range, there would be only seconds before they would strike the convoy.

"We could really use a Hawkeye up there," said Brown.

"If this goes as bad as it could," replied Stewart, "we might be the last convoy to make the crossing without a carrier in the escort."

"Good news, sir," said the radioman. "The Air Force has a Sentry airborne out of Bermuda. They're sending her our way to investigate."

"If we needed a break, that's it," said Stewart as a new icon showed up on the screen. Yet even though there was a new player, it was still a waiting game.

After five minutes, the vampire closed another hundred miles, but the E-3 Sentry managed to get a good return on the targets. Just like magic, an additional eighteen missiles appeared on the NTDS.

"Looks like your hunch was right, Earl," said Stewart.

"I'd much rather have been wrong if it's all the same, sir," replied Brown.

"I agree, XO, I agree." Knowing what they were up against didn't change the convoy's reaction. Orders were issued throughout the escort to move into a blocking position between the threat and the convoy. The missiles closed. Every man in the convoy steeled their nerves for the battle. After so long of a wait, the next few minutes seemed to hang in the air forever.

Escorts unleashed SAMs at the incoming missiles. Sea Sparrow, Tartar, and Standard missiles raced to the threat. Brown did some quick mental math and knew that the convoy was in trouble. *Arkansas* was on the north edge of the escort formation and away from the missiles that were heading right down the middle. The older Tartar missiles were nearly useless in the fight. They were failing to destroy their targets.

"Sir, Peterson reports a missile strike. She's in a bad way."

Before Stewart could react, another voice broke in. "*Knox* is hit—they're abandoning ship." The calls kept coming in.

"*Farragut* is down." Brown looked at the NTDS. This wave of missiles was passing over the escorts. He wasn't sure if the Soviets had targeted the escorts or if the missiles had just locked onto them by accident. It didn't matter—those ships were lost all the same.

"*Marshfield* reports massive fires." *Damn*, thought Brown, *those torpedoes are going to be missed.* His concern for the war effort as a whole temporarily prevented him from worrying about the fate of the souls on board.

"The oiler USNS *Neosho* is sinking."

"*Cape Edmont* is taking on water." *Damn, that's thirty-two thousand tons*, thought Brown. The calls just kept coming. By the time the Soviet missiles had taken their toll, Stewart's convoy had lost two destroyers, one frigate, and worst of all, five of their twenty cargo ships within five minutes of the first SAM being launched. Two more succumbed to their damage and had to be abandoned at sea. Nearly half of the cargo that was so desperately needed in Europe was on the bottom of the Atlantic, and they still had a thousand miles to go.

Chapter 11

5 September 1981
Texas Air National Guard
Ellington Air Force Base

Captain George "Nomad" Bush sat in the Officer's Club at Ellington Air Force Base. Across the table from him sat Captain Mike "Weezer" Olson.

"What do you think about the option?" asked Weezer.

"It's tempting, that's for sure," replied Nomad. "I applied for the same thing back during the Vietnam War, but I didn't have enough flight hours."

"That shouldn't be a problem now," replied Weezer.

"Yeah, ever since those Cuban Badgers showed up, our operational tempo has definitely given us some serious flight time."

"I know that what we do here is important," said Weezer, "but I feel like anyone with two hundred flight hours can perform our mission. The radar picks something up, you check it out, you come back home."

"It's not that simple," said Nomad. "You do realize that if we're attacked, it won't just be a lone bomber. There will be fighters in the front, with bombers in the rear. It's going to be a lot more than what we're doing now." Nomad believed every word he said, but at the same time, he understood the pull of the promise of more combat. His prolonged absence from the service led to the sometimes difficult-to-navigate instance where he was considerably older than his wingman, who outranked him by time in grade.

"That's true, that's true," said Weezer. "But at the same time, I think that having our Darts in the air will keep that from happening."

"That's an awful big risk," said Nomad before Weezer could renew his appeal. "I just think that we have to believe that this war is going to reach our shores. Hell, if what the media is reporting about those submarines mining our harbors at the onset of the fighting, it already has."

"Well, sure, I think that makes me want to move forward more than anything else," said Weezer. "Besides, mission aside, you can't tell me that you don't desperately want to fly one of those F-15 Eagles."

"You know damn well," replied Nomad, "that if you got picked up for that slot, you'd be flying a Phantom into battle."

"I don't know, they have more of those F-16s coming off the line every day. Hell, even the new F-20 Tigersharks that are in development would be lightyears ahead of the Darts."

"I'm skeptical of the Tigershark," replied Nomad. "It really just sounds like so much propaganda. You're tryin' to tell me that you staple a new engine on an airframe that's almost as old as our Sixes, and suddenly it's a world beater? I don't buy it."

"I think you're wrong on two fronts here?" said Weezer.

"Am I?"

"Yes, firstly, the F-20 isn't just about the engine. There are also massive upgrades to the avionics and weapons systems. The old F-5s couldn't carry the Sparrow missiles. These can. And you have to admit that's a major advantage."

"That's true," said Nomad. "Hell, I'd love it if our Sixes had a little more punch than the cumbersome Falcon." The AIM-4 Falcon was nearly adequate for intercepting bombers, but its use in Vietnam had proven it lacking against anything with any agility. "So, okay, you said I was wrong on two fronts. What's the second?"

"You're acting like the engine isn't one of the most important aspects of aircraft design." Nomad knew that Weezer had a master's degree in aeronautical engineering, and that he was about to get taught a lesson in the subject. "Take, for example, the P-51 Mustang in World War II."

"Okay, what about it?" asked Nomad.

"The original model of the P-51 was marginally better than the P-40 Warhawk that it was supposed to be replacing."

"Don't even try to get that past me," said Nomad. "Everyone knows that the Mustang was one of the greatest fighters of the war."

"I never said anything different," replied Weezer with a smile. "But what made the Mustang one of the best fighters of the war was an engine swap. The same idea that you're dismissing now turned a pedestrian fighter into one of the greatest."

"Okay, so the engine can make a difference, I'll grant you that."

"It's more than just a difference. It's night and day. What were some of the other 'greatest fighters' we had in the war?" Nomad thought about it. He'd grown up with stories of the Pacific war, brought so close to home by his father's service in that theater.

"The F6F Hellcat, the F4U Corsair... Those were the best in the Pacific. I suppose we should count the P-47 Thunderbolt as well."

"Damn right we should," said Weezer. "And guess what they all have in common?" Nomad stopped short, realizing that he'd just sealed the fate of his argument.

"I have a feeling," said Nomad, "that you're going to tell me."

"Damn right I am, Nomad," said Weezer. "They all had the same engine. The Pratt & Whitney R-2800 Double Wasp. Easily the best US piston engine ever designed for an aircraft."

"Okay, okay," said Nomad. "I'll grant you the point on the engine, but I'm still not sold that a souped-up twenty-year-old fighter is going to be all that."

"Be that as it may," said Weezer, "I don't think that the Air Force would be taking requests if they didn't think there was a true need."

"I can't deny that," replied Nomad. "I tell you what, I'll take it up with Laura and get her input. See what she thinks about this."

"You could just tell her that it's mandatory, and it's out of your hands," said Weezer.

"Keep thinking that way, Mike, and you'll never get married," laughed Nomad.
****

12 September 1981
Raleigh, North Carolina

It was early. Nancy was in a diner not too far from the Military Enlistment Processing Station in Raleigh. Being early was a part of the strategy that Vernon had given her. She thought back to the conversation.

"You need to understand that you don't have control right now. There are forces much bigger than you in play, and you just need to ride this out. So never show your resentment. It will only make things harder for you. And be early. Not for them, for you. You can embrace the last hours of your freedom on whatever terms you can establish. Do this, because you won't get another chance until this whole thing is over."

Nancy had no idea what the next days—weeks… years?—would hold. But she was resolved to do everything she could to do well during this unwanted phase of her life.

"Need a refill, sweetie?" asked the waitress holding a coffeepot.

"Sure, thank you," replied Nancy. The black coffee from the pot destroyed her carefully created sugar, cream and coffee ratios, and she had to reestablish them. There was a voice in the back of her head that told her to walk away. Just leave. There was no way that she could do what was being asked of her. But she'd fought this battle repeatedly over the past eleven days.

It wasn't that she didn't have a choice. She did. She could try to hide. She could try to find a country that would take her in as a refugee (Canada wasn't an option in spite of her earlier belief; they had a draft of their own to contend with). There were a hundred things she *could* do. But in her prayerful contemplations, she understood that this was something that she *should* do. It wasn't fair to Jennifer, that was true. But her parents were doting. And when Jennifer was older, she could explain the situation.

She'd sent a letter to Carlos, but whatever he was doing in Central America took him out of contact for weeks or months at a time. Even if he'd received her letter, she hadn't received a response. It wasn't as if there was anything he could do about it. *It's not like there's anything he could do about it*, she thought.

When Jennifer was older, she could tell her that there was a time when her country had needed her to make sacrifices. That her comfortable life only existed because in the past, men had made sacrifices to protect the nation. But in 1981, the country asked women to share that responsibility. Nancy was a staunch feminist. She believed in the value of women's labor and effort. She believed that Jennifer should grow up in a world where she could be anything that she wanted. And if that was the world that Nancy wanted, she needed to pay the price for that.

That price was a tour in the US military. She would gladly pay it. She'd talked the talk for years. Now she was ready to walk the walk. With that resilient thought, she took a sip of her coffee, and silently said a prayer.

Dear Lord. I don't understand why mankind must make war. I wish the Prince of Peace could come back today and make this stop. But

I understand that humans are flawed. We are sinners by our nature, and no matter how pious we wish to be, we fall short. I pray that you can help me understand what you want from me during this time. How do I remain a Christian in the face of the ugliness of war? How do I conduct myself in a Christlike manner through what is about to happen to me? I pray for your love and guidance during this difficult time.

The waitress passed by on her way to another diner. Once she'd taken care of them, Nancy said, "Can I get the check when you get a chance?"

"Sure, hon," said the waitress, who, after speaking with the kitchen crew, went to the cash register and rang up Nancy's order. She brought the check to Nancy. It was $2.25.

Nancy laid down a five-dollar bill and said,

"Keep the change." It was an extreme tip, but at the moment Nancy didn't have a lot of use for money. Better to make this waitress's morning than to carry unspendable money where she was going. She stood, and ran her hands over her blouse, and pulled her hair out of her face as she mentally prepared herself for the hardest thing she'd ever done. She left the diner and headed to the MEPS.

She walked into the building and was quickly picked up by an administrative assistant.

"Can I help you?" asked the assistant.

"Yes, I'm reporting for my draft physical," said Nancy.

"Perfect," replied the assistant. "Identification, please. I just need a driver's license or passport." Nancy handed over her driver's license. The assistant flipped through a folder, looking for a matching record. "Excellent, Ms. Rodriguez. Thank you for honoring your civic duty. I know this is a difficult time."

"Rodriguez! You need to fall in line here," shouted another drone.

"It's not as terrible as it seems," assured the assistant. Nancy nodded and walked over to the line of women who were assembled.

"Let's go, ladies, follow me." Nancy followed the woman in front of her as the women left the lobby of the building and entered a whole new world. The day was a blur. Everything happened briskly and with absolute order. It occurred to Nancy that this was what was meant by "regimented." She hadn't thought much about the military application of the term. But here it was, on full display.

The sterile, white-walled rooms reminded her of a hospital. And not just because a large portion of her day was to be spent submitting to a medical physical. No, it was more than that.

On day two, she was done with the physical. Instead, she took a number of tests. Math, engineering, English, accounting. By the end of it, she was pretty sure that the US government knew more about her than her own parents did. By the time five o'clock arrived, she was mentally exhausted.

"Rodriguez," called a tubby man in a small office. She rose and crossed the room, standing in his doorway. "Please, have a seat." He gestured to the chair on the other side of his desk. "Rodriguez? You don't look like a Rodriguez."

"It's my married name, sir. My maiden name is McNamara."

"Married?" asked the tubby man. "Shouldn't your husband be sitting here?"

"Actually—"

He cut her off before she could try to explain.

"I'm sorry, Rodriguez, it's none of my business. I just work with what I've got." She settled back in her chair. "I think congratulations are in order," he continued. "I'm excited to be able to offer you a contract as a personnelman—personnelwoman? I wonder if they're going to change that?"

"I don't—"

"Never mind about that. I'm here to offer you a contract as a personnelman in the United States Navy."

"I don't understand?" said Nancy.

"It's simple," said Tubby. "If you sign on the line here"—he pointed to a signature line—"you'll be accepting a contract that gives you the opportunity to train as a personnelman in the Navy. They perform administrative and clerical duties related to personnel records. Things like pay and entitlements. They process paperwork, maintain records, and handle financial transactions related to personnel matters. If you successfully complete your training, you'll be given an extra bump in rank."

"Oh," said Nancy. "I thought that the whole point of the draft was that I didn't have a choice?"

"Oh, that, haha. You absolutely have a choice. You can choose not to sign the contract. But then you'll still be sent to the Navy, but undesignated. That means that you won't have any kind of skilled job when you complete boot camp. If there's one thing that we've learned since the draft started inducting women, it's that women are excellent at scraping paint in a dry dock."

"Wait, what?" asked Nancy.

"It's true, and those ships aren't going to chip off their own paint. Listen, sweetie, I have to tell you, you're one of the lucky ones. Most women don't score so well on the math and accounting tests. They'll be chipping paint in no time. But you? You'll get a good professional job with plenty of experience so that when this whole thing is over, you'll be in a much better position for any employer."

Nancy was scared, confused and exhausted. She took the pen and signed her name to the contract.

Chapter 12

15 September 1981
3/6 Marines
Sangsong, North Korea

The invasion of Wonsan had been a costly one for the 2nd Marine Division. Between the losses at sea and the battle itself, they had lost nearly a third of their fifteen thousand men. This horrific casualty ratio was largely created by the successful air strikes against the task force, but the fighting on the ground was bloody and long. Once they had the beachhead, they fought west along the mountainous terrain, on their way to Pyongyang.

Kilo Company had taken more casualties than most, and they were stationed in Sangsong, some twenty miles behind the fighting. During this lull they were assimilating their replacements and trying to rebuild a sense of unity and esprit de corps. That didn't mean they were idle. Quite the opposite, in fact. They were training hard. "Pressure makes diamonds," was how Captain Beck put it.

"These mountains suck," said Private First Class Randy Harrington as the patrol made their way east.

"You can bitch as much as you want," said Corporal Phil Oliver, "but you're going to miss days like today when we're marching in two feet of snow, getting shot at by Ricos."

"Gee, thanks, Corporal, you're always looking on the bright side." Second Squad had been on patrol just outside the Sangsong Perimeter and were returning to HQ. The Sangsong Valley was well protected as it was surrounded by mountains. The Marine defenses had been built up in the six weeks since its capture, but there was always the potential for an enemy scout element to try and get some intel on the area.

As they approached their temporary home, Corporal Murphy from company HQ called out, "Hey, Evans, the captain needs you to send someone to Company HQ to collect up some supplies."

"Oliver, you and Harrington go see what's going on," said Evans.

"Roger that, Sergeant," replied Oliver.

"Supplies?" asked Harrington as the two separated from the group. "What the hell kind of supplies are we getting?"

"Yeah," said Oliver, "remember when Captain Beck pulled me out of formation and whispered in my ear?"

"No," replied Harrington, confused.

"That's because it never happened, moron," said Oliver, laughing. "I don't have any more information than you do. Murph told Evans, Evans told us, and now we're off on a new adventure."

"I don't like adventures," replied Harrington. "I like things to stay the same from one day to the next. Adventures just cause trouble."

"Good man, Harrington, I hate to say it, but you're starting to think like an NCO."

"Don't even start saying shit like that," replied Harrington. The pair of Marines entered the HQ tent and removed their helmets. They made their way to the captain's desk, where Captain Omar Beck was reading a report.

"Good afternoon, sir, we were sent to pick up supplies," said Oliver.

"What the hell are you talking about, Oliver?" asked the captain.

"Supplies, sir," replied Oliver. "Corporal Murphy told us to report to you and pick up supplies."

"Do I look like Major Ferris?" asked Beck, referring to the regimental supply officer.

"No, sir," said Oliver, never one afraid to speak his mind. "To be honest, sir, I'm just as confused as anyone, but those are my orders." Beck shuffled a few papers around, then picked one up and it appeared to refresh his memory.

"Oh, yeah. Okay." He turned his head and called out, "Jonesy!"

"Sir," said a lance corporal that Oliver didn't know, presumably Jonesy.

"Grab Ban Jung from the pool," said Beck. Jonesy acknowledged the order and scurried away. "We've got more translators, and they're being assigned at the squad level. Private Ban Jung will be Second Squad's. I want you to get him settled in the barracks and introduced to the men. The closer we get to Pyongyang, the more we're going to run into fleeing civilians and the more desperate the Norks get, the more we'll need information from them." Oliver grimaced at the captain's use of the term "Nork." Oliver could ensure that his men called the enemy by his preferred slur, "Ricos," but there was nothing he could do about the captain.

"Understood, sir," said Oliver. "We'll take care of it."

Jonesy returned with a young man wearing the same camo uniform that the Marines were wearing.

"Private Ban Jung," said Jonesy, "this is Corporal Oliver. He'll be taking you to the unit."

"Thank you, Lance Corporal, we'll take it from here," said Oliver, not wanting to spend any more time than necessary in the HQ tent. You never knew when you'd catch some kind of admin task that would numb your brain.

On their way out, Oliver decided to get the kid integrated.

"Okay, Ban, what's your background? Are you going to be an accelerator or a brake?"

"Oi'm sorry, Corp'ral. Oi'm not quoite sure I get whatcha sayin'," replied Private Jung. "And to be clear, Ban is me family name."

"What the hell?" asked Oliver. "What are you saying?"

"I just don't understand what yer askin' me?" replied Private Ban Jung.

"You're starting to sound like a pain in the ass," replied Corporal Oliver. "I'm asking if you're going to help us go forward, or if you're going to be a pain in my ass. Right now, I think I have a good idea which one you are."

"Oi, wait. No, you got it all wrong, mate. I learned me English in Box Hill, outside Melbourne. I just didn't understand yer lingo."

"That makes two of us... you're Australian?"

"I'm Korean, but me family moved to Australia when I was two. When the war broke out, I volunteered for the Republic."

"Okay, that makes sense," said Oliver. "My people came to the United States from Scotland about a hundred years ago. I bet I sound ridiculous to my Scottish ancestors."

"I'm not sure if that's a comfort or a scourge, but I'll take it," said the Korean. "Though, I still want to make sure that you understand that Ban is my surname. My friends call me Jung."

"I tell you what, Ban. If there's one thing you need to know about the Corps, it's that we call everybody by their surname. I'm Oliver, and this is Harrington."

"Pleased to meet ya," said Ban, shaking Harrington's hand.

"Grab your gear and let's get you back to the squad to meet the boys," said Oliver. The three crossed over to the Second Platoon's tent. Oliver's spirits dropped as he looked across the tent at the men assembled, some shooting the shit, others lounging in their racks. So many missing faces. Friends who'd walked down the ramp and ran up the hill but never came down.

"Hey, Evans," said Oliver, "I got yer supplies."

"Okay, what did I win?" asked Evans.

"Our new translator, Ban Jung."

"Pleased ta meet ya," said Ban.

"What the hell?" asked Evans.

"What?" asked Oliver, "you've never met an Australian before?"

"Not one that looked like that," said Evans, chuckling. "I'm glad to meet you too, Ban."

"And to be clear," said Ban, "Ban is me family name."

"I know," said both Oliver and Evans simultaneously.

"You know, we did have an hour-long training on Korean customs on the way over here," said Evans. "Even us jarheads can get edjumacated." The three men shared a laugh at that.

"Okay," said Evans. "I guess you can stick with Fire Team Two. I'm already augmenting Fire Team One, so I'd rather not put you there. Let's see." Evans looked around the tent. "Miller, Peterson, get over here." Two Marines crossed over from their racks and joined them.

"Whatcha need, Sergeant?" asked Miller, a lance corporal.

"Meet Ban. He's our translator, and before this gets confusing, he's from Australia and he sounds like it."

"Wait, what?"

"You heard me."

"Oi," said Ban, "this shouldn't be so bloody confusing. I grew up in Australia and learned English from Aussie teachers."

"What the hell?" asked Miller.

"I just told you that he's from Australia, what part of that didn't you understand?"

"I guess the part where he doesn't sound like a Korean," replied Miller sheepishly.

"No worries, mate. I get this all the time," said Ban.

146

"I'm sure you'll get along with these meatheads," said Evans to Ban. "Get settled and we'll introduce you to the rest of the squad, and a few of the others you'll want to know."

"Hey, Ban," said Private Peterson, "if you're from Australia, what are you doing here?"

"I'm just doin' me part to fight for me homeland," said Ban. "They needed all the English-speakin' young blokes they could get, so I volunteered."

"Makes sense," agreed Peterson.

"So, how does this work?" asked Harrington. "You ain't a Marine, so what are you?"

"I'm an *ideungbyeong* in the Republic of Korea Army," said Ban. "That's a private in English, mate."

"You any good with that?" asked Miller, gesturing towards the rifle propped up against a wall locker.

"I'm not gonna lie to ya, I'm a lot better at translatin' than shootin'," said Ban.

"Okay," said Oliver, "First mission for you is to get some target time. We're going to turn you into a killing machine, my Korean-Australian man."
****

28 September 1981
21st Special Air Service Regiment
South of Lübeck, West Germany

Trooper Trevor Pearce could feel the slight chill in the air that hinted of a cold winter approaching. Tonight, he was on a forested hill overlooking a flat forest below. This time and place had been chosen through a methodical process. There was no moon tonight. The position was within range of Pearce's hide spot. And most importantly, the pilots could plot a course to get there from the United Kingdom with a better-than-decent chance of not getting shot down. Now all Pearce had to do was wait.

As he did, he considered his predicament with regard to the locals. One of the leaders of *Freiheitsfront*, a Karl Köstler, had taken up the habit of enlisting German children into his unit. This was in direct violation of every principle of NATO and the United Nations, not to mention generally accepted morality. He wanted to get a report out to headquarters, but the senior man in his unit, Corporal Ralph Willis, wouldn't risk any outgoing comms, by radio or courier, unless it was mission-critical. Pearce seethed at the memory of their conversation, but he understood the corporal's point. Any outgoing communication had the potential of exposing their whereabouts and compromising the mission.

He shifted his SLR rifle to his right shoulder and again peered into the darkness. After another half hour of this, he heard the faint sound of engines. He knew that it had to be the Hawker Siddeley Andover, flying the "Hanseatic Express" a route that would allow the cargo plane to drop off supplies for at least twenty units like Pearce's. Reeves couldn't conceive how difficult the route selection must be. There were so many factors to consider: you had to fly as low as possible, only over unpopulated areas, preferably in a valley, while still hitting every unit that needed supply and not flying the same route twice, or in any kind of observable pattern.

The plane was really just a shadow in the night. Painted all black, it zipped past Reeves and continued on into the darkness. As it did, Reeves observed a pallet drop from behind the airplane. He couldn't see the black parachute that opened as it fell, but he knew it was there. Everything from the drop would be collected and used, including the nylon from the parachute and the wood from the pallet and crates. For now, though, Pearce had to wait. His orders were to observe the pallet for an hour, then he and the rest of his troop would converge on it and retrieve the supplies. Each trooper was isolated so that, in the event that one was detected, the rest could still evade capture.

The pallet sat amongst the trees for sixty minutes before Pearce made his move. He moved as quickly as he could while maintaining his stealth. Even so, he was the third trooper to reach the supplies. Corporal Willis was already rolling up the parachute while Lance Corporal Cooper snipped the wires that held the various crates together. Willis motioned to Pearce to approach.

"We're leaving the wood tonight. There's just too much to carry. We'll send locals out to collect what they can tomorrow."

Pearce nodded and went to the pallet and grabbed one of the four crates. He hefted the crate away from the pallet as Trooper Barker made his appearance. Pearce waited until the rest of the troopers had pulled their crates, then, as a team, they hefted them onto their backs, using straps that had been affixed to the crates for this exact purpose. They then began the three-kilometer trek to their safe house in Schmilau.

After the journey to the outskirts of the town, Pearce and his mates held back as Willis slunk across the street and up the driveway to the front door. He waited as Willis made contact with the residents and signaled for the team to approach. One at a time, after checking both sides of the street, a trooper would bolt across the road, and into the house. The whole process took an agonizing amount of time, but time was one thing they had. Under no circumstances could they afford to get caught.

Pearce had been here before several times. The local contact, a *Frau* Anika Kirsch, was already a war widow. Her husband had been killed in the opening days of the war. Just a man with the bad luck of being in the open when an off-target artillery round decided to explode. Tonight, however, he saw something that he'd never seen before: children. His heart sank as he remembered the coldness in Karl Köstler's voice when Pearce had asked, "What happens to the children if the enemy catches them with a load of C-4?" and Köstler had responded, "They will be shot."

Even with her husband dead, there was nothing like that coldness in Anika. Pearce considered how terrible war must be that a sweet, beautiful woman like this could be brought down to such a low standard of morality. Anika grabbed Corporal Willis by the elbow and pulled him to the kitchen. After a minute, Pearce noticed that there was something of a muted disturbance going on in the back of the house. It sounded like an argument, but both parties were trying to keep it down to avoid attracting attention.

"Eh, Pearce," said Willis, "I need you over here for a minute." Pearce looked over to the Corporal, who was in the kitchen, talking with Anika. The corporal motioned to him to emphasize that, yes, he was being summoned.

"What ya got, Corporal?" he asked as he reached the kitchen.

"I need you to translate for me," said Willis. "She's pretty agitated and won't slow down enough for me to get any idea of what she's saying." Willis could get through most of the transactional German needed for his job, but once the native left the script, he was out of his depth. Peace, on the other hand, was fluent in the local dialect.

Pearce could see the anger in Anika's eyes. In German, he tried to soothe her. "Anika, please calm down. What's going on?"

"It's the children," she replied, gesturing towards one of them, sitting at a table in the kitchen. "Karl is using them to fight in the war!"

"What do you mean they are fighting in the war?" asked Pearce.

"Exactly what I said," replied Anika. "He has been collecting orphans and teaching them the ways of war. Like how to plant bombs, and he uses them to run explosives and messages between resistance leaders. He regales them with tales of his time in the Hitler Youth during the last war." Her eyes welled with tears as she recounted what she had witnessed. "I couldn't let it continue, so I grabbed these two and brought them here for you to talk to, to see for yourself."

"We heard reports of something like this," lied Pearce, "but not to this degree. Let me talk to the corporal and get him caught up." Then, to Willis, he said, "She's found out about Köstler's child soldiers, and she's livid."

"Okay," said Willis, "this is getting too big for us to contain. It's going to damage operational effectiveness. Tell her that we need her to get a message out. Shit, I didn't want to burn a contact just yet." Willis took out a spiral notepad from his pocket and wrote something down, tore off the page and handed it to Pearce. "Here, tell her to find his man and relay the message. In fact, work with her to get the message as succinct and unemotional as you can. She needs to be very calm with this if there's going to be any chance of getting orders on how to handle this."

"I get it, Corporal, I'll do what I can." Then to Anika, he said, "I need you to get a message to this man." He handed her the torn-out page. "But you need to keep control of yourself. You can't draw any attention to yourself, or this man. Just keep the kids with you, if you can. Once we get word back on how to deal with Köstler, we'll figure out what to do with all of the kids. How many do you think there are?"

"I counted at least ten when I was last there," she replied. "There are almost certainly more. Ones who were out on 'missions.'"

"I understand," said Pearce, who placed his left hand on her right cheek and looked into her deep blue eyes. "If you can get this message out, I promise I will take care of this for you." It was all done on an impulse. At first he thought he was simply using his charm to help him complete the mission, but as he pulled his hand back, he felt as though he'd left a tiny piece of his heart with her.

Chapter 13

30 September 1981
Kremlin
Moscow, USSR

Soviet Minister of Culture, Pyotr Demichev was comfortable with his position. It was a fact that there was no truly "stable" ground if there was a change in leadership. But he understood that so long as Andropov was in charge, he was not only safe, he was prepped for advancement. That was a dual edged sword. Propaganda was his specialty. As Minister of Culture, he had a lot of influence in propaganda campaigns both domestic and overseas. The crown jewel in his own crown was the campaign in Latin America. He'd been running that program from its inception.

His position as the Minister of Culture guaranteed his dedication to the party. If he'd made any missteps, they would have been called out and he would have paid the price. But no, he was a Party Man in every meaning of the title. He looked at the General at the front of the room, gesturing at a map, and was bored.

"Comrade General Secretary," said the General, "NATO is attacking on two fronts." The General pointed his stick at a northern and southern point. "We believe that their objective is to trap the bulk of the Red Army in western Germany. If the two offensives are able to connect, they will be able to cut off resupply to our units that are preparing to move into France and the Low Countries." He paused to allow the general strategy to seep into the minds of the leadership of the Soviet Union.

"We believe that NATO is attempting to use Bonn as their fulcrum point. The northern and southern offensives will meet at Bonn, and then once our army is trapped, additional units from France, newly arrived units from the United States, and what is left of the West German forces will push through."

"This seems familiar, but yet… different," said Minister of Defense Dmitry Ustinov.

"The General Staff of the Armed Forces believes that this is a similar battle plan to that of the Germans in 1943. This is similar to the Battle of the Kursk Plain."

"But that makes no sense," countered Ustinov, "The only reason that Kursk was possible was because of the terrain. Kursk was a flat and open plain. This NATO assault, especially on the southern prong, is very mountainous, or at the very least, hilly."

"That's correct, Comrade Minister," said the General. It is the opinion of the General Staff that the Western forces have overestimated their ability to move forces via airborne assault and helicopter assault. The initial gains were accomplished with aviation attacks. But the follow-on forces are delayed. We are slowing their advance, and every metric that we have shows that they will fall short of their goals.

"And yet they advance?" asked Andropov.

"Yes, Comrade General Secretary," replied the General. "The key to defeating this attack will be to precisely time our counter-offensive. If he hit them too soon, we could wind up with a stalemate in Germany. If that happens, it will take us prohibitively long to regain the territory that we've lost."

"Prohibitively?" asked Andropov. "I'm not sure I like the implication that we are on the verge of defeat."

"No, Comrade," replied the General, visibly shaken. "It is just that the longer it takes, the more Soviet men will die. If we can simultaneously stop the assault, while attacking on the eastern flanks of both forces, we could cut them off, and deal with them piecemeal. By doing this, we can drive them out of Germany in weeks, not months." Andropov's eyebrows rose at this report.

"And you believe that this is achievable?" asked Andropov.

"Yes, Sir. But only with excellent timing. We need to marshal enough troops to accomplish both the blocking and flanking attacks. The further the enemy spearheads penetrate, the weaker they become. Their supply lines will be stretched to the breaking point. So we fall back, we give them the illusion of success. Then, when they believe they are on the cusp of victory, we will smash their lines."

I'm not sure that I believe that, thought Demichev, *but the General clearly believes it.* Demichev was adept at reading men's fascial and body language. In his role as Cultural Minister, he had to be. He couldn't create effective propaganda if he couldn't tell when his writers and artists were simply telling him what he wanted to hear. *This man isn't just telling Andropov what he knows he needs to. This man believes in this plan.* Demichev didn't know anything about military strategy, but he had faith in the general before him.

****

5 October 1981
Peñas Blancas,
Costa Rica

Join the Marine Corps… see the world, thought Carlos Rodriguez as he raised his coffee cup and took a sip. Today was his first day in Costa Rica. He and Clara Gálvez were waiting to meet someone at a small café just on the other side of the border with Nicaragua. Like the Vietcong before them, the newly formed "ComAms," the "Comunistas Americanos," were setting up camps across the borders of neighboring nations. This was done for two reasons. First, to slow the US response by adding the diplomatic layer of a separate government to negotiate with. Second, they hoped to reuse the bases when the communist revolution spread to Costa Rica. The latter was a big part of the Sandinistas rebranding. They were no longer representing Nicaraguan communism. They were representing the relentless march of communism across the entirety of the Americas.

Carlos had spent the last six weeks getting force-fed communist philosophy. It was the best schooling he'd ever had. The campus was at Pedro Gálvez's hacienda in Puerto Cabezas, and his instructor was the indomitable Clara Gálvez. From the moment she'd tied him up and pulled a gun on him, Carlos had been fascinated by her. And while she had maintained a strong front, she had softened to him a bit. She no longer seemed as though she wanted to kill him.

It's a start, thought Carlos. Once Carlos had the basics of how Marxism worked, the two of them did a deep dive on the propaganda used to bolster the movement. Clara had mentioned that she didn't have much of a background on this side of things. When she'd become a communist, she hadn't needed posters to tell her that the Somoza regime was trampling the rights of the workers. It hadn't taken a creative radio broadcast to let her know that the current system was unfair. When her fiancé had been disappeared, she'd known that she would do whatever it took to get rid of Somoza.

On this mission, though, she was going to have to talk the talk. She and Carlos needed to convince the ComAms that they were fellow travelers seeking to bring about the global communist state. So far, the road had been smooth. One of Fred's contacts was able to set up a meet with a leader in Managua. That meeting was essentially an interview to make sure that these new recruits were the real deal. Only after getting past that stage would they be given the location of an actual operational camp.

It was easy for Clara to win approval. As a local with a history of service in the Sandinista People's Militia, she was able to blend in the story of her fiancé's disappearance and even tell tales of combat from her time fighting the Americans at and near Ayapal. The latter were provided by CIA reports on how that battle had played out.

Carlos, on the other hand, was a challenge. There was no way around the fact that he sounded like a Mexican. Now he had a passport and a driver's license that confirmed this. In order to make it easier to remember, they'd recycled as much of his backstory from his first trip into Nicaragua, when he was leading a Contra patrol. He was a journalism student from the Autonomous University of Baja California Sur. He had come to Nicaragua to fight the Americans, and, like Clara, had very convincing stories of combat along the border with Honduras.

Apparently, he'd sold the story well enough that he and Clara were now waiting for a ComAm leader to make contact and bring them out to a camp where they would be integrated into the operation. Thinking back on it, he looked across the table at Clara. She was reading a book, but he didn't bother asking. Small talk generally annoyed her, and after a year of working together, he'd finally figured out that it was best to keep his questions to himself.

"Raúl said that you were pretty," said a voice over Carlos's shoulder, "but he didn't mention that you were beautiful."

"Thank you," said Carlos, laughing and turning to face the man. "My mother says I'm the most handsome boy in school." He was rewarded as an annoyed look came across the man's face. The man walked past Carlos and held out his hand to Clara, who took it.

"César Costa, at your service." He turned her hand, pulled it towards his face and gave it a light kiss. "May I?" He gestured towards an empty chair.

"Of course," said Clara. César sat down.

"I'm Clara Gálvez, and this is Carlos Rodriguez."

César nodded at Carlos.

"Raúl was impressed with your backgrounds. Especially yours, *señorita*. It takes a lot of courage to be both a schoolteacher *and* a soldier of the people."

She's blushing. What's with this clown? thought Carlos, irritated by César's intentional disrespect. *Is this some kind of machismo test? Am I supposed to keep my cool or establish dominance?* Carlos was confident that he could put this man on his ass with ease. But that really didn't seem like the best way to get his respect.

"We all do what we can for the revolution, *camarada*," said Carlos, reminding everyone why they were there.

"Indeed, *señor*," said César. "Indeed we do. And on that note, Raúl was just conducting your background check. I need to know a little more about you. But not here." He looked around the café. "The CIA has ears everywhere. Follow me." He stood and headed down a path that ran parallel to the Inter-American Highway.

They followed him to a hotel, where he led them to a room on the second floor. Once inside, they saw Raúl sitting on the edge of the bed.

"I've swept the room, Señor Costa, it's clean."

"Thank you, Raúl, you may go." Raúl gave a quick nod and left the three in the room.

"I need to understand how dedicated you are to the cause." He looked at Clara. "Your bona fides are simple enough to chase down. You fought in the revolution, and you want to keep fighting. You have already proven yourself ten times over." He turned to Carlos. "You, however… are not so simple. You are totally unproven."

"How can you say that?" asked Carlos. "I've fought the Americans in Nicaragua, I lost friends—"

"Friends that you'd known for what? Three months? No, those weren't your friends. You didn't grow up here, and you didn't feel the pain under Somoza. No, you lived a peaceful life in Mexico, then decided to throw all that away to come here and fight in a war that wasn't yours. Why?"

Carlos now understood. The disrespect and the clear attention he was paying to Clara wasn't just machismo, it was calculated to put Carlos on edge. To annoy him into giving something up in his answer.

156

He took a breath before replying. "As a student at university, I learned a lot about the corruption and oppression of the workers of the world. This was true in my own country. No, we did not have Somoza, this is true, but we did have fifty years under the PRI. The corporate pigs would get fat while poverty spread. I was ashamed of my own success. How could I stand there and do nothing when there was such clear injustice going on in the world?"

"Then why didn't you work with your brothers and sisters in Mexico? Why come to Nicaragua?"

"I'm a man of action," replied Carlos. "I'm not much for planning and plotting. I saw Nicaragua as the best way that I could do my part for the revolution."

"Yes," said César, "I think you should leave the thinking and planning to this one." He looked towards Clara. She demurred.

"And," continued Carlos, "when the revolution takes hold here, as it did in Cuba, we will move on to El Salvador. We will move on to Guatemala. Then, I will return to Mexico."

"A conquering hero?" asked César.

"No, a servant of the proletariat," replied Carlos.

"I see," said César. "You can stay here today. I need to make arrangements at the camp. I will pick you up tomorrow morning at nine. Be ready for a hike." On his way out the door, he smiled at Clara. "*Señorita*," he said as he left the room.

Chapter 14

7 October 1981
82nd Airborne Division
Bitburg, Germany

Sergeant Marlon Reeves was still trying to put all of the pieces together. It was July. They had captured the airfield. The Soviets were totally off-balance, but within days, they counterattacked. All of that was as clear as though it were yesterday. Then there was a big black hole in his memory. Between July second and August fourth, he had nothing. August fourth was what he internally referred to as the "Day of Confusion." He didn't understand where he was, or what had happened.

"There he is," said a familiar voice. Reeves shook his head and took in his surroundings. He was still in his hospital room. "You about done malingering?" asked Staff Sergeant Watkins.

"Yeah, Sarge," said Reeves. "Get me the hell out of here."

"Doc says you're good to go but that we need to keep an eye on you. To be honest, I think the nurses are just tired of looking at your ugly ass," laughed Watkins. Reeves chuckled.

"I have to admit, I will miss all of my *Fräuleins*," replied Reeves. When the Americans had liberated Bitburg, the local population had come out in support. Once the 3rd Infantry Division had linked up with the 82nd and a degree of safety had been established, the civilian hospital staff had quickly returned. This action had likely saved Reeves's life.

Reeves was worried about returning to duty. He'd been off the line for three months, but he still had a foggy feeling in his head. He felt like he was a second slow. He couldn't stay here, though. He had to get back out there with his brothers.

"I don't think you've heard, but they put you in for an Army Commendation Medal. Luca is probably getting a Bronze Star. They like to kick it up a notch when it's posthumous. But you two kept those bastards from breaking through. Hell, if you were an O-2 you'd be getting a Silver Star, no doubt." Reeves had heard the story many times. He and Kidd were back-to-back. The fighting closed in on them, and soon it was hand-to-hand. He was hit in the back of the head and Sergeant Luca Kidd stabbed the oncoming Soviet before he could finish him off.

He'd saved Reeves's life but couldn't save his own. He had died of his injuries two days after the battle.

"I'd much rather not have this head injury and not have the medal if it's all the same."

"Doesn't work that way, pal," said Watkins. "You've paid for the medal, so you might as well enjoy it."

"What's the plan? I assume you're here to check me out, right?"

"Yep, time to get you back into the soldiering business. You've got five minutes to get in uniform, gather your shit, and say goodbye to those nurses. I'll meet you out front. Welcome back, Sergeant."

His new rank still sounded strange to him. Watkins walked out of the room and Reeves hurriedly donned his green, brown, and black camouflage uniform and grabbed his pack, which contained everything that constituted his "shit."

As promised, Watkins was standing in front of the hospital, smoking a cigarette. He crushed it out in an ashtray as Reeves approached.

"So, here's what we know," said Watkins as they walked. "The Reds took some very heavy losses trying to take back Bitburg. When the 3rd ID showed up, they were off-balance and withdrew. They've fallen back to Mehren, and we're solidifying our lines and getting ready for the next big push."

"What are they going to do with us?" asked Reeves. "Do they have another airfield they want us to tackle?"

"No way," said Watkins. "We've been bled pretty dry after this battle. And that's to say nothing about the availability of airlift capabilities. Lockheed can only spit out so many C-130s at a time, even with our wartime production. Right now, we're going to be part of the follow-on forces. Once we get our numbers up, we'll be back in the action. But for now, I hope your shoveling skills are sharp as a tack."

"Oh, that's fantastic, Sarge," said Reeves. "Maybe the hospital wasn't so bad after all."

"Oh, before I forget," said Watkins, "You're taking Kidd's spot. Don't make it weird." That took Reeves aback. He knew that someone would have to fill the role, and there was no reason it shouldn't be him, but the idea of replacing his dead friend was hard for him to process.

It's going to be a while before things get back to normal..., he thought. *Normal? What's that?* he wondered as he and Staff Sergeant Watkins returned to the platoon HQ to meet up with the rest of the boys. He was greeted as soon as they crossed tent flap.

"Hey, look, it's that 'Greatest American Hero'!" said PFC Sebastian Davis.

"You look different," said Sergeant Herman Becker, the Russian translator that Reeves hadn't seen since the early stages of the war.

"Holy—what are you doing here?" asked Reeves.

"I was just passing through and Watkins told me that you were coming back to the unit, so I thought I'd hang around."

"Wow, it's great to see you, man," said Reeves. "What do they have you doing now?"

"That's classified," said Becker. "But I'll tell you this, if you see the spook shake break down and the Ninety-Seven Echoes, the Intel Spooks get the hell out of town, you'd better grab your ankles, because you're about to get something big." The tent erupted in laughter, though some of the men weren't sure how seriously to take Becker.

"I don't know," said Watkins, "I've always thought Becker was a bit too chummy with those commies. You can't trust anyone who's so good at speaking their language."

"Bah, in 1980, we were *all* too chummy with those bastards. And besides, how would you know if I'm any good at speaking Russian... unlesssss..." He strung out the last word to from an implied accusation.

"That's right," laughed Watkins, "I'm a secret agent, and my KGB puppet masters sent me on a deep-cover secret mission to hang out with this dysfunctional family. Is high-profile mishon much important to Mother Russia." The tent again broke into laughter at how terrible Watkins's Russian accent was.

"Okay, you've convinced me of your innocence," said Becker. "No native Russian speaker would ever have such an awful accent. But, hey, Reeves, I've gotta get back, but congratulations on making it back, I was really worried for you for a while there." He reached out his hand, and Reeves took it and was pulled in for a strong hug as the two brothers celebrated survival.

****

10 October 1981
345th Independent Guards Airborne Regiment
Mehren, Germany

Sergeant Misha Kozyrev and his squad huddled behind the crumbling stone wall in the small German village of Mehren. They'd lost their BMD during the retreat from Spangdahlem, so they were dismounted and left with little choice but to fight on foot. The squad had taken refuge in an alley between two buildings, seeking cover from the relentless hail of gunfire that seemed to come from all directions. The young privates, Gleb Silivanov and Vaniamin Kulakov, clung to their rifles, eyes wide with fear and determination.

An uneasy silence fell over the village, and Misha took the opportunity to assess the situation. The West German and US forces had them surrounded, and it was only a matter of time before they would be forced to retreat or face annihilation. The captain had told them that they were facing the US 3rd Infantry Division. That didn't mean a lot to Misha. What did mean a lot was that the enemy had been pushing forward relentlessly, and Misha knew that they had little chance of holding their position.

"Listen up, men," Misha whispered, his voice barely audible over the sound of a fresh artillery barrage. "We're going to have to fall back to the next defensive line. We can't hold them here any longer." He glanced at the faces of his men, their expressions a mixture of fear and resignation.

"I haven't run this much since jump school," said Taras, clearly winded from the activity. The squad moved as quickly as possible, darting from building to building, avoiding the open streets. They had only just reached the edge of the village when the silence was shattered by the unmistakable sound of a tank rumbling nearby.

"Get down!" Misha hissed, pressing himself flat against the ground. The rest of the squad followed suit, their hearts pounding in their chests. The tank rolled past them, the ground trembling beneath its weight, and Misha prayed they wouldn't be spotted.

As the tank continued down the street, Misha gave the signal to move, and the squad once again began their desperate retreat. They had almost reached the safety of a nearby wooded area when a burst of gunfire erupted from a nearby building. The sound of bullets whizzing past their ears filled the air, and Misha could feel his heart drop.

"Return fire!" he shouted, using his left hand to vector the guns. The men scrambled to find cover. The firefight was intense, the narrow streets and close quarters making it difficult to tell friend from foe. Misha unloaded with tight bursts from Andrusha's RPKS-74. He couldn't bring himself to give up the light machine gun after the disaster at Bitburg.

As Misha and his men fought, the enemy's fire seemed to intensify, and it was clear that their position was untenable. He gave the order to retreat once more, his voice cracking with the strain of the situation. In the chaos of the firefight, Misha saw one of the young privates, Gleb Silivanov, fall to the ground, his body wracked with pain as a bullet found its mark. He moved to try to render aid, but the young soldier's life had been snuffed out in an instant, leaving his comrades to grieve and carry on the fight without him.

Misha's heart ached for the loss of yet another young private, but there was no time for mourning. With a heavy heart, he led his men through the last row of buildings in Mehren. The ran as fast as they could for the woods east of the village, the sounds of gunfire growing fainter as they moved further from the battle. Misha didn't have a destination. The squad was just getting as far away from enemy onslaught as possible. They broke through branches and bushes. The cuts and bruises were of no consequence. They just needed to get away.

They approached a clearing, not sure whether to be thankful that the path of retreat would be clear or to curse that they wouldn't have any cover or concealment. Taras slowed ahead of him.

"Keep running," ordered Misha. "We may die if we run out there, but we'll certainly die if we stay here." They were a mere ten meters out of the forest when they heard the sound of diesel engines in front of them. *We're dead*, thought Misha. *We lived longer than we should have.* "Just keep going!" he shouted.

"Glory and honor!" shouted one of the privates, Misha couldn't remember which man the voice belonged to. It was an absurd thing to say, but it filled Misha with pride and washed away some of the fatigue from his body as he threw one foot in front of the other, running east— running towards home. The sound of a cannon firing echoed rang in his ears. It was followed by another and another as Misha and his men ran through the hellishness as infantry in the open.

It took a few seconds for Misha to realize that he wasn't dead. In fact, he hadn't seen any shells exploding on the ground.

"They're ours!" shouted Taras. Misha looked up and saw the rounded turret and low profile of a T-80 tank. And another. And another. The tanks were sweeping past the men to the left and the right. A tank commander popped out of his hatch and saluted the Desantniks. Misha returned the salute, amazed at how good his luck had been yet again. The retreat had been painful, and the cost had been high, but Misha knew that they had made the right choice and they were still in the fight.
****

3rd Battalion, 69th Armor Regiment

Sergeant First Class Don Mackintosh scanned the battlefield through the sights of his M1 Abrams tank. The village of Mehren was steadily falling into American hands, but the Soviet defenders were putting up a stubborn fight. The cacophony of gunfire and explosions filled the air as Bravo Company, 3rd Battalion, 69th Armored Regiment, fought alongside the infantry from the US 3rd Infantry Division to take control of the village.

Captain Henderson's voice came through the intercom. "Mack, scan the area for any antitank teams. We don't want any surprises."

"Roger that, Captain," Mack replied, diligently scanning the village through his sights. He spotted a Soviet soldier attempting to sneak up on one of their fellow tanks with an RPG. "Captain, I've got an RPG gunner at two o'clock! Engaging now!" Mack's heart pounded in his chest as he lined up and took the shot, eliminating the threat before the grenadier could take aim. The nearby tank, now aware of the danger, adjusted its position to cover the exposed flank.

"Good shot, Mack!" said Henderson. "Keep it up."

Mack felt a rush of pride at the captain's words, but he knew there was no time to dwell on it. He continued to scan the battlefield, searching for any other threats. As the battle raged on, Mack could hear the low growl of the tank's engine as Specialist Cameron "Fletch" Fletcher skillfully maneuvered her through the narrow streets, avoiding debris and staying close to the cover provided by the few buildings in the town. In the background, the metallic clanging of ammunition being loaded could be heard as Private First Class Noah Wright worked tirelessly to keep the main gun supplied.

Henderson's radio crackled to life as the platoon leader for one of the infantry platoons reported in. "Bravo Company, this is Lieutenant Tyrone Nichols from Charlie Company, 1/15 IR. We've secured the eastern side of the village, but we're taking heavy fire from a fortified position near the church. We could use some support."

Mackintosh focused intently, knowing that their support would be crucial in turning the tide of this engagement. As they approached the church, he could see the infantry taking cover behind any available obstacles, trying to avoid the withering fire from the Soviet defenders.

"Captain, I've got eyes on the target. Permission to engage?" Mack asked, his finger hovering over the trigger.

"Hammer 'em, Mack," Henderson ordered.

Mack's breathing steadied as he fired a high-explosive round, hitting the fortified position with pinpoint accuracy. The explosion tore through the enemy emplacement, silencing the heavy fire. Satisfaction coursed through him as he reported, "Target destroyed, Captain!"

"Nice shot, Mack!" Henderson praised.

Mack allowed himself a small smile but remained vigilant, knowing the battle was not over yet. With the fortified position eliminated, the infantry moved forward to secure the church and the surrounding area. The remaining Soviet defenders began to fall back, realizing that the village was lost.

As the battle for Mehren drew to a close, Mack knew that this was just one small part of the larger conflict. As though fate was reading his mind, the radio came to life.

"We've got a problem—" The transmission cut off without conveying any useful information.

"Stay sharp," said Captain Henderson, "something's up." He listened for a few seconds before relaying to his crew, "There's a major counterattack underway. This fight isn't over, not by a long shot. Wright, load sabot. Mack, we've got a major armored force bearing down on us from the east."

"Roger that, Captain," said Mackintosh, "nothing we haven't dealt with before."

"I like the confidence, Mack. Fletch, come to a heading of zero-eight-five."

"Roger, sir. Zero-eight-five," said Fletch. The captain then issued orders to the company as they pushed east in search of the enemy.

"Keep an eye on that tree line, Mack," said Captain Henderson. The tree line was to the left of the tank and was blocking their view to the northeast.

"Roger, Captain."

"Holy shit, that's a lot of tanks," said Fletch as the tank cleared the forest and hit the flat open plain.

"Target—" *Boom!* The report of the 105mm main gun cut him short. The crew was working as a fluid team. Just as before, Wright was feeding the gun as quickly as he could. This time, though, Mack felt a greater intensity. Every sabot round that he fired represented an enemy tank that could just as easily kill him. There were no HE rounds being loaded to take out infantry concentrations. This was a pure tank battle, and from where Mack was sitting, they were vastly outnumbered by the enemy.

"Captain," said Mackintosh, "we need to think about falling back, sir. I don't think HQ had any idea what Ivan was sending today. We're going to need more of everything."

"I agree," said Henderson. "We don't want to get cut off out here on the frontier, but we've got to hear it from the colonel."

"From your lips to the colonel's ear," said Mackintosh, firing another round at an enemy tank. Fortunately, Colonel Simmons wasn't a fool and could see what was in front of him: a hell of a lot of Soviet steel.

Through the roar of diesel engines and the sharp crack of cannon fire, a voice broke through on the radio. It was Lieutenant Colonel Brian Simmons, the commanding officer of 3/69 Armored Regiment. His voice was tense but controlled, an island of calm in the storm of battle.

"All call signs, this is Black Knight Actual. We are outgunned here. Break contact and prepare for organized withdrawal, over."

In the confined space of their M1 Abrams tank, the words hung heavy. Mackintosh, the gunner, exchanged a glance with Captain Henderson, their tank commander.

"Fletch, Wright, you heard the man," Henderson said into his mic, the order traveling to the driver's compartment and the loader's station. "Prepare to disengage."

"Copy that, sir," said Fletch, his voice betraying his unease at the order. The Abrams was already backing up, dust and smoke billowing from beneath its treads as it reversed away from the front line.

Wright, the loader, was silent. He was staring at the breech of the 105mm cannon, hands twitching with pent-up energy. He wanted to be loading, to be fighting. But orders were orders. His response was a resigned "Aye, Captain."

The ground beneath them rumbled with the movement of Soviet T-80 tanks, their superior firepower a constant threat. Their presence loomed like specters through the smoke of the battle, a reminder of the enemy's power.

"Black Knight Two, this is Black Knight Actual," came the voice of Lieutenant Colonel Simmons again over the radio. "Cover our withdrawal with a smoke screen, over."

"Copy that, Black Knight Actual. Smoke screen, aye," Henderson acknowledged.

"Alright, Wright," he called, "load up the smoke."

Wright's hands moved with a newfound purpose, swiftly loading the canisters into the breech. The tank lurched as Fletch navigated through the rough terrain, his focus split between the outside view and the internal comms.

"Steady as she goes, Fletch," Henderson encouraged. "Don, keep your eyes open for any of those T-80s trying to flank us."

"Yes, sir," Mackintosh replied, his gaze locked onto his periscope, scanning the terrain for any threats.

And just like that, amidst the chaos of battle, the men of 3/69th Armored began their retreat, their resolve unbroken, their spirit unwavering. They would regroup, reassess, and return to fight another day.

Chapter 15

11 October 1981
White House
Situation Room
Washington, D.C.

President Carter had assembled his entire national security staff for the latest briefing on the battle for Europe. The reports coming out in the press were scattered. It was always a challenge to tell the truth from propaganda, and this was doubly true in a time of war. Under normal circumstances, Carter would be briefed by Secretary of Defense Harold Brown. Today, however, he wanted to hear it straight from the Joint Chiefs of Staff and the Director of the CIA. In fact, it was Stansfield Turner, the CIA head, who kicked things off.

"Mr. President, gentlemen, and Madam Secretary," said Turner, getting everyone's attention. "I thought it was appropriate for me to get started with an overall assessment of what is happened as best the Agency can tell." Carter nodded for him to continue.

"Since the start of Operation Fullback, we've known that the Soviets would have no choice but to launch a counterstrike. We thought it would occur sometime in late August or early September. When that didn't materialize, we thought we might have caught a break. The Soviets were fighting off their back heel, and that's not something the Red Army is made for. So we continued to press."

"Gentlemen," interrupted Carter, "this is literally the oldest trick in the book. It was used by Joshua and the Israelites to great effect in the Battle of Ai in the Bible."

"With all due respect, sir," said Army Chief of Staff General Edward Meyer, "We didn't overextend ourselves. We didn't go racing after a fleeing enemy. We stuck to the timetable that we had developed to ensure that we would be at maximum strength in the case of counterattack."

"Then why are we suffering what looks to the interested observer like a defeat?"

"The enemy gets to make their own choices," said Turner, regaining the room. "In this case, we didn't think that they would be able to marshal a force large enough to stop our advance, much less turn it back. They're holding a lot of territory, and our attacks disrupting supply lines and depots have had a devastating effect."

"Stan," said the President, "you are in charge of the greatest, and might I add best-paid intelligence outfit in the world. You have satellites in space. You can task the fastest aircraft in the world. You have sources on the ground in every nation on this earth. How do you miss this?"

"To be frank, sir, it was a failure of the human element," said Turner. "We had some highly placed sources that had been vetted over the course of the past several years. Some of them have been proven agents for over a decade. They risked their lives to assure us that the Soviets were in disarray. The documentation that they provided was detailed and convincing. We've lost contact with every one of them. We don't know if they're all dead or if they were all playing us for all these years, feeding us crumbs over time so that they could sell the big lie when the Soviets needed it the most."

"It hardly seems to matter at this point," said the President. "Okay, that's the overview. What are the details? General Meyer?"

"Yes, Mr. President," said the general. "We were pushing the Soviets and their Warsaw Pact allies out of the German village of Mehren. Some of these troops had been falling back since the opening days of Fullback. It was mostly disorganized infantry. Most of them on foot. We have developed successful tactics of surrounding the towns with mechanized forces, then sending in infantry to clear out the enemy." Meyer cleared his throat before continuing.

"As the armored units were attempting to complete the encirclement, a previously unknown armored column engaged them from the north. The tanks took major losses, as up to that point, they had been focused on the village."

"Did you not have a reserve force?" asked Carter. He was no master strategist, but he'd read enough military history to know that no competent commander would find himself in a major offensive without reserves for just this type of contingency.

"Yes, sir," replied General Meyer, "the 4th Panzergrenadier Brigade was in support. However, they were flanked on the east by another attacking force. From what we can gather, the plan was to cut into our lines behind the 4th, cutting off the 3rd Infantry Division, which they could then decimate from both sides. It damn near worked."

"So, we have won a victory?" asked Zbigniew Brzezinski derisively.

"Well, no," replied Meyer, "But we suffered less of a defeat than we otherwise would have. The commanders on the ground could see they were in a trap, and instead of getting caught, they withdrew to reengage."

"And when did that reengagement occur?" asked Brzezinski.

"It... so..." Meyer was clearly uncomfortable. "The Soviets pressed their advantage, pushing our forces south. It was only when they stopped the attack that our forces were able to rally and organize. By that point it was determined that they needed to fall back in an organized fashion to establish a defensive position."

"So we have not been able to reestablish the initiative," said Brzezinski.

"That's right, Dr. Brzezinski," said Meyer with more confidence. "We decided to make a strategic withdrawal instead of throwing together a hasty offensive operation when we weren't even sure what we were up against. Regaining the initiative is important, but a suicidal counterattack has never been in the American playbook." Brzezinski looked away, frustrated.

"I understand that we're all on edge," said Secretary of State Jeane Kirkpatrick. "But we're on the same team, so we need to focus on the steps forward. It's unfortunate that this war wasn't easy. Until this meeting, I didn't think that any of us was under the illusion that it would be." That line hung in the air.

"Secretary Kirkpatrick is right," said Carter. "We need to know where we're going from here. How do we fix this setback?"

"I don't have that answer, Mr. President," said Meyer. "It's going to take some time to formulate a plan to get back on the offensive. Right now our biggest concern is making a defensive stand. We have to stop the bleeding before we can get back on the offensive."

"So," asked President Carter, "are we right back where we started nearly a year ago?"

"It's not quite the same, but in a manner of speaking... yes."
****

12 October 1981
3/6 Marines

Sangsong, North Korea

Corporal Oliver knew that this couldn't last much longer. Three weeks out of the shit was unheard of. Yet here they were. The thought of the return to combat was met with a combination of dread and longing. Oliver had never understood when combat veterans used the term "seeing the elephant." Then, in Iran, he had seen the elephant and it all made sense to him. It was something that couldn't be properly described. The enormity of it required a man to experience it. And so instead of trying to describe it, they just referred to it as "the elephant."

He was in the middle of a game of spades when he heard the sound. His heartbeat accelerated and he set his cards down on the footlocker that was being used as a makeshift table. *Thump-thump-thump.* It was the unmistakable sound of incoming helos.

"Hey, Ban," said Oliver, "come here, I need you to take over my hand."

"What?" said Harrington, Oliver's partner. "Ban sucks at spades."

"Sorry, fellas, I gotta go." Oliver grabbed his cover and walked out of the tent.

"Thanks a lot, Corporal," called out Harrington behind him. The rumors that they were building a Vulture Nest at Sangsong had been bubbling for a while. When Navy Seabees showed up and started clearing out the relatively level fields to the west of the village, it all but confirmed it. Oliver's eyes followed the sound of the incoming, and he could count over a dozen CH-53s coming in over the hills. He picked up his pace and jogged to the clearing.

He'd been scoping out the Vulture Nest since the beginning and knew where the operations building was. He entered the building and removed his cover. A sergeant behind the desk asked, "What can I do for you, Corporal?"

"What unit is that coming in right now?" asked Oliver.

"What's your need to know?" asked the sergeant.

"Hey, Sergeant"—Oliver looked at his nametape—"Powell, I've got some buddies flying in HMH-461. I'm hoping to catch up, or at least find out if they're still alive."

"That's not exactly regs, but, yeah, that's them coming in. Sit tight, and I'll make a call when they get settled. Who are you looking for?"

"Major Thomas and Captain White," replied Oliver. Powell was visibly surprised. Clearly, he'd expected Oliver to be chasing down a loadmaster or someone from maintenance.

"You better not be screwing with me," said the sergeant. "If I call for the colonel and you just disappear, I'm going to have your ass, Corporal"—he looked at Oliver's name tape—"Oliver. Either way, both Thomas and White are still with us, so you can rest assured on that."

"Colonel?" said Oliver. "I'll be damned."

"I'm watching you," said the sergeant as he made a motion with two fingers pointing first at his own eyes and then at Oliver.

"Got it, Sergeant, I ain't going nowhere." Oliver got comfortable. He knew the drill. He knew the checks that had to be made, and the process for end of mission. He knew it would be anywhere from half an hour to an hour. It could be even longer if they ran into any issues. But he could wait. Another Marine entered the office.

"Oliver?" said Private Peterson. "You in here?"

"Over here, Peterson, what's up?"

"Oh, okay. So… um… Evans sent me over here to find you. He said that if I found you here, he'd talk to Lieutenant Bush about putting you up for desertion."

"What the hell?" asked Oliver.

"Evans said to tell you that he's just kidding, but next time tell him before you go running after your lovebirds."

"Tell Evans that the only lovebird I'm thinking about right now is that sweet, sweet kid sister of his," said Oliver.

"There's no way I'm telling him that," said Peterson.

"If you don't," replied Oliver, "I'll have no choice but to PT you into oblivion."

"Yes, Corporal," replied the dismal messenger as he left the building. Oliver smiled. He absolutely hated when NCOs would play these fuck-fuck games with the junior enlisted. But now that he was on the other side, he couldn't figure out how to live life without them.

It was a solid forty-five minutes of waiting before the rear door behind the counter burst open and Lieutenant Colonel Thomas burst through the door.

171

"Holy shit! It's Overdrive!" said Lieutenant Colonel Jason "Ripsaw" Thomas. A smile spread across his face as Oliver cocked his head in confusion.

"Overdrive?" he asked.

"Yeah—damn, we had no idea if we'd ever see you again, especially with how bad y'all got hammered at Wonsan. But Snow and I gave it some thought and if you ever find your way into aviation, we're going to pull every string that we can to get you the call sign Overdrive. You're just too hard a charger for anything else."

"Wow, okay, I appreciate that, but to be honest, my life expectancy isn't exactly in years at this point."

"None of ours is, but we're all rooting for you. Shit, you're a legend in the community."

"Where's Snow?" asked Oliver.

"His bird came down with a fault, and they're troubleshooting it."

"His bird?" asked Oliver.

"Yeah. Oh, wait... did you think we were married or something?" said Ripsaw.

"Well, no, you were just always a team," said Oliver.

"And when I got promoted, Snow got his own chopper. Now he's flying with Quicksilver as his second now."

"Wow, that's really cool," said Oliver.

"And you're a corporal now?" asked Ripsaw.

"Oh yeah," said Oliver, "I'd rather be a PFC, just keeping my head down, but here we are."

"I don't believe that for a second," said Ripsaw. "You're Overdrive—you're the hardest charger in the herd."

"From your lips to Major North's ear," said Oliver, shaking his head.

"Don't think I won't say something," replied Ripsaw. "Listen, if you're not on duty, come on over to the Nest tonight and say hi to Snow and the crew."

"I'll take you up on that, sir. I've got a hard-charging lance corporal who owes me a favor and wouldn't mind having me owe him one for a change."

"All right," said Ripsaw. "I've got formation and debrief. Stop by around twenty hundred, we'll be shootin' the shit by then."

"Roger that, Maj—Colonel," said Oliver, offering his hand. Rip shook it and headed out of the building.

"Well, I'll be damned, Overdrive, you weren't full of shit," said Sergeant Powell. "Tell you what, if you stop by here on your way to the party, I'll hook you up with three bottles of Beam."

"No offense, but you don't seem like the gift-giving type," said Oliver.

"Ha," laughed the sergeant. "It ain't a gift. It's an 'I'll scratch your back, you scratch mine.' I could use a good word with the officers. I'm in the doghouse for some... never mind, that's not important. The point is, I wouldn't be on desk duty if I wasn't, and since everyone seems to love you, I bet your word might be a real help."

"You got it, Sergeant. I won't find a better deal tonight; I know that much." The men shook hands and Oliver went back to his unit to arrange for his absence.

An hour later, Oliver had arranged for Lance Corporal Miller to take his watch, and he slipped out to the Vulture Nest. The operations building was dark, but nonetheless, he tried the door. It was open.

"Overdrive?" asked Powell from behind the desk. It was hard to make him out in the darkness.

"Hey, Sergeant Powell," said Oliver, "What's with all the cloak-and-dagger business?"

"This plan only works if nobody knows that I was a part of it," replied Powell.

"I get that, that makes sense," said Oliver. "And I feel like I'm stealing from you, man, so here, I've got the April 1980 issue of *Hustler* magazine for you. It's got an article on the Three Mile Island disaster."

"Oh yeah, I'll be sure to read that," said Powell. "I really appreciate you doing that for me. Really, man, thanks."

"Don't even think about it twice," said Oliver. "But... those bottles of Beam?" Powell produced them from behind the desk as he took the magazine.

"Pleasure doing business with you, Corporal," said Powell.

"Right back at ya," replied Oliver, who discreetly slipped back out of the building and headed over to the Nest.

The scene was almost surreal. At the entrance to the helicopter landing area, there was a bonfire. They were far enough away from the aircraft not to create a danger but close enough that the Sea Stallions

173

could be seen as eerie apparitions in the flickering flame and smoke. The song "In America" by the Charlie Daniels Band played on a portable radio, Marines singing along. The song was over a year old, but the irresistible patriotism behind it had pushed it back out onto the radio rotation.

With these three bottles of bourbon in hand, he approached the fire.

"Who the fuck is this?" asked a belligerent Marine.

"You lost, buddy?" asked another, clearly drunk.

"Oh shit," said a third, "you found my missing whiskey." The third Marine reached clumsily at Oliver, who took a step back to watch the man fall on his face.

"Sorry, fellas," said Oliver, "this is a special delivery for Colonel Thomas." All of the formerly surly Marines suddenly regained their wits.

"Yeah, so…," the first Marine stalled. "Colonel Thomas is over there, next to the radio." He pointed in the direction.

"Thanks, man," replied Oliver. "Here." He handed the Marine a bottle of bourbon. "Don't ever let them say that Overdrive isn't kind and sharing." The Marines graciously received the bounty of whiskey, and Oliver thought that there was little likelihood that they would remember any of this in the morning.

He walked over to Ripsaw and handed him a bottle. "Welcome to Sangsong, Ripsaw, I sincerely hope you enjoy your stay."

"Damn," said Ripsaw, "you really know how to make an entrance. Check it out, Snow, it's Overdrive."

"Dear Lord," said Snow, "I didn't think I'd ever see you again."

"Don't worry, Captain," replied Oliver, "I have one for you too." And he handed over his last bottle of bourbon.

"Haha, this is déjà vu all over again." Snow turned to the rest of the crowd. "Did I ever tell you guys about the time Overdrive tried to bribe me and Rip with two bottles of bootleg rum in order to let him do the prefight checks on the Stallion?" A chorus of laughs and cheers erupted from the assembled Marines.

"To be fair," said Oliver, "you only took one bottle, so I think it was a great deal."

"Yeah, and we didn't have to preflight the chopper, *and* we got some booze."

"Hey," said Rip, "when everyone walks away from a deal feeling that they 'won,' then it's a great. deal. Besides, I'm pretty sure that Overdrive here is the only grunt in the Corps to preflight a Stallion for a combat mission." There were more cheers.

"Overdrive!" shouted the crowd as they raised their beers.

Oliver leaned in to ask Ripsaw, "What the hell is going on, sir? This is a bit much."

"I told you," said Ripsaw, "you're a legend. You're 'The Little Engine that Could' but in jarhead form."

"I'm not sure how to feel about that," replied Oliver.

"Bask in the light, my young corporal. Nights like tonight don't really happen in the real world. Just here on the crazy train."

"Amen, Rip," said Oliver.

"Somebody beer this man!" said Snow. A lance corporal appeared next to Oliver and handed him a Coors.

"You got here late," said Ripsaw, "so you're gonna have to chug that one."

"I'll do you one better," said Oliver, drawing his Ka-Bar. He stabbed the bottom of the can and jerked his knife to the right, creating a nice hole.

The crowd began chanting, "Shotgun! Shotgun!" Oliver resheathed his knife, looked at Ripsaw and said, "To the Iron Horse!" Placing the freshly cut hole over his mouth, he popped his head back, cracked open the top of the can, and gulped the beer as it rushed out of the can and straight into his belly. Within seconds, he crushed the can in his hand and tossed it into the fire.

"Overdrive!" shouted the assembled Marines.

Chapter 16

13 October
Texas Air National Guard
Ellington Air Force Base

Captain George "Nomad" Bush sat at the table with his sectionmates. They were wearing their full flight suits, sitting on alert. Major Ross "Gadget" Welch had started the betting. He tossed in a red five-dollar chip. Betting moved to Captain Mike "Weezer" Olson. Weezer looked at his cards and called the bet with a red chip of his one. Nomad didn't have to look at his cards. He knew where he stood and raised another five. The bet then turned to First Lieutenant Gregory "Speedy" Gonzalez.

"No way, Nomad," said Speedy. "They don't pay me enough to keep losing to you." He tossed his cards to the center of the table, folding. Gadget and Weezer both called.

"I'll take three," said Gadget, and Speedy handed him the cards.

"Same," said Weezer. Nomad studied the man's face as he looked at his cards and caught the hint of a smile. Just under the surface, barely perceptible.

"I just need two, thank you, Speedy," said Nomad. In reality, he could have used three cards. He was sitting with a pair of kings and some garbage. But after Wheeler's show of confidence, he thought his best bet would be to rattle him a bit. Between Speedy dropping out and Nomad keeping three cards, he thought he had a good chance to bluff his way through this round. Weezer knew Nomad well enough to understand that he wouldn't be reaching for a straight or a flush. He had to believe that Nomad was sitting on a three of a kind.

Betting was again with Gadget. He tossed his cards to the center of the table.

"Thanks a lot, Speedy."

Weezer tossed in another red chip. The squadron had a general rule of never lowering your second bet. It showed weakness. Nomad never broke eye contact with Weezer as he laid down a twenty-dollar bet. He needed enough to show Weezer that he was confident, but not so much that it looked like he was buying the pot.

"To hell with you, Nomad," said Weezer. "I know you, and you're bluffing." Weezer called Nomad's bluff. "Whatta ya got?" he asked.

"Two pair, kings and fours," said Nomad, fearing how bad he was about to lose.

"Dammit!" groaned Weezer, flipping his cards over, revealing a pair of jacks. Nomad had to laugh at his luck. He was, in fact, bluffing. He had very low confidence in his kings. But Weezer just wasn't good at cards and had no idea. Nomad pulled in all the chips, and Speedy collected the cards to deal out the next hand.

"How'd you get so good at cards?" asked Speedy.

"Oh, I got my bachelor's degree in poker from Yale, and my master's from Harvard," said Nomad, laughing.

Gadget was dealing out cards for the next hand when a barking alarm came from the speakers. There were three long gongs followed by, "Scramble, scramble, scramble!" The four men dropped their cards and ran for the door. Nomad sprinted for his Delta Dart. As he entered the hangar, he could see the main doors opening so that the aircraft could exit. He scrambled up the ladder and slid into his seat. An airman inspected the cockpit to ensure that everything was secure, then saluted the captain, said, "Good luck, sir!" and removed the ladder from the side of the cockpit.

With the scramble underway, Nomad pushed his throttle forward and taxied out of the hangar. In his experience, the "ready five" aircraft, the ones that were on the tarmac waiting to launch, would be routed towards the threat, and the alert would stand down before Nomad got off the ground... but not today. He flipped on his squadron frequency and asked, "Hey, Gadget, any idea what we're looking at?"

"It ain't the typical Badger patrol," said Gadget. "We've got a major force bearing down on Houston. The radar boys' best guess is eight Badgers with twelve Fishbeds in support. This could be the end of Cuba as we know it." The idea that Cuba would attack the United States had been absurd, right up to the point when Nicaragua had taken out an entire Marine amphibious unit a year ago. From that point forward, every possible threat was treated as the worst-case scenario.

"Roger that, sir," replied Nomad. "What are our priorities?"

"As per our standing orders, we are to engage the bombers. Do not engage any fighters." The orders were expected, but they also felt like something of a death sentence. The fighters would be gunning for the interceptors, and unless the enemy were complete idiots, the fighters would sweep in front of the bombers. At the same time, Nomad understood that their AIM-4 missiles were mostly ineffective against fighter aircraft, especially head-on.

"Lonestar Three, this is Kelly Control. Upon launch, come to heading one-three-five, angels forty-five." This was a typical intercept approach for the stray Cuban Badgers. This was a routine "Badger hunt," except that this time there were many more contacts. It was as if the past year had been a rehearsal for today's attack. Nomad continued to taxi to his launch point. By now he figured that there was no way his flight would be stood down, and for the first time in a year, he felt that he might fire a missile in anger.

The four F-106 Delta Darts of Charlie Flight 182nd Fighter Intercept Squadron of the Texas Air National Guard hurtled down the runway and climbed into the air to protect the Republic of Texas from a hostile threat.

"Lonestar Three to Alpha flight," said Gadget. "Engage data link." Nomad turned the knob of his display auto-mode switch to "Data Link Max Range." This would allow the powerful ground radars to send targeting information directly to the individual interceptors. It had the added benefit of allowing the interceptors to keep their own radars cold and preventing the Cubans from detecting them. Nomad checked his data link gauges. The enemy bearing and altitude were displayed on a compass and dial. The distance dial showed the enemy at one hundred thirty miles out.

"Lonestar Three, this is Kelly Control."

"Copy, Kelly Control."

"Lonestar Three, have your flight set their radars to standby mode."

"Understood, Kelly Control, setting radars to standby mode," replied Gadget, who then passed the word. "All right, boys, set your radars to standby. It sounds like we're going to announce our presence."

"That's wonderful," said Weezer, "we have the advantage of surprise, and we're just going to give it away well outside of our engagement range."

"Take it easy, Wheezy," said Gadget. "Do you really want a shooting war with Cuba?"

"I'm not sure they're going to give us a choice," replied Weezer.

"But we're giving them a choice. Once they know we're here, we're going to… communicate our intent and give them a chance to make a decision that will turn this thing off."

"And what is our intent?" asked Weezer.

"We just got orders to fire at the bombers as soon as they are in range."

"Wait, what?" asked Nomad, saying out loud what everyone was thinking. "We're well outside of the twelve-nautical-mile limit."

"That's right," said Gadget. "This comes from the peanut farmer himself, boys. This is provocation enough. We're not going to fall for the same trap twice. They got away with this during the sucker punch, and they won't get away with it again."

"Amen," said Speedy. Nomad checked range to target. They were closing inside of fifty miles. They would need to get within six miles to launch their AIM-4 Falcon missiles. Then they would have to wait—Nomad crunched the numbers in his head—around seven seconds before launching his second missile. God only knew where those MiGs would be by then. *Probably on my ass*, thought Nomad.

The four Delta Darts streaked into the heavens behind the four that were on Alert Five. Eight Texan interceptors stood between Houston and a potential nuclear annihilation.

"Lonestar Three, Kelly Control. Engage targeting radars."

"Engage radars, roger," said Gadget, then to his men, "All right, boys, light 'em up." Nomad reached over with his left hand and flipped the switch to engage his radar. He looked at the radar scope at the top of the central control panel on the integrated flight information system. He could see the enemy contacts ahead of him. The smaller contacts were now pulling ahead of the larger contacts they were escorting.

"Hostile aircraft, this is a United States interceptor. You are hereby ordered to come to a course of zero-nine-zero and turn away from the United States," said Gadget.

"American interceptor," replied one of the Cubans, "you have no authority over a sovereign aircraft flying over international waters."

"Hostile Cuban aircraft," replied Gadget, "if you do not come to a course of zero-nine-zero, we will engage and destroy your aircraft. Do not test our resolve. You will find it unyielding."

179

"Hostile American interceptor, I repeat, you have no authority over a sovereign aircraft flying over international waters."

"Our missiles are going to kill you, regardless of authority," said Gadget. There was no response. The two formations closed on one another. Nomad checked the range. They were crossing to within twenty miles of the bombers. He scanned the sky and noticed dots in the distance that had to be the fighters. *This is getting hairy*, thought Nomad.

"Lonestar Three to Alpha flight. Open weapons bay."

"Opening the weapons bay," said Nomad, with Weezer and Speedy confirming the order. Nomad watched as the MiG-21s flew right over his flight. He cranked his neck to track them as they passed through the merge, and as expected, he watched them grab altitude, no doubt with the intention to reverse and get behind the interceptors.

"Get ready for fire," said Gadget. Sweat beaded on Nomad's forehead. "Crossing ten miles. This is it, boys."

"They're breaking off!" said Kelly Control. "Hold your fire."

Nomad's heart was slowing. He wondered if the Cubans knew how close they had come to dying today. Just as his pulse was nearing normal, he was shocked as a MiG-21 shot over his left wing with its afterburner blasting.

"Hasta la vista, Yankees," said the Cuban from earlier. "Maybe next time you die."
****

15 October 1981
3/6 Marines
Sangsong, North Korea

Corporal Phil Oliver waited for Captain Beck to get this show on the road. The captain stood in front of the company formation, with a large map to his right. The weather was turning cold and there was a definite bite in the breeze that blew through the company.

"There's no beating around the bush," said Captain Beck, then, looking at Second Platoon's commander, added, "No pun intended, Lieutenant." There were a few laughs. "These orders are a challenge. I'm saying this as an officer who has fought with you in Iran, and all the way across Nicaragua. I was on Hill 183 when we lost so many of our brothers. Those challenges served to prepare us for this." He paused to let the gravity of the situation sink in. Oliver stood at parade rest, wondering if the captain was just trying to scare the company out of the complacency that so much time away from the fighting might have engendered.

"In an effort to accelerate our advance towards Pyongyang, we will be making an assault on Kuan-ni, here." He pointed to a spot on the map.

That can't be right, thought Oliver. Kaun-ni was a solid sixteen miles behind the current front line. In these mountains, the rate of advance was as slow as a Ford Pinto climbing Pike's Peak. The mountains meant that tanks were nearly useless. This was a grunt war.

"Once we take Kaun-ni," continued the captain, "we will hold it to allow the Seabees to build a landing strip. That landing strip will then allow us to receive resupply and reinforcements."

If we don't all die before this harebrained scheme even gets started, thought Oliver. *This is insane.*

"By taking this strategic point, we will help relieve the embattled 2nd Marine Regiment, who is tied up in the assault on Yangdok. From Kaun-ni, we will be able to disrupt the supply chain to the North Korean forces. This will bottle the enemy up in a siege at Yangdok. We will be in an excellent place to hold our position until we're relieved by follow-on forces once Yangdok is secured. At that point, we will have advanced fifteen miles and eliminated a significant enemy force in the process. I've briefed the platoon commanders, and they'll pass on your individual assignments." With that, Beck dismissed the formation.

"He has got to be shitting us," said Evans as he approached Oliver.

"What are you talking about?" asked Oliver. "This is nothing at all like the movie *A Bridge Too Far*—I don't know why you're so worried."

"What the hell are you talking about?" asked Evans.

"Never mind," replied Oliver. "But yeah, this is some bullshit. We're going to be lucky if we're still alive to hear the first C-130 landing. We have to take the village. Sure, no problem, I guess. Then we have to hold it from a Rico force with much shorter supply lines and much closer to enemy air support. What could possibly go wrong?"

The Marines met up at the platoon berthing tent.

As they approached, Marines were running to and from. The pass-down of the word was causing every Marine to wrap up local business and get ready to move out. Whatever deals were made had to be concluded before the orders to move out came down. Oliver pulled open the tent flap and was surprised that the LT had beaten them to the berthing.

"Glad you ladies could make it," said Lieutenant Bush with a wink. "I was just telling the men that we've been picked to test the resolve of our enemy. You've heard the broad strokes from the captain, so what do you think the greatest risks and challenges will be?" This was something that Oliver really liked about Bush. He knew that the men he led had a lot more experience than he did, and he tried to learn from them.

"Taking the most obvious, sir," said Gunny Page, "it won't take the Ricos long to figure out what we're up to, and when they do, they'll be able to drop a ton of arty right on top of us. That valley is really closed off... it's going to be a hell storm."

"I'm not sure that'll be a problem at the start," said Sergeant Evans. "They won't want to level the whole valley until they withdraw whatever forces they have in there."

"Yeah," agreed Oliver, "and I'm not sure that even Kim Il Sung is going to wipe out that many of his own civilians."

"I don't know about that," said Ban, his Australian accent standing out in the crowd. All eyes shifted to him. "Don't ever suggest that something is too cruel for Kim Il Sung. He would sacrifice that entire village if he believed he was under direct threat."

"Okay," said Bush, "let's say that everyone's right. Arty is a huge risk here, but maybe not immediately. How do we address that?" The Marines considered the question for a fraction of a second.

"We dig in as soon as we can," said Evans. "We hit the ground, secure the LZ, and then we start getting a trench line going."

"Bigger picture," said Gunny, "we'll want to try and round up any kind of equipment that could help us out."

"Like what?" asked Oliver.

"Like plows, and tractors and shit. We don't know how long we're going to have before the shells start falling, and anything that can speed this up would be great."

"That all makes sense," said Bush. "We'll know more when we're on the ground, but this gives me something to work with. I'll leave y'all to get ready. I'll see you out on the flight line."

Oliver went to his rack and grabbed his ALICE pack. He verified that he had his entrenching tool and opened the meal ready to eat, or MRE, that was in there. Ever since the new rations had replaced the older meal, combat individual, or MCI, Oliver had started to eat his peanut butter while riding into battle. Whether he was in the back of a truck or, like today, in the hold of a chopper, he could enjoy a nice high-protein snack. The older rations were more of a pain in the ass. You'd have to use the little P-38 can opener, and if you dropped that bastard in the back of the helo, you weren't getting it back and now you were stuck with a partway open can that was probably going to make a mess in your pack.

"Hey, Evans," said Oliver, "I kind of miss the old peanut butter."

"What the hell are you talking about?" asked Evans.

"The new MREs," said Oliver, "they're great. But I kind of miss the old peanut butter."

"Dude, that stuff tasted like the metal can it came in," said Evans.

"Maybe that's what I miss?" replied Oliver.

"Whatever, man. Just get your head right for the fight."

An hour and a half later, the fourteen CH-53s of Marine Heavy Helicopter Squadron 461 carried the shooters from 3/6 Marines over the hills and mountains of central North Korea. The flight would only take around ten minutes to cover the thirty miles between Sangsong and Kaun-ni. That didn't leave a lot of time to enjoy his peanut butter, but Oliver didn't rush it.

He thought back to his first taste of combat: Eagle Claw. He remembered flying for what seemed like eternity on the way to Desert One. He smiled, thinking about Corporal Lionel Mack, his team leader back then. Mack had died on the second night of the mission. And then there was Benny Estrada. Oliver and Estrada had been inseparable when they were stationed together. Benny hadn't bought it like Mack, but he had taken a bullet that night. *And what the hell ever happened to Sergeant Rodriguez?* he wondered.

"Hey, Peterson," shouted Oliver. The private looked at him. "What do you call a CH-53 that's not leaking oil?"

The kid just stared back blankly.

"Empty!" shouted several of the other Marines that had heard the exchange. Peterson cracked a smile at that.

"Five minutes," announced the pilot, getting everyone focused again.

"Just stick with the team," said Oliver, "and do what we tell you, Peterson. We've all been here before, and we're going to get a chance to do it again." Oliver ran his hands along the pockets and pouches of his uniform, giving himself one last check. He was satisfied that nothing had disappeared during the flight.

The helo pitched and dropped before climbing again. Oliver had been through this enough times to know that there was some enemy fire coming in. He didn't let it bother him. If the helo got shot down, then he'd worry about it. Until then, it was just wasted energy. The helo flared, and the ramp dropped.

"Go! Go! Go!" shouted the crew chief, and the Marines ran down the ramp. Peterson tripped at the bottom of the ramp and took out five of the Marines closest to him.

"Shit, Peterson, what the fuck?"

"Nice dancing, dickweed." The anonymous jeers came rolling in while the men desperately tried to get their feet under them again to get away from the helo and find cover. Kilo Company's LZ was to the north of the town. They were shielded from the main body of defenders by a sizable mountain. This gave them the opportunity to get better organized before the fighting really started. Oliver ran for his rally point and could see Fourth Platoon setting up their mortars.

"Let's go, you idiots!" shouted Evans as Second Squad started climbing the steep hill. Oliver's biggest fear on this operation was that the hill would be occupied. The fact that Kaun-ni was ten miles south of the main supply lines running through Besso-ri meant that there would be less reason for the North Koreans to heavily defend it. This, in turn, meant that there would be less reason to dig in deep on the hill that Oliver was scrambling up.

Second Squad would position themselves along the northeast face at just under the ridgeline, then wait for the signal to advance. Oliver thought back to the briefing, when he'd looked at the map and realized they'd be climbing eighty meters in elevation through thick forest to get to their staging point. At the time, it had looked formidable. In reality it was hell. It started out as a fairly gentle slope but quickly became brutally steep. *I think Command overestimated our ability to climb with all this gear*, thought Oliver as he leaned forward and used his hands to help him get traction and move up the hill.

It took Second Squad half an hour to make the climb. They had been allotted twenty minutes. Corporal Murphy from headquarters squad ran up the line, grasping for breath.

"We're going to hold here for ten minutes. The entire assault is sitting tight right now. Get your men ready and catch your breath." Murph was about to depart when Oliver grabbed him by the arm.

"Peterson!" Said Oliver, calling his junior-most Marine.

"Corporal?" replied Peterson.

"Run up the hill and tell Third Squad that we're holding for five minutes then be ready to move."

"Roger that," said Peterson, who took over for Murphy as the relay man.

"Get a drink of water, Murph," said Oliver, handing over his canteen.

"Oh damn, Oliver, thanks for that," replied the corporal, taking a knee, then raising the canteen to his lips for a quick drink.

"I just hope Peterson gets back before the balloon goes up," said Oliver. "You goin' in with us, then?"

"I suppose so," said Murphy. "I was supposed to go in with Third Squad, but that was just because they were my last stop." Oliver took back his canteen and took a pull. Sweat beaded down his forehead, and he wiped it away with his sleeve.

"This op is going to lead the Marine Corps to add 'Vertical Running' to the PFT."

"I'm going to puke just thinking about it," replied Murphy. Peterson scrambled back to his position in the line.

"Good work, Private," said Oliver. "I'll make sure Sergeant Evans hears about it."

"This is it, Second Squad," said Sergeant Evans, "we're advancing to contact with the enemy. Move out!" As one, Second Squad rose and advanced. There was another ten yards of uphill climb, and Oliver's hamstrings stung at the effort. But then they were over the crest

185

and coming down the other side. Running down the west face of the hill was every bit as difficult as climbing up the east face. The difference was that if you lost control, you were liable to tumble for twenty yards or more before you could get your balance.

"Oh, shit!" Lance Corporal Palmer cried out as he lost his balance and rolled down the hill.

"Mouthwash down!" said Oliver, trying to insert some levity into the situation. *A cheetah can't change his spots*, he thought, remembering how, once upon a time, such a smart-ass comment would have been expected from Private First Class Oliver. Oliver saw mortar rounds exploding in the village below. Fourth Platoon certainly had spotters on the hill, dialing in fire wherever they could find troop concentrations. The only surprise for Oliver was how few shells were coming down. He'd expected a much bigger weight of fire.

As they got to the bottom of the hill, they were struggling to find targets.

"Someone, find me something to shoot at," shouted a voice Oliver didn't recognize. Second Squad took up positions in a row of buildings on the east side of the village and held position, waiting for orders. They'd secured their objective without so much as a round fired.

"Palmer's pride was our only casualty," said Oliver when Evans asked him about his team. It was another half an hour before anyone decided to clue them in.

"This place is more or less abandoned," said Lieutenant Bush. "The heavy weapons guys dropped what they suspected to be the municipal police and government buildings, and Lima Company captured about a squad of Rico regulars who had no idea what hit them."

"Okay, let's get to digging, then," said Gunny Page.

"Amen," agreed Bush. Now that 3/6 Marines had taken Kaun-ni, they would have to fight to keep it.

Chapter 17

16 October 1981
White House
Situation Room
Washington, D.C.

"We knew this was a possibility," said Zbigniew Brzezinski.

"Well, yes, Zbig," replied President Carter, "but we anticipated some warning here. Why didn't the Chinese tell us that this was their breaking point?"

"Firstly," said Brzezinski, "I imagine they wanted to preserve the element of surprise. Secondly, perhaps they felt that after 1950, this was self-evident."

"I hardly find that credible," said Secretary of State Jeane Kirkpatrick. "I think it's more likely that with the war in Europe going poorly for us, they've decided they wanted to be on the 'winning' side."

"I don't like the sound of that," said President Carter.

"It's a bleak pronouncement," said Kirkpatrick, "but that doesn't make it untrue. By interceding in the Korean conflict, they can signal their alignment with their communist brothers while only engaging in a land war near their own borders. They don't have to cross an ocean or a continent. Just the Yalu River."

"I think Jeane has it right," said Brzezinski.

"What are we looking at?" asked Carter, looking to the Chairman of the Joint Chiefs of Staff, General David C. Jones.

"Well, sir, it looks like the Chinese have dedicated 16th Army Group. The best we can tell is that they intend to throw as many men into the meat grinder as they need to in order to turn the war effort around for the DPRK."

"Can we overcome this new threat?" asked the President.

"Of course," said General Jones. "But we're going to need help."

"Japan?" asked Carter.

"Yes," replied Jones. "Without Japan's equipment and manpower, we're going to get tied up in the mountains of Korea. The 2nd Marine Division is going to be in severe peril because the North Koreans will no longer need to pull troops from the South to fight the

Marines. That means there's no relief heding their way. We have a massive advantage in technology, and heavy weapons, but the Chinese can just keep coming for them."

"What about the efforts in the South?" asked Carter. "Will China commit troops to fight in South Korea?"

"They have no reason not to," said Brzezinski. "They've already stabbed us in the back—there's no reason they wouldn't twist the knife."

"Will Japan commit?" asked Carter.

"It's more a question of *can* Japan commit," replied Kirkpatrick. "Their constitution of 1947 prohibits the use of their Self-Defense Forces in offensive military operations. So, according to the current law, they can't attack China unless and until China attacks them."

"Are you saying," asked Carter, "they'll have to change their constitution in order to join the fight?"

"There's the possibility that the Prime Minister could argue that the threat posed by China is an imminent threat and the only way Japan can preserve their sovereignty is to act preemptively. But that's a flimsy argument and there's no way it will get past their courts."

"So we're back to needing a constitutional amendment?" asked President Carter.

"I'm sorry," interrupted Brzezinski, "have we asked Prime Minister Suzuki if he's willing to do this?" There was a silence at the table, broken after a few seconds by Kirkpatrick.

"It hardly matters, Zbig. We need them to commit, so we need to know what we're looking at to make that happen. Of course, if you have some kind of secret plan to defeat the Chinese, I would hope you could mention it now."

"Let's not lose our heads," said Carter, trying to bring the temperature down a tick. "You're both right. Yes, we need a plan for bringing this up to Prime Minister Suzuki. But the generals are going to need to know how long this is going to take, if it does work, so that they can plan. Jeane, please continue."

"It could happen fairly quickly. But it's anyone's guess how this will play out. The Prime Minister would need to convene an extraordinary session of the Diet, then propose the amendment. That could be voted on within the week. The real issue is the next step. There must be a national referendum on the amendment. This will take some time, and we are by no means a lock to win this referendum."

"Yeah," replied Jones, "we did kind of take the fight out of them back in 1945." The joke hung in the air and died without laughter.

"We have news in the Atlantic Theater as well," said CIA Director Stansfield Turner, trying "The CIA conducted a study back in July, trying to understand how *Kirov* was able to re-arm so quickly. One of the possibilities is that they had a resupply station in a friendly African port."

"Kirov is no longer a problem," said Brzezinski.

"No, but in response the Agency put some resources on the ground in some African ports, including Luanda, Angola. The tactic paid off. We have solid intel that Minskiy Komsomolets, the Soviet submarine that sank the *Eisenhower*, is re-arming at Luanda." There was a pause, as the room digested the information.

"Minskiy Komsomolets is much more dangerous than *Kirov* was," said Admiral Thomas B. Hayward, the Chief of Naval Operations. "We need to hunt her down and sink her."

"What do you need for that?" asked President Carter.

"I have everything I need. I will work with Stan to get our forces in the best position to make this attack. Once that submarine is neutralized, I'll sleep better at night."

"Okay," said President Carter, "we know what's ahead of us, and we know what we need to do. Thank you all," said Carter, shuffling papers to see what was next.

****

17 October 1981
3/6 Marines
Kaun-ni, North Korea

Corporal Oliver hit the dirt with the spade and pushed hard with his foot. The digging wasn't easy, but fortunately, he'd procured himself a proper shovel.

"Hey, Corporal," said Private Peterson, also digging, "why did you call Palmer 'Mouthwash' the other day?"

"I could tell you, Pete, but then I'd have to kill you." The younger Marine was clearly saddened by this. "And don't get it in your head to call him that yourself. Palmer'll kick your ass, and I'll just watch." Oliver furrowed his brow as he considered that there were only about four men in the squad that had been there on the night Palmer had immortalized himself. Some had rotated out, but most were casualties. It had been a hell of a war so far. As if on cue, Palmer came over with another shovel to join in.

"How's it hanging, Oliver?" asked Palmer.

"A little to the left," replied Oliver.

"Did you hear," asked Palmer, "that the LT and Gunny stole an excavator from Regimental HQ last night and dug out a decent platoon bunker?"

"You just hearing about this?" asked Oliver. "I was all over that story from the start."

"Yeah, right," said Palmer. "Like you were there."

"I was," replied Oliver. "Shit, it was my idea. And it was a good one. But Gunny and the LT were on board, and they took the blame."

"Seriously? I should have figured," said Palmer. "How'd you come up with the idea?"

"It was simple. I saw the dinosaur—that's what we called it— being used by the major, and thought, *I bet that thing's just going to be sitting there tonight.* Now, the LT said that we should file a request to use it." Palmer nodded. "But I suggested that if we went to the captain with this idea, and he went to the major, well, that would probably mean that someone *else* would get the dinosaur. See, once we pointed out that it was available, someone with more seniority would slide right in and take it."

"That's pretty ballsy," said Palmer, chucking another shovelful of dirt out of the trench and onto the pile above.

"Yeah, it was pretty hairy," said Oliver. "Gunny has some interesting skills he picked up in his youth. The LT and I took the muffler off one of those shitty Chinese jeep things, then we drove over to the motor pool, and wouldn't you know it, somehow a Ka-Bar had punched a hole in one of our tires." Palmer smiled, imagining the situation.

"Then Lieutenant Bush starts ripping my ass, hard." Oliver laughed, thinking about it. "It was all, 'What the hell are you doing, Corporal? How did you *not* see the obstruction in the road? You are the dumbest son of a bitch I've ever had as a driver.' It was quite the scene."

"Sounds like it," agreed Palmer.

"So," continued Oliver, "the noise from the jeep was ridiculous. And with the LT screaming at me, of *course* all eyes were on us. While we were making a scene, Gunny slipped into the dinosaur and drove it out in a wide circle. By the time I'd changed the tire, Gunny was halfway back to the platoon, and nobody was the wiser."

"Until Gunny took it back," said Palmer.

"Yeah, that was the plan. We knew that we couldn't provide a diversion for the return, so Gunny and the LT took it back with an apology for the theatrics."

"They getting into any trouble?" asked Palmer.

"I have no idea. Whatever happens to the LT will probably stay with the zeros," said Oliver, referring to the officers. "I imagine Gunny will know, and he'll probably tell me... and if—" Oliver was cut off by the sounds of sirens.

"Shit, get small!" he said.

He, Peterson, and Palmer ran to the south, where the trench was already deeper. Shells whistled through the air. Before the first shells landed, the thunder of 155mm howitzers indicated that 2/10 Marines were already sending counterbattery shells in reply. The barrage didn't last long, and it wasn't as close to Oliver as many previous barrages he'd been through. He shuddered as he remembered Hill 183. As silence fell again on Kaun-ni, the Marines returned to digging.

"Hey, Oliver," said Peterson, "whattaya think about the Chinese entering the war?"

"I think those rat bastard ChiComs showed us who they really are," said Oliver. "They pretend to be our friends, and then as soon as we need their help, *bam!*"—he slapped his hands together to emphasize the point—"they go back to their Soviet masters."

"You think they're going to be tougher than the Ricos?" asked Peterson.

"Don't matter how tough you are when some 5.56 knocks yer brains out the back of your head." The two other Marines nodded in agreement as they shoveled, digging the ever-deepening trench.

Chapter 18

18 October 1981
US Navy Recruit Training Center
Orlando, Florida

Nancy Rodriguez stood in the position of parade rest just past the entrance of her barracks. It was dark and quiet. While it was true that Nancy would rather be asleep, she really didn't mind the midwatch. There wasn't much chance of anyone hassling you, and you had time to think. That was something that she had taken for granted before the Navy had sent her to boot camp. The days were constant movement. There was physical training, classroom training, and damage control training. If someone screwed up bad enough, there was physical training *during* classroom training. They had an hour between the end of the day and lights out, which she used for letter writing. So, the midwatch was about the only time she could just think.

She wondered what it had been like for Carlos when he'd gone through Marine Corps boot camp. From everything she'd heard, that was way tougher than what she was enduring. Nevertheless, she would have to compare notes with him the next time she saw him. The thought made her smile. She was making a lot of assumptions with that one. Would he survive the war? Would she? Would he want to reminisce about their time in the service? *A girl can hope*, she thought.

"Rodriguez," grunted a five-foot-tall fireplug of a woman wearing a Navy uniform. Nancy jumped. "What is your Fourth General Order?"

"Ma'am, my Fourth General Order is: To repeat all calls from posts more distant from the guardhouse or the quarterdeck than my own."

"Who said, 'Surrender? I have not yet begun to fight'?"

"Ma'am, John Paul Jones said, 'Surrender? I have not yet begun to fight.'"

"Wrong!" said the fireplug. "He said 'I have not yet begun to fight.' I added the 'Surrender?'... Drop!"

Nancy fell on the ground with her hands in front of her.

"Down."

Nancy lowered her body until her arms were parallel to the floor. "Up." Nancy extended her elbows pushing herself back up. This was repeated again and again. Mercifully, after twenty push-ups, the company commander was satisfied.

"Who's your relief?"

"Atkins, ma'am," said Nancy, thankful that she'd checked the duty roster when she'd first started her fire and security watch.

"Go get her and tell her to report to me." Nancy was amazed. She'd just been relieved early... or had she? She walked over to Atkins's rack and shook her foot.

"Wha—?"

"Atkins, it's your watch."

"Nah... it's..." She rolled away from Nancy.

"Atkins, Muncie is here, and she's waiting on us." It was as if by magic. Atkins leapt from her rack and began straightening out the uniform she'd been sleeping in. Petty Officer Vera Greene had picked up the nickname "Muncie" among her recruits due to her short stature and tenacity. Within the first week of this training company, someone had compared her to Chuck Muncie, the fullback for the Super Bowl champion San Diego Chargers.

With Atkins getting it together, Nancy realized the trap that had been set. She practically ran away from Atkins to get ahead of her, then took her position at the entrance and stood at parade rest.

"What are you doing here, Rodriguez?" asked Petty Officer Greene.

"Ma'am, I haven't been properly relieved." Nancy wondered if Muncie had smiled, but she'd never know because she was staring straight ahead.

Atkins approached, and when she was near enough, she said, "Sentry for the barracks watch, you are relieved."

"Drop!" said Greene. Both Nancy and Atkins fell forward into the position. "Rodriguez, recover." Nancy was surprised but quickly stood and returned to parade rest. She stood and stared straight ahead as Muncie counted out twenty-five push-ups before ordering Atkins back to her feet. "Details matter, Atkins. Details are the difference between life and death in this business. I am not fucking with you because I think it's fun. I'm not making this shit up as I go. This is important. And if you can't figure out something as simple as how to relieve the fire and security watch, how can the Navy expect you to figure out something more important, like how to connect a high-priority communications network when lives are on the line?"

"I'm sorry, ma'am," said Atkins, choking back tears of frustration.

"Sorry doesn't fix a damn thing, Atkins. Rodriguez, how do you properly relieve the fire and security watch?"

"Ma'am," said Nancy, "The relieving watch will review the watch log, then request and receive a pass down from the standing watch. Upon completion of the pass down, the relieving watch will say 'Sentry of the Barracks watch, you are relieved."

"That's correct. You stand relieved, Seaman Recruit Rodriguez." Relief washed over Nancy as she made her way back to her rack and tucked herself in for the next few hours before morning colors, when the whole crazy routine started over.

****

22 October 1981
21st Special Air Service Regiment
South of Lübeck, West Germany

Anika Kirsch was aware of the effect she had on Trooper Trevor Pearce. Every time he came her way, she caught those extra glances in her direction. It was tempting to throw all caution to the wind—she *was* lonely after losing her husband, and in a war, one never knew how long one's life expectancy was. But she had something that she wanted from Trevor, and Anika was aware that if she gave in, she would lose any leverage, any hold she had on him.

Klaus Köstler was a special kind of evil, and Anika was determined to stop him. She could not fathom the moral depths that one would have to stoop to in order to rationalize using children as mules for explosives. There were even rumors of them scouting Soviet positions, and even standing watch for resistance meetings. If any of them were ever caught, they would be shot, or possibly killed in a less merciful way and turned into an example.

Anika had been pregnant once, although she had lost the baby. She had always wanted to be a mother, and if she couldn't hold her own child, then by God, she was going to fight for these children in whatever way possible.

Knock, knock.

Anika rushed to the door. She let in Trevor and his supervisor, whom she only knew as Willis. As Trevor passed her, she casually touched his biceps and watched as the hair on the back of his neck stood on end.

Good, she thought. *Maybe he will be ready to listen to me.*

She led the men to the kitchen, where they all sat, as had become their habit. Anika pulled an envelope out of her bag and slid it across the table to Willis, who opened the envelope and flipped through the pages. Once he reached the end, he started over again on the first page. Anika had come to expect this. She once asked him about the habit, and Willis had told her that the first pass was just to make sure that nothing appeared to be missing, while the second pass was to understand the nature of his orders.

As Willis read through the paperwork, Anika reached out with her foot and gave Trevor's leg a light stroke as she shot him a coy look. She could tell that he fully understood what was happening. She'd overheard others in his unit joke about his prewar exploits.

"Pearce," said Willis, "read this." He handed over the orders. Anika watched and waited for her opportunity. She couldn't let Trevor leave without making her impassioned plea. When Pearce finished his reading, he handed the orders back to Willis.

"Sounds straightforward enough," said Pearce. They never mentioned the contents of the envelope to Anika. On the one hand, Willis's German language skills weren't the best at conveying abstract ideas. On the other hand, Anika's inability to speak English extinguished any chance that there could be a leak. But Pearce was fluent in German. In fact, he was fluent in the local dialect. So he had to be careful to keep her out of the secrets. She couldn't accidentally let slip information that she didn't know. And if, God forbid, the Soviets ever captured her, this way she wouldn't be of much use beyond cracking down on the local resistance unit.

"If you don't mind, ma'am," said Willis, standing, "do you mind if I use *der Wasserklosett*?" This was her chance.

"Of course, Mr. Willis, it's down the hall to the left.

195

As soon as Willis was out of the room, Anika placed her hand on Trevor's shoulder. "Trevor, we really must stop Klaus Köstler. I saw it in your eyes the last time we spoke about it. I know that you agree with me."

Trevor sighed. "Anika…I think he is a horrible monster, but the last time I so much as criticized Klaus to his face, Willis told me in no uncertain terms that I was to stand down."

"Why?" she asked. "I don't understand how your people can tolerate what he's doing."

"Willis doesn't want to burn our contact," Trevor explained. "We're totally exposed out here, and we need every ally we can find."

Anika shook her head. She had to try something else.

"Why did you join the Army?" she asked,

"Well…to protect my country," he replied.

"Do the children of my country not deserve your protection as well? You are fighting in Germany. You are fighting *for* Germany. Protecting those children is the right thing to do." She paused, getting ready to really pour it on. "Listen, in my country, there have been some terrible atrocities in our history. Surely you know about the Jews that were killed in gas chambers or worked to death in camps?"

Trevor nodded.

"Imagine if someone had the opportunity to sabotage one of those gas chambers and decided not to."

The sentence hung there uncomfortably. Finally, Trevor said, "But, Anika, what do you want me to do—assassinate him?"

"Heavens no, *mein Schatz*," she replied, using a German equivalent of sweetheart. "Men like Klaus respond to power. I think all he really needs is a show of force."

Just then, Willis returned from the restroom. He gave the pair a sideways glance. "Am I breaking something up?" he teased.

Anika and Trevor shifted farther apart from each other. "No," replied Pearce, "Anika was just telling me about the history of the area. Very interesting."

Willis chuckled. "Well, I've seen that playbook before," he replied good-naturedly. "Don't fall for his hallway, Anika."

What the hell? she thought.

"He means *Falle*," corrected Pearce. "Don't fall for my trap." Anika blushed. "Hey now…war matures a man," Trevor replied, standing straighter.

"We'll see," Willis shot back.

As the two of them left, Anika watched, hoping for a sign that her persuasion techniques had been fruitful. Trevor looked back and gave her a slight nod. It was enough.

****

31 October 1981
USS *Coral Sea*
Sea of Japan

Lieutenant Sam "Pharaoh" Bell looked at the bars on his uniform in the mirror of his stateroom. They still felt out of place. Under normal circumstances, he would have needed another six months of time in grade before this promotion, but with the combat losses sustained by the attack squadrons, combat experience meant more than time. The Navy needed lieutenants, and Pharaoh was the closest thing they could find.

He left the head and walked to the ship's chapel. Since the Battle of the Sea of Japan, he'd been spending a lot of time here. He had never been a spiritual man, but with so much death, he had to wonder, *What happens next?* He'd never dwelled on it. Sure, as he got older, he thought he'd wonder. The older you get, the closer you are to your death, so yeah, that just made sense.

But to have death shoved into your face with such vehement force seemed to age him both physically and spiritually. He'd had a lot of death. They'd lost eleven aviators on July 25, including their commanding officer, Commander Clinton "Rerun" Duncan, Lieutenant Will "Heaver" McGuire and Lieutenant Nathan "Scooter" Hayes, Pharaoh's wingman on his first combat mission over Iran so long ago.

"Hey, Heaver," he whispered as he sat in one of the chairs in the dim room. "Remember just before my first combat mission, you told me, 'Don't screw up, or we're both dead?' Man, that scared the shit out of me, but you really got me focused. I always appreciated that. I wish I had been around on the night you earned your call sign. It sounds like it was an incredible party." He looked up at the altar, about to leave, when he remembered, "Oh, they promoted me. I got my bars early." With this addition, Pharaoh surprised himself.

These trips to the chapel were used to try to make sure he didn't forget his dead friends. He wasn't actually talking to them. He didn't think they could hear him. He just wanted the memories preserved so that, one day in the far, far future, he could tell his grandchildren about the men he'd fought with so he could avoid telling them about the horrors of war. So to give Heaver an update about his own life… that really was talking to the dead. He wondered if his time in this place was changing him. *Or maybe living through this war is changing me*, he thought.

He left the chapel and made his way to the ready room. Since the Battle of the Sea of Japan, life had gone back to what he had known from before then: air-to-mud. The Maces had been slipping between SEAD, or Suppression of Enemy Air Defense, and CAS, or close-air support missions. It was grueling work, but nothing like facing the Soviet fleet. He could still remember watching the tracers nearly take off his wing. It chilled his blood to this day.

"So, you decided to show up?" said Commander Gerald "Chops" Armstrong, VA-27's new commanding officer. "You think lieutenants don't have to be on time?" Pharaoh looked at the room. Everyone else was here. He looked at the clock. He was two minutes early for the briefing.

"Wait, what? I've got two minutes to the briefing," protested Pharaoh.

"Five minutes early is ten minutes late," said Lieutenant Carroll "Buzz" Barber. In the squad, Chops had started to bring in the old Vince Lombardi rule of preparation. It was taking Pharaoh some time to adjust.

"All right, gentlemen," said Chops. "Pharaoh, have a seat. Okay, boys, it looks like the jarheads might have bitten off more than they can chew. You've all heard that the Chinese are on their way to save their communist neighbors. There's a reinforced Marine Corps battalion that's about to face the brunt of those ChiComs. It's our belief that most of our missions for the foreseeable future are going to be dedicated to trying to save that battalion." There was some murmuring between the aviators.

"The Chinese are considerably more mechanized than they were the last time we saw this movie," continued Chops, "but they're still largely an infantry force. Our goal today is to eliminate as many of those men as possible. Intel has found troop concentrations thirty-five miles north of Kaun-ni, where the Marines are holding fast. If those Marines are going to have any hope of surviving, we will be going after the ChiCom forces relentlessly. We're going to be strung out and used by the time this is over, gentlemen. I know we're understaffed, and overextended, but this is the mission, and those men need us."

The briefing continued with the specifics of the mission. They'd be carrying the maximum load of six Rockeye II cluster bombs. This was the first time that Pharaoh was concerned about the lack of any Sidewinders. Against the Sandis in Nicaragua, they hadn't had to worry about it at all. Nicaragua didn't have an air force to speak of. Even the past few months off the coast of Korea, they'd rarely run into fighters. But this... they would be going *deep* into North Korean territory, and they would be fighting the Chinese, whose air force, while technologically unimpressive, was still plenty enough to shoot down a defenseless Corsair.

"Fortunately," said Chops, "we'll have Intruder support to seek out targets and assign aircraft for strikes." Pharaoh knew that the Intruder's target recognition and attack radar provided them with a significant advantage that the A-7 couldn't compete with.

"In order for our strike to have the maximum impact," said Chops, "we will need to stay on top of this mission tasking. I don't need any of you blowing up some dumb ChiCom column that some other unit is assigned to kill. Remember, this isn't just about killing the enemy. If we want to beat back the Chinese, we're going to have to do it *efficiently*. There are just too many of them for us to mess around. You men got that?"

The question came out a bit more hostile than Pharaoh had expected. That helped it land all the more. *That's doubly true for me*, thought Pharaoh. If he screwed this up, he wouldn't just be wasting his own ordnance; as the section leader, he'd be wasting another Corsair's ordnance as well.

"All right," concluded Chops, "that's what we've got. Those Marines are depending on us, and we *cannot* let them down. Dismissed." The Royal Maces cleared out and headed to maintenance control, then to the lockers to suit up.

As he was gearing up for the mission, it occurred to Pharaoh, *I wonder what Scooter thinks about the Chinese Air Force?* And then he remembered that Scooter was dead and didn't have an opinion.

"Hey, Rhodie," said Pharaoh. "You think the ChiComs are going to contest the air?"

"If they ever will," replied Rhodie, "it'll be a day like today. It's early in the fight and they want to preserve as much of that ground force as they can."

"That's great news," said Pharaoh with a sigh.

"Cheer up, Pharaoh," said Lieutenant Junior Grade Dustin "Oxy" Turner. "It'll be a great chance to make new friends." That elicited laughs from several of the aviators. Oxy was a nugget who had endeared himself to the unit with his reckless bravado when talking before the mission and his cool calculation when in the air. That was how he'd earned his call sign. It was short for Oxymoron. There was quite a debate in the squadron about which half of the word they'd use. At the end of the day, he was well liked, and "Oxy" stuck.

"I'll be sure to introduce you," said Pharaoh, trying to keep up his end as he patted himself down to check for all of his bits and pieces before heading to the hangar deck to check out his ride.

The thrill of the launch wasn't quite the same as it was the first time Pharaoh had launched into combat, but it never ceased to be magical. He'd never not smile while feeling the g-forces pushing him back into his seat as he was flung down the steel deck and then into the air. *If they could bottle this feeling, there'd be an awful lot of addicts out there*, thought Pharaoh. He climbed into the air and headed out to his rendezvous point. He looked over his right shoulder and saw Oxy sitting pretty off his right wing. This wasn't Pharaoh's first time as section leader, but it was his first time as *Lieutenant* Bell. That held some significance to him.

Once formed up, the Maces grabbed altitude on a heading of two-nine-five. They overflew the allied-controlled territory at high altitude to conserve fuel. They would orbit at their rally point and wait for orders. At some point, the A-6E Intruder would call in and order up a strike. Depending on the target and priority, Chops would then detail his men to swoop in and blow shit up.

The three-hundred-and-twenty-mile flight was blissfully boring. It occurred to Pharaoh that he might never complain about being bored ever again. At the rally point, he flew lazy eights with Oxy on his wing. The enemy columns were outside of the town of Yongha. While there were some serious hills around the town, in this mountainous terrain, it was damn near a prairie. That was the reason that Command had picked this as the best spot to hammer them.

"Charger Actual, this is Battery Three."

"Battery Three, Charger Actual. Send it." Battery Three relayed a target area to Chops, who dispatched Buzz and his wingman to deal with it. Pharaoh kept station in the formation and cut his lazy eights. The pattern repeated again and again. Pharaoh was on the verge of napping when the call came in.

"Charger Six, stand by for tasking." Chops then relayed the nine-line brief to give Pharaoh the details of the target.

"Roger that, sir. Engaging," replied Pharoah. "Oxy, on me."

"Roger that, Pharaoh, I've got ya."

The two Corsairs peeled off from the formation and dove for the deck as they came to a course of two-nine-five.

"All right, Oxy," said Pharaoh, "just follow me in. We'll grab some alt just before we drop. Pickle your eggs five seconds after I call it. We'll light up these ChiCom assholes." Pharaoh didn't want Oxy to be dropping on more or less the exact same real estate that he was.

"Roger that, Pharaoh. Delay five seconds." The hills had funneled the enemy columns into narrow target areas. VA-27 was punishing them for the choice to try to move through the rough terrain, even though there was nothing the Chinese could do about it.

Pharaoh flew the hills at near-treetop level. As he came to the last hills between himself and his target, he pulled back on the stick.

"Climbing, get ready to drop," said Pharoah.

"I'm with you," replied Oxy. The two Corsairs popped up over the hill, and Pharaoh could see the masses of enemy men and vehicles in the valleys below.

He extended past the poor defenseless infantry beneath him. Once he'd crossed enough distance, he cranked his stick and rudder to flip his Corsair on its back and pulled back on the stick to dive towards the ground. As he came out of his dive, he could see the column of Chinese infantry heading south. They were defenseless. Just men in trucks.

Bad luck for you, thought Pharaoh as he lined up the enemy on his display.

"Dropping," said Pharaoh, starting Oxy's timer. Pharaoh's Rockeye II cluster bombs fell towards the unprotected convoy. Pharaoh knew that before the Rockeyes struck the target, they would burst open, ejecting hundreds of bomblets. The bomblets would then tear through everything on the ground. The destruction would be massive.

"Dropping," said Oxy as the two Corsairs dropped as low as Pharaoh dared and they darted away to the south, running for home. "That was intense."

"Just think of all the Marines you may have just saved," said Pharaoh. "They're going to need a lot more runs just like that."

Chapter 19

1 November 1981
Minskiy Komsomolets
Mid-Atlantic Ocean

The menacing shape of *Minskiy Komsomolets* slid through the depths, hunting. By this point in the war, she was the most feared submarine in the world. Sailors kept watch throughout the Atlantic, praying that they wouldn't cross paths with him. In the opening days of the war, Captain of the First Rank Dmitriy Usatov had been named Hero of the Soviet Union for *Minskiy Komsomolets*'s sinking of the American aircraft carrier USS *Eisenhower*.

His second cruise was less glamorous but still of vital importance, as he'd managed to sink seven cargo vessels bringing supplies for the NATO forces in Germany and the Low Countries. As soon as he fired his missiles, Usatov made for the port of Luanda, Angola, for resupply. It took more time than he would have liked to load the missiles. The port facility had never seen anything like *Minskiy Komsomolets*. They had been trained to load the P-700 missiles onto *Kirov*. However, with *Kirov* resting on the bottom of the Atlantic, *Minskiy Komsomolets* was the only ship in the fleet that could fire the state-of-the-art antiship missiles.

Usatov looked at his orders again and frowned.

"What is troubling you, Captain?" asked Maksim Yermolovo, the ship's political officer.

"I fear that we may be the victims of our own success," replied Usatov. "Read this." He handed the orders to Yermolovo. The *politruk* read the orders and raised his eyebrows.

"I suppose you should be flattered," he said, handing the orders back to the captain.

"In the abstract, you're absolutely right. The idea that the enemy has decided that we are dangerous enough to send a task force to kill us is a bit flattering. But forgive me for not celebrating."

"You are forgiven," joked Yermolovo in a rare show of humanity. "On the other hand, we have always been hunted, and we have always approached significant enemy targets. Therefore, I don't know how much this increases the danger."

"There is definitely an element of truth to that," said Usatov. "But when we sank *Eisenhower*, it was an ambush. Command knew when and where she was, and we had those old submarines to sacrifice to establish our radar contact. Now the board is cleared, and those older submarines have almost all been destroyed. There won't be any sacrificing a pawn to take out a rook at this point in the game."

"That's true. However, I, and Stavka, have every confidence in your being able to employ a new and different gambit to bring down more enemy shipping."

"I appreciate your support, comrade," said Usatov, rereading his orders and the warning about the extra attention being paid to his ship. "In the end, I believe that you are correct. The fact that they are hunting us simply means that we won't have to seek them out. They will come to us."

"And when they do, comrade Captain, we will make them pay for having the insolence to attack the mighty *Minskiy Komsomolets*!"
****

USS *Arkansas*

Commander Earl Brown, the executive officer of USS *Arkansas*, had his coffee in hand and was making his way from the wardroom to the bridge. As he entered the bridge, he was greeted with the latest scuttlebutt.

"Did you hear that one of our passengers has been restricted to his stateroom?" asked Lieutenant Stephen Jenkins, the ship's intelligence officer and the current officer of the deck.

"No, I hadn't," replied Commander Brown. "What's that all about?"

"Seasickness," laughed Jenkins. "Poor guy had only ever been out on a carrier and had never hit any rough seas. He was puking his guts out. The docs had to sedate him and send him to bed."

"That's really too bad," responded Brown. "Don't get me wrong, it's funny as hell," he chuckled, "but I want those guys to finish their job and get the hell out of here. A warship in battle is no place for civilians, no matter how smart they might be." During their last stop in Norfolk, the Navy had brought on engineers from McDonnell Douglas to install a pair of Harpoon missile quad launchers and a pair of Phalanx close-in weapons system, or CIWS, guns. The Phalanx was a pain-free installation. The Harpoons, on the other hand, were another issue altogether.

The missiles hadn't been operational when the orders to find and sink the Soviet Oscar-class submarine had come down. The solution was to send a team of five experts out with the cruiser. They'd be transported to *America* by helicopter when done, then flown back to land as soon as it was practical.

"Yeah, I can see your point," said Jenkins. "I don't know why they sent them out with us in the first place. It's not like we're going to find a surface ship to shoot at."

"You don't think Ivan's going to come steaming out of Severomorsk to save their submarine?" Jenkins looked to his XO to see if he was being serious. Brown grinned at him and the two laughed. "Now," continued Brown, "if they could get us an ASROC with that kind of range, I'd be interested."

"Yeah, though, from what I hear, the Oscar can hit us from way beyond the range of the Harpoon."

"Well, sure," said Brown, "but they won't be able to detect us from those ranges. Even though the missile has the range, the detection systems don't."

"Tell that to the *Ike*," said Jenkins.

"Yeah, or *Virginia*," Brown agreed, citing the lead ship of the *Arkansas* class that had been sunk on the same day.
****

USS *America*
Ship's Signal Exploitation Space

Lieutenant JG Richard Rogers stared at the copy of *Jane's Fighting Ships* in his lap.

"This could be more vague," he said to his boss, the ship's intelligence officer, Lieutenant Edward Diaz.

"What do you expect? It's a brand-new ship." Rogers looked at the page again. There was just a simple drawing of the profile of a submarine, not even a single photograph. The printed details were just as slim. Lots of question marks. Diaz reached over Rogers's shoulder and pointed to the words "Missiles: 24 tubes for SS-N-19."

"That's all we need to know at this point. Don't forget, the last time we tangled with those missiles was when *Kirov* attacked the convoy. Those twenty missiles took out nine ships. The extra four missiles that the Oscar carries would likely equal another one or two losses." Rogers nodded. "And the worst of it for us personally is that we'll be the targets of the next batch. When *Kirov* attacked, it was clear that she was after the cargo ships. If she'd wanted to sink us, we would have been sunk. This time, we're going to be the primary target. If Oscar gets a clean shot off on us, you'd better pray that we can get off the ship before she's a crab mansion on the bottom of the Atlantic Ocean."

"Sheesh," replied Rogers, "thanks for the motivational speech."

"If your survival instinct can't motivate you, I don't know what to tell you, Rogers. But hey, if you want some more motivation, think about this: any submarine that we run into on this mission will likely be a newer, more capable platform than our first crossing." Rogers tilted his head, not quite following the logic. "During our first crossing, what did Ivan throw in our way?"

"Well…" Rogers thought. "There was the Charlie II, then a Victor." He paused as his eyebrows went up with understanding. "Then a Juliet and a Zulu."

"That's right," said Diaz. "How many operational Juliets or Zulus do you think have survived this far into the war?"

"That would be zero, sir," replied Rogers.

"That's exactly my point. We're going to be fighting off Victors and Charlies, and this Oscar."

"That makes sense. I guess it's a good thing that we got a lot of great experience engaging the old rust buckets at the start of the war."

"Are you trying to look on the good side?" asked Diaz.

"That is my nature, sir," replied Rogers.

"Okay, then let me rain some more pessimism on you. Any sub skipper that we run into will have survived ten months of World War III in the Atlantic. We aren't the only ones who have learned from experience these past months. Anyone who's still in the game is varsity. All the JV guys are crab food."

"Iron sharpeneth iron," said Rogers with a grin. There was a knock at the secured door to the SSES.

"Were you expecting company?" asked Diaz.

"Yeah," said Rogers, crossing the room to receive their visitor. "I ordered some Chinese food." He opened the door and saw a young yeoman standing in the passageway.

"Skipper wants to see Lieutenant Diaz in the CIC." Diaz peeked out from behind a rack of radio equipment.

"Any reason I can't bring Rogers?" asked Diaz. The seaman seemed confused.

"He didn't say anything about Rogers, sir." Diaz turned to Rogers.

"Come along—if they don't want you there, they'll let you know."

"You think they've got a contact?" asked Rogers as they briskly walked towards the CIC.

"I have no idea," replied Diaz. "Maybe they just want to have a cup of coffee with their favorite intel weenies." They reached the entrance of the CIC and left the well-lit passageway and entered the darkened electronic world of the combat information center.

"Diaz, over here." Rogers looked and saw Captain Darin Ingram, *America*'s commanding officer, motioning for them to join him. "I see you brought your protégé along."

"Yes, sir," replied Diaz. "I've got to get him trained up so I can get promoted out of this billet." The captain laughed at that. "What do you need, sir?"

"Well, we were just trying to understand our enemy and thought you might be able to lend us your expertise."

"Sure thing, Skipper. What are you looking for?"

"Basically," said Ingram, "if you were driving this Oscar, how would you go about it? How would you conduct the operation?"

"Yes, sir, I understand the assignment," said Diaz. "I'd start out by looking at my motivations. What's my mission?" The officers around him nodded. "The last time out, I attacked a convoy. With the war going so well for my land forces, that's still my number one mission. To sink shipping."

"I don't disagree," said Ingram. "However, I will point out that her first shots fired in anger sank *Mighty Ike*."

"Yes, sir, that's right. I've put a lot of thought into that attack, and the more I think about it, the more I'm convinced that that was a play that was set in motion at the start of the war."

"What leads you to that position?" asked Ingram.

"Well, sir, at the start of the war, they knew exactly where *Ike* was. It wouldn't take an intel genius to determine that she would head south to clear the shipping lanes, or to go after *Kirov*."

"How would they know that *Kirov* was detected?" asked an ensign that Rogers didn't recognize.

"They didn't keep it a secret," replied Diaz. "They announced in the United Nations that they were sending *Kirov* to the Persian Gulf. Then they sank the USS *Philadelphia*, so we had a pretty good idea where she was at."

"Oh," replied the ensign sheepishly.

"But getting back to the setup," continued Diaz, "all I would need to do is have several older missile boats arranged in a picket. Given the range of the SS-N-19, which we now estimate to be in excess of three hundred miles, Oscar could sit in the middle with a huge net. As soon as one of the picket boats picked up *Ike*, she'd fire a salvo at the fleet, causing *Ike*'s task force to radiate their air-defense radars and announce her position to Oscar, who sent everything she had, and it was more than enough."

"I see," replied Ingram. "You weren't lying when you said you'd put a lot of thought into this. So you don't think that they would send Oscar out on an anticarrier strike without knowing where a carrier is?"

"That's my thought," agreed Diaz. "On the other hand, if I, as the captain of the Oscar, stumbled into a carrier battle group, I imagine my orders would insist that I sink it. But those wouldn't be my primary orders. I wouldn't be hunting for carriers."

"That's good news for us, I guess," said Ingram. "Anything to add, Rogers?"

"Wait, what? I mean, no, sir," replied Rogers, surprised at the question and angry with himself for missing the opportunity to wow the CO with his knowledge.

"So, if we think Oscar is hunting convoys, I suggest we do everything we can to look like a convoy." Again, there were nods around the room. "Ops"—he looked at the operations officer, Commander Ryan Schultz—"I need you to get on the STU and get with your counterparts to put together a dispersion that looks like a small convoy. And make sure everyone knows that we need some sloppy station keeping to really sell the rouse."

"Understood, sir," replied Schultz.

"Anything else, Diaz?" asked the captain, turning back to Diaz.

"Only this, sir," replied Diaz. "This all relies on the fact that the Oscar doesn't know we're gunning for her. I don't quite know what to do with this, but if she's onto us, she'll be hunting specifically for us, and our looser formation will put us at risk."

"What's more likely, in your opinion? That they are aware of our orders, or that they are not?"

"Actually, sir," replied Diaz, "I find it highly unlikely that they would have any idea that we're coming for them."

"Agreed. In the end, whether they think they're shooting at a convoy or a task force, nothing changes. In fact, if they know we're after them, it should speed things up. I, for one, would like to complete this mission and move on to the next." The captain collected his thoughts before continuing.

"Right now, all we know is that this Oscar left Angola two days ago. We have P-3 Orions detached to Augusto Severo International Airport in Brazil, and the Brits have a squadron of Nimrod MR2 at Lungi International Airport in Sierra Leone. They can cover a lot of water on either side of the Atlantic. We're going to cruise down the middle, trying our damnedest to look like a Brazil-bound convoy. We need to sprint to this point here." He indicated a point on the map that was in the middle of the empty Atlantic Ocean.

"From there, we will make a solid eight to twelve knots on a course for the Brazilian city of Belém. If we don't make contact on the way in, we'll depart and try our luck as a northbound convoy. Any questions?"

"Begging your pardon, sir," said Rogers.

"Spit it out, son," replied the captain.

"Wouldn't it give us a better chance of success to have the P-3s hammering their patrol areas with active buoys, to discourage the Oscar from moving too close to the shore, then our task force moves from the northwest to the southeast down the middle of the lane."

The skipper considered the proposal.

"What about your boss's analysis? Do you disagree?" asked Captain Ingram.

"Oh, no, sir. Diaz has it right," said Rogers. "The Oscar is definitely hunting convoys. It's just that the odds of encountering the enemy in this vast space"—he waved his hand at the map—"would be greatly improved if we were running head-on at each other instead of at a ninety-degree angle."

"I see your point," said Ingram. "But I think you're forgetting that if the analysis is correct, the Oscar may well be sitting in the shipping lane waiting for us."

"Yes, that could be true," said Rogers, feeling like he was getting in over his head and suddenly wishing he'd kept his mouth shut. "But I don't think the Oscar will really care about a convoy going to or coming from Brazil. This is the most advanced naval asset the Soviets have. She'll be heading to the North Atlantic to take out an American or Canadian convoy."

"What do you think, Ops?"

"The kid's got a point. If we want to try the convoy ruse, it'd be a lot more convincing in the North Atlantic, but we'd be giving up our main strategic advantage here."

"And what's that?" blurted the unknown ensign. Rogers didn't think he could see anyone actually roll their eyes, but he wouldn't have been surprised.

"That we know exactly where the Oscar was two days ago," said Commander Schultz. "We know where she is, and we know, more or less, where she's going. There's"—he looked at the map and worked the lats and longs—"seventeen hundred miles between Sierra Leone and Brazil. That's a lot of territory, but that's nothing compared to the thirty-five hundred miles between New York and Brest. If we miss her transiting now, this job will be infinitely more difficult."

"Rogers's plan," said Diaz, "also has the benefit that it will allow us to travel along our course at the speed of our choosing. We can run as fast or slow as we want, without having to sprint to our starting point, then making like a convoy. We can send *Arkansas* and her screening force ahead while our helicopters and S-3s can expand the search even further out, all searching along the reciprocal bearing of the Oscar's most likely course."

"All right," said Ingram, "I'm not a hundred percent sold, but you've given me something to think about." He gave Rogers an approving nod before turning back to Schultz. "I guess you can belay that order to turn us into a convoy."

****

1 November 1981
21st Special Air Service Regiment
South of Lübeck, West Germany

Trooper Trevor Pearce had been mulling over his conversation with Anika since they'd last spoken. The words had played over and over in his head. She was right—those kids deserved his protection. He couldn't condone the use of children, especially orphans who didn't have anyone to speak and act on their behalf, as soldiers in the war. Klaus and his supporters would argue that they weren't really soldiers. But Pearce knew exactly where this would lead.

He came to feel that if he didn't intercede on behalf of these innocent children, he would bear the responsibility for whatever happened to them. The weight of that responsibility was too heavy to ignore.

Pearce didn't say anything to Willis. If he knew what Pearce had planned, this little escapade would be over before it started.

The potential consequences of defying Corporal Willis could be severe. On the other hand, they were at war, deep behind enemy lines. Pearce doubted that anything too serious would happen to him. Hopefully.

This was one of those rare missions that had the entire cell out at the same time. With the NATO forces pushing hard against the Soviets farther to the west in Germany, the resistance was stepping up their attacks in the rear areas. Pearce's cell was emptying their weapons caches. Everything except their personal weapons was being transferred to the partisan forces.

Pearce's heart jumped when the stable came into view. It had been months since he'd been here and two weeks since he'd decided that he had to do something drastic the next time he came. They used the same caution and procedures to scout out the stable and ensure that nothing was out of place. Under the cover of darkness, they crossed the road and Reeves stepped to the door and knocked.

"*Was brauchst du?*" asked a familiar voice on the other side.

211

"*Ich brauche Frösche*," replied Pearce. The door opened a crack, and Pearce kicked it in, knocking Klaus backward. Before the man could regain his footing, Pearce laid into him with a fierce right cross to his jaw, sending him to the ground. There were several German men in the room, and as they made their move towards the fracas, Pearce heard the charging of three SLRs charging, and his mates shouting at the Germans in English to get on the ground.

Pearce followed up his punch by grabbing the man by his shirt collar and slamming the back of his head into the ground. Once he felt he'd gotten the man's full attention, he slapped him in the face with his open palm to make sure he understood who was in control here. Pearce then grabbed Klaus's head in both of his hands and brought the man's ear to his lips.

"If I ever lay eyes on ya, or even catch wind of ya usin' kids in this bleedin' war effort, I'll fuckin' do ya in, mate. Proper slow and painful like."

"Pearce, at ease," shouted Willis. "Trooper, get off the man, or I'll have Coop put a beatin' on ya."

Pearce spat on Klaus and dropped his head before he stood up and walked back to his team.

As Pearce crossed paths with Willis, Willis pulled him close and whispered, "I've a right to properly kick your arse, trooper. But before that, I need you to translate this for me. I don't want to spend any more time here than we need to." With that, the two British soldiers turned to the shocked German assemblage.

"Who, besides this man, is in charge?" asked Willis, pointing at Klaus.

Pearce translated, for the Corporal. The Germans looked at each other before one stepped forward.

"We are bringing you the last of our explosives and weapons. We need to make as much noise as we can to help our brothers in the west so that they can liberate your nation."

Pearce again translated, but at the end of the statement he added, in German, "If anyone asks, your friend their got his ass kicked by a Soviet. Do you understand?"

"*Ja, ich verstehe*," replied the German man.

"*Sehr gut*," said Pearce. Willis turned to leave, and Pearce followed.

212

"The bloody hell was that?" asked Coop as soon as they were clear and in the forest, heading back to the shelter.

"Shut it," said Willis, "we'll deal with this complete shambles when we get home."

Home, thought Pearce. *That's what it has become. What utter madness.* The trek back to the MEXE shelter was long and silent. But when they eventually made sure the area was secure and began meal preparation, Willis got everyone's attention.

"Trooper Pearce, are you retarded?"

"No, Corporal, I'm not retarded."

"Then why did you act so retarded during this mission?"

"Corporal, someone had to do something. I couldn't just stand by and watch as he got those kids killed."

"Wait, what?" asked Will Gardner, who hadn't said anything other than "Get on the ground" since the mission had begun.

"Yeah," said Pearce before he was cut off by Willis.

"Pearce is correct. That sack of shit was using kids as runners and… frankly, soldiers. There have even been rumors that he's been buggering some of the ones he most fancies."

"What the 'ell?" asked Pearce, horrified.

"Stand down, Trooper," sighed Willis. "Look, you're right. He needs to be stopped. He's an absolute monster. My orders were that he was hands-off and protected. We were not to intercede. This was an internal German issue, and we were to stay out of it. But I think you're right. We were the only people who could protect those children. There is no German government to deal with the issue. The Soviets sincerely don't care, and the provisional government is toothless. The only Germans that could stop this are the ones in the resistance, and apparently there weren't enough of them to override what was happening."

"That's not entirely true," said Pearce. "Anika Kirsch was doing everything that she could to put an end to it."

"Ahhh, I get it now," said Willis. "She bats those pretty brown eyes at you, and you decide that one German bird has more authority than the entire British Army?" Pearce looked away. "Well, to be honest, lads, I think that Pearce telling them that the Soviets beat up their friend and not him while glaring at them menacingly will probably keep this from going up our chain of command." Pearce cocked his head at that. "My German isn't that bad—I picked up the drift of your 'translation.'"

"Thanks, Corp—"

"Shut it," repeated Willis. "You broke discipline, and you disobeyed orders. In any other circumstances, you'd be duly punished. Don't go thinkin' that you have some kind of moral authority that puts you above my authority. This ain't the church."

"Understood, Corporal," replied Pearce, thinking of Anika, and how crazy the events of the past few weeks had been.

****

1 November 1981
Minskiy Komsomolets
Midatlantic Ocean

"What do you think the Americans will do?" asked Maks Yermolovo, the *politruk* on *Minskiy Komsomolets*.

"Actually," replied Captain Usatov, "I'd be curious what you think the Americans will do."

Yermolovo thought for a moment.

"I believe that they will place their fleet in a central location, so that if we are detected, they will be in position to intercept us. I believe that this strategy would require them to remain fairly far north, so that we don't get past them."

"That's an interesting strategy," replied Usatov, "and one that merits consideration. However, let me first ask, why? What causes you to think that they will use this... let's call it a 'protecting the goal' strategy"? Sports metaphors didn't come naturally to Usatov, but he understood hockey well enough and knew that Yermolovo was a fan.

"Because, in their hearts, the Americans are cowards. They have an advantage in numbers, so they will hide out and not put themselves in danger until they are sure that they can put that force into action where they can most safely deal with the dangers. The capitalists are cowards, but don't let them fool you, they are shrewd cowards."

"I see," replied Usatov, "but I disagree." Yermolovo looked disappointed. "The Americans can be shrewd, this is true. However, I don't think they are cowards. In fact, quite the opposite; I believe they have bravado to the point of hubris. They have spent the last thirty-six years believing in their invulnerability, and while their Army is learning the truth of that lie, their Navy has yet to. But we will teach them that lesson."

"And how do you plan to do that?" asked Yermolovo.

"The Yankee brutes will come straight for us. They know our starting point and can fairly assume that they know more or less where we are going."

Yermolovo looked alarmed.

"In such a case," he said, "shouldn't we change our plans and put ourselves in a position that they won't be expecting?"

"I applaud your tactical thinking," replied Usatov, "but that sounds almost like cowardice."

Yermolovo turned red. Usatov didn't think it was cowardice at all; he was just rebuking his *politruk* for his assumptions about the American enemy.

"It is no such thing," protested Yermolovo. "It's merely sound strategic thinking."

"Tactical," corrected Usatov. "And, yes, that could be a sound plan, but what's worth more, evading the enemy, or knowing when and where they will be at the time of our engagement?" Yermolovo looked confused. "If we evade the enemy, how will we engage him?"

"We won't," replied Yermolovo. "We will slip past his grasp and hunt for convoys in the Atlantic."

"I see," said Usatov. "Your reading of our orders is that the convoys are our priority?"

"Absolutely."

"I disagree. Protecting the ship is the first priority. And we will not be able to engage any convoys with this task force breathing down our necks."

"With respect, Captain Usatov, the orders specify that our mission is to engage the convoys to reduce the supply of men and materials delivered to NATO forces."

"Then why did they include the threat of the American task force?" asked Usatov.

"To provide you with information that you needed to use in order to execute your mission of engaging the convoys," said Yermolovo.

"No, there's more to it than that. They know that for the first time since the start of the war, we know when and where an American aircraft carrier will be, and our mission is to sink it."

"Again, sir, with respect," pleaded Yermolovo, "if Stavka wanted us to hunt the carrier, they would have explicitly called for it in their orders."

"You are very well versed in the needs of the Party, Yermolovo. But you have a lot to learn about military operations. I appreciate that the subtleties are lost on you, but that's not your fault. You're a *politruk* and not a line officer."

"What are your intentions, Captain?" asked Yermolovo.

"We will proceed exactly as the Americans would expect. Directly northwest through the Atlantic Ocean, making for the shipping lanes between Texas and France. However, we'll be doing it fully aware that we will have a mighty Yankee aircraft carrier in our way. Once we detect them, we will send them to the bottom of the Ocean, then return to *Zapadnaya Litsa* to reload our missiles."

"That's a sound plan," replied Yermolovo. Usatov shot him a look of mild scorn to let him know that he wasn't particularly interested in what the *politruk* thought of his plans.
****

Yermolovo excused himself and made his way back to his stateroom. He'd been serving with Captain Usatov for over a year now. The past ten months had been in combat. Like many *politruks*, he didn't have a great relationship with the commanding officer of the submarine he was stationed on. There was almost always a power struggle that erupted when the CO had a man on board who fell outside of the direct chain of command.

Even so, Yermolovo had done everything in his power to ingratiate himself to the captain. In Yermolovo's opinion, it had been effective. Usatov was much more open and accepting of Yermolovo than he had been at the start of their service together. Though it would be a stretch to call Usatov a friend, it wasn't unreasonable to call him a fond acquaintance.

That was right up to the point where the Americans had sent an aircraft carrier to assassinate the man. In some ways, Yermolovo believed that Usatov was listening to his own echo. His success in combat was leading him to believe that he had all the answers. It wasn't just Yermolovo either. Usatov had been going against the advice of trusted officers. From what Yermolovo could tell, Usatov's success in combat and the added pressure of this latest mission were compromising his ability to command the ship.

It didn't bother Yermolovo that Usatov had a different plan for engaging the Americans. Yermolovo was no naval tactician. It was Usatov's reading of the orders. There was nothing in them to indicate that they were to engage the American aircraft carrier. It was just a warning that they needed to be aware of an extra challenge to their mission. Yermolovo was reminded of Rodion Raskolnikov, the protagonist of the novel *Crime and Punishment*. His pride was going to be his downfall. And the only one who could see it was Yermolovo. Now he had to figure out how to stop it.

The Soviet government was, by its nature, paranoid. *No. Not paranoid*, thought Yermolovo. *The selfish grabbing capitalists are everywhere, and always trying to stop the advancement of the proletariat. That's not paranoia, that's a fact.* That was the reason that the *politruks* were assigned to ships like *Minskiy Komsomolets*. These vessels were prizes to be stolen or sabotaged by capitalist infiltrators. That was why the *politruk* was there. To find these plots before they could succeed and report them to their bosses in Moscow.

Yermolovo didn't think that Captain Usatov was a capitalist sympathizer or anything like that. However, the same communication channels that could be used to alert leadership of officers with insufficient loyalty to the Party could inform that same leadership of a man at the breaking point who was disregarding orders and putting his crew in danger.

When Yermolovo reached his stateroom, he opened his locker and removed a simple notebook. He flipped to the first blank page and began writing a message. He read it over, then closed the book. He took ten deep breaths, then opened the notebook again and reread his message. With this ritual performed, he ripped the page from the notebook and placed it in his pocket.

Once he had his message written out, he checked his watch and headed to the enlisted galley. Outside the galley, he flagged a sailor who was heading in and told him that there was an important matter that needed attention.

"Captain Usatov requires the presence of Senior Seaman Solomonov in the communications room. Please pass along this message. This is classified, do not read it!" The message was clear to the poor sailor who took the paper. No enlisted sailor would ever think to confront a *politruk*. With the message delivered, Yermolovo headed to the radio shack to wait for Senior Seaman Solomonov.

"Captain Lieutenant Yermolovo, this is unexpected," whispered Solomonov.

"I need that message sent out as quickly as possible," said Yermolovo. "Our very lives depend on it."
****

USS *America*
Ship's Signal Exploitation Space

"I remember before the war," said Lieutenant JG Rogers. "I remember a sensation that I used to get during deployments. It was as though I had nothing to do, and it agitated me. It was an existential crisis."

"Boredom, Rogers," said Lieutenant Diaz, "You're thinking of boredom.'"

"Yes! That's it," laughed Rogers, impressed that Diaz had figured out his game so quickly. Diaz was a hell of an analyst, and word games were no different than sorting out data and turning it into actionable intelligence. "I used to get bored out here. But now, boredom is a luxury. I can't even remember the last time I was bored."

"Maybe if you hadn't been so bored you would have gotten your surface warfare quals done more quickly." That earned Diaz a look. Rogers lowered his nose and shot daggers at Diaz. "Hey, it's not a lie."

"Be that as it may," said Rogers, "I'm not here to rehash the past. But I was wondering, do we have a count on total Soviet submarines sunk in the Atlantic to date?"

"Nope," replied Diaz. "And it's unlikely that the flags are going to give us that information. They want us on our toes and don't want to give us *any* reason to take our foot off the gas. Nope. As far as Command is concerned, every submarine that was on the board on day one is out there trying to kill us."

"I suppose that makes some sense. But it's still annoying."

"Write your congressman," said Diaz. "Wait, what have we here?" He pointed to the NTDS, which showed the disposition of the carrier task force and her screening surface action group, or SAG. To the southeast of the fleet, Rogers saw what had gotten Diaz's attention. An unknown submarine contact.

"It could be anything," said Rogers.

"I'm not telling you that it's the Oscar," said Diaz, "but it is curiously where we expected to find the Oscar."

"Either way, they're about to end up with a hell of a lot of helos and Vikings swarming all over it. Everyone in the fleet is champing at the bit to get this done and move on to the next mission. Anyhow, I'm just saying, let's not start the celebration early."

"Fair point," said Diaz. The two watched the NTDS as the contact was prosecuted.

"Look at that," said Rogers after about fifteen minutes, "I swear the latest contact shows that it's moving to the southwest."

"These are faint contacts," said Diaz. "You can't really get a fix on them, but I do like that you're going there. What does that mean to you?"

"It could mean one of two things," replied Rogers. "It could mean that the Oscar is zigzagging, or otherwise trying to hide their course."

"Okay, and the other possibility?"

"That it's not the Oscar, and that this submarine is heading in from the northeast."

"Both are plausible," agreed Diaz. "Which do you think it is?"

"I think we have a new player on the field," said Rogers.

"Why?"

"Because the Oscar is an offensive weapon developed to hunt convoys and aircraft carriers," said Rogers. "I just don't think that she'd be lingering around out here. I think that she'd be making her way north at all costs and only doubling back if she was engaged."

"Maybe she is?" said Diaz.

"I thought about that, but we aren't getting a secondary cont—"

"ID is coming in," interrupted Diaz. Both sailors started at the NTDS. The contact was suddenly clear. It was moving at thirty knots when the torpedo appeared on the display.

219

"Not so fast, Ivan," said Rogers, staring at the display. The submarine's speed pushed past thirty-five knots.

"Damn, she's got some shoes," said Diaz. The torpedo was homing, but the target crossed over forty knots.

"Alfa?" asked Rogers.

"I think so," agreed Diaz. "The only other sub that can make that speed is the Papa—"

"And she's been sidelined as far as we know," concluded Rogers.

"Yeah, I mean, I suppose it could be her swan song, but—"

"The odds are better that it's an Alfa," finished Rogers.

"Exactly."

"I think he's going to make it," said Rogers.

"I'll take that action," replied Diaz. "Even odds, twenty bucks."

"You're on," said Rogers. Again, the two intel officers stared at the screen, more engrossed than in a football game on Thanksgiving. The torpedo was behind the fleeing submarine, but it was closing. It looked like the race was going to go to the torpedo when it disappeared from the NTDS display.

"What the hell?" asked Diaz, demanding that the display unit explain the situation to him.

"Check out the depth on that Alfa," said Rogers. "She's gone deep. I'm talking John Holmes deep." The words were barely out of his mouth when a new torpedo contact appeared in front of the Alfa.

"Ha!" said Diaz.

"That doesn't count," replied Rogers. "I've already won the bet." The two watched as the new torpedo contact closed on the Alfa at eighty knots. The Alfa made a turn and dive, but it was too little too late. The torpedo detonated, breaking the sub's keel in two. Diaz reached into his pocket, pulled out his wallet and fetched a twenty.

"You should at least have the decency to buy me a beer the next time we have liberty."

"You got it," said Rogers, shoving the bill into his khaki slacks.

They went back about the ordinary course of business, preparing tomorrow's brief for the captain and reading through the reports coming in from the satellite imagery and signals intelligence, looking for anything that could give them a clue as to where the Oscar was.

****

Minskiy Komsomolets

Maksim Yermolovo stared at the "Unified Information Management and Control System on the Vessel," or ESU TZ. His sonarmen had picked up a submarine fighting for its life to the north. It didn't take long for his crew to figure out what was happening. A Soviet *Lira*-class submarine tried her one single trick: running. It worked at first, but you just couldn't outrun aircraft.

The emphasis on speed in that class was folly, thought Yermolovo, letting a bit of criticism of the communist system creep in. Internally he admonished himself for such a transgression.

"I believe that was a distraction," said Captain Usatov.

"How's that, comrade Captain?" asked Yermolovo.

"Stavka sent that *Lira* to guard our flank. Only a submarine with that kind of speed could reach us from the Northern or Baltic fleets. She was sent to help us find the Americans, and now we know exactly where they are. We simply need to make a course to the point where the *Lira* was sunk. From there we can find the American fleet."

Or, there are only so many submarines in the fleet, and one of them was heading down here to hunt Brazilian convoys, thought Yermolovo. *Usatov isn't letting go of this obsession with the task force that is hunting him.*

"With apologies, Captain," said Yermolovo, "but I have some reports to attend to."

"Very well, Yermolovo." Captain Usatov reached out a hand in an unusually friendly gesture. Yermolovo took it and gave the captain a curt nod before turning and leaving the command center. He made his way through the narrow passageway and climbed a ladder before taking another passageway and coming to a door, which he opened. When he entered the communications room, all eyes were on him. Most of those eyes showed fear.

"Senior Seaman Solomonov, there have been some disturbing reports of your anti-Party beliefs and your fomenting discontent among the men." It was as though Yermolovo had issued magic words. Four of the five-man crew found a sudden and irresistible need to get the hell out

221

of the communications room, leaving Yermolovo and Solomonov to have a conversation.

"Was that necessary?" asked Solomonov.

"I'm afraid it was," said Yermolovo. "We are running out of time. The captain's hubris is causing him to delude himself. He's beginning to incorporate any new information he gets into his hubris. He's going to throw us at this American force, and he's being reckless about it."

"I see. Okay, yes. I'm glad you came. Listen, I received word from the top that you are to use your discretion to stop the captain. We need to get in contact with Captain Sakharov," said Solomonov, referring to the boat's executive officer. "Between the two of you and the orders I have in the encrypted file, we can take control of the boat." Yermolovo swallowed hard. A mutiny wasn't his first choice. He'd hoped that orders would come down from Stavka, explaining that the priority of the mission was the convoys and that the American task force should be avoided.

"This is an extreme measure," said Yermolovo. "Did leadership not give us any alternative?"

"No, sir," said Solomonov. "There were concerns about Captain Usatov that were observed both when we returned to Polyarny after our first cruise and in Luanda, Angola, after our second cruise. From the limited information I have, there is a fine line between confidence and hubris, and Captain Usatov was diagnosed as being likely to fall into the second category."

Yermolovo looked at the young radioman with respect. This man was an inferior in the chain of command, yet he was clearly a wise and intelligent man. It humbled Yermolovo to remember that on the ship, he was in power and Solomonov was not, even though Solomonov showed plenty of intellect. This was causing a misfire in Yermolovo's sense of self. But he'd have to set that aside until the crises at hand abated.

"I will speak with Captain Sakharov," said Yermolovo. "This could make or break our operation. If he refuses to go along with us, I fear that we will be jailed—or worse, shot."

"If Usatov chooses to shoot a *politruk*, he'll be signing his own death warrant. But jailing… yes, you could find yourself in the brig. And it will become my sole mission to get you out."

"I appreciate that, comrade," said Yermolovo. "When the comms staff comes back, explain that this whole thing was a misunderstanding about a fight you had with an uncle. Just let me know what lie you come up with, so I can confirm it later."

"Thank you, sir," replied Solomonov. "I appreciate the consideration."

"It's the least I could do for a true believer," said Yermolovo as he exited the communications room, and made his way back down the ladderwell, then into another passageway. This time he headed forward towards the bow of the ship, stopping at a door on his right and knocking.

There was a momentary rustling on the other side of the door before it was opened and a burly man asked, "What the hell do you want?"

"Comrade Captain," said Yermolovo, "I'm afraid I need your counsel."

"I'm not on duty for another four hours—can't this wait?" asked Captain Sakharov.

"I'm afraid not. It's an emergency."

"Very well." Sakharov opened the door, and Yermolovo entered.

"We have a major problem with Captain Usatov."

Sakharov wiped the sleep from his eyes.

"I don't understand."

"Captain Usatov is no longer following the orders that he was given by Stavka. He has instead decided to throw this vessel at an American carrier battle group that is searching for us."

"That just makes good sense," said Sakharov. "Sinking an American carrier is of considerably more value than putting seven more cargo ships on the bottom."

"You fool!" said Yermolovo. "This war will not be won at sea. It will not be won at all if we cannot stem or stop the flow of supplies to NATO. *That* is our mission."

"If that is the case," said Sakharov, "why were we given such high honors for sinking the *Eisenhower* and not for those seven merchants?"

"That was a show for the people!" said Yermolovo, surprised that he had to explain this to a captain of the second rank.

"You are an apparatchik. You have zero experience or understanding of naval tactics or strategy," said Sakharov.

"I have a very clear understanding of my orders, and I would recommend that you get on board with them before we are all cast into doom by Captain Usatov's terrible decisions."

"If that is everything, comrade *politruk*, please leave my quarters."

Yermolovo was shocked at the reception. The orders were clear. Usatov's instability was clear. It occurred to Yermolovo that the one thing he'd underestimated was the dedication of the crew to the man who had led them through such heroics over the course of the last eleven months. Under the pressure of combat, Usatov had created a team that was more loyal to him than to the Soviet Union. Preventing this was literally his job, and he was failing.

Chapter 20

USS *Arkansas*

Commander Earl Brown took a sip of his coffee. It was a bit hot but within acceptable parameters for drinking. The combat information center was a better place to get all of the information you needed to fight the ship, but he much preferred being able to see the sea and the sky from the bridge. Whenever his duties didn't require him to be in the dungeon, you could find him here.

"How's the coffee today?" asked the officer of the deck, Glen Hopkins.

"Mr. Hopkins," said Brown, "The coffee today is exactly the same as the coffee was yesterday, and it is exactly the same as the coffee we'll have tomorrow. I wouldn't serve it at my niece's wedding, but I'll gladly drink it every day while we're bobbing in the Atlantic."

"Fair enough, sir," said Hopkins, "but I reserve the right to ask you again tomorrow."

"Are you hoping that I'll come up with a different answer?" asked Brown. "I literally said the coffee always tastes the same."

"Maybe you'll decide to mix up the sugar and cream ratio?" asked Hopkins.

"Hopkins, you should understand that I like my coffee like I like myself: black."

"That certainly makes it easier, Commander," said Hopkins with a smile.

"Any excitement today?" asked Brown.

"Negative, sir," said Hopkins. "Nothing since the mad dash of the Alfa."

"I don't know if that's good or bad anymore," said Brown. "We've spent the past ten months hoping that we *don't* find submarines, and now we're spending every day upset that we *didn't* find any submarines."

"If it's any consolation, sir, if we find that Oscar, we can go back to avoiding submarines."

"That's a good way to look at things, Lieutenant," said Brown.

The speaker overhead came to life. "Commander Brown to the CIC."

Brown picked up the mic. "This is Commander Brown, I'm on my way." Then to Hopkins he said, "Don't crash into anything while I'm gone."

"Well, sir, I was going to make a run at *John Young*, but I guess that'll have to wait."

Brown made his way to the CIC, where he huddled up with Captain Stewart. "What's the word, Skipper?"

"One of the S-3s picked up something pretty far out there," said the captain, referring to the S-3 Viking antisubmarine warfare aircraft that was flying off *America*. "If the Oscar was cautiously heading for the shipping lanes, this is about where we'd expect her to be."

"I see," said Brown. "So, assuming that this isn't a biologic, or a phantom signal, the analysts think we might have our quarry?"

"That's the long and short of it," agreed the captain.

Brown looked at the NTDS readout.

"So, we're already in range of those Shipwrecks?" he asked, using the NATO code name for the deadly Soviet antiship missiles.

"That we are," said Stewart gravely. "The saving grace here is that there's not a lot of chance that she knows we're here. She'll need to get a lot closer to get a firing solution."

"There are a lot of ways that this can go wrong. A data link with a satellite overhead. Maybe one of those Delta Bears lights us up and Oscar receives the data that way," said Brown, referring to the Tu-95 Bear D, which was used for maritime patrol.

"You're not wrong to be concerned, Commander," said Captain Stewart. "We need to be on our A game out here. But there's nothing we can do about it, so don't let it get you down."

"Oh, I understand that, sir. I'm just looking at the possibilities. Hell, that Alfa might have been sent down here to get our position."

"This is going to play out over some time, but I thought you'd want to know what we're looking at. You can go back to daydreaming on the bridge if you'd like," said Stewart with a grin.

"Those native island girls aren't going to conjure themselves up without me," said Brown, leaving the CIC and making his way back to the bridge.
****

USS *America*

226

Ship's Signal Exploitation Space

"What do you think?" asked Lieutenant Diaz, looking at the faint track of the unknown submarine.

"I don't have a lot to go on," said Rogers. "That could be our Oscar, or it could be a whale fart."

"That's not a very well-rounded analysis of the situation," replied Diaz.

"But you can't say that I'm wrong," said Rogers. "But let me expand. Right now it's the only lead we have, and it's credible. So it bears further investigation. That investigation will be done by the S-2 and S-3 helos. Once they disprove the whale fart theory, we can update our report, and they can continue to bring us more information, up to and including a solid firing solution for one of their torpedoes. Then, it's Miller time, and we all grab a beer."

"Not bad," said Diaz. "What are some of the risks you associate with the contact?"

"First and foremost," said Rogers, "submarine detection is hard." Diaz put his face in his hands. "No, hear me out. There are so many variables that go into detecting an underwater contact. Depth, water temperature, salinity. All of these factors make it so that we have to devote major resources to investigate this contact, which may or may not be the Oscar. That means that there is the very real possibility that the Oscar is somewhere else and getting closer by the minute."

"It's rather sobering, isn't it?" Said Diaz. With the novelty of the new contact wearing off, the two officers went back to their daily routine, sifting through data and reports looking for anything that they could turn into actionable intelligence to report to Command. Over the course of the next hour, Rogers would occasionally glance at the NTDS to see the ASW aircraft heading to and from the contact until the contact disappeared.

"Whale fart," said Rogers.

****

1 November 1981
Minskiy Komsomolets
Mid-Atlantic Ocean

"Contact!" said one of the sonarmen on duty. "Bearing three hundred, range unknown."

"All stop," ordered Captain Usatov. With only a line of bearing to go on, he made his boat as quiet as possible to give his sonarmen every opportunity to firm up their contact. He waited patiently for more information. He knew the enemy was out there, and they were hunting him. If he was rash at this point, he would ruin his chances to sink the American aircraft carrier.

"Captain," said *politruk* Maks Yermolovo, "what are the chances that this is just shipping moving through the ocean?"

"Until we have more information, we have no way of knowing," said Usatov. "However, once we get a little more information, we can make an educated guess."

"What would be your best-case scenario?" asked Yermolovo.

"Best-case would be that one of these wizards"—he gestured towards the bank of sonarmen—"can identify the contact by the noise it makes. But that is unlikely. Realistically, our best-case scenario is that we'll be able to pick the contact up again and establish a heading."

"What will that tell us?" asked Yermolovo.

"Nothing definitive, perhaps. If the contact is heading towards us, I would bet that it is our American friends. But, if it's heading towards Brazil, or towards Europe, it might be a convoy, or it might be our American friends hunting for us."

"Captain," said a sonarman, "contact is bearing three hundred and five degrees. Initial estimates are a course of one hundred twenty-two degrees, speed fifteen knots."

"That makes it quite interesting," said Usatov. "Navigation, calculate an intercept course based on current information, with our speed at five knots."

"Understood, comrade Captain." The man dutifully started making the calculations before ordering the helmsman to make the adjustments to their course and speed.

"Playing it a bit cautious is probably for the best," said Yermolovo.

"This again?" asked Usatov icily.

"I beg your pardon, sir?" asked Yermolovo, taken aback.

"During our last attack on the enemy, you all but called me a coward for firing from such a long distance."

"No, sir—"

"Be silent! I am sick of your constant second-guessing of my orders."

"But I agree with—" Usatov cut him off again.

"Navigation, recalculate our intercept with a speed of fifteen knots."

"Understood." The navigator went back to his calculations.

"Captain Usatov—"

"Shut your mouth, Maks."

"No," said Yermolovo, the word hanging in the silence that followed it. "This is reckless, and you are putting the Rodina's most valuable naval asset at risk, to say nothing of the lives of every man on board. At this speed, the enemy will be certain to detect us. You know as well as any man in the fleet how many ASW assets an American carrier task force can bring to bear."

"And this defeatism is coming from a *politruk*? You should be prosecuting yourself for defeatism and cowardice."

"It's not cowardice to stop a madman who is suffering from hubris."

Smack.

The punch clearly caught Yermolovo by surprise. His jaw snapped shut midsentence and his head whipped back before he lost his balance and fell to the floor.

"Get this coward out of here," said Usatov to the pair of marines standing watch in the control center. "Lock him in his stateroom." Then to Yermolovo, who was rubbing his jaw as he opened and closed it repeatedly, he said, "I will deal with you when this is over." The two burly marines took Yermolovo and carried him out of the bridge.

"Sir," said the sonarman who had reported the contact initially. "We've lost the contact."

"That's to be expected, Seaman Anrep, but thank you for alerting me. Once we have closed with the enemy, we will reduce speed and regain contact."

****

Yermolovo was hauled down the passageways of *Minskiy Komsomolets*. The two marines who had taken custody of him brought him to "Officer's Country" but then stopped.

"Which way, comrade *politruk?*" asked the sailor on Yermolovo's right.

Rather polite, given the circumstances, thought Yermolovo. He supposed that the fear the men had of the *politruks* remained even in these circumstances.

"Third stateroom on the left side, comrade *matros*," said Yermolovo. At this point his guards released him and let him walk with whatever dignity he could regain to his stateroom.

He entered, and before he could close the door, the marine he'd just spoken to said,

"You are being detained and are in our custody. Should you try to leave your room, we will prevent it."

That's pretty straightforward, thought Yermolovo before nodding in acknowledgment and closing the door behind him. Now that his stateroom had become his prison cell, what had once been a warm and comfortable place was claustrophobic. It was a tight space under any circumstance, but adding to that was the idea that he couldn't leave. Worse than that was the idea that he was going to die here, if he couldn't find a way out.

We knew this was a possible outcome and we discussed it even if at a superficial level, he thought. *Solomonov will come for me, but then what? How is he going to overpower the two sentries at the door?*

That wasn't even the worst of it. Yermolovo knew that even if he could get out of the room, then what? Sending a message to Stavka wasn't going to do them any good. It would simply risk detection, and he doubted that they would be able to receive the message, craft a response, transmit it to the boat, and have it delivered to Captain Usatov before they were all dead.

But that's the only chance we have. If there are direct orders from Stavka to stand down, perhaps it will break this obsession of Usatov's, he thought. It was his only choice, so he sat at his small desk and began to draft his outgoing message. If the submarine was destroyed while he was sitting at this desk, then so be it. He would have died doing everything he could to save his ship.

The one saving grace was that naval warfare was a very slow affair before the missiles were flying. Then it became a very rapid and terrifying affair. But with luck, he would have enough time to bring this plan to action.

After some time, there was a commotion outside his room. He stood from his desk and backed away from the door. When it opened, he was relieved to see the face of Senior Seaman Solomonov.

"We need to move," said the seaman in a tone that surprised Yermolovo. As he left his stateroom, he saw the still and lifeless bodies of his two jailors. There was blood pooling on the deck as Solomonov urged him ahead. Solomonov's manner reminded Yermolovo of exactly how the now-dead jailors had treated him.

"We must get to communications and get a message to Command," said Solomonov.

"How did you know that I was detained?" asked Yermolovo.

"The boys in the radio room know everything that happens in the ship, comrade. Everyone owes us favors or wants us in their debt because we are the only chance they have of ever getting word to or from the outside world."

"How did you... kill—"

"Comrade, those are not the first men I've killed. I didn't learn how to use this radio equipment at the School of Communications of the Soviet Navy. I learned at the Andropov Institute." That took Yermolovo aback. Typically, a submarine wouldn't merit a fully trained and skilled KGB operative. Simply a dedicated and cleared enlisted sailor who checked some boxes would do.

It occurred to Yermolovo at that moment that Solomonov was a replacement who had been added after their first cruise.

"They sent you on this boat because they were worried this would happen," said Yermolovo.

"Yes, comrade. Captain Usatov's reaction to his successful first mission, becoming the first Soviet submarine commander to take out a US carrier, and their *newest* aircraft carrier, raised some red flags. He seemed to be ascribing the victory to his own abilities as a commander and not to the system that put his submarine in position to fire missiles, as well as offering the lives of seventy-five Soviet sailors to get him the fix on the carrier. This individualism warranted intervention."

They were coming up to the communications room when Solomonov said, "You need to order everyone out. They'll listen to you, and I don't want to have to kill any more of my countrymen today." Yermolovo nodded, then banged on the door. The sailor who opened the door had no idea what had just hit him as Yermolovo pushed past him.

"Everyone out!" It was a simple command, and everyone in the room understood that the man who had been placed in confinement by Captain Usatov was in their presence. In every navy in the world, the commanding officer was feared and revered. He was God at sea. But the Soviet Navy had something that no other fleet had: a devil. As much as the radiomen loved their God, they feared their devil even more and they ran.

"We won't have much time. If there's one thing I've learned on this assignment, it's that radiomen love to talk."

"Okay, I've got the message drafted. How are we sending it?"

"We don't have a choice," said Solomonov. "We have to use a buoy." That was distressing to Yermolovo. That meant that sending this signal could be what doomed the submarine.

"Wait," said Yermolovo. "What if sending this message is what alerts the Americans to our position? Could it be better to let Usatov carry out his attack without this action?"

"You were detained because the captain was making a rash attack on the enemy. They will find us regardless of this buoy. You have to be a man right now, Maks."

"You're right," said Yermolovo, and he handed the paper over to his KGB associate, who turned and began keying it in. The man was lightning on a keyboard, and within a minute, he'd entered the entire message and began the process of launching the communications buoy.

"The chance that this works would be scientifically inexplicable," said Solomonov. He reached behind one of the equipment bays and retrieved a Makarov pistol. "Help me barricade the door." Solomonov pushed a chair against the door and wedged it against the doorknob. Yermolovo picked up a piece of equipment that he didn't recognize and slid it against the bottom of the door.

"What do we need to keep in order to get Stavka's reply?" asked Yermolovo.

"Nothing," replied Solomonov as he pointed at the deck above them. "The intelligence officers will receive that communication. I don't have a high enough clearance." He winked as he said it. The two men continued to pile equipment against the door until there was nothing that wasn't solidly bolted down. Yermolovo didn't think that it was going to be enough of a barricade, but it was what they had. Well, that and Solomonov's pistol.

****

"Sir," said Seaman Anrep, "we've just released a communications buoy."

Captain Usatov was taken aback by this. He hadn't issued orders for a buoy, and no routine launch was expected.

"Captain Boreyev," said Usatov, "were you expecting a communications buoy?" The question appeared to take Boreyev by surprise. That wasn't a good sign, since Captain Boreyev was the senior communications officer on the boat.

"No, sir," replied the captain of the third class.

"Find out what the hell is going on!" ordered Usatov.

"Sir! Understood," said Boreyev, making speed to get the hell out of the crucible that had become the command center of *Minskiy Komsomolets*.

Captain Usatov was now struggling. The communications buoy was going to be detected. In the absence of the buoy, his instinct had been to slow and reestablish contact with the enemy. Now, though, staying near the buoy was suicide. As soon as it started transmitting, any aircraft or ship would know exactly where they were. *I don't see that I have any choice*, thought Usatov as he issued the orders.

"Dive officer, come to five hundred meters, Helm, increase speed to twenty-five knots." Usatov was taking the boat below her test depth, but he wanted to put as much distance as possible between the comms buoy and his boat. "Anrep, do you have any trace of the contact?"

"Negative, sir," replied Seaman Anrep. This wasn't a surprise, but better to be sure than to be surprised. Now he just had to decide how long he wanted to make this dash. There was a fine line between being too close to the buoy and being too close to the enemy. He also didn't know how long he would have before the buoy started transmitting and getting the attention of the enemy ASW aircraft. If he timed it right, whoever had released the buoy might have done him a favor, since the enemy would be focused on an area far behind him.

He picked up the microphone and switched the channel. "Security, Command. Send a pair of marines to Comrade Yermolovo's quarters."

"Sir, I already have two—"

"Just do it!" *What the hell is going wrong with everyone?* thought Usatov. He looked around the command center. The faces of his men were impassive. He could tell that they were hiding something, and that was unusual. This crew had been an efficient fighting force, but as with many of the best crews Usatov had served on, there was a family unity that was absent from the room. *It must just be this business with Yermolovo. The children don't like it when their parents fight.*

"Command, Security, I have sensitive information for you." Usatov put on a pair of headphones and plugged them into his intercom.

"Security, Command, you are cleared to release sensitive information."

"Sir, Yermolovo is missing, and two of my marines are dead."

"You need to get as many men as you can to the communications room. I doubt Yermolovo is alone—it's not in his nature or ability to kill your men. Thank you for your discretion on this. We can't have the crew coming apart in the middle of an attack run."

"Understood, Captain. Security out." This complicated things further.

"Sir," said Seaman Anrep, "the buoy is transmitting."

"All stop, come up to fifty meters," said Usatov instantly.

"All stop, set depth to fifty meters," repeated the helmsman. The ship's inertia carried it forward as the propulsion stopped and the crew leaned forward as the nose of the boat rose.

"As soon as you have something, Anrep." The seaman nodded. "Weapons, prepare the *graniti*," said Usatov, referring to the twenty-four antiship missiles that made *Minskiy Komsomolets* the menace of the Atlantic.

"Sir, we are beginning preparations to launch the *graniti*." Some skippers might consider it premature to start weapons preparation when they didn't have a target, but Usatov knew that he'd have a very brief period of time where he could launch.

"Command, Security."

"Security, Command, you are cleared to send sensitive information."

"Sir, the communications room is barricaded. We do not know how many people might be on the other side."

"Understood. Do not attempt to breach the room. We can't afford the noise at this point."

"Very well, Captain. We will contain the traitors in the communications room and await further orders."

"Contact," said Anrep. "Bearing two-eight-seven, range seventy-three kilometers." Usatov waited as more contacts were defined. The speed with which the task force was moving made Anrep's job much easier. Though the Soviet submarine had one of the most advanced sonar suites ever built by Soviet engineers, it was not able to provide specifics beyond the comparative sizes of the contacts. Even so, the formation of the enemy task force was taking shape on the display in front of him.

"It looks like a screening force, followed by a big fat American carrier," said Captain Sakharov, who had entered the command center without Usatov noticing.

"Indeed, I agree," said Usatov.

"Seventy-three kilometers is practically point-blank range for the *graniti*," said Sakharov. "They won't know what hit them."

"Oh, they'll know," replied Usatov, "and for the last few minutes of their lives they will be frightened by the knowledge of their impending doom. This is the price the Americans pay for coming after us. Weapons, fire a spread of eight missiles at the screening force, followed by the remaining sixteen at the carrier group. Six missiles target the carrier, additional missiles spread out evenly across the escorts."

"Understood, sir." The weapons officer made the calculations and entered the values into the boat's computer. "Ready to fire."

"Fire!" ordered Usatov, feeling a primal savagery in his soul.
****

USS *Arkansas*

"Oh, shit. Sound general quarters," said Lieutenant Tom Grant, the officer of the deck. The klaxon sounded and the 1MC urged everyone to their battle stations.

"That's a lot of missiles," said Captain Stewart, telling everyone what they already knew. "Ops, engage the Big Eye, and let's get firing solutions on these bastards. Weapons, as soon as you get a clear shot, take it. Don't wait on me."

"Understood, sir." Within a minute of the first reports of incoming missile, the two twin-rail launchers on *Arkansas* were firing SN-1 missiles as quickly as they could. The reloading time seemed agonizingly long as the launchers went vertical, received two new missiles, retrained on the target, and launched, just to repeat the process. From the CIC, Captain Stewart watched as the groups of four missiles raced to the enemy SS-N-19 missiles.

"Code-naming those things Shipwreck was a bad omen," said Grant.

"We could have called them Fluffy Puppies and they'd still be bad news," said Stewart. "We just need to knock down as many as we can." He watched the screen and could see that they were in grave danger.

"How the hell did they get so close?" asked Grant.

Stewart looked at the NTDS.

"They tricked us," said the skipper. "They deployed that signal buoy to get our attention, and to cause enough noise to let them sneak up on us."

"Devious bastards," said Grant. "For all the good it's going to do them. Look." He pointed to the swarm of ASW helicopters that were rapidly closing on the point of origin of the missiles. "There's no way that they're going to get away this time."

"Sir, *Knox*-class has taken a hit. She's gone, sir."

"Damn, there's practically no chance for a ship that small to survive one of those thousand-pounders," said Stewart. He looked at the NTDS and his blood ran cold. "Sound collision!"

"All hands, missiles inbound forward, prepare for impact." The words were still echoing through the CIC when the ship shuddered and the lights went out, then came back on red.

"Damage report," said Stewart on the 4MC, the damage control circuit, as he had practiced countless times during drills.

"Sir, we are reporting massive flooding forward. It looks like the missile punched us right in the face."

"Is the flooding controllable?" asked Stewart.

"Unknown, sir."

"Find a way to know, dammit," said the captain before ordering, "Counterflood aft, get this under control."

"Understood, counterflooding aft."

"Bridge, CIC. Earl, I need you to get your ass down to the CIC and fight the ship if we can get main power back on."

"Understood, sir," said Commander Earl Brown. When Brown emerged into the darkness, Stewart pulled him aside.

"I'm going forward to take command of the DC efforts. Did you see anything that might help?"

"Just the explosion itself, sir. The missile came in jinking and just hit us on the low end of an evasive maneuver. Had she hit us coming down instead of heading back up, we'd both be dead and the ship would be underwater."

"Very well. I've begun counterflooding aft. Just try to keep her afloat while we fix this problem." Stewart turned and left without waiting for a response. He didn't have time for pleasantries. Men were moving forward on the starboard passageway, heading to the damage control party.

Stewart kept moving forward until he found a group of men dogging a watertight door. He looked at the wall where the frame and deck, were painted and grimaced. They were on the third deck, frame twenty-five. They were about twenty-five percent of the length of the ship, and they were trying to seal up the watertight doors.

"Is there flooding in that compartment?" asked the skipper, yelling over the chaos around him.

"Negative, sir," replied a boatswain's mate who was soaked from head to toe.

"We can't give up here. If we let the ship flood to this frame, we'll lose her." The presence of the captain was enough to calm the panicked men. "We need to advance as far as we can and rescue any of our shipmates. Come on, you'd want them to do it for you." With that, he began to advance, frame by frame. He opened the doors, and they would look for injured sailors, who would be helped aft by their shipmates.

By frame sixteen, water was starting to come in. Stewart made a quick assessment.

"We've got cracks in the bulkhead. Get a shoring team up here," he said, hoping that the team would be able to jam enough wood or metal into the cracked bulkhead to stop the flooding. He was very tentative about moving forward at this point. The water coming in was one thing. That could be from flooding happening further forward. But the crack in the bulkhead was most likely the result of the missile impact, or

237

secondary explosions. He was entering the blast damage area, and things would only get worse from here.

He pushed forward, opening the next hatch. More water came rushing in.

"I'm going to dog this hatch while I make my assessment," said Stewart, not wanting to let in any more water than he had to. The joint between the bulkhead and the overhead on the forward port side had buckled and water was spraying in. He wasn't sure that they'd be able to seal it off. It was going to take more than some wood and a few hammers. He returned to the previous frame and dogged the hatch behind him.

"It's bad in there—we're going to need to patch it. We need a welding crew and some scrap metal."

The ship's forward trim had increased dramatically in the next few minutes while the welding team was brought forward. The pressure on the shoring job in this compartment was starting to leak, causing the shoring crew to hammer away at the wood stopping the water.

When the welding team made it to the compartment, Captain Stewart turned the wheel to open the hatch. Just as the dogs cleared the coaming, the hatch exploded inward, knocking Stewart in the face as the rushing water threw him against the bulkhead, killing him instantly.
****

USS *America*
Ship's Signal Exploitation Space

"I know that you're not a religious man," said Diaz, "but I think it's time to start praying."

Rogers looked at the display on the NTDS.

"I've found Jesus," he said, and he meant it. Every time he'd mocked someone for their faith, every time he'd held himself superior because he didn't believe in an old man in the sky, or a Jewish zombie, came rushing back as he began asking, even begging, for both forgiveness and salvation.

"Look," said Diaz, "we have leakers getting past the screen."

"The Oscar doesn't care about the screen," said Rogers. "Any missiles that hit the cruisers or destroyers were probably accidental."

"I doubt it matters to that cruiser that just got hit," said Diaz. "You know anyone on *Arkansas*?"

238

"Negative… it's a big fleet out there. You?"

"Carlson—Lieutenant Commander Dan Carlson. We were stationed on Forrestal together back in the day."

"I hope they can save the ship," said Rogers, knowing that it sounded pathetic.

"I hope he can get out," said Diaz, showing a degree of optimism.

"Attention! Missiles inbound, forward. Brace for impact!" The 1MC startled both men, even though they were watching the digital representation of the missiles approaching.

"Oh shit," said Rogers, "*Long Beach* just took a hit." *Long Beach* was the cruiser directing forward of *America* and was the last defensive unit between her and the incoming swarm of missiles.

The giant aircraft carrier shook as though Poseidon himself was pissed off at her. There were repeated shocks in succession. Rogers knew that they had taken multiple hits from the incoming Shipwrecks. The strap securing a rack of radio equipment broke, and the gear spilled all over the SSES. The ship was immediately down by the bow. As Rogers stood up, he pitched over forward, falling into the tangle of equipment. He felt a sharp pain in his left arm and he hit the deck.

"Fuck" was all he said as he rolled to his left and tried to get his his feet under him again. Diaz reached over and offered Rogers a hand, which he took with his right hand.

"We've gotta get out of here," said Diaz as the 1MC began to broadcast again.

"All hands, abandon ship. All hands, abandon ship."

"Holy shit, the damage must be devastating," said Rogers as the two men opened the safe door and entered the passageway outside of the SSES. The ship's degree of pitch was growing.

"I think they must have ripped the entire bow off the ship," said Rogers as the two men climbed up the passageway, trying to make their way to a ladder to get them up to the weather deck. The klaxon blaring in the background was deafening. The deck was at a forty-five-degree angle by the time they made it to the ladder.

Getting up the ladder was easier than usual because it was almost parallel to the horizon. Rogers slipped, racking his nuts on the ladder and slamming his arm on the railing on his way down. He immediately vomited. Diaz reached back to grab him, but Rogers fell back to the deck and rolled down, towards the SSES. Diaz scrambled back down the ladder and ran after his shipmate. Rogers was grabbing his crotch and rolling on the deck.

"You have to get up or we're going to die here," said Diaz. Rogers shook his head and in a moment of clarity realized that he was about to die. He pushed the pain to the back of his mind and started back up the steepening deck. "We're almost back to the ladder, you can do this."

"I'm going to die, Diaz," said Rogers, losing hope.

"You are not going to die," said Diaz. "There is nothing life-threatening about your injuries. You need to get your head out of your ass and get topside. That's all. We get topside and we'll make it."

The two men crossed the ladder again, and this time Rogers was able to get all the way across. The hatch to the flight deck was open, and as they crossed into the daylight, they could see life rafts deploying. The two men crossed the ladder again, and this time Rogers was able to get all the way across. The hatch to the flight deck was open, and as they crossed into the daylight, they could see liferafts deploying.

"Listen, Rogers, we need to jump. Just get into the water, then inflate your vest, then kick as hard as you can away from the ship."

Rogers looked at Diaz and gave a faint nod. The pain of his injuries was overtaking his ability to reason. Diaz made a running jump over the side. Rogers steeled his nerve, pulled the CO_2 triggers on his vest, and jumped over the side.

When Rogers hit the water, both of his shoulders dislocated. The immense pain caused him to pass out. With his useless arms above his head, his vest slid over his comatose body. While Rogers slid into the depths, his vest rose to the surface.

****

Minskiy Komsomolets

"Helm," said Captain Usatov, "dive to five hundred meters, flank speed, course one-two-zero."

"Depth five hundred, course one-two-zero, flank speed, understood," repeated the helmsman.

Usatov picked up his mic and keyed his security detail.

"Security, Command. Break down that door and find out who these traitors are."

"Understood, Captain." Just before the signal cut out, Usatov could hear a loud pounding sound.

"Anrep, what can you hear?"

"There's a lot of noise out there, but the fleet has increased speed. It's hard to get specifics—the engine noises are overlapping each other, making a real mess out of it."

"Very well—"

"Splashes, sir. Sonobouys to our port forward."

"Are they active?" asked the captain.

"Affirmative, sir. They are pinging."

"Helm, get us under the layer," ordered Usatov. Getting under the layer wouldn't ensure that they could avoid detection, but it would improve their chances. Of course, given the number of ASW units up there, they'd no doubt be dropping buoys with hydrophones under the layers as well as above. If there was a saving grace right now, it was that too many active buoys could create enough noise contamination to confuse each other, allowing *Minskiy Komsomolets* to slip away in the chaos.

****

Yermolovo wished he had a weapon. Anything to give him a chance to hold on long enough for orders to come through from Stavka. That was when he felt the ship tremble. He'd felt this exact feeling twice before. *Minskiy Komsomolets* was firing his missiles at the NATO task force.

"That's it, Comrade Yermolovo. We have lost," said Agent Solomonov.

"What do we do now?" asked Yermolovo.

"It hardly matters. If our analysis was correct, we will all be dead soon."

"I'm not sure which is worse," said Yermolovo, "dying by a Yankee torpedo, or dying by Usatov's orders." Outside the door, there was a pounding sound.

"I've killed my countrymen today," said Solomonov. "I wish to spare the men on the other side of this door from the same fate."

"You are sympathetic to this treachery?" asked Yermolovo.

241

"The men trying to root us out are not traitors. They are patriots following orders. As far as they know, we are the traitors, and we are just as deserving of death as you think they are."

"So then, surrender?"

"Not yet," said Solomonov, "but yes, surrender before there's more bloodshed in this fool's errand." Solomonov pulled the Makarov pistol from his waistband, dropped the magazine, and charged the handle, ejecting the chambered round. Then he pulled the slide back, locked it, rotated the takedown lever, and released it, allowing the slide to fly off the pistol and onto the floor before he tossed the rest of the gun to the other side of the communications room.

The mass of radio equipment stacked against the door surged inward. Solomonov bent down and put his shoulder against the pile.

"Push, dammit!" he said. "We need to keep that door closed for as long as we can."

It occurred to Yermolovo that Solomonov had just given them "empty work," something meaningless to do while they passed the time. A savage shove from the other side pushed the door open for a second before it slammed shut again. "We can't let them get the door open like that!"

****

"Explosions, sir," said Seaman Anrep, "best guess is that the picket ships have taken hits."

"Pathetic," said Usatov. "We weren't even trying to kill them, just keep their attention long enough to get our main strike through against the carrier." He shook his head with disdain.

"I have additional sonobuoy splashes," said Anrep.

"They are getting desperate," said Usatov. "Every missile hit that we achieve will make them angrier, and they will continue to make mistakes in their rage. Helm, what is our depth?"

"Crossing two hundred meters now, sir," replied the helmsman.

"Change course to one-seven-five."

"One-seven-five, understood," replied the helmsman.

"Sir, it's a mess, but I'm fairly certain that one of the escorts is sinking. It's hard to tell with all the noise out there."

"Understood, Anrep," said Usatov. "Keep up the good work. You are our eyes right now."

"Torpedo detected!" shouted Anrep, shedding his calm facade in the wake of his greatest fear. "Bearing zero-four-five. It's circling." The American aircraft didn't have to worry about a torpedo "coming back" on them, where the torpedo would start searching for a target and find the firing sub. Instead, with the firing platform safe in the air, they could fire what Soviet submariners referred to as a *beshenaya sobaka*. A mad dog that would attack anything that it came across.

"Weapons, release an acoustic decoy. Helm, come to course zero-four-zero." It was unlikely that a noisemaker would make enough of a fuss to keep the actively pinging torpedo from detecting them, but Usatov wasn't about to leave any arrows in his quiver.
****

Yermolovo was sweating. Some of that was from the exertion, but more of it was from the stress. In his years as a *politruk*, he'd never been in any actual danger. Now, there were men on the other side of that door who wanted to kill him for the crime of doing his job. None of this made any sense. A part of his brain wanted to trivialize this as the madness of war, but he refused to reduce it to that. This was personal. He was good at his job and, more importantly, he was *right*. Usatov was a madman who had probably already gotten all of them killed, and they just didn't know it yet.

The deck shifted as the submarine changed course. *We're running now. It's just a matter of time before the enemy runs us down*, thought Yermolovo.

"Stop daydreaming and push!" said Agent Solomonov. There was another shove from the outside, and the door popped open for just a second. It was a second too long. Yermolovo watched as something came flying into the room. Solomonov shoved him out of the way and grabbed the object, but it was too late—a thick haze of gas was spewing out of it. Solomonov chucked it at the door, trying to get it back into the passageway on the other side, but it bounced off the door as the security detachment closed it.

The CS gas quickly filled the room, choking the two KGB men. Yermolovo had enough. He'd done everything he could. He sat down being the pile of radio equipment as coughing fits racked his body. The more he coughed, the deeper he breathed. The deeper he breathed, the

more CS gas he inhaled. The more CS gas he inhaled, the more he was racked with coughing fits.
****

"More explosions, sir," reported Seaman Anrep. "These are in the main fleet."

"Targets?" asked Usatov.

"Unknown, sir, but given the target priority and numbers, I believe that we've sunk our second carrier." There was no cheer in the command center. Everyone who had been fighting the ship was nervous from the fight between Usatov and Yermolovo, as well as the fact that there was at least one torpedo in the water hunting them.

"The torpedo's pinging is increasing," said Anrep. "I think she has us."

"Weapons, deploy another acoustic decoy, Helm, emergency blow." It was a risk, but Usatov was running out of cards to play. The massive submarine shot through the water as it grabbed for the surface.

"Sir, the torpedo is still homing. Time to impact in thirty seconds."

"Sonar, deploy the Rubikon." The order was ridiculous.

"Aye, sir," said the sonarman to the right of Anrep without hesitation. Usatov knew that deploying the *Minskiy Komsomolets*'s towed array would only stop the torpedo if he were living in an adventure story. In real life, he was just...

The submarine shook violently. Water began spraying through the control room.

"Helm, once we are on the surface, get us back under!" ordered Usatov. *We should already be dead*, he thought. "Damage report!" he shouted into his mic on the main damage containment channel.

"Sir, we've lost contact with the Rubikon."

"No shit?" said Usatov, annoyed at the obvious statement. "What about the rest of the boat?"

"Shock damage, but nothing we can't handle. We're rerouting some cooling systems, and checking for hull damage, but we're looking good."

"Very well," said Captain Usatov, thinking the conversation was over.

"Sir," continued the damage containment officer, "there's no telling what our structural integrity is. I don't recommend going any deeper than we must."

"You contain damage, I will fight the boat," said Usatov as he slammed the microphone on its cradle. "Depth?" he called out.

"Just about to surface," said the navigation officer.

"Get us back underwater as soon as you can," insisted Usatov.

"Multiple torpedoes in the water!" said Seaman Anrep.

Usatov had known that this was a possibility. He had survived the first torpedo, but only by ensuring that the capitalists would swarm him before he could recover. Usatov felt the vibrations as an enemy helicopter overflew her within mere meters of *Minskiy Komsomolets*. The waters around the boat were roiling as she desperately tried to dive.

****

Yermolovo had puked out every bit of food, water, or bile he had in him, but he was still heaving. The rocket-ship rise of the boat was lost on him as he thought he was going to die in the communications room of *Minskiy Komsomolets*. Suddenly, he felt something new—a pressure against his back. The pile of equipment jammed against the door was pushing back against him.

"*My sdaiomsya!*" shouted Solomonov, telling the incoming troops that he and Yermolovo surrendered. The security detail began clearing the obstacles when the entire submarine shook. Several of the security men fell in the sudden trembling of the boat. The air cleared as the door was opened and the men entered.

Solomonov looked at Yermolovo, reached out a hand, and said, "I serve the Soviet Union."

Yermolovo grasped it and said, "I serve the Soviet Union." Without warning, the bulkhead burst as the explosive payload of a Mark 46 torpedo ripped into the side of the submarine as it tried to escape. The water rushed in, and Yermolovo had gone from suffocating on unbreathable gas to drowning in water. His dying thought was that Solomonov had achieved his goal of nobody having to kill their countrymen.

Chapter 21

10 November 1981
Communist Camp
Mountains Outside
Peñas Blancas, Costa Rica

It had been over a month since Carlos had become a communist insurgent. It made his skin crawl just thinking about it. He always worried that no matter what he did on this assignment, he'd be putting Americans and innocent Nicaraguans in danger. Poole had told him that this was what had to happen in order for them to have any hope of bringing down the larger group, but Carlos hated it nonetheless.

The camp was situated in the mountains just across the border from Nicaragua. The terrain reminded Carlos of the camp he'd raided at the Reserva Natural Serranía de Amerisane. The mountains and the forest provided excellent cover and concealment, but, as at Serranía de Amerisane, the same features that made it a good hiding place also made it vulnerable to an attack by an intelligent adversary.

The accommodations were about the same as the location. They were well suited for their purpose, but nothing beyond that. It was all canvas tents with the occasional light wooden structure. It was more or less what Carlos had been living in for the past eighteen months.

I wonder if it's easier for Clara, he pondered. *She's spent so long with the Sandinista movement, the precursor to these AmComs. I wonder if she's going to switch sides again…*

"This camp is run by idiots," said Clara, returning from a quick trip into town for supplies.

"Keep it down," replied Carlos, a bit spooked that perhaps Clara could read his mind.

"César knows what he's doing, but these idiots." She shook her head. "Nobody knows what they are doing here, and mostly I think they are only here to hide out from their responsibilities."

"How are they avoiding their responsibilities?" asked Carlos.

"They should be working and rebuilding the country. But instead, they hide out in the mountains, playing revolutionary."

"You say that like it's a bad thing," replied Carlos.

"I don't know what to make of it," replied Clara. "Even back at the start of the Sandinista movement, we always had the 'lazy parasite,' but here, they seem like they're the standard."

"I'm with you," said Carlos. "So far, this whole expedition seems like a major waste of time and effort. These idiots aren't going to foster a revolution any more than I'm going to flap my arms and fly to the moon."

The door to their communal residence opened, startling them both.

"Thank you for making your supply run," said César.

"I don't see the point," replied Clara. "These idiots are more interested in beer than bullets. None of them actually seem to understand the struggle between the proletariat and the bourgeoisie."

"I can see how it appears that way," replied César, "but I wouldn't be too hard on them. Right now, they are recovering from months of intense fighting against the imperialist Americans. They are hiding out and preparing to move forward. I'm sure they will get back into fighting shape soon. We just need to get them there."

"How, exactly," asked Clara, "are we getting them there if all they do is hide in the jungle?"

"If we push them too quickly," replied César, "they'll just leave, and we can't have the movement shrinking."

"Right now, all they are doing is using up supplies that could otherwise be used by actual fighters. If they don't want to fight, let them walk."

I don't like the way this is going, thought Carlos. *She really seems intent on making this unit much more effective.*

"I've seen the instruction materials the Soviet have given us," continued Clara. "We need to start using them. We need to teach our members how to build the bombs. We need to train them in marksmanship. They need to learn how to perform dead drops. There is so much to do, and we don't have time to sit around on our asses."

"Okay," sighed César, "you win. We'll start holding the men accountable for some kind of improvement."

"I'm glad you two sorted that out," said Carlos. "On that note, I'm going to go down to the first observation post and wake up Roel. His siestas are going to get us killed one day." He started up the trail to the observation post above. After ten minutes of quick hiking, he came upon the sleeping Roel. He kicked the man's boots.

"Time to wake up, dude," said Carlos. "Man, you give us Mexicans a bad name" Roel had found himself trapped in Nicaragua at the start of the war.

"Screw you, Carlos," said the man, wiping the sleep from his eyes.

"Clara just came back from town," said Carlos. This was calculated to ensure Roel left the hill. The one thing he liked more than sleep was food.

"Oh, yes, good. I should check in with César," he said as he started to ramble down the trail. As soon as Carlos was sure he was alone, he made his way off to the west and up the hill a bit. One of the first things he had done upon reaching the camp was to hide a PRC-77 radio. He was worried that it would be a challenge to get it past the communists and thought that he'd just say it was captured equipment that he'd learned how to use to spy on the Americans. But the less-than-enthusiastic nature of the men here allowed him to stash it without any drama.

He picked up the handset, put it to his ear and said, "Albacore, Barracuda. Do you read?" There was no reply. "Albacore, Barracuda, over."

"I've got you, Barracuda," said Fred Poole. "Good to hear from you—I was beginning to worry."

"I assure you, Albacore, you have nothing to worry about. The situation here is bizarre to say the least. This unit is combat-ineffective. In fact, it's action-ineffective. I don't think this group could organize a cookout, much less a revolution."

"Understood, local participation is limited," said Poole.

"You're not listening," insisted Carlos. "These guys don't have the will to fight."

"But what about all the evidence of organization?" asked Poole. "What about the propaganda we've uncovered? What about the terrorist attacks we've been tracing back to these guys?"

"I don't know what the disconnect is, Albacore," said Carlos. "Maybe our sources are just scapegoating these idiots, but this is a dry hole. I think we should slip out of here and try to find someone more serious."

"Understood, Barracuda. Sit tight for now. Don't blow your cover, but try to make contact in the next few days. I'll have some answers as to what Langley wants us to do here. This just doesn't make any sense."

"Roger that, Albacore. Barracuda out." Carlos stashed the radio and quietly made his way back to the observation post. He stopped short as he found César standing behind the embankment.

"Did you get lost?" asked César.

"Had to take a leak," replied Carlos nonchalantly. That seemed to placate César.

"I've already told Clara about this, but we're going to be relocating in order to give her the training and action that she's looking for."

"Relocating?" asked Carlos.

"Yes, we have many camps, not just this one. I think that we'll get a better response a little further inland. A little farther from Managua."

"Hey, like I told you on the day we met," said Carlos, "I'm a man of action. I agree with her that we've been idle for too long, and I'm looking forward to getting back to taking the fight to the *burguesía.*"

"I assure you, you will get your chance," said César.

****

18 November 1981
US Navy Recruit Training Center
Orlando, Florida

The feeling of the sun on Nancy's face was surreal. It wasn't that she hadn't been in this sun nearly every day since reporting here. No, today was different. Today was the last day that she'd be a recruit at RTC Orlando. After graduation ceremonies, she'd no longer be a recruit. She'd be a seaman's apprentice in the United States Navy. She shook her head. She couldn't believe that something that had been so meaningless to her could become so important so quickly.

More than that, though, was the twenty-four-hour liberty that the graduates would have, starting this evening. Nancy would get to see her beautiful daughter for the first time in two months. She couldn't believe it had been so long. Inside she was terrified that Jennifer wouldn't remember her. Or that Jennifer had come to accept the idea that Mommy was gone and her little heart had attached itself to Grandmama, Nancy's mother. Tears began to well up in her eyes. *Get it together, Rodriguez*, she chided herself.

"Rodriguez," called out Petty Officer Vera Greene, one of Nancy's company commanders.

"Ma'am." Nancy came to the position of attention.

"Relax, Rodriguez, you've made it. The sooner you figure out that I'm just an NCO and not some kind of minor deity, the better."

"Yes, ma'am," said Nancy,

"That's the first thing you need to knock off," laughed Greene. "You only call officers sir and ma'am. I'm just normal, regular Petty Officer Greene, no more, no less."

"Oh," said Nancy, trying to break free of two months of intensive indoctrination. "Thank you, Petty Officer Greene. I appreciate the heads-up."

"Don't mention it. You have plans for tonight? You don't look like the kind of girl that would be hitting the discos tonight."

"What?" laughed Nancy. "I have it on good authority that I'm hot enough to be a stripper."

"I'm not really in a position to judge," said Greene, smiling. "I just want to make sure that you have a plan. Sometimes the older sailors don't find a landing place once the chains are loosened."

"Oh, that's not a problem for me, ma—Petty Officer Greene. I'll be spending the evening, night and tomorrow with my parents and my daughter."

"That's fantastic, Rodriguez. You'll be a lot better off than a lot of your shipmates, that's for sure. By the way, I've got your orders." She handed Nancy a nine-by-twelve orange interoffice envelope.

"You could have told me this first," said Nancy excitedly.

"I know, but then you wouldn't have told me about your plans, and I really wanted to take care of that first." Nancy opened the envelope and pulled out a firm packet of papers. She scanned the top page and flipped it over. She read and flipped and read and flipped. Finally satisfied, she returned the packet to the envelope.

"Well?" asked Greene.

"Millington," said Nancy, referring to the city in Tennessee that was the home of Naval Support Activity, Mid-South.

"You knew that the day you signed your contract," said Greene. "What's your follow-on duty station?" Rodriguez hesitated.

"Rota, Spain," she said.

"That's not bad. At least you aren't going to Japan. Spain is pretty far from the front, but it's a vital port. You'll be doing a lot of good for the war effort, and you can be proud of your service."

"Thank you, ma—Petty Officer Greene," said Nancy.

"It'll take a few weeks before you get used to it," said Greene. "And for the love of God, watch your language when you're hanging out with your family. The men can get away with their... 'colorful' new vocabulary, but it doesn't play too well for the women." Nancy laughed at the thought of telling Jennifer how fucking happy she was to see the little shit.

"Thanks, Petty Officer Greene, I owe you so much."

"Bullshit," said Greene. "You earned everything that you got out of this place. You weren't given a damn thing."
****

18 November 1981
Communist Camp
Parque Nacional Guanacaste,
Costa Rica

The detachment of ComAms was pretty ragged as far as Carlos was concerned. They walked with a casual gait, which César said was to keep them from attracting attention. Carlos felt like he was a member of a thuggish gang and not some kind of communist conspiracy. The four of them, César, Clara, Roel, and Carlos, had taken a bus from Peñas Blancas to the speck of civilization that was Guapinol. From there, they casually walked through town and up into the mountains.

After an hour of silent walking, Roel, who was at the front of the group, made an abrupt left turn and headed up the mountain and into the forest. After what Carlos believed was a few hundred yards, Roel again turned off the path. He began to clear brush and camouflage netting to reveal an old Willys Jeep. Carlos wondered if it had seen service in the Korean War, or maybe even the Second World War.

Roel sat in the driver's seat and turned the engine over. The labored engine cranked but didn't catch.

"*Pedazo de mierda*," grunted Roel, and he flipped the hood latches and pushed it up while swinging the hood brace into place. "Carlos, you know anything about engines?"

"Just that you need fire, fuel and air," said Carlos.

Roel grunted again.

"Get in and turn the ignition when I tell you to."

Carlos obliged, uncomfortable with Roel seeming to have more value in the moment than he did. He watched Roel messing around inside the engine compartment, but the raised hood kept him from seeing what exactly his Mexican comrade was doing.

After a few minutes, Roel said, "Try it now."

Carlos turned the key and the engine again cranked over and over but didn't catch.

"Knock it off," shouted Roel. "You'll kill the battery." Roel went back to fiddling. After a few minutes, he again said, "Try it now."

Carlos turned the key, and the engine cranked a few times, coughed, sputtered and stopped.

"Again," said Roel, still under the hood. This time the engine caught immediately, then died again. Roel continued whatever he was doing under the hood. "Try it now," said Roel.

Carlos again turned the key, and the engine caught and continued to run. It was rough at first, but as the engine warmed up, the hiccups and lapses disappeared and the engine began to run with a constant and predictable rhythm.

I'll be damned, thought Carlos, *this idiot has some real talent.*

Roel appeared at Carlos's side and said,

"I'm driving."

Carlos had no idea where they were going, so he gladly slid out of the Jeep and let Roel take the wheel. The four of them rode up through paths that were barely wider than the Jeep itself. It was nearly impossible for Carlos to recognize the path that they were on, which led him to believe that either they didn't move up the mountain much or they had multiple paths that they took. After the last month outside Peñas Blancas, he was surprised by this attention to detail.

After an eternity of plowing in between the trees while at a constant incline, Roel pulled the Jeep over to the left and found an indentation that he slid her into it.

"All right," said César, "we're here. Let's cover the Jeep." As Carlos and Clara were getting out of the Jeep, César and Roel were already pulling camo netting out of the depression that they'd stopped in. Once the jeep was covered, César called everyone over.

"Listen, you all need to stay close. Anyone who gets lost in these hills will more likely than not end up dead." The sudden hush that fell over the group was intense. Carlos had had to use stealth many times in his life, but this approach was so strange because Roel and César had never shown any skill of any kind when it came to soldiering.

The foursome quietly padded up the hill. There was no talking, noise discipline in effect. They came to a trail crossing, and César held up his hand to stop everyone. Carlos looked left and right, trying to see why they had stopped. He couldn't see anything marking the position. Suddenly there was movement just outside of his focused vision. He turned his head to see a man with a rifle stepping towards them. The rifle was at the low ready, but it wouldn't take but half a second to become deadly.

"César, good to see you." The guard nodded to Roel, who returned the gesture. "These are friends of yours?" The rifle shifted enough to let Carlos know of the danger he was in.

"*Sí*," replied César, "they have been working in the camp over by Peñas Blancas for the past week or so."

"Ah, yes, Camp Siesta," said the guard, laughing quietly. He held out a hand to Clara. When she took it, he wrapped his hand around her fingers and brought the back of her hand to his lips and gave her a gentle kiss. "Diego Compos, at your service," he said with a wink.

"Clara Gálvez, charmed."

"And I'm Carlos Rodriguez," said Carlos, offering his right hand.

Diego took it and gave it a firm shake. "If you have passed César's tests, you are welcome here. This battle is just beginning, and we have a long road ahead of us."

"Keep up the good work, Diego," said César as he made his way past the checkpoint. The four of them continued up the mountain. *César's tests*, wondered Carlos. *What the hell were César's tests? All we*

*did was sit around on a mountain, bored out of our heads and wanting
something, anything, to do.*

Carlos and Clara froze at the sound of small-arms fire in the
distance.

"There is no cause for alarm—at least not yet," said César.
"Those sounds are coming from our firing range. Of course, we'll verify
that as we get closer, but I'm very familiar with that sound."

"How much range time do your men get?" asked Carlos.

"Enough," said César. "It's less about how long they spend
shooting and more about how well they shoot."

"Fair enough," agreed Carlos, though inside he wanted to argue
that the amount of training time correlated well with someone's ability
to shoot accurately. Then it occurred to Carlos that César hadn't actually
answered the question. Now he couldn't go back to it without raising
suspicion.

"What other facilities do you have here?" asked Clara.

"It's mostly around training and indoctrination. We have a
small field hospital where we train our soldiers in first aid. And of course,
the classrooms for learning Marxist-Leninist philosophy. It's very
important that everyone here know exactly why they are here and what
we are trying to achieve. I was hoping that you might want to take a turn
teaching a few lessons. You have a command of the material and the gift
of teaching."

"I would be delighted to teach our comrades," said Clara. "Do
you have materials on comrade Castro and the Cuban Revolution? I find
that those are well received by my countrymen."

"Of course. Our own model is more or less based on Castro's
governance. Essentially, Leninism for warm climates," said César,
smiling at his own wit. The party came to another checkpoint. This time
there was a fence with a gate and two guards. It looked much more like
a formal military guard post than the relatively relaxed garrisons of the
Sandinistas he'd seen.

One of the guards snapped a sharp salute, "Welcome, Señor
Costa."

"Thank you," replied Costa, returning the salute. They walked
through the gate and into the compound. There were men and women in
various training regimes, some working on close combat, some running
on a path that wove through the camp. The crack of rifle fire told Carlos

254

that even more fighters were training with firearms. The whole thing was surreal. This was nothing like what he'd seen at the other camp.

Oh, shit, thought Carlos. *My last report to Fred was that this whole movement was a joke. I've got to figure out how to get another report out. If things go wrong, we're going to need a lot of support!*

Chapter 22

20 November 1981
20,000 meters over Prüm,
West Germany

This is more like it, thought Lt. Colonel Dmitriy "Germes" Bogdanov as he cruised high above the battlefield in the latest reconnaissance plane, the MiG-31 *Lisa*, or Fox. The men had started to refer to the aircraft as the Fox when they heard that the NATO designation for the MiG-25 was "Foxbat." As with the MiG-25, there were both interceptor and reconnaissance variants of the MiG-31. Germes loved his new mount. It wasn't quite as fast as his previous MiG-25R, but it more than made up for it with the improved sensor suite and longer range.

Besides, I remember what happened the last time I used that max speed, thought Germes, remembering being stranded behind enemy lines and ending up on the run with a ragtag band of paratroopers. At the time, freezing in the German forest, he'd considered that death would be the better option. But he'd held fast, unwilling to let those army dolts see him flinch. And his steadfast determination was rewarded with his survival, and returning to fly again.

He had some nostalgia for the MiG-21R that he'd been flying for the past five months. It was the mount he had originally been trained in, and though it was ancient by aviation standards, it still had a role to play on the modern battlefield. He reached over to the control panel for his Zaslon-M ELINT collection computer. He switched it into SIGINT mode to scan the airwaves for radio broadcasts.

Unlike his previous efforts to collect radar signatures, which required additional strike fighters to make enough of a threat to energize radars, his current mission only required that he get close enough to enemy transmitters to pick up the communications they were sending. In the rapid retreat out of Germany, NATO was becoming increasingly sloppy with their communications security.

Sometimes, Germes would tune his cockpit radio into the frequencies that the computer identified as having military value. He'd try to determine if the operators were speaking French, English, or

German. He didn't speak any of these languages, but it was sort of a game that he played to pass the time.

"Stol Three, come to course two-seven-five, maintain altitude." The disembodied voice of his ground-based controller made him jump, but he quickly moved his stick to the right and adjusted his westerly course by five degrees. He wondered what his controller had found that caused the mild course change.

"Stol Three, this is Avangard One." That got Germes's attention. Avangard One was the A-50 Mainstay Airborne Warning and Control System aircraft on station. "I have multiple contacts heading in your direction from the vicinity of Liège Airport."

"Understood, Avangard One," replied Germes.

"Stol Three, maintain course," said his ground controller.

This doesn't bode well, thought Germes. Ground Control was sending him right at the incoming threat.

"Avangard One, do you have a detailed contact report?" asked Germes.

"Stol Three, Avangard One. I have four contacts climbing in your direction at Mach 2."

Blyat, thought Germes, *Could be Phantoms, could be Eagles— hell, it could even be a French Mirage. Best-case scenario, they're French and I have some time before those Matra missiles are in range.*

"Control, Stol Three. I have interceptors heading my way. They'll be in missile range soon."

"Understood, Stol Three. You are to maintain course. We need you to collect as much signals intelligence as you can."

"Control, Stol Three, I understand that. At the same time, it doesn't matter how much I record if I can't live to deliver it back to base." It was true, and self-evident, but Germes never would have said such a thing a year ago. His status as a lieutenant colonel with significant combat experience gave him some flexibility.

"Understood, Stol Three. I wouldn't be asking if it wasn't important."

"It's in good order, I understand," said Germes. He knew he was being painted by ground-based radar deep in Belgium and France, and it seemed unfair that they could see him but he couldn't see them, so he flipped the switch to energize his air search radar. The results were almost instant. He could see what looked like two contacts heading directly for him.

Could be two, could be four, he mused. Interceptors often flew in close formation to mask their numbers. *I need to assume it's four. Better to be relieved by overestimating than to be shocked by underestimating.* There before him were at least twelve medium-range missiles. They were rapidly approaching and nearing firing range. And he could do nothing but fly on course, collecting the signals that leadership needed to continue the drive against NATO. Each second brought the launch closer.

"*Vnimaniye! Vnimaniye!*" shouted his radar warning. He was being painted by the incoming aircraft.

"Control, Stol Three, I'm being locked by enemy radar. Request permission to evade."

"Negative, Stol Three, maintain course."

Sweat beaded on Germes' forehead. As much as he resented the orders, he knew that this was the mission. To stare down the enemy with the knowledge and understanding that you would survive. His classmates at the Frunze Academy thought he, and those who were assigned to the recon squadrons, were insane. To fight without weapons was madness. Germes had never bought into that idea. Until now.

"Stol Three, Avangard One, we have identified the incoming aircraft as four F-15 Eagles."

"*Vnimaniye, zapusk!*" shouted the radar warning, indicating that the enemy was launching missiles at him. The warning rang over and over. *Blyat! Worst-case scenario*, thought Germes.

"Control, Stol Three, I am under attack. Enemy missiles are inbound. Request permission to evade."

"Stol Three, evade the incoming missiles and return to base."

Germes wasted no time. He rolled his Fox onto its back and cranked back hard on the stick. The g-forces drained the blood from his head as he neared blackout. As soon as his vision returned and he was 180 degrees from his initial direction, he pushed the throttle to the wall and ran like hell. He put the MiG into a shallow dive to gain as much acceleration as he could. He would need every meter he could get if he was going to get out of this situation alive.

The MiG pushed past Mach two, and Germes marveled at how smooth everything was. In the MiG-25, you could feel the speed by how much the airframe shook. In the 31, it was as smooth as butter. For a second, Germes even wondered if this new wonder-plane could be pushed past its limits like he did his old 25. In the end, he chose not to tempt fate. He wouldn't push the engines. The radar warning continued to yell at him while he dashed away from the enemy missiles.

At some point, they would close to a fatal distance, or they would fall into the ground below them. He watched the radar screen in the middle of his control panel. They were closing. His *Lisa* was nearing Mach 3, but the trailing missiles were closing at Mach 4. He did some quick math in his head and realized that he wasn't going to make it. He slid his hand down his stick to the chaff button and waited for the missiles to get closer. Externally, he was collected and calm. Internally, he was scared to death. He had to time this perfectly. The missiles closed in.

Suddenly, his radar picked up additional contacts. They were heading towards the Americans. The Eagles dispersed as multiple missile contacts chased them down. As the American fighters broke lock, the Sparrow missiles went stupid and just flew in a line. Germes grabbed some air, and the enemy missiles simply fell away. It was only after he was safe that it occurred to him that it was possible his mission was twofold. First, to collect the signals intelligence, and second to bait those Eagles into a trap. He was sure that he'd never know, but he was thankful for the knowledge that he wasn't being sent on a suicide mission.
****

30 November 1981
345th Independent Guards Airborne Regiment
Prüm, Soviet-Occupied West Germany

Senior Sergeant Misha Kozyrev was sure of two things. One, he was pleased with his promotion. Two, he was not pleased with being reduced to serving in a motor rifle battalion. He was a Desantnik, an elite warrior. But the current needs of the Red Army were for heavy infantry. So now Misha and his team had been quickly trained up on the differences between the BMD that they'd fought in from the start of the war, and his new BMP, the bigger, tougher cousin. Now they were part of the 50th Guards Motorized Rifle Division.

In moments when Misha could put aside his professional ego, he had to admit that not much had changed in how he experienced the

259

war. He hadn't made a jump since day one. Ever since then, he'd been grounded and fighting just like the infantry. In the months since his squad was running for their lives in Germany, they'd been taken off the line, given a week of rest, then dropped into their new unit to fight their way back across the German frontier and right to the edge of Belgium.

When he thought about it, it bothered him that NATO's plan had nearly worked. From his perspective, if the Soviet counterattack hadn't stopped them when it had done, there was every chance that the Western forces would have linked up with their allies in the north and cut off the bulk of the Soviet forces in western Germany. It would have been catastrophic. The Soviets would be fighting their way out of the trap instead of advancing on France. This would give the Americans the chance to get even more men and equipment onto the continent and make a successful push all but impossible.

Now, however, the Soviets were back in their element: attack. They had fractured the American forces and chased the survivors across Germany and into the Low Countries from whence they had launched their doomed counterattack. Scholars would debate this as the "turning point" of the War to Liberate the West, but for Misha, there was no argument: the Battle of Mehren had changed everything.

"What are you philosophizing about, professor?" asked Misha's driver, Taras Knyazev, entering the squad tent and sitting next to his squad leader.

"Just reminding myself that we're very lucky to be alive," replied Misha.

"Yes, and if there's one thing I've learned in the last year, it's not to take that for granted. I can't count the things I can't wait to take for granted again," concluded Taras.

"How's that?" asked Misha.

"I can't wait to live for a week where I totally expect to remain alive. I want the day to come when I'm eating a hot meal cooked by my loving wife and I never even consider that there might be a day I go without."

"Your wife?" asked Misha. "So... this is a story of fiction, then?" He smiled as he delivered the insult.

"I may not be a pretty boy like you, Misha," said Taras, "but I'm more than enough man to win the love and affection of many a farmer's daughter."

"Oh, of that, I have no doubt, Romeo." He changed the subject. "How are the men?"

"The new guys are still getting used to the team," replied Taras. One of the changes that the VDV troopers had to get used to was that they had an additional three men in the squad. The BMP, by nature of not having to be air-dropped, had a bigger meat box. Instead of the five riflemen in the BMD, they now had eight in the BMP. The extra three troopers gave them a considerable boost in presence on the battlefield. But Misha also felt like the bigger team lacked some of the cohesion he'd felt with the smaller squads in the VDV.

"Everyone is in good spirits," continued Taras, "Private Zavyalov is a damned menace with that PK at the range."

"How's that?" asked Misha.

"He's great at the care of the weapon. He can break it down, clean it, assemble it. He's even a decent shot. But... that *durak* has no idea what a controlled burst is. It's like as soon as he depresses the trigger, he loses his head and just... unleashes."

"I suppose there's a time and place for that," said Misha.

"I don't know. The second he runs out of ammo, we'll get overrun," said Taras.

"What happened to the optimistic sergeant that sat down a few minutes ago, going on and on about his loving wife and the amazing meals she made him?"

"I have to keep that sergeant on a short leash, lest I dare to dream too long and never wake up."

"All right, I'll talk to him. We need to get the whole team working at the highest state of readiness. I don't think that Belgium is going to be a fun party. If NATO is going to make a stand, it's going to have to be here, don't you think?"

"I'm a mere sergeant in the Soviet Red Army, my friend," replied Taras. "I don't try to grasp grand strategy. I simply follow my orders and try my damnedest to survive the day."

"Agreed, my friend. Agreed."

****

30 November 1981
3rd Battalion, 69th Armor Regiment
St. Vith, Belgium

The past six weeks had been brutal for 3/69 AR. The promising drive into the heart of Germany had come crashing down. The Soviets positioned a dug-in infantry force to slow the advance while agile armored units attacked along the flanks. At first, Sergeant First Class Don Mackintosh thought it was a temporary setback. Then the word came that the Soviets units that the Americans were attempting to "bottle up" and were not attacking from the west. If they didn't fall back, and fast, they would be the ones cut off and unable to get supplies.

"Belgium, man," said Fletch from his driver's seat, "How the hell did we end up in Belgium?"

"I guess we just ran out of Germany to be in," replied Mackintosh from his gunner's position.

"What do you think?" asked Fletch, "We got another counteroffensive getting ready to go? Something like Operation Fullback?"

"More like Operation Fallback," said the team's loader, Noah Wright.

"You're lucky that the captain ain't here," said Mackintosh. "Don't ever let him hear you say that crap," said Mackintosh. "In fact, don't let *me* hear that again. That's defeatist BS and I don't want to hear it."

"Understood, Sarge," said Wright, a bit defeated, "it won't happen again."

"As to your question, Fletch, I'm no grand strategist, but yes. There has to be something else in the works. We always knew that the key to winning this fight was going to be holding off the Reds for long enough for our units to get here from across the Atlantic." Fletch nodded in agreement. "I believe that's still true. We've been spinning up new units for the past eleven months. Those units must be readying in Belgium and France as we speak. Fullback is what gave them the time to get organized and ready for the fight."

"That sounds right," said Fletch. "I hope they take us off the line for a while."

"I wouldn't count on it," replied Mackintosh. "If we're going to beat back the Russkies once and for all, it's going to be a total team effort. Heads up, here comes the old man." Mackintosh liked referring to the much younger captain as the "old man." It made him feel a bit less

262

old himself. The captain climbed up the tank and dropped into his position as the tank commander, or TC.

"Okay, boyos, I hope you've been missing Germany, because we're going back." This got the crew's attention.

"Those are pretty open-ended orders," said Mackintosh.

"But wait, there's more," said Captain Henderson. "It's not a bad mission. The company is being sent forward as a rear guard element. We're going to deploy in and around Winterspelt, Germany. Our role will be to engage any incoming enemy units, then get the hell out of there."

"So, shoot and scoot?" asked Mackintosh.

"More or less, yeah," replied Henderson. "We're not trying to hold on to the town or anything. We just need to slow the enemy down and buy some time for the rest of the regiment to evacuate."

"I'm sure getting tired of moving west," said Fletch.

"Me too, Specialist," said Henderson, "me too." The captain got on the radio and spread the word to his men. Once they were all on the same page, the company headed southeast on the N646 towards Winterspelt.

"They really think the Russkies are going to make it this far today?" asked Fletch as he guided the command tank along the Belgian roadway.

"They think it's *possible*, and that's enough," said Henderson. "We might sit here all day and night without anything more dangerous than a refugee on a bicycle. Or we might be in another life-and-death struggle. Gotta be ready for anything."

The column reached the town and Mackintosh listened to Henderson deploy his eight tanks. They had started Operation Fullback with fourteen tanks. Mackintosh reflected on some of the friends he'd lost over the course of the last four months. Good men who'd deserved a much better fate.

There was high ground on either side of the town, and Henderson positioned one platoon on each hill, spaced out to prevent the enemy from being able to concentrate fire. *It's a decent little ambush*, thought Mackintosh. Once the tanks were in position facing the egress bearing of three-zero-zero and the gun pointed backwards facing the town, the crews went about concealing them. Camo netting was deployed and augmented with what local foliage remained in the forested

263

November hills. By the time they were done, the sun had set, and darkness was quickly falling.

"Anyone got a deck of cards?" asked Fletch.

"That hasn't been funny since ever," said Mackintosh.

"Cheer up, Sarge," said Fletch. "One day you aren't going to have me around and you'll be really sad about it."

"It pains me to say this, but you might be right."

"I was thinking," said Henderson, "what if you could trade living celebrities for dead ones?"

"Um, Skipper, you feelin' alright?" asked Mackintosh.

"No, I'm serious, hear me out," replied Henderson. "I was thinking about this Sylvester Stallone production of *Pork Chop Hill*, and I got to thinking about how much cooler it would be if it could star the Duke back in his prime."

"Do you have any other examples?"

"Yeah," said Henderson, "I'd definitely trade that Han Solo guy for Humphrey Bogart."

"That's crazy," said Fletch. "Harrison Ford is amazing!"

"Kid, you need to see a few more movies, but… I'll grant you that he's not terrible, like the other guy in those movies."

"I'd trade Burt Reynolds for Cary Grant," said Wright, trying to get into the conversation.

"Hate to tell you," said Mackintosh, "but Cary Grant isn't dead, he's just old."

"Yeah, but I'd take young Cary Grant," replied Wright.

"Captain, can we get a ruling? Can we de-age living actors?"

"Negative, Sergeant, they have to be dead."

"You're just making up the rules," said Wright.

"I am," agreed Henderson.

"I've got something on the thermal," said Mackintosh, breaking up the conversation. He was referring to the AN/VSG-2 thermal sight that could track enemy vehicles by their heat signatures.

"Looks like a recon element," said Henderson. "I'm counting three—no, four BTRs."

"We gonna hammer 'em?" asked Mackintosh.

"Negative," replied the captain. "They aren't a threat to the division. We just need to keep an eye on them. If they get behind us, we'll have an issue, but otherwise, they're not our concern." Henderson got on the radio and reminded the rest of his tank commanders that they were not to engage the enemy unless and until they encountered a serious threat. Mackintosh and Henderson watched as the eight-wheeled armored personnel carriers fanned out before coming to a halt. They were fixated as enemy soldiers further spread out.

"They've got good position in those hills," said Mackintosh. "We'd better hope our boys did a great job on their concealment. Otherwise, we could have a real problem here."

"We'd better hope that *our* camo is on right and tight," said Henderson.

"If it ain't," said Fletch, "we'll probably be dead before you have time to write anyone up."

"I wonder if they have those laser designators that we've been hearing about?" asked Wright.

"I don't want to think about that," replied Mackintosh. "It's bad enough that they can call in arty or an air strike."

"Whoa, whoa," said Henderson. "Mack, you seein' this?"

Mackintosh peered through his sights. In the distance, past the hills where the recon element had set up, there was an armored column of some kind.

"What do you make of it, sir?" asked Mackintosh.

"Maybe those recon units are actual forward observers?" said Henderson.

"You think the Russkies are going to make a run on Winterspelt tonight?" asked Mackintosh.

"I think it's *possible*, and that's enough," replied Henderson, repeating his mantra from the start of the mission. He got on the radio and let the rest of the company know what they might expect.

"They must have a massive column on the other side of that hill," said Mackintosh. "If they're planning on taking the town, they won't be coming in piecemeal. It's going to be 'The Ride of the Valkyries.' Pure power and force."

"I think you're right," agreed Henderson. He then got back on the radio and told the company to be ready to initiate the start-up process. He didn't want to give the enemy any advanced warning of their presence, either by the sound of the gas turbine "jet" engines, or from the heat they would throw. At the same time, he needed everyone to be ready to move, because when the enemy came pouring over those hills, they would be on top of Henderson and his men in no time. There was the sound of big guns firing in the distance.

"Arty?" asked Mackintosh.

"I think so," said Henderson. "Everyone grab your asses. If those spotters found any of us, we're about to be in a world of hurt." The men in the tank could do nothing. They simply had to wait and pray. Mackintosh wondered how far away the guns were. That would help him understand—

The bright blast blinded him. He thought he was looking at the sun as he waited for death to take him. Instead, he realized that he was staring at an illumination flare, slowly falling to the earth.

"Not yet," said Henderson over the radio. Mackintosh agreed with the call. No sense getting spooked into action at this point. If the enemy knew where they were, they would have dropped live rounds on them.

The enemy raced over and down the hill, coming straight at them.

"Drivers, start 'em up!" said Henderson. "Gunners, as soon as you get the okay from the drivers, fire! Then we're getting the hell out of here." Henderson's men had rehearsed the start-up procedures countless times and were experts at it. But they couldn't change the laws of physics. Everything had to happen in a specific order, and it took time. As that time ticked off, the enemy advanced.

One of the Abrams off to their left fired off her 105mm cannon.

"That's an impressive start-up speed," remarked Henderson.

"I just hope they actually got her started," said Mackintosh.

"We're good, Mack, I'm ready to run!" said Fletch.

Mack fired a round at an incoming tank. "Go! Go! Go!" said Mackintosh. The tank lurched out of its hiding place as Fletch pushed the accelerator to the floor. As they took off, Mackintosh caught an explosion off to his left. Either the gunner of that tank had fired before he was ordered to, or the driver had skipped some crucial step in the start-up procedure, causing an engine failure. Either way, it didn't matter. That tank was added to the list of casualties, and Mackintosh found himself hoping against hope that there were somehow survivors.

Chapter 23

1 December 1981
21st Special Air Service Regiment
South of Lübeck, West Germany

The MEXE shelter was always cramped. But at the start of the war, it was almost a home. It provided a warm and safe shelter from a world gone mad. After almost a year, it was feeling more like a prison than a home. The men were starting to feel a bit of cabin fever. Nobody believed that they would be here for a year when the war started. The war would be over in a few weeks or months.

The additional stress of realizing that there was an evil and cruel element to their own stay-behind organization that was employing child soldiers. There hadn't been much fallout from the incident a month ago. The backlash that Corporal Willis had feared never came. It turned out Command had bigger problems to worry about. In retrospect, Trooper Trevor Pearce wondered if he might not have gotten away with killing the man.

"We're getting bad news from the front lines," said Willis to the other three troopers in the shelter. "Two months ago, I honestly believed that the Army of the Rhine would retake this area by the new year…" He trailed off. "That ain't happenin' boys." There was a murmur among the men before Willis continued. "We're too far behind the lines to get resupply. Command is looking to get us out, so that we can rejoin the fight closer to the front."

"What about the locals?" asked Pearce. "I don't think they'll last long without us."

"It's not our finest hour, no," agreed Willis. "But we've done all we can do here."

"What's the plan?" asked Lance Corporal Josh Cooper. "How are they getting us out?"

"They are still working on that," said Willis. "From what I can tell, we're going to have to sneak out to the Baltic coast outside of Boltenhagen."

"That's about forty, forty-five kilometers," said Pearce. "That's not too bad, but it is heading east, closer to Ivan."

"Yeah," replied Willis, "but with the fighting all to the west of us I don't think it's going to be too bad."

"We have a time frame?" asked Coop.

"'Soon' was all they gave me," said Willis, "so we need to make sure we have everything we need to make the trek at a moment's notice, understood?"

"Any orders before we pull out?" asked Pearce, hopefully.

"Negative," replied Willis. "Command is concerned that if the locals find out that we're leaving they will... prevent that from happening." There was a silence in the shelter as the men let that sink in. Command didn't trust their friends and allies to let them leave, even after the past eleven months. "Some of that is directed at you, Pearce."

"What?" said Pearce, surprised.

"Yeah, if we tell the locals that we're leaving, that Klaus character might put a bullet in your head."

"Fair point," said Pearce. The men ate dinner and, after a while, turned in. Pearce had the watch and waited for his mates to fall into a deep sleep before he slipped out of the shelter and made the five-and-a-half-kilometer hike to Anika's. He was unburdened with gear and was able to move at a quick pace. If this had been a straight line, he could make it in under eighteen minutes. In the darkness with the terrain, he hoped he could cover it in half an hour.

As he ran in the night, he wondered what the hell he was going to say. He didn't know what he wanted. He was torn between his dedication to his team and his nation and the feelings he had for this relative stranger. The whole thing was absurd. He couldn't stay. But he wanted to. Hell, he'd already violated orders for this woman. He was violating the most basic orders of any soldier by abandoning his post during a watch.

It was a brisk twenty-five-minute run in the cold December air when Pearce creeped across the street and up to Anika's door. He knocked lightly, hoping to avoid waking any of the neighbors. She wasn't expecting him, and he had every reason to believe that she would be asleep. After a minute, he considered knocking again but first tried the doorknob. It was locked. He knocked again, this time louder. After another minute, he heard a familiar voice call out in German.

"Who's there?"

"Anika, it's Trevor."

"What are you doing here?" she asked, unlocking the door and opening it. He slipped inside.

"I can't stay long," he said. "But I couldn't leave without seeing you."

"Leaving?" asked Anika, rubbing the sleep from her eyes. "Where are you going?"

"They're pulling us out. We're being sent west to fight the Russians."

"Oh my God," gasped Anika. "What will become of the resistance?"

"You're going to have to keep up the fight when we leave. Never give up." Anika began to softly weep. Trevor reached out and pulled her to him. She flung her arms around him and fell into his embrace. He held her for what seemed like forever. Slowly the shaking of her sobs subsided. She sniffled several times and pushed away.

"When are you leaving?" asked Anika. "Will I see you again?"

"No," said Trevor quietly. "I had to sneak away tonight to see you." There was a pause. Trevor had expected her to say something to that. "I don't want to leave, Anika, but I don't have a choice."

"You could stay," she pleaded. "You could help us in the resistance."

"I can't," he said. "I have a duty to my country."

"And what of my country?" asked Anika.

"I'm so sorry. Anika, I love you." The words just tumbled out of his mouth.

"If you love me, you'll stay." It was laid out there like a brutal fact. He knew that this wasn't going the way he wanted it to.

What the hell were you expecting? he asked himself. He quickly fished out a piece of paper he'd been carrying all night.

"Here," he said while handing her the paper. "This is my parents' address in Leicester. Once we've won this thing, please, send word to them. I will come for you as soon as I can."

"And if I don't want you to come?" she asked. He was shocked at the response, but her stern face melted into sadness. "I'm sorry, there's just too much to take, and no time to process it."

"I know, and I'm sorry. I wish there was another way," said Trevor. "I need to get back before anyone misses me."

"Thank you for everything you've done for me, Trevor. Thank you for everything you've done for my country." Trevor nodded and turned for the door, somewhat disappointed. As he walked out, she whispered, "I love you."

Trooper Trevor Pearce smiled as he ran down the driveway and into the night.

****

5 December 1981
Texas Air National Guard
Ellington Air Force Base

"What's the word?" asked Captain George "Nomad" Bush as he sat down and ordered a beer at the Officer's Club. His friend, Captain Mike "Weezer" Olson called him up and told him to meet him at the club for a news scoop.

"We're getting the Ns," said Weezer, referring to the AIM-4N, an update on the venerable but outdated AIM-4 Falcon missile that the F-106 Delta Darts carried. Those missiles were state-of-the-art in the 1950s. They could knock down the Tu-16s that Weezer and Nomad encountered six months ago.

These new missiles had improved everything. Hughes had started development on them eleven years ago, but they were shelved when the F-4 Phantom with AIM-7 Sparrow missiles took over the role as the "Defender of the Homeland." As soon as those Phantoms started to get rotated out in favor of the older Delta Darts, Hughes dumped a ton of time and effort to get the missiles upgraded to something that could compete on the modern battlefield.

"Wow," replied Nomad. "They kept mentioning the possibility, but I was starting to think that it was all so much nonsense. Any word on performance."

"Range is boosted to twenty miles," said Weezer. "It has improved maneuverability, and they've added a laser proximity fuse along with improved infrared homing for terminal guidance."

"I guess we're not going to put the Sparrows out of business," said Nomad. "But this is a major upgrade for sure. I wonder if we'll get to fire off a few live rounds for training."

270

"There's no chance of that," said Weezer. "The process for firing hasn't changed, just the likelihood of a kill once you've fired it."

"That's no fun, but it makes sense," replied Nomad. "I really hope it has a better-than-average chance of taking down a MiG-21 if called to."

"Yeah, that really should have been the goal," agreed Weezer. "I felt so defenseless the last time we were up there, knowing that while we could get the bombers, we didn't stand a chance against their escorts."

"I was right there with you, man," agreed Nomad. "Those bastards knew it too. But with the Ns, we can launch on the incoming force from twenty miles out and then beat feet home, and they've got nothing that can catch us."

"It's not exactly very macho," laughed Nomad, "but speed equals life, and running for friendly SAM coverage is a valid lifesaving activity."

"I put my packet in," said Weezer.

"No kidding?" replied Nomad. "What made you finally take the plunge?"

"Like we talked about before. Any junior pilot can do what we're doing down here. I've got enough airtime and experience; I think it would be best for everyone if I go active and some fresh kid comes out here to get some experience of his own."

"That's a good way of looking at it," said Nomad. "I'm not going to lie, I'm a bit envious."

"You don't have to be," said Weezer. "You can always put in your packet."

Nomad thought about it. It was hard enough on Laura with his spending so much time in Houston while she was in Midland. They had been planning to start a family, but those plans had been put on hold with the war. She'd come up a few times and stayed with Nomad's parents in the Memorial neighborhood of Houston, and that helped a lot.

But was he doing enough here? There was no doubt that this mission was important to US national security. But maybe Weezer was right. Could any young up-and-coming pilot take this billet and be just as effective?

"Nomad, Weezer. Comms check, over?" said Weezer, waving a hand in front of Nomad's eyes.

"Sorry, lost in thought," said Nomad. "I think that we both have different answers to this question, and they are both perfectly valid. In your case, you're younger, you don't have a family, and you're still looking to make a name for yourself." Weezer nodded, following along with Nomad's line of reasoning. "I'm older, I've got a wife and we want a family. And while maybe you're right that anyone can fly these air intercept missions of ancient Soviet bombers, this unit still needs experienced pilots in the organization to ensure that it runs smoothly."

"Any FNG might be able to get to altitude and paint a Badger, but the administrative duties to ensure that pilot has the training, the chow, the paycheck and all the things that are required to put in in the position to be successful... those can't be done by someone fresh out of flight school."

"I can't argue with anything you've said," replied Weezer. "I mean, I *could* argue with it, but I'm not going to. I think you have a very good point, but if I get in, I'm going to miss having you on my wing."

"That makes two of us, my friend." Nomad raised his glass and toasted his friend. "Good luck, and kill a dozen of those commies for me."

Chapter 24

7 December 1981
White House
Situation Room
Washington, D.C.

Eleven months ago, President Carter had similarly grown weary of meetings with nothing but bad news.

"The French have withdrawn all of their units from the High Countries," said Secretary of State Jeane Kirkpatrick.

"Have they given an explanation?" asked President Carter. "Do we think they are preparing to sue for a separate peace?"

"Right now the French are blaming NATO's combined command for the loss of Germany, and they say that they cannot rely on NATO to prevent France from falling to the same fate."

"They know that they can't stand alone against the Soviets, don't they?" asked Carter.

"They haven't addressed that," replied Kirkpatrck. "There are numerous NATO units within French borders, and the French haven't ordered them out. Basically, they want the best of both worlds. They want our help fighting the Russians, but they don't want to commit any of their troops to defending their neighbors."

"President d'Estaing must be feeling a lot of pressure from his right wing," said Brzezinski. "He's in a delicate position. Even with the war on, he barely beat Mitterrand in the election this year. So he's got pressure on both sides and I'm afraid his government might collapse under that pressure."

"Be that as it may, Zbig," said Carter, "we have problems of our own, I'm afraid."

"No doubt, sir, no doubt," agreed Brzezinski.

"It's been a week since we pulled out of Germany. Where are we now?" asked the President.

"The Soviets pulled up as they neared the border, sir," said Defense Secretary Harold Brown. "Intel believes that they were highly concerned about prepared defensive positions. They've been shelling the border for the past week."

"How long with this last?" asked the President.

"We don't know. At best we'd be guessing at what the Soviets were guessing at how deeply dug in the Belgians were."

"I see," said the President. "Can we take advantage of this lull in the fighting?"

"We're trying to position newly arrived units for the defense of Liège," said Brown, "but there's no telling if it will be enough. These new units are raw. We've been adding returning combat veterans to try to round them out, but we won't know how they're going to perform until they are in the fight."

"Sir," said General David C. Jones, the Chairman of the Joint Chiefs of Staff, "we need to rethink our position—"

"I will *not* be the first person to use nuclear weapons, General," said Carter. "I said the same thing on the first day of the war, I said it six months ago when the Soviets first pushed us out of Germany, and I'm telling you today, dammit. I will not destroy the world in a misguided effort to save Brussels."

"Yes, sir," said General Jones, "I understand. With respect, my job as the Chairman of the Joint Chiefs of Staff is to advise you. My advice is to use one or two Lance missiles on Soviet troop concentrations in Germany. I'm aware that you don't agree with this advisement, but I stand by it on the record."

"I understand that you're doing your job, General," said the President, sighing. Then, more to himself than anyone else, he continued, "I wonder if this is how Truman felt when MacArthur demanded the use of nuclear weapons in Korea?"

"Sir, are you asking for my resignation?" asked General Jones.

"No, no," replied Carter, "nothing like that. It's just exhausting having the same conversation over and over."

"I'm sorry, sir," said Jones, "but just as much as your position hasn't changed, neither has mine, and I can't do my job without advising you with every escalation of the danger. Soon, we will be in a position that a tactical strike will not dissuade them. Once we lose that option—"

"Don't," said Carter. "Do not mention a strategic nuclear first strike. That is not on the table, and it never will be. If the Soviets launch on us, we'll return the favor. But until then, you can keep that advice to yourself. Am I clear, General Jones?"

"Crystal clear, sir," said Jones icily.

"We're getting mixed signals out of Nicaragua," said Secretary Kirkpatrick, changing the subject before it became any more heated. "Some reports have come in suggesting that the communist uprisings are ridiculously incompetent, while others are coming in that allege the communists have a well-funded and equipped paramilitary organization that rivals the likes of the Vietcong. We're having trouble figuring out which one it is."

"We can't exactly make policy without knowing what we're up against," said President Carter.

"I understand that, sir," said Kirkpatrick. "I would suggest that we work from the assumption that they're well-funded and well organized. The communists have been a step ahead of us every step of the way in Nicaragua."

"Do we have a feel for other nations in the region?" asked Zbigniew Brzezinski. "El Salvador? Guatemala?"

"We don't have exact details, but the number of terror attacks by communists in both of those nations is on the rise. In fact, in all of Central America, these attacks are on the rise, with the sole exception of Honduras."

"Look, everyone," said Carter. "I appreciate that the focus is on Europe and Korea. But we can't forget that this is much closer to home. I don't need to remind anyone here about how bad it was in October of 1962, when the Soviets put missiles in Cuba. Now imagine long-range missiles in Guatemala, or short- range first-strike missiles in Mexico."

"Sir," said Kirkpatrick, "I've worked with Stan and the Agency to put together what we think we're going to need to assess and begin to address the communist threat in Latin America." She reached into her briefcase and handed a file to the President. "It's a modest force of Army intelligence, a few state resources, and a few more CIA assets." Carter flipped through the file, quickly digesting the basics.

"This doesn't look unreasonable," said the President. "Please disseminate this to the group. I want everyone to have a look at this and come back tomorrow with your assessment." He turned to his Chief of Staff, Hamilton Jordan. "What else do we have?"

"Only this," said Jordan. "Local law enforcement units across the country are reporting small pockets of communist protesters showing up at city council meetings and holding rallies. Individually, they aren't much, but when looked at as a whole, it's pretty clear that there's some

275

kind of central organization. Things have gotten violent in some of these cases, but so far we've managed to keep it out of the national news. That won't last."

"I don't understand how American citizens can attack their own institutions," said President Carter, "in this time of crisis."

"It's precisely this crisis that is causing the communists to push," said Jordan. "They can cause us to fight amongst ourselves while reminding everyone that Europe might fall. At some point, people will start to listen. Basically, the Soviets want no part of invading the United States. They just don't have the logistics for it. But if they can bring us down from the inside…"

"They can win without fighting," Carter shook his head. "It looks like we're going to have to bring in Bill Webster to these meetings." Carter was referring to the FBI Director. With a domestic threat being tied in so closely to the foreign threat, they all needed to be on the same page.
****

15 December 1981
Kremlin
Moscow, USSR

Soviet Minister of Culture Pyotr Demichev did not enjoy the military briefings. He was required to attend, he was required to understand the information being conveyed, but he wasn't required to enjoy it. From his perspective, the matters on the front line were of little interest. He preferred to concentrate on what was happening *behind* the lines. His ministry was fighting the propaganda war.

So while the generals droned on and on about "strategic withdrawal" this and "counteroffensive" that, he was ready to get back to pacifying the occupied territories and convincing the Latin American populations to rise up and join the revolution. *A pity we can't just dispense with all this and get to the heart of the matter*, he thought. Then something caught his attention.

"… lessening over time," said the general giving the briefing.

"I'm sorry, comrade General," said Demichev, "can you repeat that?"

276

"Of course, comrade Minister," replied the general. "We have noticed a significant decrease in the effectiveness of enemy resistance groups in Germany. We believe that with the complete conquering of the country, they are demoralized, and their effectiveness will continue to lessen over time." Demichev nodded, and the general continued.

Those damned resistance groups have been causing me so much frustration, he thought. *It will be nice to get past them to get to the real work of indoctrination.*

"Thank you for your presentation, comrade General," said Soviet Secretary General Yuri Andropov. He waited as the general nodded and withdrew, closing the door behind him. "I believe that the military situation is where we wanted it to be in order to move to our next phase." This was met with silence, as expected. Every man in the room understood that the next phase was playing with a nuclear fire that could spill out of control and kill billions of people.

"Our contacts in Paris have assured us that they are ready to move," said Viktor Chebrikov, Andropov's personally picked successor as the Director of the KGB. "We have every confidence in our operatives on both our side and the French. While it is true that much can go wrong with this operation, there is simply too much to gain for us to shy away."

"Remind me again, comrade Chebrikov," said Nikolai Shchelokov, the Minister of Internal Affairs, and the only skeptical voice in the room, "what are those gains that you promise?"

"I promise nothing, comrade Shchelekov," replied Chebrikov. "I only offer that our ability to remove France as an enemy without requiring us to fight like a fish against the ice would be a major gain."

"And at what cost?" asked Shchelokov. "I don't see the value in occupying France once it's a radioactive wasteland."

"Comrade Shchelokov," said Andropov, "I would remind you that your hyperbole is not appreciated when we are making decisions of this nature. You can leave those schoolboy tactics to your arguments with your family." The rebuke was felt by everyone present, but Shchelokov wasn't finished.

"With respect, comrade General Secretary, it is not hyperbole to suggest that NATO will escalate the exchange once it is initiated. We all expected NATO to have used nuclear weapons by now, and I believe it is possible, even likely, that once the first exchange occurs, we will not be able to prevent it from growing to a strategic exchange ending only with the death of nearly all of humanity."

"My agents are convinced to the point of certainty that the American President will not escalate a nuclear exchange," said Chebrikov. "We will have the French in our pocket by then, and the UK won't dare move without the Americans' leadership."

"Have you not listened to the rhetoric of Margaret Thatcher?" asked Shchelokov. "Are you certain that woman won't launch a strike to spur the Americans to join? What if you are wrong about d'Estaing? What if he orders a full strategic attack?"

"We are satisfied with our research, and you have no idea what you are talking about," said Chebrikov. "D'Estaing would never launch a strategic attack because he doesn't have enough weapons. We currently project that he has no more than three hundred warheads, and many of those are low-yield battlefield weapons."

"Comrades," said Andropov, ending the debate, "we have been over all of this before, and while I understand that Comrade Shchelokov feels the need to retrace our previous discussions, I see no reason to continue on this track. I'm suspending this discussion, and I would like to move on to logistic considerations." Shchelokov lowered his head, defeated.

"Dmitriy, have we dispersed our forces along the French border?" asked Andropov.

"Comrade General Secretary," replied Minister of Defense Dmitriy Ustinov, "it has been a challenge, but we have done what we can to minimize our troop concentrations in the areas we feel are most likely to be struck."

Andropov nodded before adding,

"Have we chosen our sacrificial lamb for this operation?"

"Indeed we have," replied Ustinov. "In looking at the units that are in the vicinity of the French border, and comparing that list to the effectiveness of those units, we looked to find the most expendable unit available. To that end, we have selected the 27th Mechanized Regiment of the 2nd Polish Mechanized Division to lead the invasion of France. The 27th is an uninspiring unit that has failed to achieve much honor in the war so far. In fact, they have shown themselves to be more interested in their own survival than advancing the front." The men around the table, with the exception of Shchelokov, nodded in approval.

"They will be sent across the border in a probing maneuver. It will be business as usual as far as they are concerned."

"Until they are obliterated in a nuclear hellfire?" asked Shchelokov.

"Yes," replied Ustinov coldly.

Chapter 25

20 December 1981
2nd Polish Mechanized Division
Schengen, Luxembourg

Staff Sergeant Krzysztof Donica was nervous. Being summoned to the Company Commander's office was generally not a good thing. The 27th Regiment had taken up positions in Schengen once the bulk of the fighting was done, and Donica wasn't very interested in expanding the frontier. But he put on his best face as he entered the room.

"Sergeant Donica reporting as ordered, sir," he said as he ambled up to his captain's desk.

"Sergeant Donica," said Captain Fabian Kalata, "great news. We have orders. We will be scouting the French frontier. Our commanders have been holding off on the invasion of France until after Germany is secured, and the low countries are on the defensive. We will be probing French defenses so that Command can determine the best plan for the actual invasion."

"Sir, that's great news," lied Donica. "We will collect all of the information that we can."

"That's right, Sergeant Donica," said Kalata, "We'll be conducting a recon by fire." Some of the blood drained from Donica's face. "We will attack any French or NATO forces along the border, then report the composition of the defense back to Command, who will then determine how to take them out."

This is madness, thought Donica, *we'll be lucky to get any report off to Command before we're overwhelmed.* He studied Kalata's face for any betrayal of his outward demeanor. In the brief silence, Donica was sure he caught a slight wincing in Kalata's expression. *He knows this is bullshit.*

"Sir, I will let the men know that we will be heading out soon," said Donica, "Do we know when we'll be moving out?"

"Negative, Sergeant," replied Captain Kalata. "It's going to happen fast, so just get your men and vehicle ready so that as soon as the orders come down, we can move out."

"Understood, sir," said Donica before offering a two-fingered salute, then turning and leaving the office.

Donica headed back to the tent where his squad was berthed. When he entered the tent, he saw the whole squad was present.

"Strom, Krzycki, I need a word," said Donica. The junior enlisted soldiers knew how to read that and quickly filed out of the tent.

"What's up, Sarge?" asked the squad's gunner, Czesław Strom.

"We've got orders," replied Donica.

"What are we looking at?" asked the squad's driver, Dawid Krzycki.

"Don't tell the boys, but we're heading into France," said Donica.

"Why are we keeping this a secret?" asked Krzycki.

"Because there's something not quite right about it," said Donica. "Captain Kalata wasn't quite himself in relaying the orders. There was definitely something that he knew, or suspected, that he wasn't sharing with us grunts."

"That's not unusual," said Strom. "The captain is always hiding details from us, and the major is hiding details from him, all the way up the chain of command."

"You're not wrong," agreed Donica, "but today he was very agitated."

"What can we do about it?" asked Strom.

"There's nothing to be done but to keep alert. If you see anything out of the ordinary, let me know. We need to be alert on this mission, or we're going to pay for it."

"Understood," said Strom.

"Understood," agreed Krzycki.

"Good," said Donica, "now go round up the squad and and get the BMP ready to go."

It was four hours later when the word came down. The radio came to life, ordering the company to assemble and prepare to depart Schengen. Donica was sitting in his vehicle commander's chair when the call came in.

"Squadron, assemble," he yelled, trying to ensure that all of his men could hear him regardless of how far they may have strayed. The same call was erupting from every BMP in the area, so it was impossible for any soldier to miss it. He watched as men slipped into the troop compartment behind his command station. Strom and Krzycki dropped into their respective hatches as the gunner and driver, respectively.

281

"Okay, men, we're going to go pay our French friends a visit," said Donica. "Everyone stay fresh and ready. We don't know when or even if we're going to have to deploy. We're playing it with a delay today," said Donica, using the Polish expression that meant roughly "playing it fast and loose." The company moved out to the south in a dual-column formation.

"Do you think the Frenchies are going to put up a fight?" asked Krzycki. "The last time anyone punched them in the nose, they quit."

"Almost every French soldier bears the stain of the capitulation to the Nazis," said Donica. "I think they're going to have an enormous splinter on their shoulder. They are going to fight us tooth and claw. Do not expect anything less." The crew went silent upon hearing their leader's resolve.

The radio came to life. "Five kilometers to the border. Everyone stay vigilant." Donica pressed his forehead into his view port, searching for anything that might give him a clue as to the danger ahead.

"See anything, Strom?" asked Donica.

"Negative, Sergeant, the battlefield is empty at this point."

"I don't believe for a second that they will let us walk right into France without a fight. It must be a trap."

"What can we do about it?" asked Strom.

"Nothing. Just press forward and be ready for whatever the enemy brings."

"Crossing the border now," came across the radio.

"If something's going to happen, it's going to happen soon," said Donica. Yet there was nothing. The column rolled into France unopposed.

"You were saying something about the fighting spirit of the French?" asked Krzycki.

"It won't be the first time in my life that I've been wrong," said Donica, feeling an unfamiliar hope. He tried to focus on anything out of the ordinary. He was searching the terrain for any indication of an enemy unit. There was nothing out of the ordinar—

There was a flash to his west. The intensity grew exponentially. Within a fraction of a second, Donica was blinded by the flash. His eyes didn't have enough time to send his blindness to his brain before the entire BMP was engulfed in a blast wave that bathed the vehicle and crew in a nuclear hell storm that erased any trace that they ever existed.

****

20 December 1981
Ballistic Missile Launch Detection Facility
Serpukhov, Russia, USSR

The "Oko-1" launch detection facility was one of the most advanced in the world. It was originally scheduled to be built in 1982, but with the coming war, the Soviets ensured that it was ready for this moment. The wide open operations floor was lined with computers. The computers maintained a datalink to the many *Oko,* or "Eye" satellites that were designed to detect ballistic missile launches.

Thus far in the war, neither side had taken aim at the enemy's launch detection satellites. Both sides well knew that any attack on these systems would cause the other to believe that an atomic first strike would follow.

Tonight, Senior Supervisor, Damian Durov paced the watch floor as he did every time he stood the watch. He could operate any of the consoles on the floor, but his real gift was ensuring that his true gift was getting the most out of the people under him. He was a stern man, but he was fair. Only the most juvenile and lazy operators could call him unfair.

When everyone was doing their best and the watch floor was operating like a well-oiled machine, Durov could be downright affable. Right now he was smiling as he thought of a time, not that long ago, when he and his new wife had a picnic on the banks of the Moskva River. With the war on, and his duty to country taking so much of his time, such a small event held more value than he could have imagined before the war.

Whamp! Whamp! Whamp! The sound of the launch warning snapped him back to the here and now. He was a red light flashing over one of the operator stations. He ran to the position as quickly as he could.

"Junior Sergeant Maksimova, what do you have?" he asked.

"Single launch from the vacinity of Metz, France," replied Junior Sergeant Lydia Maksimova as she stared intently at her monitor. "Wait. Multiple launches. Five total." A man stepped next to Durov.

"Missile artillery?" he asked.

"We'd better hope so," said Durov. "This doesn't correspond to any of the pre-war positions of French atomic forces, but that really doesn't mean anything today." Durov stepped to one of the many pillars on the watch floor that had a telephone mounted on it. "Sir, we have detected six individual launches coming from Metz, France... No, sir, we won't have that information until the rockets reach their apex... Understood." He hung up the phone, flipped a switch on Maksimova's computer console, then entered a code on the keypad to the right of the switch.

The *Whamp! Whamp! Whamp!* of the alarm again rang out, but this time it was followed with a recorded message.

"Attention in the facility. Possible atomic attack initiated. All personnel assume war posture black." The alarm and the warning repeated three times as red flashing lights put everyone on notice that their worst fears were being realized.

"Wait, sir, sixth launch," said Maksimova.

"That's odd," said Durov. "Keep an eye out for a second salvo."

"Understood," replied Maksimova her eyes glued to her monitor.

"Maksimova," said Durov, "I need estimated targeting the moment those missiles start their downward course."

"Understood Comrade Durov," said Maksimova," you will have it." The phone next to Durov range. He picked it up and listened. After a moment, he again entered a code into Maksimova's console.

Whamp! Whamp! Whamp! the alarm blared once more. This time the message chilled everyone to the bone.

"Atomic launch release has been granted." Again, the alarm and the message repeated three times while the red lights flashed. The tension in the room was palpable. It took another five minutes before Maksimova broke her silent vigil.

"Sir, it's too soon to tell for sure, but the targets appear to be along the German and Luxembourg borders."

"That's consistent with rocket artillery," said Yeromeyev.

"Six rockets, on six different targets?" asked Durov. The phone rang again. "This has all the hallmarks of an atomic attack." He picked up the phone.

"Sir, the targets are all along the French border. It appears that this is an atomic counter-force attack... no, sir... with respect... but... yes, I understand." He hung the phone up.

"Comrade Yeromeyev," said Durov, "I sincerely hope that you are correct. If this turns out to be an atomic attack, Marhsall Votintsev has authorized a full strategic atomic response."

"Maksimova," said Durov, "was there any follow on for the second salvo?"

"Negative, sir. It was as though the last rocket malfunctioned."

As the crew on the watch floor of the Oka-1 facility held their breath, the launch preparations began all across the Soviet Union. The R-36M multiple warhead intercontinental ballistic missiles at Plesetsk Cosmodrome in northern Russia were rapidly being readied for launch. A thousand miles away at the Baikonur Cosmodrome in Kazakhstan, older UR-100 missiles were similarly being readied. In between those two facilities, there were a dozen missile farms that were performing the same steps. The entire might of the Soviet nuclear threat was being placed on a hair trigger, waiting for one last piece of data.

"Atomic detonation, sir," said Maksimova, her low voice emotionless. Durov looked at the telephone. He had to decide. He couldn't hide the truth forever. Within an hour, Marshal Votintsev would know the truth. Durov ran both of his hands across his face, wiping the copious sweat away, and picked up the phone.

285

From Alex Aaronson

I'm so glad that you've kept up with me though the first three volumes of the Soviet Endgame! I hope this book has left you on the edge of your seat, waiting for the next volume. I'm working on it as you read this, and we'll get it out to you as soon as we have a quality release worthy of the series.

The next book in the series is not yet available for preorder, but if you sign up for my mailing list, I will let you know as soon as you can sign up. To join the mailing list, just click this link: https://frontlinepublishinginc.eo.page/alexaaronson

I love interacting with the readers. This is no BS, I really do engage on social media, so please join me on:
Twitter: https://twitter.com/AlexAaronson80
Facebook: https://www.facebook.com/alexander.aaronson.102
Facebook group (if you don't want to be Facebook friends with a stranger!): https://www.facebook.com/groups/833777043807871
Instagram: https://www.instagram.com/authoralexaaronson/
YouTube: https://www.youtube.com/channel/UCCulp1Ru2EkO3pknPcGkb_Q

I have the most interactions on Facebook and Twitter, but the YouTube channel is where you'll find "behind the scenes" videos as well as a few World War III movie reviews and a bunch of shorts relating to the series.

If you have a chance, I would greatly appreciate it if you could stop by Amazon and/or Goodreads and leave a review of this book. It's a very competitive market out there, and ratings and reviews are a tremendous help in bringing in new readers. Unless you thought the book sucked and you just skipped to the end to find out how to contact me to blow up my accounts with hate posts. In that case, please don't review the book.

Finally, if you enjoyed this book and you haven't checked out the rest of the Front Line family, please take some time to do so. I'm partial to the Monroe Doctrine series, since I helped write Volumes IV and V, and the Crisis in the Desert series, since I did a little ghostwriting on those.

Thank you so much for taking the time to read this. Writing this novel has been a dream come true and I hope you stay with me as we continue the journey together.

From James Rosone

I have really enjoyed working with Alex Aaronson over the last two years. It has been exciting to see one of my fellow veterans take wings and fly. He has embodied everything that I had hoped would come true when I started this project to mentor other vets in this writing business.

If you'd like to be added to my personal mailing list, you can do so by clicking on this link. This will help you keep informed of any new releases as well as any upcoming promotional deals.

I enjoy connecting with my readers online. If you'd like to connect, you can find me on:
Facebook (https://www.facebook.com/groups/803443733408830)
Twitter: @jamesrosone

Facebook private reader group
(https://www.facebook.com/groups/803443733408830)
Our YouTube page is
(https://www.youtube.com/channel/UCCExLcHFoPmwC8IKikNsVvg/videos) if you'd like to listen to some author interviews I've conducted of some fellow writers as well as some of our thoughts on the Ukraine war and the performance of the Russian military and how this plays into China, Taiwan, and other topics.

You may want to see what other books I have written. To find a full list, visit frontlinepublishinginc.com

Abbreviation Key

1MC	The main communications channel on a US Warship
4MC	The damage control channel on a US Warship
AA	Anti-aircraft
AAV	Amphibious Assault Vehicle
AC/DC	An Australian rock band
ACV	Amphibious Combat Vehicle
ADCAP	Advanced Capability Torpedo
AEGIS	Advanced Electronic Guidance and Instrumentation System
AFB	Air Force Base
AGM	Air to Ground Missile
AIM	Air Intercept Missile
AK-74	Standard Infantry Rifle for Soviet and Soviet aligned forces
AKS-74	A Combat Rifle used by Soviet Paratroopers
ALICE	All-Purpose Lightweight Individual Carrying Equipment
AMTI	airborne moving target indicator
AN/PAQ-1	A Laser Designator used by the US Military
AN/PRC-77	A man-portable radio used by the US Military
AN/PVS-5	Night vision goggles
AN/SPS-59	surface search radar
AN/VRC-12	A medium sized radio used by the US Military
APC	Armored Personnel Carrier
ARM	Anti-Radiation Missile
ASAP	As Soon As Possible
ASW	Anti-Submarine Warfare
ATGM	Anti-tank Guided Missile
AWACS	Airborne Warning and Control System
BLUF	Bottom Line Up Front
BMD	Russian Paradropped infantry fighting vehicle
BMP	Russian infantry fighting vehicle
BOHICA	Bend Over, Here It Comes Again
BTR	Russian armored personnel carrier
C & C	Command and Control
CAS	Close Air Support

289

CIA	Central Intelligence Agency
CIC	Combat Information Center
CCP	Casualty Collection Point
CIWS	Close-In Weapon Systems
CNO	Chief of Naval Operations
CO	Commanding Officer
COMSEC	Communications Security
CRT	Cathode-ray tube
DLAB	Defense Language Aptitude Battery
DMZ	Demilitarized Zone (area along the border of North Korea and South Korea)
DOD	Department of Defense
DOJ	Department of Justice
DPRK	Democratic People's Republic of Korea (North Korea)
ECM	Electronic Countermeasures
ERA	Equal Rights Amendment
ETA	Estimated Time of Arrival
FARP	Forward Arming and Refueling Point
FBI	Federal Bureau of Investigations
FSO	Foreign Service Officer
FUBAR	F***ed Up Beyond All Recognition
GAU-8	A very large rotary cannon fielded by the A-10 Thunderbolt II
GOP	Grand Ole' Party. The Republican Party in the United States.
GQ	General Quarters – Battle Stations
GRU	Soviet Military Intelligence
HE	High-Explosive
HEAT	High-Explosive Anti-tank
HQ	Headquarters
HUMINT	Human Intelligence
IBM	International Business Machines
ICBM	Intercontinental Ballistic Missile
ID	Infantry Division
IFV	Infantry Fighting Vehicle
IR	Infrared
JP-4	A type of jet fuel
KGB	Soviet Intelligence Service

KH-11	An American Photo Reconnaissance Satellite
KIA	Killed in Action
KPA	Korean People's Army
LAW	Light Antitank Weapon
LCAC	Landing Craft Air Cushion
Lieutenant JG	Lieutenant Junior Grade
LT	Lieutenant
LZ	Landing Zone
MAC	Military Airlift Command
MANPAD	Man-Portable Air-Defense System
MAB	Marine Amphibious Brigade
MAU	Marine Amphibious Unit
MD	Mechanized Division
MP	Military Police
MRLS	Multiple Rocket Launch System
NATO	North Atlantic Treaty Organization
NCO	Noncommissioned Officer
NMCA	National Military Command Authority
NSA	National Security Agency
NTDS	Naval Tactical Data System
NVG	Night Vision Goggles
OPEC	Organization of Petroleum Exporting Countries
PA	Public Address
PFC	Private First Class
PFT	Physical Fitness Test
PI	Philippine Islands
PLA	People's Liberation Army (Chinese Army)
PO2	Petty Officer, Second Class
POL	Petroleum, Oil and Lubricants
PR	Public Relations
PT	Physical Training
PVO	Russian Air Defense Forces
PVV-5A	Soviet explosive compound. Similar to C-4
QRF	Quick Reaction Force
R & R	Rest and Recreation
RAF	Royal Air Force
RF	Radio Frequency
RHAW	Radar Homing and Warning

RIM	Radar Intercept Missile
ROE	Rules of Engagement
ROK	Republic of Korea (South Korea)
RM3	Radioman, 3rd Class
RP	Rally Point
RPG	Rocket-Propelled Grenade
RPKS	Soviet light machine gun used by paratroopers
RSO	Regional Security Officer
RTB	Return to Base
RTO	Radio Telephone Operator
RWR	Radar Warning Receiver
S2	Intelligence Officer
S3	Operations Officer
SACEUR	Supreme Allied Commander, Europe
SAG	Surface Action Group
SALT	Strategic Arms Limitation Treaty
SAM	Surface-to-Air Missile
SAS	Special Air Service (British Army Special Forces)
SEAD	Suppression of Enemy Air Defense
SEAL	Sea-Air-Land (Naval Special Warfare Development Group)
SF	Special Forces
SIGINT	Signals Intelligence
Sitrep	Situation Report
SM	Standard Missile
SRBOC	Super Rapid Bloom Offboard Countermeasures
SSES	Ship's Signals Exploitation Space
TASS	Tactical Air Support Squadron
TOW	Tube-launched, Optically tracked, Wire-guided
TRAM	Target Recognition Attack Multi-sensor
UN	United Nations
USSR	Union of Soviet Socialist Republics
VA-##	Naval Attack Squadron
VADS	Vulcan Air Defense System
VDV	Russian Airborne Infantry Forces
VF-##	Naval Fighter Squadron
VLS	Vertical Launching System
VP	Vice President

VTOL	Vertical Take-Off and Landing
XO	Executive Officer

NATO Equipment

A-6e Intruder	US Navy Heavy Attack Aircraft
A-7e Corsair II	USN/USAF Light Attack Aircraft
AH-1 Cobra	Attack Helicopter
Austin Class	Amphibious Transport Dock
AV-8A Harrier	VTOL Attack Aircraft
Blue Ridge-Class	Command Ship
C-130 Hercules	Medium Transport Aircraft
C-141 Starlifter	Heavy Transport Aircraft
CAR-15	Colt Automatic Rifle. Used by US Special Forces
CH-46 Sea Knight	Medium Transport Helicopter
CH-53 Sea Stallion	Heavy Transport Helicopter
Charles F Adams	Guided Missile Destroyer
E2C Hawkeye	USN AWACS Aircraft
E-3 Sentry	USAF AWACS Aircraft
F-14 Tomcat	USN Fleet Interceptor
F-4 Phantom	US Built Multi-Role Fighter
F-5 Freedom Fighter	US Built Multi-Role Fighter
Iwo Jima-Class	Amphibious Assault Ship
JetRanger	Civilian Passenger Helicopter
Leahy-Class	Guided Missile Cruiser
M113	Armored Personnel Carrier
M16	US Military Standard Combat Rifle
M-163	VADS Air Defense Vehicle
M1911	.45 Caliber handgun
M2	.50 Caliber Machine Gun
M203	40mm Grenade Launcher
M60	Squad Automatic Weapon
M60a1 Patton	Main Battle Tank
M72 LAW	Single Use Light Antitank Weapon
Midway-Class	Aircraft Carrier
Model 37 Shotgun	Tactical Shotgun used by US Special Forces
Nimitz-Class	Nuclear Aircraft Carrier
RF-8 Crusader	Reconnaissance Aircraft
SH-2 Seasprite	ASW Helicopter

Spruance-Class	Destroyer
Tarawa-Class	Amphibious Assault Ship
Thomaston-Class	Dock Landing Ship
UH-1	Utility Helicopter

Warsaw Pact Equipment

A-90 Eaglet	Ground Effect Vehicle
AKS-74	Compact Combat Rifle used by Soviet Paratroopers
An-12 NATO Codename "Cub"	Medium Transport Aircraft
An-72 NATO Codename "Condor"	Heavy Transport Aircraft
BMD	Airlift Capable Infantry Fighting Vehicle
BMP	Infantry Fighting Vehicle
BRDM	Combat Reconnaissance/Patrol Vehicle
BTR	Amphibious Armored Personnel Carrier
KM	Prototype Ground Effect Vehicle
Mi-24 NATO Codename "Hind	Attack Helicopter
Mi-8 NATO Codename "Hip	Transport Helicopter
MiG-23 NATO Codename "Flogger	Multi-Role Fighter
MiG-25 NATO Codename "Foxbat"	Interceptor/ Reconnaissance Aircraft
MiG-27 NATO Codename "Flogger"	Dedicated Attack Version of the MiG-23
Osa Class	Missile Patrol Boat
RPKS-74	Light Machine Gun used by Soviet Paratroopers
SA-8	Surface to Air Missile
Su-20 NATO Codename "Fitter"	Multi-Role Aircraft
Su-25 NATO Codename "Frogfoot"	Medium Attack Aircraft
T-72	Main Battle Tank
Tu-16 NATO Codename "Badger"	Medium Bomber

Made in United States
Troutdale, OR
10/28/2023

14102173R00166